BANNON
BROTHERS
TRUST

Also Available by Janet Dailey

LET'S BE JOLLY
HAPPY HOLIDAYS
MAYBE THIS CHRISTMAS
SCROOGE WORE SPURS
EVE'S CHRISTMAS
SEARCHING FOR SANTA
MISTLETOE AND MOLLY
AMERICAN DREAMS
AMERICAN DESTINY
SANTA IN A STETSON
MASQUERADE
TANGLED VINES
HEIRESS
SOMETHING MORE

From the Calder Series:

SANTA IN MONTANA
CALDER STORM
LONE CALDER STAR
CALDER PROMISE
SHIFTING CALDER WIND
GREEN CALDER GRASS

BANNON BROTHERS
TRUST

JANET DAILEY

KENSINGTON BOOKS
http://www.kensingtonbooks.com

FIC
DAI

KENSINGTON BOOKS are published by

Kensington Publishing Corp.
119 West 40th Street
New York, NY 10018

All Kensington titles, imprints, and distributed lines are available at special quantity discounts for bulk purchases for sales promotion, premiums, fund-raising, educational, or institutional use.

Special book excerpts or customized printings can also be created to fit specific needs. For details, write or phone the office of the Kensington Special Sales Manager: Attn. Special Sales Department Kensington Publishing Corp, 119 West 40th Street, New York, NY 10018. Phone: 1-800-221-2647.

Kensington and the K logo Reg. U.S. Pat. & TM Off.

ISBN-13: 978-0-7582-6714-6
ISBN-10: 0-7582-6714-2

First Trade Paperback Printing: August 201

10 9 8 7 6 5 4 3 2 1

Printed in the United States of America

BANNON
BROTHERS
TRUST

CHAPTER 1

High clouds drifted above the Blue Ridge Mountains as a hawk swept down from a barren granite summit, its wings spread wide, soaring over the rolling terrain below. Wheeling only once, the hawk flew through vast, moving shafts of light that cast farms and fields into alternating bands of sun and shadow. Sheltered by nature, the rich land of Virginia's valleys had been tilled for generations and tamed long ago, unlike the ancient mountains that rose abruptly from them, clad in their namesake haze of indigo. The hawk made a banking turn, spotting a moving object below. Its sharp eyes quickly identified a vehicle traveling along Route 231. But it took no interest in the dark-haired man behind the wheel and swung west toward the Shenandoah.

With eyes as keen as the hawk's, the driver saw it lift away, then refocused his attention on the road ahead, catching glimpses of forest on the verge of spring. A pair of sunglasses shielded his eyes from the morning glare. The cut of his cheekbones and jawline were on the hard side. Although only in his early thirties, RJ Bannon looked more experienced than that.

As he let a truck pass him, he glanced again at the steep slopes of Old Rag, a solitary outcrop of the Blue Ridge, the only one with a bare rock summit. A smile of remembrance softened the line of his mouth as he recalled climbing that mountain as a boy, scrambling over giant boulders to beat his brothers and father to the top.

The experience got him into rappelling and free climbing by the time he was twenty, something he very much doubted he could do now, twelve years later.

Bannon sat up straighter when he felt a twinge near his spine, an unwelcome reminder of the bullet still lodged there. In most respects, he was as strong as ever, something his brothers had taken into account when they'd asked him to open the backcountry cabin the three of them shared. He'd gone up two days ago, a jolting drive over ruts that the winter had deepened, to look the place over. Nothing too dire. The roof was still on, minus a few shingles. The well was working and, after a little persuasion with a wrench, so was the plumbing. A critter or two had taken up residence beneath the floorboards—he'd flung open all the windows and gotten into the crawl space with a flashlight to make sure it had vacated its winter lodgings. Nothing there but drifts of fur.

After that it had been nice to get out into the air and do the hard work of clearing away and chopping fallen branches around the property for firewood and kindling. When he was done, he hadn't wanted to leave. But now that he was on the road, he wasn't sure when he'd get back out again. With Deke and Linc out of the state on assignment, Bannon didn't feel much inclined to hang out at the cabin on his own.

He drove on, humming some old song to himself, toward Wainsville. He could see it in the distance. Not his hometown, but he'd been happy enough there, wanting to live in a town that time forgot, until Wainsville had been "discovered." Now its friendly old houses were overshadowed by condos and too many trees had been taken down to make room for them. The town even had a couple of office parks on land that had been bought cheap and developed with no thought to tradition. The surrounding area was still beautiful and largely rural, but an influx of hedge-fund titans who'd cashed out had come here. Their new, outsize mansions were everywhere and their nouveau riche attitude rankled the locals.

Bannon scowled as he passed a just-built monstrosity that sat on raw soil, an eyesore from any angle. Construction debris was half-heartedly controlled by an orange plastic fence that flapped in the breeze. He didn't have a good reason to feel superior. After all, he lived in a condo, mostly so he wouldn't get stuck maintaining a home. Being a cop, you made decisions like that. He stopped at his condo long enough to pick up an envelope of paperwork and headed out again.

The sun grew brighter as Bannon drove through town, turning left at a small complex of textured cinder-block buildings on the other side of Wainsville. Someone had made an effort to landscape around headquarters—yellow daffodils, the eye-popping yellow of crime scene tape, were blooming in rows of unvarying straightness. He bet the chief of police approved.

He parked in what had once been his slot and switched off the engine, looking up at the narrow windows under the eaves. They were too high to see in from the outside, but it was a safe guess that everyone was right where they usually were. Except him.

Out of habit he used the reflection of the wire-gridded glass to look behind him as he went up the front steps. What would it be like, he wondered, to not feel compelled to check every corner, every shadow, every movement for danger? But the habit of constant watchfulness had been drilled into him the hard way.

Bannon spared a fraction of a second to check himself out before he opened the door. His dark hair was windblown and his jaw was outlined with stubble after two days up at the cabin. Forget the uniform. He still wore the torn jeans, scuffed work boots, and banged-up leather jacket that had served him out in the woods. Too bad. He was here and he was on time. Chief Hoebel would have to deal with him the way he was.

His boots were old and they didn't make much noise on the gleaming tile floor of the hallway as he walked down to the young officer on desk duty. Fair-haired and freckled, Kyle Rasmussen was a rookie, a fact almost anyone could conclude just from his spotless uniform and shiny new gun belt, laden with forty pounds of regulation-issue junk.

"Can I help you?" Rasmussen studied him with curious, almost innocent blue eyes.

It took Bannon a second to realize that the new cop didn't recognize him. He'd been out of the office for too many months, thanks to a drug dealer with fairly good aim and a chief who didn't like him for being a hero—and for a few other reasons he was beginning to figure out. Without saying a word, he reached inside his jacket and flashed his badge. The officer shrugged, looking a little surprised, and went back to reading a binder with bulleted lists and line illustrations, a manual on police techniques that no one took seriously. Bannon suppressed a smile and headed down the hall to where the chief's office was located.

When he reached the outer office, Bannon flicked a glance at the closed door to the chief's inner sanctum, then focused on Chief Hoebel's assistant behind the desk. The blond and blue-eyed Jolene Summer had the phone cradled to her ear—with both hands. That, and the low flirty tone of her voice, made it easy for Bannon to guess she was talking to her boyfriend.

Looking up almost indifferently, she cupped a hand over the mouthpiece and whispered, "The chief had to go out. He said to leave your paperwork with me."

"Okay. Here." Irritated that he'd come this far without getting to talk to Hoebel, Bannon smiled at Jolene anyway and passed her the manila envelope with his paperwork.

"I'll try to get him to sign it today," she added in the same low whisper. "It's not going to be easy. You know he's got it in for you."

"Really? I hadn't noticed." He winked at her and left her to flirt with the lucky guy on the other end of the call.

Retracing his steps, he headed back to the front. Near the door to the basement, he automatically glanced at it and hesitated when he read the sign there.

Doris Rawling. Case Files Manager.

An image of the fiftysomething woman flashed in his mind—average height, slim build, iron-dark hair with stylish streaks of silver-white, warm brown eyes, and lips that were always ready with a smile for him.

Bannon looked at the new title again, realizing she had been promoted from evidence clerk sometime in the last several weeks. But he had a feeling she hated being stuck in the windowless basement with its chill-inducing cement floor.

As he opened the steel door, he called out a greeting and descended the studded metal stairs. When there was no reply to his call, he ventured forward. The floor-to-ceiling metal grates that enclosed the Evidence Control Unit blocked the lines of sight. Bannon looked through them for a person on duty, then swung around a corner, spotting the top of Doris's head at a makeshift computer workstation.

"Hey, RJ," she tossed over her shoulder. Doris was about the only one who called him RJ; to everyone else, except for his mother, he was just Bannon. Doris put a document from the huge pile beside her into a scanner and closed the lid. A thin bar of light moved from one end of the machine to another as the scanner emitted a faint hum. She looked into her monitor and clicked the mouse a few times to make the image fit a format, then saved it with another click. Turning, she flashed him a smile, a pair of reading glasses perched on her pudgy nose. "It's been a while. How are you?"

Bannon shot a glance around the area. "Fine. Are you alone?"

Eyes dancing, she peered at him through her half-glasses. "What the hell do you have in mind, kid?"

He winked at her. "Just wanted to know. Who's handling evidence now?"

"Hoebel's son-in-law Petey. He leaves early."

Bannon nodded, then waved a hand at the tall stacks of file folders surrounding her. "So what's all this?"

"We're going paperless. I'm archiving old case files," Doris said, adding, "Hoebel gave me a month. I'll never finish in time."

RJ looked over his shoulder, then turned back to her. "I was supposed to meet with him but he's out. Want some help, or is that against the rules?"

"Sure. He doesn't have to know." One shoulder lifted in an uncaring shrug. "Hardly anyone comes down to this dungeon."

"Good. Hey, I forgot to say congratulations on your promotion." He lifted his coffee cup in a salute and caught her faint smile of pride.

"I guess it's worth the extra work." She pushed aside the pepper-and-salt bangs that fell into her eyes when she leaned forward to peer closely at the document on the screen. "The information is going to be shared with the new national databanks."

"State and federal, right?" He crumpled up his takeout coffee cup and tossed it in the nearest wastebasket, then looked over the files spread out in irregular rows.

"That's the idea. Connect the dots, catch the criminals."

"About time," RJ said. "Some of these old cases could be charged or cleared."

"The chief thought so. For once I agree with him." She stopped what she was doing to swivel her chair and actually look at him. "So what brings you here?" she asked.

"I had paperwork for Hoebel to sign. Continuance of claim, that kind of thing."

"Are you still on official leave?"

"Yup."

"Take your time about coming back, RJ. You did get a settlement after the shooting, right? Enough to live on?"

"For a while. Not indefinitely."

Doris sniffed. "After being used for target practice, you should have gotten plenty."

"Tell that to the insurance company and the top brass," he replied. "Getting better was all I wanted to do."

"Ever think about catching the guy who shot you?"

"All the time," he said. "Who did Hoebel assign to the case after the first guy quit? Hope it's not the baby boy on the desk."

"No, it's not him. I think right now it's up for grabs, actually," she replied.

He threw up his hands. "Nice to know a shot cop is such a high priority around here. Is it me? Is it Hoebel? Is it something I said?"

"Uh, he does think you're a loose cannon—"

Bannon had to smile. "From him, that's a compliment. But I guess he didn't appreciate my noticing where his new car came from."

"Refresh my memory, dear."

"Remember that college kid who set fire to the gas station at the crossroads just for the hell of it?"

"Yes. The charges were dropped before it ever got to court."

"Of course. Because his daddy owns the Big, Fast, and Ridiculously Expensive dealership out on the highway."

"Ah." Doris nodded sagely. "I understand. I did notice that Hoebel was driving a Beefer. Well, he needs the extra belly room."

"So will I," Bannon said ruefully, looking down at his midsection and slapping it. Physically, he was most of the way back to what he had been, thanks to a rigorous exercise routine he'd devised to rehab his body. "Someday," he added quickly. Too late. Doris was laughing.

"Yeah, maybe in fifty years," she teased him. "Anyway, getting back to you being shot, it's hard to believe there are still no leads in the case." There was an edge of disgust in her voice.

"Who cares?"

"I do, RJ. Anyway, welcome to Cold Case City. Guess that makes me its mayor." She glanced back at her computer screen. "I wish this was over. I'm only halfway through."

"Take a break," RJ said.

"Don't tempt me."

"It's a beautiful day, Doris."

"And the Art Walk is going on. Wish I didn't have to miss it." She gave him a dejected look. "Days like this make me eager to retire."

"Really?" he asked. "You don't look old enough."

"Aww. Aren't you sweet," she mocked in amusement.

RJ returned his attention to the files on the table, wondering if any of his older cases were among them. They had been laid out in alphabetical order, he noticed. "Okay. Where do you want me to start?"

"Are you really that desperate for something to do?" She sliced him a doubting glance.

"What letter are you up to?" he asked.

"*M.*" She slid off her chair to come over to where he was and picked a thick, crammed folder from a group. "The Montgomery case is next. This is the main file." She set it in front of him.

"It's a monster."

"You volunteered," she reminded him and sighed. "This one's a mess, and there are ten others."

"Mind giving me a summary of it?"

One eyebrow went up. "You can read, right?"

He grinned. "Big type. Small words. You know me, I just sit on a stump and shoot tin cans for laughs."

"Don't make me believe it, Detective Bannon." She patted the file. "Get started. Do what you can."

"How come it's so big?"

"Oh—there are lots of Montgomerys around here, for one thing." He noticed that she had dodged his question. "The family goes back twelve generations in this part of Virginia. The historical society even gives tours of the ancestral mansion outside of Wainsville—one of those big stately homes that got built, oh, in the eighteen hundreds. Haven't you seen it?"

"No. I usually get assigned to drug dealers in double-wides, remember?"

"Of course I do." She nodded, then smiled wryly. "Somehow I don't think the Montgomerys would know a double-wide if one snuck up on them and bit their butts. They're rich and always have been." Her dry tone made the social divide between the Rawlings and the Montgomerys more than clear. "Still and all, they're not as snooty as some of the newcomers around here. And the Mrs. Montgomery in that file definitely wasn't a blueblood."

"You read it?" Bannon challenged.

Her face was a study in patience. "I knew her—not well, though. We went to the same church when we were younger. Before she married and I didn't. Luanne was always nice."

Something about her thoughtful tone made him curious. Very curious. "You going to tell me more about that?"

"Later. Maybe."

"I'm holding you to that," he responded.

Doris turned back to her work. "Go ahead and start sorting what you can. I'll finish the one I'm working on while you do."

"Okay. Take your time."

He took off his leather jacket and slung it across the back of a folding chair, then settled his long frame into the seat, ignoring a sharp twinge in his back when he sat down. RJ opened the Montgomery file and noticed that the earliest forms had been completed on a manual typewriter. He picked up the first piece of paper and read the basics.

Victim: Ann Spencer Montgomery.
Adult/Child: child.
Age: 3.
Nature of crime: abduction.

At a later date, someone had scrawled four bleak words across the paper.

Still missing. Presumed dead.

Presumed dead. Not declared dead. Officially still considered missing. Curious, Bannon began turning pages of the thick file and soon became engrossed in it for the better part of an hour. "This is one hell of a case," he said softly and glanced at Doris. "How come I never heard of it?"

"You were a kid when it happened, Bannon." She sounded a little surprised by his interest. "It was before your time. Before you knew it all," she added in a teasing way.

"Yeah, sure. But—Ann Montgomery was abducted at the age of three." He grabbed a pad of paper and pencil and jotted down some quick figures. "That means she would be twenty-nine now if she somehow survived."

"That's correct," Doris agreed.

Pulling out the old reward poster and the bank document clipped to it, Bannon scanned them both. The money was held in a trust that would terminate on Ann's thirtieth birthday. "There's a year to go on this reward." He couldn't imagine why the case was being closed. The female victim was still officially classified as missing and a million-dollar reward was still in force for information leading to her safe return.

Decades had gone by. Her family had faith, he'd give them that. Some people would cling to hope forever when no body was found. A few abducted children had turned up alive, years later, but the odds were solidly against this little girl. He flipped through the documentation, feeling a rush of hunting instinct. It felt good. Like his old self was back.

"Yes, I noticed that," Doris replied. "What's your point?"

"Fake Anns might start showing up. I wouldn't call this case cold."

"It's been forgotten, RJ. Don't spin your wheels."

RJ leafed through another section of documents. "I don't get it. Did you ask Hoebel about this? What could it hurt to keep it open for one more lousy year?"

"As a matter of fact, I did, RJ. But he said nothing doing—every case more than five years old with no activity and no leads is officially cold. He wants these off the shelves. The actual files are going into a document storage place in a week. It's about a hundred miles from here."

RJ frowned. "Not this one. It could be a gold mine of information. Every scrap of paper counts. This was a kidnapping, for chrissake."

"Hoebel knows that," she said, "but he doesn't care. He wasn't working here when the Montgomery case was headline news. Bye-bye, files."

"But why—"

"Did you get through everything in that one?" Doris was asking.

"I skimmed most of it."

"Finish reading," she ordered in a schoolteachery voice.

"Yes, ma'am." RJ sank his chin into his hand and pored over the last miscellaneous pages. When he was done twenty minutes later, he glanced at Doris, a thoughtful frown creasing his forehead. "I still don't understand. Tell me why a case with a million-dollar ticking clock and a missing child gets closed."

"More like two million. Don't forget the interest," Doris pointed out.

He flipped back to the bank document and noted the date on it. "Eight per cent, compounded, low tax. Yeah, two million is probably about right."

"Now look at the date on the last document in the file."

He found it—a memo from a detective, now retired, whose name he remembered only vaguely. It was about something minor. RJ read the date aloud. "Okay, that was fifteen years ago. So?"

"It's ancient history, RJ. We don't have the manpower or the money to stick with cold cases, even a high-profile one like this.

Our budget keeps getting cut." She scowled into her screen. "Hoebel has a master plan to streamline some of us out of existence, you know."

"But you just got promoted."

"Which means I have to prove myself, right? I intend to get every single file down here entered in my lifetime. Which is getting shorter every day." She picked up a staple remover and snapped the tiny jaws at him. "Getting old really bites. Just you wait."

"I'll take your word for it." He sat up and clasped his hands over his head, stretching out his back. "Are there other Montgomery files? I feel like I'm missing something."

"Like I said, there are ten on that table. It's possible some already went to the storage place, but I can't be sure until I find the master list of files. That thing runs to about three hundred pages all told."

"What about the record of evidence? Where's that?"

Doris's reply was matter-of-fact. "Evidence? There wasn't any to speak of. Not a drop of blood or a sign of a struggle. Whoever took Ann left virtually no trace."

RJ favored her with a look of disbelief. "That can't be. Who handled the investigation?"

She wagged a finger at him. "Did you forget I wasn't working here then?"

"What's that got to do with it? You just said you looked into all the Montgomery files."

Doris gave him an annoyed look. "RJ, you'd know as much as I do if you'd really read the material."

"Brief me anyway. For old times' sake."

She sighed and tapped her pencil on the tabletop. "Half the cops in Virginia were working on it for months. Every sheriff who could keep his pants up over his gut got in on the action and dragged his deputies along. Search and Rescue went out with tracking dogs. The woods around the Montgomery house were gone over inch by inch."

"And nothing was found?" His tone was skeptical.

"The dog handlers couldn't pick up a scent trail and the searchers found zip. Whoever took her was extremely careful. I don't know if you noticed it," she added tartly, "but the FBI sent a profiler to try to match the MO to their list of known offenders."

"Where's that file?"

"I'm not sure." She looked his way. "Maybe to your left."

He set aside the file he'd been leafing through to look for something labeled *FBI* and got distracted by another one labeled *Photos. Montgomery, Ann.* Bannon instinctively steeled himself.

This was where it got real.

After five years as a cop and five more as a detective, there were things he never wanted to see again. Crime scene photos that involved kids were among them. Granted, Doris had said there was no evidence, but the way he'd tensed up made his back twinge again. Damn bullet.

Two years ago it had stopped perilously close to his spine, just short of severing it. The surgeons had left it in. Bannon thought of it as a souvenir of his own unsolved case, a meth lab bust that hadn't gone too well. The dealer had used his young sons for a human shield and Bannon had no choice but to drop his gun, unable to ignore the terror in their eyes. But the dealer had opened fire.

Two other bullets had been successfully removed from his chest. He had them somewhere, maybe in his sock drawer. The dealer's sons were on the lam with him as far as anyone knew. RJ would give anything to set them free. But he wasn't going to get the chance.

He had lived—Bannon was grateful for that. And he planned to keep on living. But he'd learned you never knew, that was all.

Opening the file, he looked through the faded photographs of a smiling little girl, pale blond hair caught back in ribbons, clad in a smocked dress. A photo-studio shot showed her holding a favorite toy, a pink teddy bear with flowered tummy and paws. There were others of her: most with her parents as a baby, as a toddler, as a three-year-old.

Nothing he could go on now.

"No age-progression images, looks like," he said absently.

"They didn't have the software back then."

"Guess there were no sightings of the suspects. There's no police composite either," he said. "For what they were worth. I've heard they used to give a cop a crayon and hope for the best."

Doris snorted. "I know what you mean."

Looking at the photos stirred feelings in RJ that went beyond a mere hunting instinct. Protectiveness was chief among them. A vulnerable child had vanished. That kind of crime got under the skin and stayed there.

Apparently not with Hoebel, though. The chief was declaring the case cold exactly when anyone who knew the particulars of the reward might come forward. Stupid bastard. Still, he had to concur with Hoebel on the probable outcome of the kidnapping.

Ann Montgomery hadn't lived long. Somewhere there was a shallow grave that had never been found. A small one.

Someone ought to be behind bars, facing the maximum penalty for that, no matter how long it took to make it happen. Bannon knew it was wrong to let this one go.

He put back the drawings and sketches of Ann at three. What was the point? He knew the odds that little girl had lived for more than a couple days after her abduction weren't good.

"What else needs to be organized?" he asked briskly.

"Every freakin' file on that table. Pick a letter," she said absently.

RJ went one row down to the *N* files and opened folders for other cases that were a lot less sensational, sorting police documents by date and methodically dealing with the miscellaneous papers in them.

After a couple hours of sitting in one place, his back began to ache, a warning signal that he needed to move around if he didn't want it to start stiffening up. Right now a break and some fresh air had a welcome sound to it.

Pushing his chair back from the table, he stood up. "I have a couple errands to run, Doris." Truth to tell, he didn't, but it was a good excuse. "I'll be back in an hour or so, okay?"

Doris acknowledged that with a nod. "Off you go. Give my regards to the real world."

"Want anything?"

She made a face. "A vacation would be nice."

"I meant something to eat. Or is there food at an Art Walk?"

"We are below the Mason-Dixon Line, therefore there is food.

It's the unwritten law of the South. But I'm not hungry. Thanks, though."

"You're welcome. See you later." RJ put the folders he'd been working on into some kind of order and left, taking the stairs up from the basement two at a time. At the top he hesitated and glanced down the corridor. There was Jolene, still talking on the phone. When she caught his questioning look, she gave a negative shake.

Still no chief. No problem, he thought and realized it was probably a good thing Hoebel wasn't back. If he saw him right now, Bannon suspected he would argue with him over the decision to archive the Montgomery case. Considering that he needed Hoebel to sign off on his leave extension, a confrontation wouldn't exactly be a wise move.

Outside the sun was bright and the air smelled fresh and clean after the basement's staleness. With no particular agenda other than movement, Bannon decided to drive around and see what else was new in Wainsville besides just the Art Walk.

Without really thinking about it, RJ took the routes he'd favored when he was still a patrol cop, before he'd made detective. It wasn't like he knew every inch of the streets—he'd grown up outside of Arlington with his mother and two younger brothers after his dad died—but he liked the town, had made a home for himself here. One hand on the steering wheel, he looked up idly at trees that hadn't leafed out yet, their trunks damp from the recent rain. A few skinny shrubs were trying.

When he turned the wheel to take a shortcut through the community center parking lot, he remembered the Art Walk and headed that way.

A professionally made sign with a holder for brochures stood at the park entrance. Beyond it was some lightweight scaffolding that supported framed photographs, watercolors, and oil paintings. Attached to the big sign was a smaller one, made by hand. HOME-MADE PIES, CAKES, AND MUFFINS.

That got Bannon's attention. He rolled down the window, doing a recon of the baked-goods table strategically positioned near the entrance to the park. The pies looked good at a dollar a slice and so did everything else—their money jar was filling up. Sunlight glinted on a gigantic coffee urn that he guessed had been borrowed from a church or a restaurant.

Decision made. Bannon parked and got out, walking over to the short line at the table, ready for some pie and coffee to soothe his soul. A plump woman was putting slices of fruit-filled pie onto paper plates while another woman was serving.

"One slice, please. And coffee. Black," he requested when he reached them. RJ slid a five across the table and shook his head when the plump woman started to make change. "Keep it," he said. "The pie looks worth the extra."

"It is. I made it myself." A shyly proud smile dimpled her cheeks an instant before she turned to the next customer.

Bannon walked away and leaned against an empty concrete planter, idly looking around while he ate and drank. Noticing the number of artists still setting up, he realized the event wasn't in full swing yet. He took a brochure and read it, surprised to find he recognized a few of the participants' names. A lot of them had studios or homes in the Rappahannock area, which was turning into a cultural mecca of sorts.

With a slight lift of curiosity, he let his gaze wander over the exhibit area. Near the far end, a young woman stood next to a display of framed watercolors, something proprietary in her stance. From this distance, Bannon couldn't identify the subjects of the paintings, but the young woman was another matter. A little taller than average with silky dark hair and a slender build that curved in the right places, she triggered all his male interest.

Unfortunately, he wasn't the only one. A lanky, tall guy was eying her too. There was something off-kilter about him, like he was made of spare parts and secondhand clothes. His gaze was hooded but he still managed to stare fixedly at her, hands jammed in the pockets of his dirty pants.

Bannon made short work of finishing the pie and coffee, disposed of the plate and cup, and strolled over to give the creep a move-along look. He had strange eyes too. Narrow and cold, with a feral quality. Bannon didn't speak—he didn't have to. The guy seemed to understand instinctively that Bannon was police.

RJ watched the guy walk away casually, an uneasy feeling coming over him as he tried to remember if he'd seen him anywhere before, drew a blank. Then he was gone. Bannon returned his attention to the young artist and went over to look at her exhibit.

"Afternoon," he said in greeting, glancing from the framed artwork over to her. Up close like this, he saw that she was worth the walk. In that split-second moment, he memorized her face—out of that same damn cop's habit of constant and detailed awareness—taking note, with some pleasure, of her delicate features and sensual mouth devoid of lipstick. Silky, dark brown hair tumbled over her shoulders, not styled, but brushed to a high shine. He didn't want to stare into her eyes like a jerk, so he didn't. Even if they were china blue with long dark lashes.

"Oh—hello." She seemed almost surprised that he'd spoken to her.

Self-consciously, she adjusted the position of one of the framed watercolors, a dramatic study of galloping horses. In fact, they were all of horses.

"Are these originals? They're really good." He meant that. "Are you the artist?"

"Yes." There was something touching about the faint swell of pleasure in her expression.

"You must ride."

She shook her head. "Not anymore. I wish I could. Growing up, all I had was an old farm horse, and he was too smart for me. He only let me on his back every once in a while. After a minute he would walk into the pond and float me off."

"So you're a country girl." Funny she didn't sound like one. Bannon was curious as to how she would respond.

"Sort of." She seemed almost to regret that she had previously been so forthcoming.

It wasn't a reply that invited him to ask questions about where she lived and where she was from. *Try something safer,* he told himself. "Did you go to art school?"

"No, I taught myself. And believe it or not, I make a living at it." Confidence was in the assertion.

"Good for you." He really didn't want to pepper her with questions, despite his curiosity. "You have a lot of talent. So, what else do you do—" RJ stopped himself when she gave him a wary look. "I mean, as far as art. Portraits, anything like that?"

She relaxed visibly. "Yes, sometimes. I've done people and even houses. Houses have a lot of personality when they've been lived in for a while. It's fun to try to capture that."

"I bet it is."

She definitely wasn't the chatty type and seemed content to let him look at the art rather than to talk to him about it. RJ took his time to study the framed works on the table, not wanting her to think he'd only come over to check her out.

"Tell me more about these," he requested, grateful he was the only visitor at her display. "These are wild horses, right?"

"Yes, they are." She smiled at him but said nothing more.

RJ felt damn close to dazzled by that one smile. A little disconcerted, he glanced back at the painting of a herd of horses galloping through mist. "It can't be easy to paint animals moving that fast." Done in subtle washes of dark color on white paper, outlined with sure-handed strokes of ink, the painting conveyed speed and power.

"It isn't. But I did that one from memory. I happened to see them out at Chincoteague at dusk," she said, "running on the beach as the fog came in. There was something so mysterious about them, it just stayed with me."

"You did that from memory? It's fantastic," Bannon responded, aware she'd handed him a reason to ask if she was from that part of Maryland, but instinct told him it wasn't the moment to follow up on it. One thing at a time. In some indefinable way, she seemed as leery of strangers as the horses she painted.

"Think so?" She seemed pleased. Leaning over the table, she took it off its stand. "I have to admit it's one of my all-time favorites."

"Is it for sale?"

She nodded.

Taking it from her, Bannon studied it. "I can almost hear the thunder of their hooves," he mused.

She was kind enough to smile.

"Okay." He set the painting back on its stand. "I think I have to have it. How much?"

She told him the price.

"Well worth it." He would have paid double. Bannon dug in his back pocket for his wallet. He pulled out several twenties and waited to hand them to her. She wrapped the framed picture in brown paper and string, adding a cardboard tube for a handle as he watched.

"Thanks," he said. "That'll make it easy to carry."

She took the money and stuck it into her jacket pocket, then extended a hand. "You're welcome. I'm Erin, by the way."

"Erin. Okay." He waited for a last name, which she didn't offer. And there were no business cards on the table. "I'm RJ Bannon," he said easily. "Nice to meet you. Are you going to be here tomorrow?"

She shook her head. "The Art Walk is for one day only."

"Did the sign say that? Too bad." He let the matter of her last name go for now. He could always get her full name from the event organizer, and maybe even a phone number. An e-mail address for sure.

She passed the wrapped painting over the table. "Is this for yourself or for a gift?"

"Myself." He took it from her, handling it with care, but the corner knocked over a smaller, postcard-size watercolor of a solitary horse. It lay flat on the table and he looked down at it, searching for something he hadn't thought of until that moment. A full signature, if it was legible.

Yes, there was one in the right-hand corner—but it was just her first name. He got the unspoken message. She went by Erin, just Erin, professionally. Maybe she had her reasons. Considering how that lanky guy had been staring at her, Bannon respected those reasons.

"Oops." She righted the watercolor, but not before she caught the odd look on his face. "Don't worry," she reassured him. "No harm done."

Bannon set his purchase on the edge of the table, letting the wrapped painting lean against his chest. "Good," he said. "I'll take that one too. It'll be a present for a friend."

She looked happy to hear that and wrapped it up just as quickly. "There you go. Can you manage both?"

He gave her the last of his twenties. "Sure can. And thanks again, Erin. Uh, see you around. I assume you get into Wainsville now and then."

"Sometimes." She nodded and seemed about to say something more when an older couple came over. Oblivious to his presence, the friendly woman started to chat with Erin while her white-haired husband looked at the thickening clouds above and flipped up the hood of his nylon windbreaker.

Bannon saw the first drops of rain hit the brown paper wrapping and realized he'd look like a fool if he hung around. Erin got busy throwing a light plastic tarp over her artwork and someone with an Art Walk badge ran over to help her. The visitors streamed back to their cars and he went with them.

Whistling, he slid the wrapped paintings into the well between the back and front seats so they wouldn't bang around. He was feeling good, even confident. Finding Erin again wouldn't be too tough. But right now he had to get back to the station.

CHAPTER 2

Moving fast in the downpour, Bannon closed the distance between his parked car and headquarters in long strides. The yellow daffodils bent their heads, hammered by the steady rain as he went past them and through the front doors. The cinder-block building was almost deserted. Late in the afternoon, the people on the day shift cleared out in a hurry. But he knew Doris would still be there. He went down the basement stairs, the small wrapped watercolor in his hand.

Doris glanced up when he entered. She was sitting at the table, the documents from the Montgomery file spread out in front of her. "Back for more? You're a glutton for punishment." She straightened in her chair and rubbed her neck wearily. "I've been glued to this since you've been gone. Big mistake."

"Take a break."

She managed a smile. "That's good advice. Did you get your errands done?"

"Yeah." He'd almost forgotten that white lie. "I went by the Art Walk. Thanks for the tip." He patted his stomach. "I scored some pie."

"Did you bring me some?" she asked with mock annoyance.

"You said you didn't want anything to eat. But I got you a present. You like horses, right?" He held up the wrapped package.

"I like to bet on horses. Other people can ride them. What's that?"

RJ handed it to her. "Open it and find out."

Doris slid off her swivel chair. "It isn't my birthday, is it? Am I getting so old that I forget my own birthday?"

He smiled. "Just open the damn thing."

Doris laughed and took her time, unpicking the knot in the string with care. The watercolor of the horse glowed under the overhead fluorescent lights, a touch of nature in the ugly basement. "That's really nice, RJ," she said with pleased surprise. "It's not a print, is it?"

"No, it's an original."

"Local artist?"

"She didn't say, but I think so."

"Aha. She." Doris put the small framed painting where she could see it and studied him for a moment. "Was she pretty?"

"Damn straight."

"That's what I thought." She grinned. "Still, it's a beautiful little painting. Thanks."

"My pleasure."

"So, are you going to see her again?"

RJ only shrugged.

"You don't have to stay, you know," she chided affectionately. "Go chase girls. Leave me in the basement to suffer."

"Feeling sorry for yourself?"

Doris got up, stretching a little. "A little."

RJ glanced at the table and the rows of files. "Let's just do what we can in an hour and call it a day, how about that?"

"All right with me." Returning to her workstation, Doris clicked in and out of various programs as he handed her documents she asked for from the Montgomery files. He deliberately didn't read them. Right now he didn't want to be ensnared by the grim futility of the kidnapping case. He'd much rather be tracking down a certain artist with dark hair and incredible blue eyes.

He handed the faded reward poster to Doris. She used the staple remover to unclip the bank document from it, pulling the thin metal prongs out with a hard yank.

"It's just plain wrong for all this dough to go back to Hugh Montgomery," she muttered. "The money ought to be given to Ann's mother if no one's going to claim it." She slid the first page of the bank document into the scanner and closed the lid firmly. "Did you read the fine print in the trust?"

"I glanced at it. Fine print or no fine print, Montgomery can't be accused of stealing his own money," Bannon reasoned. "And he doesn't have to give it away if the trust is set to expire in another year. Considering the girl has never been found and the police are about to close the case on it, it's a logical end."

"It may be logical, but it still sucks," Doris grumbled and picked up the last page of the bank document to slide it in the scanner. "Especially this." She waved it in emphasis. "I'd bet anything Montgomery set up this trust as a tax shelter. It's like he had a feeling that Ann was never coming back."

"How much does anyone really know about Montgomery?" RJ asked.

"Not enough. But I doubt he's the pillar of the community he pretends to be," Doris said.

"Maybe so. But he hasn't broken any laws, right? Anyway, what happened to Mrs. Montgomery?"

"No one knows, RJ. I doubt that she uses the name anymore."

RJ shot a sideways look at his older colleague. "Did you ever see Luanne after she married him? You know, go out for coffee, have a chat, something like that?"

"I ran into her in town once in a while," Doris answered after a beat. "It wasn't anything we planned, but we would catch up and laugh about old times. That kid was cute as a button."

"So you met Ann."

Doris took a deep breath. "Yes, I did."

"What do you remember about them?" He watched her with close attention.

"Ann and her mother? They were both sweet. Even though she was getting written up in the society pages, Luanne was shy and kind of naïve. I know she didn't tell me everything, but I didn't like what I heard about her and Hugh Montgomery. All he cared about was his money."

"And after Ann was abducted," Bannon said bluntly, "what happened between the two of them? If you know," he added.

"Nobody really knew much, but everyone had an opinion. Montgomery was devastated. He coped by throwing himself into his work. He was cold to Luanne, so cold that her heart got broken twice. He shut her out completely." She heaved a sigh and crossed her arms over her chest as if she was protecting her own heart from some unknown danger. "That's what men do."

Bannon thought about his dad, who had sometimes shut all of them out. That was part of being a cop. He himself wasn't as good at it, though. His mom had done some sensitivity training on him and his brothers.

"Let's get back to the money," he said. Seemed safer. "He put up plenty of it to get his daughter back," Bannon reminded her. "Interest or no interest, that reward had to be a record."

"Believe me, he could afford it," Doris said. "By the way, I found the records of a few attempts made to claim it."

Bannon nodded. "Bound to be." He hadn't noticed those records himself, but with a reward like that, it was a given that there would be a large number of claimants.

"Montgomery had his people check out every one, I'll grant him that," Doris added grudgingly. "You wouldn't believe who comes out of the woodwork for a million."

"Yes, I would, so what else don't I know?"

"A lot." She looked down at the heaps of manila folders and the papers spilling out of them. "What's the use? I shouldn't get caught up in it again."

"No, you shouldn't," Bannon agreed. He spoke bluntly, but with a gentle tone. "At this point, about all anyone might learn is what happened to Ann, maybe locate her remains. We have the technology to read disturbed soil decades later, you know that—hell." He broke off when he noticed her stricken expression. "Never mind."

Doris didn't seem to be listening. "There wouldn't be much to bury after all this time," she whispered.

"But with DNA testing—" He realized a little too late that there were tears in her eyes she was valiantly holding back.

"What are they going to test if they don't find anything, RJ? The air?" she asked quietly.

"I'm sorry." Bannon held up his hands in a silent gesture of surrender.

In all his time with the Wainsville police, he had never seen Doris Rawling get emotional about anything. But she was now. In an attempt to cover it, she moved away from her computer and started fussing with the files on her end of the table. Busywork. His trick. It was useful. He turned in his chair to pull together the Montgomery folders.

An hour went by before he glanced her way. Doris had cut a substantial pile of material down to size and seemed like her old self again.

Deciding it was safest to stick to business, Bannon asked, "Is that FBI profiler report over there?"

"No, it's somewhere by you," she said crisply.

RJ finally found it and flipped through grainy, photocopied photos of convicted criminals and psychological profiles, then skimmed the stapled pages of the profiler's assessment.

"Nothing definitive in here. Could have been a man, could have been a woman," he muttered, frowning. "From here, from away. Maybe middle-aged. Maybe not."

Doris pushed her half-glasses back up her nose to look at him. "The profiler didn't have much to go on except for the sightings. People were calling in for months, coming in to give reports." She indicated the file those reports were in and RJ located it. "I haven't read them myself."

More out of idle curiosity than anything else, Bannon picked up the file and skimmed its contents, interested only in the high points. As expected, there was nothing of any real value there. He leafed through it again, checking dates, then closed the folder and gave it a toss onto the table.

"I can see why this is headed into cold case storage," Bannon declared, then paused long enough to check the dates in another file. "It's been nearly eighteen years since there's been anything that remotely resembles a lead to follow."

"Of course there hasn't been a lead," Doris shot back. "Nobody's looked at any of this in years. So how could there be any new information? It's been forgotten . . . and that isn't right," she ended with a telltale tremor in her voice.

"And it would take a new lead to keep this case active," Bannon admitted, thinking out loud. On the heels of his comment came a possibility that had the corners of his mouth lifting. "I think I know how to accomplish that."

Doris turned to him, suddenly hopeful. "Are you going to investigate it, RJ? On your own?"

The question was met with a short, negative movement of his head. "There's a slim-to-none chance that I could turn up something solid enough to warrant reopening this case. Actually, I had someone else in mind."

Totally puzzled, Doris frowned. "Who?"

"The bane of all law enforcement," he said with a smile. "The media, of course."

Understanding dawned in her expression. "That blond television reporter you dated for a while. What was her name?" She snapped her fingers, trying to recall it.

"Kelly Johns," Bannon filled in the blank for her. "And I didn't go out with her all that long. By the third date, I could tell that she was looking at me as a 'confidential source' in the police department."

Doris sniffed disapproval. "My mother always said not to trust anyone with two first names."

Bannon let that little pearl of wisdom pass without comment. "Kelly just happens to be ambitious as well as intelligent."

"Not to mention gorgeous," she inserted, a little cattily.

Bannon just smiled. "She is easy on the eyes."

"What makes you think you could talk her into looking into this?"

"Simple. The anniversary date of Ann's abduction is coming up. It should make an interesting feature—missing child of local Virginia aristocrat, two-million-dollar reward. Old or not, that's the kind of stuff the media feasts on."

From her expression, it was obvious Doris conceded that point. Almost to herself, she mumbled, "I hope you split up with her on friendly terms."

"I know I've been accused of lacking diplomatic skill, but I'm smart enough to know that you never want to make an enemy of anyone on that side of the police tape."

"Thank goodness for that," she declared, then watched in bewilderment while he pulled folders out of the stack and started a different pile. "What are you doing?"

"Before I contact her, I need to make sure I have the facts straight in my mind."

"But, RJ, you aren't on active duty," Doris protested. "You can't take original documents out of here until you're officially back on the force."

"I know that." He picked up the new stack and carried the folders to the copy machine. "I'm only asking you to let me have this stuff overnight."

"I shouldn't."

"Clap, clap." Bannon pretended to applaud. "I admire your character. How did we get this far?"

"I really shouldn't." She held out a hand. "Give me that stuff back."

"Too late. It all started with a fateful step," he intoned. "I saw your name on the door to the basement. And down I went. And there was the Montgomery file."

"RJ—"

"I have to stop opening doors," he said conversationally. "I keep catching bullets."

"That was two years ago."

"True." He arranged the old snapshots carefully on the glass, face down. "I could do these in black and white, but I'll lose a lot of detail. I'm thinking you could scan the visuals and send me jpegs. Or burn 'em on a CD."

She folded her arms across her chest. "All traceable to my computer. No."

"Then let me have them." He gathered up the photos with one hand like it was a done deal. "Just temporarily."

Doris hesitated, not saying yes or no.

"You can always send them into storage later. Just say you forgot or something."

"What if Hoebel checks up on me?"

Bannon shook his head. "He won't. The man is all memos and no action. And Jolene isn't going to come down those stairs in sky-high heels."

"You noticed."

"Years of training."

With a surrendering lift of her hands, Doris went back to her computer and Bannon took what he thought he would need, as well as the photographs. He got everything into a single big envelope, reasoning that he had entered the building with an envelope and wouldn't attract any notice leaving with another.

"See you," he called to Doris as he went back up the stairs.

At the top of the stairs, he looked around. There were more empty cubicles than not. The entering cops on the night shift were talking to each other, their backs to him, or staring into monitor screens. He was happy to be ignored as he eyeballed the huge whiteboard where current cases were listed on a grid, their status to the right. Two at the top had been solved. Ten unsolved. Doris was right about the lack of manpower. Most had been on the board for a few weeks.

Needing to breathe and collect his thoughts, he took a roundabout way home that wound through the country. No sunset. The evening sky was shrouded by clouds. Cold air came his way from the quiet, leafless woods that surrounded him. He went over a low bridge, not stopping to look at the river below. But he did wonder if Ann Montgomery's abductor had brought her down it somehow. What he remembered of the police maps in the file showed the same river upstream, not far from the family mansion.

It began to drizzle as he drove on. Bannon pondered the convoluted facts of the old Montgomery case without reaching any conclusions that made sense to him. After a while, he turned off the country road and headed back into town, feeling kind of blue. He hadn't had any time to decompress between coming back from the cabin and picking up the claim forms for the chief to sign that morning. He thought of Erin, the one bright spot in an otherwise mostly depressing day. It was definitely worth finding out more about her. Whatever it took, he would do. Short of acting like a stalker.

The windshield wipers were slapping at raindrops when he pulled into his space in the condo's lot. He took a minute to find a plastic bag under the seat large enough for the envelope with the photocopies. The bag went inside his jacket as a fail-safe to protect the contents. With his free hand, he managed to hoist the large wrapped watercolor of the wild horses. He had to set the painting down to unlock the door of his condo.

Inside he put the plastic bag on the coffee table and then lifted up the painting onto the fireplace mantel, promising himself to unwrap it later and look for a framer's tag on the back, another possible lead to follow, in case someone at the Art Walk committee was reluctant to give him Erin's contact info and last name.

A partially muffled but decidedly impatient yowl came from the direction of the living room's sliding glass doors, followed quickly by the sound of claws on mesh screen. Without hesitation, Bannon altered his course toward the rear patio where a tiger-striped tomcat stood on his hind legs, demanding admission. Bannon took one look at flattened ears and wet fur spiked by the steady drizzle, smiled, flipped the lock, and slid the door open.

Immediately the cat came down on all fours and padded into the living room, grumbling his irritation at being kept waiting when he passed Bannon. "Like you would melt in the rain," Bannon scoffed.

A pair of golden eyes sliced him a look. In the next second the cat sprang onto the stretch-limo-sized black leather couch and proceeded to rake his tongue over his wet fur.

Bannon watched him for a moment. Big and muscled, the tomcat resembled a boxer—right down to the tattered ears. A year ago, his brother Linc had handed him an open cardboard box. Inside was an injured, scrawny kitten, half-wild.

"He was getting the short end of a fight with some big tom when I rescued him," Linc had told him. "I thought you two could recuperate together. You know what they say—misery loves company. Meet Babaloo, your company."

Compared to Bannon's, the cat's wounds had been minor, so Babaloo had recovered more quickly than he had. As for the company part, Linc had known what he was talking about. But Bannon wasn't likely to ever admit that to him.

Leaving the cat to his grooming, Bannon doubled back to the kitchen where he opened the refrigerator and surveyed the shelves. Slim pickings. There was a chunk of cheese with suspicious white spots and a wrinkly apple. He picked up both and tossed them into the garbage, then took out a leftover cooked salmon steak wrapped in foil.

Babaloo strolled into the kitchen, nose twitching.

"I take it hunting wasn't very good today." Bannon unwrapped the salmon, cut off a piece, and tossed it in the cat's food bowl.

The cat demolished his share in two gulps and licked his whiskers appreciatively when he was done.

Bannon grinned. "You were hungry." He put a dollop of mayo for dipping on a paper plate, then cut the salmon steak in chunks. Cold protein. It would do. He didn't feel like cooking. But he looked at the plate and added a few slices of tomato from a lidded container, for his health.

Taking a bowl from the cupboard, he filled it with ice and jammed three unopened bottles of beer in. It had been a long day; he was entitled.

Back in the living room, he cracked open beer one and set the bottle on the floor to guard against a spill. Next he separated the copied papers from the photos, then sat down and spread them out on the coffee table.

He skimmed.

The wistful quality of the little girl's gaze pulled at him. She clung to her mother in a few shots and shyly peered out from the folds of her skirt in one. The only shot of Ann with her father showed Hugh Montgomery smiling affably into the camera, his hands thrust into the pockets of his expensive suit. He was standing a few feet away from his tiny daughter, who looked up at him. Her uncertain expression said a lot about that relationship.

Bannon put the photos down with a sigh, wanting to look at the drawing of Ann at age three again. Just as he reached for it, the phone rang.

Smiling when he saw the caller ID, he picked up the receiver. "Hi, Mom. What's up?"

"How are you, RJ? It's not like you to not call. Haven't heard from you—"

He finished the sentence for her. "For a whole day." He cracked open beer two and kicked back to relax.

His mother laughed. "Okay, I'm a worrywart. Sue me."

"I don't mind, Mom. Good to hear your voice." He meant it. She was on her own since his father's death and there was nothing he wouldn't do for her. Which didn't mean that Sheila Bannon didn't drive him crazy now and then.

"Oh, RJ. So what are you doing?"

"Eating." He waited for what he knew she would say. "Yes, leftovers. How did you know?"

"I just do. Are you alone?"

When the tiger-striped cat sauntered into the room, Bannon glanced his way. "Babaloo is keeping me company. That's about it for excitement around here. I was thinking of watching the Discovery Channel with him. He loves nature documentaries."

"That's funny. He's a good cat. You should get out more, though."

"He's fine company."

"You know what I'm talking about, RJ. Find a girl, have fun again."

"I did, as a matter of fact. Today. She seems nice. Her name is Erin. I'll keep you posted."

"What does she do?" Sheila Bannon just had to make sure that his dates didn't make a living wrapped around a stripper's pole.

"She's an artist, mostly watercolors."

His mother pondered that. "Oh. Well, that's nice. Not much money in it, though."

"I didn't ask for her tax returns," he said dryly. "Like I said, I just met her."

"It's a start. You can't live alone forever."

"I don't plan to, Mom. But Gina isn't coming back unless there's a big fat diamond in it for her."

"How do you know that?"

"I told you that story. Not very romantic. She let me know how many goddamn carats she expected. Too many."

He waited impatiently while his mother said something sympathetic, but not about him.

"I was flat on my back with a bullet in me, Mom, waiting for an insurance settlement—how was I supposed to pay for a rock like that and in a platinum setting? And from an expensive jewelry store in Washington, DC? You know it—where the senators shop for the women they actually sleep with. Not their wives." He stopped to take a breath. "Sorry. I'm ranting."

"You never told me the name of the store."

Was that ever a Mom thing to say. He couldn't figure out why she would want to know, but he named it. "That was the beginning of the end, believe me. It's been a year already, Mom. Can't say I miss her."

His mother was silent but not for long. "See what I mean? You're getting grumpy."

"No, I'm not," he said soothingly. "Look, I gotta go." He said an affectionate good-bye before she got on his nerves and hung up with a promise to call the next day.

He had deliberately not mentioned anything to her about the favor he was doing for Doris on the Montgomery case. And he probably wouldn't when he saw her this weekend either.

The Montgomery case. Drawing a deep breath, he reached for the top folder and flipped it open to begin his fact gathering. Kelly Johns would likely do her own, but Bannon wanted to be well-armed when he talked to her.

An hour later, he knew a lot more about Montgomery, none of it very good. Montgomery's financial empire had been founded on what was left of the family fortune and bolstered with smart horse trading. Right now the guy was touting a shaky-looking hedge fund that amounted to selling shares of winning Thoroughbreds.

There were several offshore accounts in Caribbean countries and a few in Europe. A joke postcard from Switzerland showed a fat cat in pinstripes kissing a banker. It was blank on the back. Bannon figured that Montgomery had clipped it to his tax returns to amuse his accountant.

On it went. Montgomery had never been investigated or indicted for financial misdeeds, but it didn't take a forensic accountant to see that the man was wildly overextended, a polite term for being in a colossal amount of debt. He owed millions and seemed to be paying his debts off by borrowing millions more from people who were either naïve or plain greedy. That was going to catch up with him—and the luckless investors who didn't do due diligence.

The tax analysis made for dry reading. Then Bannon noticed that the man treated himself to a generous charitable deduction every year for allowing the Wainsville historical society to give tours of the family mansion.

He could understand why the family had pulled up stakes; few would willingly stay in a house after a tragic kidnapping, especially once it was clear that the child was gone forever. Even so, deducting its use by a nonprofit was legal but didn't smell right.

It struck him that Montgomery played every angle for his maximum benefit. Maybe the guy wasn't as rich as the press clippings and Internet mentions made him out to be.

Sliding the financial reports back in the file, Bannon got up to take a break, feeling the mellow buzz of two longneck beers. The wrapped painting on the mantel caught his eye. He was ready to open it and see if he'd actually bought something good or been under the spell of the artist.

The brown paper was noisy when it came off. Babaloo opened an eye but not all the way.

"Disturbed your sleep, did I?"

When the paper dropped to the floor, Bannon pushed it against the wall with his foot. A search failed to locate a framer's tag, and he concluded Erin had probably framed it herself. It looked professional, though. Maybe she'd learned how in her starving artist days, which he suspected were behind her.

He turned back to his laptop, touched a few buttons, and typed in *Erin*, *horse*, *painting*, *Chincoteague*. Bingo. She'd been in a group show out there. But still under just the one name. There was no link or contact info on her. With a defeated sigh, Bannon closed the lid and let his gaze wander over the watercolor.

It was as good as he remembered, better, even. Dramatic. And mysterious.

Chincoteague horses, huh? He'd never been to that part of the Maryland coast—he was more of a mountain man. Briefly he considered taking a trip there. It was still the off-season; the place wouldn't be swarming with tourists. He'd bet anything her work would be exhibited at a gallery there. He ambled over to an arm-chair that faced the painting he'd bought and helped himself to beer three on the way.

Leaning back, Bannon supported his head on the muscle in his upper arm, trying to remember every single detail about Erin. Her face, her figure—he hadn't really seen that, because the weather hadn't been cooperating. But she had a lithe way of moving that let him know her body was good. He'd liked the warm pitch of her voice and her hesitation in talking about herself.

Bannon sipped his third beer and contemplated his next moves where she was concerned.

First you have to find her, he reminded himself cheerfully enough.

CHAPTER 3

Tired and sweaty from his three-mile run at dawn, Bannon walked the last hundred feet to his condo. The big tomcat waited for him at the door, sprawled across the mat, looking all smug and satisfied.

"Back from your midnight wanderings, I see." Bannon dug the key from his pocket and inserted it in the lock. "Who was she this time? The cute little calico on the next block or the fluffy white angora from Unit Nine?"

At the click of the lock, Babaloo rose and stretched with a muscled ease that Bannon envied greatly at that moment. He gave the door an inward push and the cat strolled through the opening ahead of him.

"Wise cat." Bannon followed him inside. "It's never smart to kiss and tell."

Crossing the kitchen, he threw a glance at the clock and stripped off his damp sweatshirt. He paused in the living room long enough to turn on the television and switch to the local news. Kelly Johns smiled back at him, her brown eyes gleaming with intelligence, the curving sweep of her blond hair brushing the top of her shoulders. Her ever-so-subtle tan gave her a healthy-looking golden glow.

"We'll be right back with Ron and his forecast for this week's weather." Her voice had a well-mouthed tone, pitched neither too low nor too high. In short, it was perfect for television, like everything else about her.

Bannon punched the Mute button and headed straight for the shower. By the time he shed the rest of his running clothes, the water was hot and he stepped under its pummeling jets, letting them beat the ache from his muscles.

After about five minutes under the invigorating spray, he felt half-human again, killed the jets and toweled himself mostly dry, then used a corner of the cloth to wipe off the moisture steaming the mirror. He ran a skimming glance over his own reflection, absently noting the dark brown hair, hazel eyes, strong chin, and the crooked line of his nose from a previous break. A razor made short work of the dark stubble shadowing his lean cheeks. Finished, he splashed on some after-shave lotion and winced at its sting, then headed into the bedroom.

He dressed less casually than usual for Kelly's benefit, pairing jeans and a crisp striped shirt with a camel sports jacket. With his cell phone, wallet, keys, and loose change stuffed in various pockets, Bannon backtracked to the living room. He verified the local news was still on, switched off the television, and headed for the door.

Babaloo snaked outside first and trotted off. "No 'have a great day,' 'good luck,' nothing?" Bannon challenged as he locked the door behind him.

The tiger-striped cat spared him a look and issued an indifferent "Meow."

"So glad you care," Bannon murmured dryly and struck out for his car.

After reversing out of the parking slot, he pulled onto the street and took aim on the downtown area. The first of the morning rush had just started, filling the lanes without slowing speed yet.

His cell phone rang, drawing a half-smothered sigh of irritation from him. He slipped it from his pocket, noticed the caller ID was blocked, and flipped it open.

"Bannon," he offered in clipped greeting.

"RJ, it's Doris." A car in the next lane honked impatiently at a less-than-alert driver slow to accelerate when the light turned green. "Where are you?"

"In traffic. Can't you tell?"

"I wasn't paying that much attention," she admitted. "Where are you going? Do you have a minute?"

The anxious and slightly harried note in her voice warned Bannon that this conversation wasn't likely to be a short one. He started looking for a place to pull over. With the traffic thickening, he didn't want his attention divided.

"I was on my way to Kelly's favorite espresso bar."

"Do you have a meeting with her?"

"Not yet. . . ." He pulled into the lot of a combination gas station and quick mart.

"You mean you haven't talked to her? I thought you'd call her last night."

"What is this? The second degree?" Bannon challenged, then muttered, "You sound like my mother."

"What did you say? I'm sorry, I didn't catch that."

"I was just saying that I was busy with other things last night." Namely, the Montgomery files. "You obviously called me for a reason, Doris. What is it?"

"I—I've got a call coming in. Hang on. I have to take it." For an eon of seconds he watched the vehicles rolling by on the street and waited until she came back on the line. "I'm back. Are you there?"

"Still here."

"That was a friend of mine at the bank. Montgomery just filed the paperwork to have the monies held in trust for the reward revert to him."

"A friend, you say. Can you get her to refund my bounced check fees?"

"No, she can't, and I would never ask her. Now, be serious. We have something to talk about."

Bannon stifled another sigh. "We've already been over this. Montgomery funded the trust. Therefore, he can dissolve it."

"Even though his daughter was never officially declared dead?"

"I'm not a lawyer, so I don't know whether it matters that he never petitioned the courts to have her declared dead. My gut says that it probably doesn't."

"But why is he doing it now, after all these years?"

"Well, from what I read last night, I got the impression Montgomery's had some financial difficulties. At the least, a cash flow problem." He checked his watch. "Look, I'd love to go into it with you, Doris, but if Kelly sticks to her usual pattern, she'll be popping into the espresso bar sometime between ten and twenty after. I'd like to be there ahead of her, which only gives me ten minutes."

"How can you be sure she'll even go there?" Doris protested. "I know you're trying to be subtle in your approach, but you could have done it all with a phone call."

"Maybe so, but only an earth-shattering news story would stop Kelly from grabbing her morning jolt of java." He shifted the car in reverse and glanced into the rearview mirror. "We'll talk later."

As Bannon started to lower the cell phone, Doris shouted, "Don't hang up! I haven't told you the most important thing."

Something in her voice made him ask, "What's that?"

"I found the master list for the files. The Montgomery evidence folder is gone."

Bannon frowned. "But you said there wasn't one."

"RJ, I said there wasn't any evidence to speak of. But that doesn't mean there wasn't a file for it. There was—I mean there is—and Hoebel signed it out. The question is, what's in it?"

"I see what you're getting at." He nodded, considering this new wrinkle.

"Why would he do something like that, RJ?"

"How should I know?" A thought occurred to him. "Does Hoebel know Montgomery?"

Part of her reply dissolved in a crackle of static. ". . . I was thinking the same thing . . . reopen the case."

He held the phone away from his ear, not sure if he'd heard her right. What the hell was going on at headquarters?

"Do you actually have some dirt on Hoebel? Mr. Rules and Regulations himself?" Bannon strained to hear her reply.

"No, but there has to be a connection. Get this—the Montgomery evidence file was the only old case that the chief signed out. All the others were current ones."

"Interesting," Bannon said slowly.

"There's more. This missing one apparently has letters, along with fill-in-the-blank reports. Or so said the master list."

"Big deal." Bannon shrugged it off. "Kidnapping cases generate a ton of mail. Mostly from cranks."

"I know that. But the list specified a letter from someone calling herself Ann's new mother, quote unquote, to Montgomery himself. So that got my attention."

New mother. The phrase opened up a whole other aspect to the case that he hadn't previously considered. "There was never any ransom demand made, was there?" he recalled.

"Not that I ever heard about, and there wasn't any mention of one in the evidence master list."

Subconsciously he must have registered the lack of reference to one, Bannon realized. Without it, he had automatically jumped to the assumption that the little girl had been taken by some perverted child molester. In those instances, a child rarely lived longer than a matter of days. But if she had been taken by someone seeking to fill a void in his or her own life—for the first time Bannon thought there might be a real chance Ann Montgomery was still alive.

"Was that letter dated, Doris?"

"The master list didn't say. But what with the chief signing out the file and not returning it—and Montgomery trying to dissolve the trust—well, I don't know about you but I want to know what's in that letter."

"Me too."

"And I want to know why that file got sent to storage ahead of all the other *M*s."

"It may not be in storage, Doris." It crossed his mind that it could be smoke wafting out of an incinerator by now.

"I'm going to call in sick and drive down to the warehouse where the first batch of cold case files were stored. I could be gone a couple of days."

"You're running the risk that somebody there could call Hoebel," Bannon warned.

"I've been to the place before. The staff sleeps sitting up when they're not watching TV. It's not like the files are trying to escape. In the meantime," Doris added, "we have to keep Montgomery on a short leash. The best way to do that is by going public. He's less likely to grab back that two million dollars if he thinks it will make him look bad."

"Agreed. That's where Kelly comes in."

". . . I'm gone."

The connection was broken. With a smiling shake of his head, Bannon flipped the cell phone and returned it to his pocket. Seconds later he was back in the flow of traffic and headed for his "coincidental" rendezvous with Kelly Johns.

Due in no small part to the green lights that met him at every intersection, Bannon pulled into the espresso bar's parking lot in eight minutes flat. As he stepped out of the car he caught the back view of a slender blonde in a belted lightweight coat and high heels just entering the coffee shop. Though he couldn't swear to it, he was certain it was Kelly Johns.

Two steps inside the door and his suspicion was confirmed. It was Kelly there at the counter, standing in profile, still in television makeup, a pair of designer sunglasses resting atop her head.

As luck would have it, there was no one in the line ahead of him and he walked up behind her. "Let me guess." He peered over her left shoulder at the capped cup the attendant pushed across the counter toward her. "Double shot latte with skim milk and drizzles of caramel."

She turned with a small start, her dark eyes lighting up with recognition at the sight of him.

"Bannon. This is a surprise. And more of a surprise that you remembered this." She picked up the cup and gave it an indicating lift.

"Remembering details is my business," Bannon reminded her and ordered a regular coffee. "Sometimes the seemingly minor ones turn out to be important."

"I'd ask how you are, but you look so strong and fit, the answer seems obvious." She waited next to him while his coffee was poured. "Are you back on duty?"

"Not yet. Which is probably just as well since they'd more than likely restrict me to desk duty and I'd hate it." With his coffee delivered, he gestured to an empty table. "Do you have time to sit and drink that?"

After the smallest of hesitations, she smiled easily. "I can steal a few minutes."

"Good." He guided her to the table.

Once seated, she ran a thoughtful look over his face. "I don't know if anyone told you or not, but I went to the hospital to see you a day or two after the shooting. But at the time, they were only allowing immediate family members in to see you. I stopped again a week or so later, and you'd already been released."

"I'm sure someone mentioned it to me, but as drugged as I was, I don't even remember my family being there."

"I understand. I'm just glad that you've fully recovered—or almost."

She meant that. Bannon could tell. And he also believed that she had come to see him back then out of genuine concern for his well-being. But he also knew she'd probably been hoping she could talk him into an exclusive interview.

While wasting a couple of minutes on idle chitchat, Bannon acknowledged to himself that she was still beautiful, intelligent, and very easy to talk to—all things that had originally drawn him to ask her out those many months ago. But when he compared her with Erin, even though he had just met her, Kelly came up lacking on many levels. It was an observation he wanted to explore. Then he caught her glance at her wristwatch and knew he was running out of time.

"So, what story are you heading off to track down this morning?" he asked, then held up a silencing hand. "I'll bet you're going to try to dig up a fresh angle on the Montgomery case."

"Montgomery. You mean—Hugh Montgomery?"

He could almost see all her antennae go out, and worked to hide a satisfied smile. "The one and only."

"Oh. Right. Just to be sure we're on the same page, which case are you talking about? His name's been mentioned in a couple of financial investigations that didn't go anywhere." She was careful to show only a mild interest.

"His daughter's abduction. Either this week or next, it will be twenty-odd years ago that it happened. I just assumed your station would run a feature on it to mark the occasion. After all, it has all the hooks—a wealthy old Virginia family, beautiful little daughter missing, a two-million-dollar reward for her safe return."

"Of course. You know we will," Kelly assured him. "A juicy cold case report always boosts the ratings. We run them on our website for days sometimes." She paused—deliberately, Bannon thought. "It was before my time, but we recycle a lot of stories. I'm trying to remember." A thoughtful little crease marred her smooth forehead. "The police never had much to go on, did they? No blood-soaked little dress or anything like that?"

"Not that I know about."

"Too bad. I know it sounds sick, but our viewers seem to like those gory visuals."

"Not surprising when you consider the popularity of horror movies. Anyway—" Bannon gave a small shrug. "I'm sure you can dig up a ton of still pictures of the little girl and old footage out of the station's image bank. Combine that with a computer-generated picture of what the girl might look like today, and you'd have a good feature."

"Mmmm." She made a vaguely agreeing sound that sounded far from happy. "But that wouldn't be much different from any other station. Unless—" She stared at him for a long second. "I have an idea. Excuse me, I need to make a quick phone call. Don't go. Just stay right there."

Clearly hot to pursue this idea, Kelly was out of the chair with her cell phone in hand before she ever finished talking. Amused by her avidity, Bannon sat back in his chair and sipped at his coffee to disguise his study of her.

After taking a few steps away from him for privacy, she partially turned her back to the table, punched a couple of keys on the cell phone pad, and raised the phone to her ear. The connection was almost instant as she started talking in quick, hushed tones.

As conversations went, it was short, but television news had a reputation for brevity. Judging by the Cheshire cat–like uplift to the corners of her mouth when she walked back to the table, Bannon guessed that she had been successful.

"That was my producer I called." Resuming her seat, she reached for her cup. "She liked my idea."

"Good."

Her dark eyes danced with amusement as she smiled at him over the rim of her cup. "You might not think so when you hear what it is."

"Why?" What is it?" he asked, suddenly on guard.

"For an interview with you to be part of the piece."

"Me?" he blurted in stunned disbelief.

"Remember that weekend we spent at Virginia Beach?"

"What about it?" Caution was in the flatness of his voice.

"I don't think I ever showed you the picture I took." Kelly rolled the cup between her hands and studied him with suppressed amusement. "I know you're not conceited, but you're very photogenic. In the interview you're going to come across as tough and sexy. And that sells just as well as blood and guts."

"Yeah, well—you know that I can't divulge any specific information. About all I could do is comment on police procedure in cold cases such as this."

"No problem." A shoulder lifted in an eloquent shrug. "Do you agree to the interview?"

The wheels had already been turning, so his hesitation was minimal. "On one condition."

Kelly cocked her head, intrigued by his response. "What's that?"

"That I'm guaranteed to get a look at the viewer responses you receive."

Her interest sharpened, all her reporter instincts surfacing with a rush. "Are you going after the reward, Bannon?"

Was he? After his conversation with Doris, Bannon admitted to himself that the reward was not entirely out of reach.

"Let's just say I'm curious."

He could tell that Kelly didn't buy his answer. She paused fractionally, then gave him a decisive nod. "All right then. You've got a deal."

"Good." Something told him that she hoped to extract a price for this favor later on.

"Are you free to do the interview this morning?"

It was Bannon's turn to shrug. "Why not?" Now that he'd agreed to it, he was eager to get it over with.

"Then let's go." Kelly rose.

* * *

The local television station was two blocks from the espresso bar. Kelly led him into its dim and cool inner sanctum and handed him over to her producer, a fortysomething, no-nonsense woman by the name of Carla Frazier. With a smile and a wave Kelly was gone.

The producer motioned to a chair in front of her desk. Bannon sat down as he made his usual visual survey of his surroundings. There on the monitor screen was a photograph of a little girl. Bannon recognized it immediately as being identical to one he'd seen in the Ann Montgomery file. Carla Frazier hadn't wasted any time retrieving information about the case following Kelly's phone call.

"It'll be a few minutes before they're ready for you in the studio," she informed him. "The questions are all scripted. Try to keep your answers short."

"No problem." Bannon had testified in enough court cases to know that you never gave a five-word answer when *no* would do— and you never volunteered information.

"Might as well get the releases handled while we're waiting." She opened a drawer and pulled out several forms, then slid them across her desk toward him. "Sign here and here." She stabbed the paper with the tip of her pen before handing it to him. "Basically it says that we have the right to edit your interview for content and length. And no, you don't have prior approval of what goes on the air."

"What a surprise," he muttered under his breath and scratched his signature across the appropriate blanks.

"Yeah, well, not everybody gets their fifteen minutes of fame." She gathered up the releases in a neat stack and sized him up with one glance. "Kelly thinks the camera's going to love you. If it does, so much the better. If not, we'll do the story with our anchor and the visuals we'll create."

"My feelings won't be hurt if I end up on the cutting-room floor," Bannon assured her.

She shot him a skeptical look, but said nothing.

An hour later, he found himself in a small, soundproof chamber with a photographic blow-up on one wall that looked vaguely like a city at night. There was one chair, for him. He felt like a perp in an interrogation room.

Everything happened fast. A skinny kid clipped a tiny mike to his shirt and a tech told him to look directly into the camera lens when he spoke, pointing to where it came through the other wall. A young woman came in to take the shine off his face with a powder-laden brush and frowned at his hair but left it alone. Bannon was grateful. He didn't want to be gelled, thank you very much.

She was replaced by a man who didn't give his name but squatted out of camera range, giving a countdown and then reading the scripted questions aloud in a monotone. Not ones Bannon was expecting, but they got what they wanted in two takes.

The whole business was about as exciting as waiting for a bus. He wasn't expecting much . . . when and if the segment appeared on TV.

Two days later, a production assistant left Bannon a message on his cell phone, telling him the piece would air on the evening news slot. But Bannon didn't pick the message up in time. He missed the broadcast and forgot about looking for it on the station website.

RJ opened the door of his fridge and heard the cat come running on soft paws. The suck of the rubber seal got Babaloo's attention every time. Too bad there was nothing on the shelves worth eating for either of them.

His cell phone buzzed in his jeans pocket.

"Sorry, pal. That has to be Doris. I'll make a supermarket run after I hang up."

The cat sauntered away as RJ extracted the phone from his pocket, flipping it open without looking at the screen to see who it was.

"Hey," he said. "Are you all right?"

"Am I speaking to RJ Bannon?" The male voice was cordial, but not remotely familiar.

"Who is this?"

"Olliver Duncan. Senior partner at Duncan, Hobert, and Giles. You don't know me—"

"Let's keep it that way," Bannon said, cupping the phone in his hand to flip it shut. He stopped when he heard the man's faint reply.

"I represent Hugh Montgomery."

Bannon brought the phone back to his ear. "And . . . ?"

"We saw the segment on Ann's kidnapping on the news today."

"You're one up on me. I didn't."

"I see." There was an infinitesimal pause. "Mr. Montgomery and I would like to talk to you about that and some other things. At your convenience, of course."

Frowning, Bannon considered the unexpected request. But there was only one way to find out what was behind it.

"Where and when?" he asked.

Olliver Duncan gave the address of his law firm. "Would one o'clock tomorrow work?"

"Fine." Bannon flipped the phone shut and let his mind sift through the possibilities.

The glass doors of Duncan, Hobert & Giles were immaculately clean. Either they weren't doing much business or they had a guy with a squirt bottle of glass cleaner who did nothing but run out and eradicate every fingerprint an instant after a client arrived. It fit. Bannon had done his homework on Olliver Duncan. He had started out in criminal law, but he only represented white-collar crooks who stole millions with the stroke of a pen. No riffraff for him. Duncan had made a fortune and moved on. The clients on his current roster were generally respectable. And filthy rich.

The thought made Bannon smile grimly as he pushed one door open. He softened the smile when the young receptionist looked up.

"Mr. Bannon?" she said eagerly.

"That's right. I have a one o'clock meeting with—"

"Mr. Duncan," she finished for him. "You're early. He's not back from lunch yet." She tapped the eraser end of a pencil on the large appointment book spread open on her desk. "I knew it was you the second I saw you open the door. I recognized you from the cold case segment on the news last night." She gazed at him as if he was a movie star.

"Sorry, I haven't seen it myself."

She darted a quick look over her shoulder. There was no one there. "Really? But wasn't it taped?"

"Yes." He offered no further explanation.

"If you want, I could show it to you on my monitor. I'll keep the sound down low. It's only a few minutes long."

Without waiting for his answer, she clicked away on her mouse, looking for the video clip online. Then she turned the screen around and tipped it up, beaming around the side of it at him.

He watched himself. It was excruciating. The thoughtful answers he had given sounded wrong, mainly because the smooth-talking anchor had changed the questions to suit his on-air persona. He emphasized the outstanding reward, directing viewers to the station website for details.

Bannon winced. The guy was putting a spin on the facts that made him want to punch something. The short segment concluded with the software-generated image of Ann Montgomery as she might be now, done by the station's graphics department. His eyes widened when he saw it.

They'd blown that too. The features were just too perfect and the hair color was pale blond. They'd made her look like a glamorous model, not a real young woman.

"This is . . . Ann Montgomery," he heard the anchorman say in a deep, phony voice. "Missing for over twenty-five years in the most sensational kidnapping in Virginia. But she may be alive. Have you seen her?" The image of Ann faded away as the anchor came back on. He stared intently into the camera as if he, not Bannon, was on the case. "Contact us at . . ."

The receptionist heard someone coming and hastily turned the monitor back around, clicking out of the website and pretending to work.

An older woman whom Bannon took for the office manager appeared. "Put these in order for filing, please," she said as she handed the girl a sheaf of papers, then surveyed him. "And you are . . . ?"

"This is Mr. Bannon," the receptionist said innocently. "He has a meeting with Mr. Duncan at one o'clock."

"I see." The older woman looked him up and down in a scornful way before going back to the inner offices. No offer of a cup of coffee or other friendly overture for the likes of him. He figured that her low opinion of him was the official one. So much for the adoring young receptionist.

Bannon headed for a maroon leather sofa, its heavy walnut frame outlined with bronze studs. It was a huge piece of furniture designed to impress legal clients—or intimidate the opposition.

He stretched out his long legs and waited, but there was no getting comfortable on this thing. He looked around at the tasteful, nondescript framed art on the paneled walls and the potted palm, its luxuriant fronds as well-groomed as everything else. The atmosphere of affluence and privilege was almost suffocating.

The glass doors swung open behind him. Two men walked by and Bannon had a chance to scope both of them out for a few seconds. One was tall and powerfully built for an older man. Hugh Montgomery. The other—the short one—Bannon pegged instantly for a lawyer. He had on an Armani suit and a gold watch so heavy Bannon was surprised he could lift his hand to wave to the receptionist.

"Hello, Mary. Any calls for me?"

She tore off message slips from a spiral-bound book and kept the carbon copies underneath. "Here you are, sir. Your one o'clock is here." She nodded in Bannon's direction.

He was already standing when both men turned around.

He met the gaze of the taller man. Hugh Montgomery was older and balder than the photos Bannon had seen of him, but he still possessed a masterful air. He looked the part of a modern-day Virginia aristocrat. Old school. Wealthy. The kind of man who appeared in the winner's circle at major horse races or profiles in upscale magazines. His eyes held a fierceness that Bannon had somehow expected to see.

"Hello." Montgomery extended a hand and Bannon had to shake it.

The attorney was next, coming over to where he was and clapping him on the shoulder. "Mr. Bannon, you are punctual. My apologies. This is Hugh Montgomery, of course. First names, every-one? Hugh, RJ. Were you waiting long? Come into my office, gentle-men. Mary, hold my calls."

Bannon went with him, keeping exactly to the side of Hugh Montgomery. He didn't want those eyes boring into the back of his head.

They reached Olliver's private office, which at least looked like a working office, although it was about the same square footage as Bannon's condo. The vast desk was piled high with stapled docu-ments and other paperwork. More stacks were on the floor. But there was a cleared-off table in one corner and armchairs arranged around it. Maroon leather, of course.

"Make yourselves at home, you two," Olliver said. "Be right there. Sara!" he called through the open door, then turned to them. "Anyone besides me want coffee? There's tea too. Or bour-bon, if you prefer."

"Nothing for me, thanks," Bannon said.

Montgomery echoed his words. His voice was deep, with a weary edge. He rested a large hand on the table. Bannon got the impression of controlled power—barely controlled. The older man was drumming his fingers on the surface.

The lawyer came back with a cup of coffee that the office man-ager handed through the door. He set it on the table and took the chair between them.

"So why am I here?" Bannon decided he might as well get to the point.

Olliver stirred his coffee with a spoon. "We saw the segment after it aired. Actually, a colleague alerted us. My client wanted to know more. Needless to say, he has a few questions for you."

"Go ahead."

The lawyer set the spoon to one side. "I should explain that he wanted me to be present. It's been years—you understand."

Bannon didn't. But he followed Montgomery's lead and let the lawyer do the talking. Olliver was getting paid for his time, no doubt. Bannon wasn't.

"No adversarial intent. This isn't a deposition or anything, you know. Just a friendly chat."

One with sharp teeth, Bannon thought, catching a glimpse of the shark behind the lawyer's affable smile. "Okay."

"We wanted to know, first of all, if you were officially reopening the case."

The case. Neither man had mentioned who was at the heart of the case: Montgomery's missing daughter. Bannon glanced at the stern, deeply carved face of the older man, not seeing little Ann's delicate features in him at all. "I really can't say."

"All right." Olliver nodded. "Were you speaking on behalf of the Wainsville Police Department?"

Bannon shrugged. "You could find that out with one phone call."

"Well, we did make a few inquiries. I was curious to hear what you had to say. I take it your answer is no."

Bannon looked at him steadily. "I didn't think I answered the question."

The attorney picked up his coffee and took a sip. "You're not on trial. You don't have to answer."

Damn straight. Bannon was suddenly very much on his guard.

"I understand you're on extended departmental leave," the attorney went on. "For a very good reason, of course," he said to his client. "He was shot during a criminal altercation."

Montgomery acknowledged that with a nod. Bannon was sure the other man had been thoroughly briefed in advance. The chief must have given Olliver Duncan an earful. Hoebel had never been famous for his discretion or his brains.

"Getting back to the case you seem to be so interested in," Olliver continued, "do you know something we don't?"

"No," Bannon replied, pausing, then dragging the bait. "Not yet, anyway."

Attorney and client regarded him expectantly. Bannon held his silence. There was a hidden agenda to this meeting and he couldn't figure it out. He was getting an idea of why Doris had such a low opinion of Hugh Montgomery, though. So far there hadn't been a single mention of his daughter.

Olliver glanced at his client, then centered on Bannon again. "A lot of calls came in to our offices immediately after the broadcast. It surprised me, considering you didn't mention the firm on the air. Mr. Montgomery even received some unwanted calls at his house, and that number is unlisted."

"Is it? I wouldn't know."

The attorney sighed. "Naturally you didn't have anything to do with that."

"No. I didn't," Bannon said. "Complain to the phone company. Not like they care—"

"But," Olliver interrupted him, "the police database does allow you access to all phone numbers. I'll be honest with you—my client is under a considerable amount of stress lately and the broadcast didn't help. I'm sure you share my concern."

Bannon looked at him levelly. "That's true about the database, but anyone can find out a phone number these days. All it takes is money. Everything's available online for a price, from incriminating photographs to financial records." He shook his head regretfully. "There is no such thing as privacy anymore."

Montgomery's fingers drummed on the table.

The lawyer took another sip of coffee. "This case is a little different. It was long ago, for one thing. So it rarely crops up in databanks."

Bannon thought of Doris, slaving away to enter information for the benefit of the state and the nation. *Wait a week, Duncan*, he wanted to say.

"I have to say, the broadcast came as a shock. The anchorman was over the top. But the news is theater, these days. All fake. You weren't, though. I liked the way you outlined it without giving too many particulars."

Faint praise. But the last comment wasn't quite what it seemed. Bannon had structured his answers to keep the crazies at bay, not to make the Montgomerys happy. The lawyer had to know that.

"We'd like to continue keeping the details confidential if at all possible. To protect the family. Whatever the cost," the lawyer added.

Were they planning to buy him off? Bannon looked from one man to the other.

"Of course, we can't unring a bell," Olliver admitted. "The story is news again, thanks to you. Just one year before the reward will be withdrawn." He glanced at Bannon over the rim of his cup. "Interesting timing."

"Twenty-five is one of those milestone numbers." Bannon was getting wise to Duncan's game. Act friendly, catch his opponent off guard, stick in the knife.

"Tell me, do you really think Ann might be alive?" The lawyer's tone was bland, almost casual. Yet somehow lethal.

"I have no idea," he replied.

Hugh Montgomery gave Bannon a look that damn near pinned him to the paneling. But he kept his deep voice controlled and smooth. "Would you mind keeping us in the loop on your investigation?"

"I don't recall saying I was investigating anything," he reminded them.

"Exactly what are you doing?" Montgomery challenged.

"That would be my business alone." Bannon went to the door without a backward glance at Montgomery or Duncan, then opened it and went out, closing it behind him to take swift strides down the hall. He could hear the two men talking heatedly, but didn't get the exact words.

The receptionist looked up as she saw him go past, then turned her head when Duncan came running after him.

Bannon was waiting for the elevator when the lawyer caught up.

"Look," he puffed, "we really are on the same side—here's my business card. We're going to keep a confidential record of the incoming phone calls and e-mails, both to the office and to Monty's house. We'll give you printouts, okay?" Duncan gave him a fake-friendly clap on the shoulder. "We're in this together."

"If you say so." Bannon was thinking that the law firm's printout could be easily manipulated to send him on wild-goose chases. But it might be interesting evidence, if it came to that. "Send it to me. I'm sure you have my home address."

He stepped in when the elevator doors opened and turned around, getting one last look at Duncan. The lawyer's face was unreadable. Bannon was relieved when the doors shut.

* * *

Bannon pushed the right side of another set of glass doors at the
TV station across town. The décor was so damned trendy, it was
hard to see the receptionist, just like the first time. There he was,
under the exposed ductwork, in an ironic argyle sweater.

"Is Kelly Johns in?" Bannon asked him.

"Do you have an appointment?"

"No, but—" He stopped. She was coming toward the reception
area.

"Hey, RJ. What are you doing here?"

He tried not to look at how short her skirt was. "Just thought I'd
stop by. I finally saw the segment."

"What did you think of it? We got about a million hits on the
website." She led the way to her office with long-legged strides that
distracted him from answering until she pointed to a chair for him
to sit in. Kelly settled herself behind her desk, glancing at her monitor, then at him.

"That many?"

"That many," she confirmed with a smile. "The bean boys were
impressed with our ratings for that one bit. Through the roof."

"Good for you."

"You know it was." She clicked the mouse on her desk. Behind
her, a printer started spitting out paper. "We received everything
from e-mails to pictures. I assume you can use some of it."

"You never know."

Click. Click. Click. "I'll forward the list for your reading pleasure
and give you a hard copy as well."

"Thanks."

"We already had an intern screen out the lunatics and the cell
phone pictures of Bigfoot, by the way."

"Thanks for that too."

"Want to do another segment?" Kelly asked. "The ratings were
high," she reminded him again. "They could go higher. Our execu-
tive producer thought it might be a good idea to interview you
live."

"Not just yet."

"If you did, you'd be fielding tougher questions."

"Such as?"

"Like," Kelly paused for effect, "what's in it for you?"

Bannon smiled coolly, thinking of his meeting with Montgomery and his lawyer. "Maybe I just like trouble."

Her dark eyes widened in approval. "Intriguing answer. A touch of mystery. Don't lose it."

There was more than a touch of mystery to this case. But Bannon didn't voice that thought.

Kelly twisted in her seat and got a fat sheaf of paper out of the printer. "Here you go. Stay in touch, Bannon. And let me know what happens."

"Sure thing." The phone on her desk rang. Bannon stood. Picking up the receiver, Kelly waggled her fingers in a blithe good-bye.

Back home, Bannon forced himself to look again at the TV segment, pulling it up from a video website on his laptop. Ann Montgomery's adult face just didn't seem real. The station's graphic artist had started with a photo of Ann as a child and had gone overboard. Computer-generated imagery was only as good as the person who created it, RJ thought sourly.

He paused the segment on the CGI face. Generic, not smiling but confident, with a rich-girl glow. It didn't remotely jibe with his sense of who Ann Montgomery might be now, not that he had a damn thing to go on. If she was alive, the resemblance to her baby pictures could be definite or not there at all. Some faces really changed as kids grew. No matter how much people wanted to believe in age progression, it wasn't a science.

Bannon wondered what Hugh Montgomery had thought of it. He could add that to the list of questions he was never going to get to ask.

He went into the kitchen and found a forgotten container of takeout lasagna. Good enough. He'd nuke the germs out of it. Food was food. While it was in the microwave, he returned to the living room and sent the TV station list from his laptop to his huge plasma TV.

One click opened the file and then the microwave beeped.

He got up to deal with his dinner and slung the lasagna on a plate, returning to the living room. He waited for the food to cool off some while he got comfortable. Scrolling down through the e-mails, he wasn't surprised by what he saw. A couple of wackos the intern hadn't caught. Fans of cop shows who wanted to be detectives. Natural-born busybodies. And, of course, a few that began, "I am Ann Montgomery." Yeah. And he was Captain Kangaroo.

Bannon clicked it closed and concentrated on his food. It was delicious, for week-old lasagna.

The thing to do, he decided, was to go with the verifiable ones first. If the name, address, occupation, and other personal data could be checked out, that might cut the huge task down to manageable size. If the responder sent an image or described a woman who was too young or too old, nothing doing. If some sightings by different people recurred in a geographical area, that counted as a clue right there and a further verification.

He had a monumental task ahead of him. And for what? He pushed the dirty plate away, feeling the lasagna settle in his stomach like a lump of cement.

The whole thing had started out as a favor, more or less, for Doris. Yet, in just one week, he'd made an enemy out of Montgomery, and he wasn't even getting paid for this.

He dragged a hand through his hair and tossed a glance at Babaloo. "Can curiosity really kill a cat?"

The phone rang. Bannon flung himself over the end of the couch to reach it, peering at the number. Doris's cell number. So she was back from the storage facility.

"Hello?"

"RJ?"

"Who else? I'm glad you're back."

"Are you? You sound awful."

"I just ate the Lasagna of Death. I may not make it until morning."

She didn't laugh. "RJ, you have to get the visuals back to me. Hoebel's on the warpath. He got a call right before he left today, Jolene told me. From Hugh Montgomery. The chief wants me to get him all the Montgomery files by tomorrow so he can go through them."

"Did you mention the missing file he signed for?"

"Hell, no. Are you crazy? Why would I do that?"

Brave words. She sounded genuinely scared. "Just asking. What did you find out?"

"The original Montgomery evidence file wasn't there or I couldn't find it. I went through every box with a Wainsville label—they do have the cold cases up to the beginning of the *M*s. And Hoebel authorized only the cheapest storage in rooms below ground level. So I couldn't get a cell call out, and when I got back to the motel, I found out that the damn battery was dead—"

"You went to all that trouble for nothing?"

"Not quite nothing. I did find a file with documents photocopied from the originals, but not the originals. It was in the wrong box," she said. "The transmittal form had Jolene's initials on it and last month's date. So it was sent down before you and I got interested."

Bannon nodded. "Any idea why it was copied?"

"Damned if I know. It was all letters, and like you said, they were mostly from cranks. But there was that one, supposedly from Ann's 'new mother,' that I would swear was the real deal."

"Why?"

"The tone of it. And that's how she signed it."

"It wasn't necessarily written by a woman," Bannon pointed out.

"Don't say that," she begged. "I don't want to think about a man abducting Annie."

"Statistically, that's what we should be thinking about." She went quiet and Bannon changed the subject. "Just a photocopy, huh? That means no original fingerprints and no envelope with DNA licked onto it. But it's better than nothing."

"Maybe. Their photocopier was busted. I wrote out what it said by hand."

"Good going." It was too bad the actual letter had been lost, but she had risked too much as it was.

"Look, Doris, I'm hoping the TV piece works."

"Me too. Unfortunately I missed it."

"You didn't miss much," he said dryly.

"You'll have to tell me about it later," she said. "I shouldn't be calling you from here at all, RJ. I just wanted to make sure I caught you so you can bring back the photos and whatnot that I gave you."

"Are you at headquarters?"

"Yes. But I'm about to drive home. I don't think you should be wandering into the station late at night—I can get away with it, but you can't."

She was right about that. Bannon could just imagine Hoebel reviewing the footage from the security cameras and seeing his least favorite detective's face over a midnight time slug, especially after Montgomery had called Hoebel.

"Meet me at my place as soon as you can," she was saying. "Call when you're a block away. Then I'll rush back to the station and say I forgot my wallet or something. I can put everything together in the files, nice and neat for review."

"On my way."

He scrambled off the couch and swept every picture of Ann that he could find into the nearest envelope, leaving the photocopied documents from the file on the table. Babaloo moved into the warm spot he left and settled down. Bannon scooped up his keys and hurried out.

Doris was at her house, her car pointed out of the driveway when he drove up on her left. She rolled down the window and took the envelope, muttering something that ended with a low-voiced *thanks*, and drove off immediately. Bannon stayed where he was, the engine running but the headlights switched off to watch her go, thankful that no vehicle swung out after her. Her taillights dwindled to solitary dots of red down miles of empty road before finally disappearing. Bannon's best guess: She wasn't being followed.

Which didn't mean the handover hadn't been watched or even photographed. Sitting in the dark, he scoped the perimeter of her house and yard, looking for movement in the shrubs, along the foundation, anywhere. Nothing. He had compulsively checked his rearview and sides on the way over and hadn't spotted anyone on his tail.

What the hell had she said to him besides that pointless thank-you? He scowled, trying to remember something besides her frightened eyes. Just a couple of words. Then they came to him. *Lie low.*

He backed out of her driveway, still looking intently around, and didn't turn on his headlights until he'd turned a corner. There was nothing to see but a fat raccoon on a night foray for garbage, its low-slung body almost concealing its small paws as it ran.

Driving home, he kept an automatic eye on the mirrors while he considered the development of the photocopied letter she'd found. Doris had a well-honed sense of what was fake and what wasn't, in his judgment. The most interesting thing about the letter to him was that someone had obviously tried to make it disappear from headquarters but hadn't destroyed it outright—unless the copy had simply gone astray. He suspected it wasn't the only letter from whoever had written it.

Unfortunately, Doris had been too pressed for time tonight to provide her transcription of it, and he couldn't blame her. The letter would have to wait.

An hour later, he was back in his condo, not eager to return to his painstaking work. Driving at night with the windows down, on full alert for surveillance on him, had brought out his animal energy. The adrenaline he'd been missing coursed through him full-blast, a hot rush of sensation.

He didn't have time to blow it off with a run. If truth be told, Bannon didn't want to. He had to get as much done as he could before things really hit the fan.

By midnight, combing through the e-mails from the station, he'd narrowed the search area to the same part of Virginia as before. The responses varied in style and content: Some were carefully composed, some were ungrammatical. Most of the senders asked to remain anonymous. Remembering the veiled menace behind his confrontation with Montgomery and his ass of a lawyer, Bannon could guess why.

He rubbed his weary eyes. There were almost too many to have to check out by himself. Asking for backup was not an option. He was on his own.

So far, he was cool with it, but he wasn't so sure about Doris. She was the one who had to lie low. And he had to make sure the trouble they were stirring up was his problem, and not hers.

CHAPTER 4

A shrill but distant ringing pierced the fog of his sleep. Bannon struggled up to a half-reclining position, resting on one bent arm as he reached for the phone with the other.

"Hello?" he said gruffly.

A male voice that was an echo of his own chuckled. "Rise and shine, Mr. Famous."

Bannon gave a growl that scared the cat next to him off the bed. "Up yours, Deke. It's six-thirty. Do you know what time I went to bed?"

His brother didn't seem to care. "I saw you on the news."

"You did? Are you back in Virginia?"

"Nope."

Even half-asleep, Bannon knew better than to expect too many details from Deke when he was on assignment.

"A guy on my team caught the segment on the Web, asked if you were my brother," Deke went on. "What could I say but yes? Ugly as you are."

"Thanks."

"I watched it a few times, RJ. Sounds like you got yourself a new case."

"Yeah. And I don't think old man Montgomery wants me on it. The hell with him. There's something there worth investigating. I think." He scrubbed a hand over his face, sitting up all the way, feeling stiff and creaky. Christ, he was tired. He needed coffee, bad.

"You talked to him?"

"Let's say I was summoned to his lawyer's office after they saw me on the news. I didn't say much to them. But then I really don't know much. Just starting. You know how it is."

"I hope the TV hounds in your viewing area give you some leads. How many responses did you get, about ten million?"

"Not that many. And they don't come to me, they go to the station website."

"Yeah? Wish I could pull a stunt like that."

Bannon looked around on the floor for his sweatpants and slid them on, keeping the phone receiver cradled against his shoulder. "I'm not going to ask why."

"Go right ahead, bro," Deke said. "What I'm doing isn't classified—not all of it, anyway. Oughta hit the news tonight. Someone threw a billionaire arms dealer out of his private plane over open ocean. No jurisdiction. The government called us in."

Bannon wasn't going to ask which government, either. "You calling from a safe line?" he inquired, standing up and stretching. "Or are you looking to get whacked?"

"My uncle says it's safe. But he doesn't know about you."

"Your uncle—" Bannon got it. "Oh. Good ol' Sam."

"While I'm on that subject, you might want to update your firewalls. Have you looked at your Facebook page?"

"Not for a year and a half. Why?"

Deke laughed. "You have a lot of new friend requests. Check it out. You are one popular dude after that segment."

Bannon swore. That should have occurred to him. It hadn't. Still, he didn't have to accept a single one. But he felt invaded.

"One or two of the requesters might be smart enough to trace your ISP address. It's not that hard, you know. Just keep peeling the onion. Layer after layer."

"I'm taking the page down. Today." He could hear Deke grinning.

"Look at it first. You never know."

"Yeah. Will do."

The brothers exchanged a few more ribbing remarks and Bannon hung up, mad at himself. He made some double-strength, super-hot coffee and took a sip before flipping open his laptop and staring into the screen as it came to life.

He checked the national headlines, then the local news, putting off the inevitable for a little while. Then he went to the site and looked to see who was trying to friend him. A long list of Anns with a bunch of different last names met his bleary gaze.

Before he got started on that, he answered a rude comment from his brother Deke, and another from Linc, with zings of his own. Then Bannon scrolled on through the list of wannabes, not really registering them. Fakers. Some people needed to get a life and not waste other people's time with tabloid-type fantasies.

Still, he had only himself to blame for not taking his Facebook page down in advance. He really had forgotten about it.

No matter what he and Doris might find, or what leads panned out, he still would bet a lot of money that Ann Montgomery had died long ago. Swilling the unpleasant brew, he jabbed at the down-arrow button, wondering how long it would take. A single name stopped him short.

Erin.

Wow. His Erin?

Bannon shook his head to clear it. Then he looked up at the painting of wild horses on the mantel. The artist wasn't his by any stretch of the imagination, and this might not even be the same Erin. But . . . he hadn't called anyone at the Art Walk committee, after all. What if it was her?

He accepted her request. Then got busy. He wasn't going to glue his eyes to the laptop waiting for an instant message like he had nothing better to do.

An hour later he got one.

Hello. Erin here. I saw you on the news.

Bannon winced, wondering what she'd thought of the segment. Only a conceited jerk would ask. She was adding a little more. The typed sentence appeared in bits.

Sad story. I know it was a long time ago. I hope you find out something.

Interesting response. She didn't automatically get misty, thinking a missing vic would be found just like that. Erin was smart. And if she was as beautiful as he remembered, well—If one good thing came out of reopening this case, he hoped like hell it was her.

I'm working on it, believe me.

Not a bad answer. He didn't want to sound like he was playing hero or putting himself in the limelight just for the hell of it. Mulling over what else he could say, he took the time to check out the handful of photos she'd posted. It seemed like a professional page, not personal. For one thing, it wasn't loaded with the usual girl's-night-out shots of happy inebriated pals squeezed together.

There was one photo of her at an easel, dressed in a loose, tattered shirt that looked like it belonged to a man, with jeans under it. It was a little frustrating to not see more of her, but that was beside the point. She was working on a half-finished watercolor, using a magazine image of horses that was propped to her right. Not his painting, but one that was about as good. Bannon jealously wondered who'd taken the picture—or given her his old shirt to paint in. He didn't see a single mention anywhere of a significant other.

His hands poised over the keyboard, he thought some more. His goal was to see her in person, not chat online indefinitely. But at least they were communicating.

It's great to hear from you, Erin.

He waited. She wasn't the kind to rush through an answer, and he was grateful she didn't use those dumb-ass acronyms to reply, because he couldn't remember any of them.

Thanks.

One word. He tried not to read more into it. She asked about the painting he'd bought. He assured her that it had pride of place on his mantel. And so it went. An hour went by without his realizing it. Then she typed something that made him sit up straight.

Bannon—I almost forgot to say why I contacted you.

He sucked in a breath, watching the rest of her typed words appear one by one.

I painted the Montgomery mansion for the Wainsville historical society. They're doing an illustrated book on grand old houses in the area.

That was information he didn't have. It called for an immediate reply.

I hadn't heard that.

Brilliant, he told himself wryly.

Do you know the director? She went to high school with your mom in Arlington. They're e-buddies now (she's Mrs. Judith Meriweather—I don't know her maiden name).

His mother was all over the Web lately, he knew that. But he didn't know Mrs. Meriweather. He was grateful to her, though. Obviously he had been thoroughly vetted in advance. That fit the wariness he remembered about Erin.

Want to go to the house? I can get the combination for the keypad from her. It's not tour season yet.

Bannon's eyes widened. *Down, boy. Don't sound too eager*, he told himself.

Sure.

Erin suggested that they meet at a country restaurant north of Wainsville and he grinned, glad she couldn't hear him. He knew the place, though he'd never been inside. It was a converted barn by the side of the road, famous for its traditional American fare with a gourmet twist. Sign him up. Then she asked a question that stunned him.

Today?

Did she mean it? He typed an answer fast.

Hell yes. Looking forward to it.

She replied after a minute, as if she'd gone off to do something else in the meantime.

Me too.

Bannon signed off with an oh-so-casual *see you there*. Then he realized that he still didn't know her last name or anything much about her at all.

Erin was waiting outside the restaurant, sitting in the sun, when he showed up. The long, light dress she had on fluttered in the warm breeze and her dark hair fell over bare shoulders—well, not quite bare. There were thin straps between here and paradise. She was gorgeous. He couldn't believe his luck.

He reached out to shake her hand, noticing the strength in her slender fingers.

"Hello."

"Oh, hi." She rose gracefully just as he let go and they stood there, awkward as a couple of teenagers on a first date.

"Uh—shall we go in?"

Erin smiled slightly and nodded, preceding him inside. The back view of her was just as tempting. Bannon looked up, startled, when the hostess asked him a question. "Two?"

"Yes," he said quickly, almost placing a hand on Erin's waist as they followed the hostess, then thinking better of it.

"How's this?" the hostess asked, motioning toward a secluded table by a window. Its panes were made of old, wavy glass that revealed the flower garden outside in a shimmer of colors.

"Okay with you, Erin?"

"Sure." She swept the folds of her light dress under her thighs as she took her seat, a very feminine gesture that got a reaction from him. He sat down across from her as quickly as he could.

A smiling waitress replaced the hostess. She handed them menus and took out her pad. "Anything from the bar for you two?" she asked, pencil poised.

"Ah—not for me," Bannon said. "Water's fine." One beer could turn him into a fool for love. It had happened.

"Same here," Erin said, returning the waitress's smile.

"Okay, water it is." She signaled the busboy to fill their glasses and launched into a brief description of the day's specials, then left them to think it over.

"Nice place." He looked around approvingly, noticing the massive, hand-hewn beams overhead and the chinked planks that made up the walls. "Do you—come here often?" He caught himself, realizing how stupid that sounded. "Sorry. That's none of my business."

"I've been here a few times," was all she said. Her downcast gaze was on the menu, but her mouth turned up just a bit at the corners.

"Anything you would recommend?" Bannon told himself to concentrate on the food.

"The roast chicken with fennel was really good," she offered. "I might have it."

"Fennel? I'm not even sure what that is."

"It's a vegetable. The taste is sort of hard to describe." She peered over her menu to look at his and tapped it halfway down. "You could have the steak with frites. That's definitely man food."

He looked where she'd pointed. "Sounds good. And frites are . . . ?"

"French fries."

When the waitress returned, Erin gave her order first, and then he did. He returned his gaze to her face when the waitress finished taking their order. She was looking out the window at the flower garden, the fingertips of one hand just touching the pane. "I love this old glass, don't you? It makes everything you see through it look like a watercolor."

He glanced outside. "Yes, it does."

They looked into each other's eyes at the same moment, and Erin actually blushed. Which made him feel good all over.

"So," he said after a few seconds, "I guess I should tell you—I was meaning to look you up before the Montgomery thing went on TV."

"Really?"

"Yeah. You didn't have a website or anything. But I did find your work in a Chincoteague gallery listing." He took a breath. "Do you live out there?"

She shook her head. "I visit sometimes, rent a room at an inn so I can paint. I used to spend summer vacations with my mom and dad there, though."

"Oh, okay." Something in her tone told him that her parents were no longer living. But he'd wait for Erin to confirm that.

"My dad liked to fish, so he went off with his rod and reel while my mom and I wandered around the seashore trails with binoculars. Kind of geeky, huh?"

Bannon shook his head. "Binoculars? No. Gotta have them on a stakeout."

"Oh, right. Then I don't feel so geeky. Anyway, off we went. Most of Chincoteague is marsh—there are lots of wading birds. And wild horses, of course. In the distance."

"Sounds nice. So you go out there alone now?"

She looked at him sharply, brushing a stray lock of brown hair away from her face. "How did you know that?"

"Ah—just a guess," he replied, knowing he'd said something tactless. Erin seemed suddenly distant and he wished to God he could take the question back.

"It's a good one." She pressed her lips together before she said anything more. "My parents died three years ago, within months of each other."

"I'm sorry."

She shrugged, but he could see that she was holding back a fair amount of emotion. "I came along late in life for them. They were so much older—well, I wasn't that close to either of them. I miss them sometimes. But in answer to your question, it was a while before I went back to Chincoteague and yes, I was alone when I did. Just easier that way."

Bannon nodded, noting the waitress returning with their entrees. The plates set in front of them gave off the tantalizing aroma of excellent food, and he was grateful for the distraction.

Erin picked up her knife and fork, and he followed her lead. She tucked into her chicken and ate several bites before taking a breather. "This is really good," she said, leaning back. "Keep eating. I'll tell you the rest of my life story. Might as well get it over with, right?"

Bannon's mouth was full and he didn't know what to say to that odd question. So he nodded. If she wanted to talk, he was happy to listen.

"I grew up on the other side of the Blue Ridge," she began, naming a town he'd never heard of, "and I was homeschooled. My mom was a teacher, but she didn't work outside of raising me. She had emotional problems, I guess you'd say. I had an older brother who died before I came along."

Bannon was paying attention. *Came along.* She'd said it twice. Not born. He wondered if she'd been adopted. Erin's casual tone wasn't telling him a lot. He finished his steak and fries, and set down his cutlery.

"Anyway," she continued, "it was always just us three, me and Mom and Dad, way outside of town on our own forty acres. No grandparents or anything. No cousins."

"What did your dad do?" Bannon asked.

Erin's expression softened. "He was an inventor, actually. We lived off the income from a few patents he held. I used to like to hang around in his workshop because it was so neat—you know, a place for everything and everything in its place. It seemed safe."

He could fill in the blanks. Troubled mother, remote dad. And one sensitive little girl who didn't get much from either of her parents.

"You know something?" he asked lightly. "You never did tell me your last name."

She seemed taken aback. "I didn't? Well, it's no big secret. It's Randall. Ordinary as can be."

"You're anything but ordinary, Erin," he said in a low voice. He looked up at the waitress, who'd returned with dessert menus even before the table was cleared. Several other customers had come in, and a couple of large groups. They must need the table. He decided to skip the sweet stuff and ordered coffee, but Erin ordered Raspberry Glory, whatever that was.

"Thanks for the compliment." She negated it with a wave of her hand. "Even though I hate compliments. Now tell me about yourself."

Bannon kept it short. "I have two brothers. Hell-raisers."

"And you're the angel."

"Um, no." He grinned at her. "I'm the oldest. I showed Deke and Linc how to raise hell, put it that way."

Erin laughed and the sound warmed him all over. "Your parents?"

"My dad was a cop, like me. An outdoorsman. He liked to take us up to the family cabin and teach us woodsy lore and whatnot. He passed away a few years ago. Mom is still going strong. She hovers over us all."

"Mrs. Meriweather mentioned that. And she said you'd been on departmental leave for a while. After that shooting."

"Yeah," Bannon said wryly. "I knew you knew everything about me as soon as you said those two reunited online." He liked her even more for stopping where she had and not asking a whole bunch more questions. That quietness of hers was something like kindness.

He pulled the coffee cup that the waitress set down toward him with the saucer and waited for Erin to be served.

She was smiling at his reply. "Only a little. So what do your brothers do?"

"Law enforcement. But not police work."

Her dessert arrived and she seemed willing to let it go at that. "And you guys are close."

"Yeah. Very."

"You're lucky." The wistfulness in her voice struck him. Overall he got an impression of loneliness, even isolation, in her upbringing. But not why. Hell. There was time enough for that conversation, and if it didn't happen today, he was fine with that.

Bannon watched her spoon up the homemade berry sherbet with the same thoughtful care with which she seemed to do just about everything. The sight was erotic and oddly pure at the same time. He stuck with black coffee, stirring it to give himself something to do besides gawk at her, even though there wasn't any sugar or cream in it.

They took both their cars to drive out to the Montgomery mansion. He followed her, taking note of the license plate under her hatchback just in case he might need it in the future. Getting her last name had taken long enough, he thought.

He couldn't shake the feeling that Erin was a very private person. He'd do well not to ask her too many questions at this point.

She raised the arm that she'd crooked in the open window on her side, pointing ahead. Bannon snapped out of his abstracted mood and looked. There was the Montgomery mansion, looking even more grand than it had on the historical society's website. Two full stories and a half story atop those. Columns. A double-height veranda. Nice details like carved swags of classical garlands under the eaves. Outside the tall, spiked iron fence that surrounded the house were towering old oaks, with a few smaller and much plainer structures well behind those. Probably had been the washhouse and sheds once upon a time. A neatly made, small shack undoubtedly covered a well.

They parked under a porte cochere to one side that was wide enough to shelter a couple of four-horse carriages side by side. Erin rubbed her arms when she got out. "It's chilly here."

Bannon looked around. They were in the shade of the huge house, that was one reason why. It had been built on a rising swell of land that caught the spring breeze from the valley below.

She bent into her car and retrieved a sweater from the backseat, throwing it over her shoulders. Then she picked up a canvas bag with paint splatters on it and started hunting through the contents. "Mrs. Meriweather wrote down the keypad combination for me.

Give me a sec to find the piece of paper. It's okay to go on up the stairs. I'll be right there."

Bannon nodded. "Okay."

The view from the lower veranda was spectacular, a sweeping vista of the valley. The house was well out in the country, away from the sprawl around Wainsville.

"I'll play tour guide," she told him, coming up the stairs with her long dress lifted a bit by one hand, pretty as a picture. He felt like he ought to bow and take her arm. Gallant? Him? The truth was, she had that effect on him, filling him with an old-fashioned desire to court her.

"You're on," he grinned.

"The house was built in 1810. It's never passed out of the Montgomery family."

"Quite a place. Ever been inside?"

"Nope." Erin looked at the piece of paper in her hand and went to the door, entering numbers into a keypad lock with one finger.

A small light on it flashed and she turned the doorknob. The huge carved door swung inward almost soundlessly. Well-oiled and well-maintained, Bannon thought. Just like the scion of the family himself.

"Walk on in. Pretend you're a Montgomery."

"I'll have to think about that." But he went in ahead of her and she followed him inside.

The furnishings were as grand as the exterior. They looked like antiques, good ones, even to his untrained eye. Meaning there had to be security, above and beyond the keypad lock. Instinctively, his gaze swept the light fixtures and moldings, looking for discreetly placed devices and finding nothing. A prickling on the back of his neck told him they were there, though.

Every surface gleamed, free of dust. The Montgomerys might have left the house just yesterday and not twenty-some years ago.

"It's so perfect," she said. The house seemed to swallow Erin's soft words. It wasn't empty, but it echoed.

"The society keeps it up, don't they?"

She nodded. "I think a couple of volunteers come out every week. And Mrs. Meriweather said something about a caretaker."

Bannon raised an eyebrow. "No sign of him."

"I don't remember whether he lives somewhere on the property or not. When I was painting the place last year, I didn't see anybody around."

"Hmm. This stuff looks valuable." Hands in his pockets, Bannon surveyed the large rooms that opened off the foyer. Parlor, music room, library—each was an example of the gracious old South, but it wasn't a house he could ever imagine living in.

"It is." Her answer was perfunctory. In silence, they moved from room to room. Bannon walked near her. He couldn't help noticing that Erin seemed to hesitate before entering each room.

"Dining room, second parlor, study," he said under his breath before she opened doors that had probably been closed to save on heat.

"How do you know that?" she asked.

"Ah—" He had pretty much memorized the police diagrams of the house. "Just guessing. Am I right?"

Erin opened each door and peeped inside. "Yes."

Her gaze moved over everything, as if she was memorizing it herself.

He studied an oil painting of a pair of Thoroughbreds from the Montgomery stable. "Not as good as yours."

She came over. "Different style. Not what I do, really."

"Right."

He followed her as they came to a small room that opened off a corridor. "I looked through the windows of this one from outside," she said softly. "It's not like the others. A woman decorated this just the way she wanted it, don't you think?"

"Maybe so."

She played tour guide again, pointing things out. "That delicate pattern on the wallpaper and the sewing table with the piecrust edging—very nice."

He picked up on the funny note of longing in her voice and then looked where she was pointing, realizing just how good her eye for detail was. If she had a house, she would probably have things like this.

"I wonder—" Erin stopped and looked at a small oval painting of a little girl. It was half in shadow, but she didn't seem inclined to turn on the light. "I didn't see this from outside. Is it her? Ann Montgomery?"

Bannon moved forward. "Yes. I think so. There was a photo something like it in the files."

She studied the painting, then backed away. "It's strange to see her. It's like she's still here. Waiting."

Bannon wanted to say that he knew exactly how she felt. But he didn't.

"Should we go upstairs? Mrs. Meriweather said the bedrooms are just the way they were when the family still lived here. Not on the official tour, of course. Stairs are a liability."

He looked at her curiously. The same wistfulness he'd seen in her at the restaurant shone in her eyes. "Are you sure you want to?"

"If you're investigating, you should."

"I could do that on my own. Go upstairs, I mean."

Erin gave the slightest shake of her head. "I'll go with you."

"But—"

She held up a hand before he could form a question. "Don't ask why. I just want to."

In silence, they went back the way they'd come and stopped at an inner staircase that led to the second floor, not the grand one of the front hall. She went ahead of Bannon, unclipping the velvet rope that kept visitors on the first floor of the mansion and handing the brass end back to him. He clipped the rope again where it fastened when he'd gone up a couple of steps. Just in case someone came in, like the caretaker. Or someone else. He still couldn't shake the feeling of being watched, though he had yet to spot a surveillance device. A little noise, a few seconds of warning—he wanted both.

She was already on the landing, looking through another massive door. Bannon joined her. He peered over her shoulder. A baronial bed decked out with fringed scarlet hangings took up the center of the room. Had to have been Hugh's. The room was entirely masculine, with heavy side furniture and dark wood. Bannon guessed that the wife had been summoned to it. He hoped it hadn't been too often, for her sake.

"Now this is some serious furniture," Erin said, looking around and adding with a smile, "but those hangings would be great for a kid playing hide-and-seek, don't you think?" She closed the door without making a move to go in. Like the great front door below, it shut almost without a sound.

The bedroom adjoining was more feminine. He took in the lace runner on the dresser, and the ornate silver-backed brush and comb set in front of the mirror. Its patina told him that it was the real deal. There had to be security, very good security. Anyone could slip that into a pocket and walk off with it. Then he reminded himself that tourists weren't allowed up here.

Even so.

Erin continued down the hall, stopping at a door with a painted cut-out of a bright-eyed bunny attached to it. Below it was Ann's name.

Bannon exchanged a long look with Erin, who didn't say anything as she slowly turned the knob. He was right behind her when she walked in.

The room was decorated in pastels. Even the antique crazy quilt on top of the dresser was made out of pink and yellow scraps from long ago. It was piled high with stuffed toys that didn't look like props on a set. They looked like a real little girl had played with them a lot.

Bannon realized that he was looking for the bear—the pink bear in the photo of Ann. It wasn't there. Maybe the kidnapper had let her take her favorite toy. To keep her quiet. The idea sickened him.

"What's the matter?" Erin asked.

"Huh? Oh—just thinking. There was a toy bear in one of the photos of Ann. Pink. Flowered tummy. It's not here."

She turned around to study the heap of toys. "I had a bear like that," she said.

He thought. "It would have been about the same time period. They probably sold about a million of them."

"No, my mother said she made it. I always thought my bear was the only one." She seemed lost in the memory for a moment—it must have been a poignant one, considering that her mother had passed away only a few years ago.

Bannon wasn't too surprised. "Could have been from one of those printed kits. My mom used to make toys from those."

"For you and your brothers?"

"No. Her nieces. We would have yanked out the stuffing and made ninja headbands out of the cloth."

Erin smiled. "I loved my pink bear. Guess it's a girl thing."

"Do you still have it? Might be interesting to compare it to the one in the old photo, see if I could find a manufacturer or something like that," Bannon said. "You never know what's going to be useful when you reopen a case."

"Oh. It's probably somewhere in one of the boxes from our old house. I haven't thought about that bear in years."

"Well, if you happen to find it, call me—"

"I'll look." Her lips lifted in a smile. "If I bring Pinky in, go easy on her, okay?"

"You bet."

He was on the point of asking if he could come over and help her look. Not yet. It wasn't the right time to put any kind of move on her. The vibe in the Montgomery house was making him nervous, but she seemed oddly at home. Then again, she'd been there before, if only on the outside. He hadn't. And she wasn't looking high and low for surveillance equipment the way he was doing—why would she? They left the little girl's room, and Erin closed the door as gently as if there were a child asleep in it.

A row of family portraits in gilt frames stared at them when they rounded the corner of the hall, heading for a different wing. Generations upon generations of Montgomery men. He guessed the wives had their own wall somewhere else.

Erin paused at each one, studying the subjects closely. Bannon only glanced at them. The bland expressions told him nothing—maybe Erin was studying the technique. He stuck his hands in his pockets and walked through his mental map of the place.

Being here gave him a better understanding of the bedroom layout. But how the hell had the abductor gotten Ann out without anyone knowing? The hall floors creaked and so did the stairs. Inside job? A servant? It had to have been someone who knew the house, one way or another. He was lost in thought, until he noticed Erin was standing in front of a portrait of the last male in the Montgomery line.

"That's old Hugh," he said. "Did he ever stop by when you were painting?"

"No. Mrs. Meriweather told me he never comes here." She focused all her attention on the painting. "He seems so authoritative in this. Maybe that's not the right word. But whoever painted him saw through that pose. There's something sad in his eyes. Maybe the portrait was done after the kidnapping."

Bannon nodded. "You could ask Mrs. Meriweather about that." He wasn't going to talk about meeting Montgomery or what he and Doris had turned up in the files about Ann. Who knew what it all meant? He didn't. Suddenly he just wanted to get the hell out of there.

Erin turned and looked him full in the face. The expression in her eyes was distant, almost dreamy. It puzzled him.

"I've seen everything I want to see," she said lightly. "Let's go, okay?"

"Fine with me."

"I had a nice time today, so—" She hesitated, but not for long. "Maybe you could come visit my place. It's out in the sticks—you'd have to follow me."

He'd follow her anywhere. "Sure. Name the day."

"Soon. Let me check my social calendar," she teased him.

She led the way down the hall and back down the stairs, exiting with him through the front hall, carefully punching in numbers on the keypad while he waited. This time he took her hand as she put her foot on the first outside step. Erin didn't pull away.

A tall figure stood outside the glass doors of Duncan, Hobert & Giles, his expression lost in the subdued lighting of the office building at night. He scowled when Olliver Duncan came hurriedly down the hall and unlocked the door from the keypad on his side.

"Hello, Hugh," Olliver said a little breathlessly, holding open the door, "come on in. Sorry to keep you waiting. I was alone—"

Hugh Montgomery swept past, ignoring his lawyer's greeting and heading down the hall to the office where they usually transacted business.

"Did I interrupt something?" Olliver asked, catching up and rounding his desk to go to his swivel chair. "Sit down, please. You did say to contact you if Bannon—"

"Here I am. Get to the point."

"Right." Olliver Duncan put on his glasses and began to type on his computer keyboard. "Let me see if I can pull this up—shoot. No. Wait a minute—"

Montgomery slammed a hand down on the desk. "I was at a horse auction. And I want to get back. There's a party afterward and people I need to talk to."

"Of course, of course," Olliver said soothingly. "Now I have it." He turned his monitor around so Montgomery could see the screen, then got up and stood behind him, holding the tiny remote control for the computer and clicking its arrowed button.

"Good." The single word from Montgomery held icy condescension.

"After the story broke on the news, I assigned our security tech to review the daily tapes—well, these aren't tapes, of course. It's all digital now. Much better images."

"I hope so. The system is costing me a fortune."

In jittery black and white, Erin and Bannon made a fast-forward entrance to the house and went through the rooms again and again. Olliver paused the digital feed here and there when Hugh told him to.

"There's our boy," the lawyer said. "Wonder what he's looking for."

"Spycams, what else," Montgomery said dryly. "I didn't get the feeling he was stupid, did you?"

His lawyer didn't answer that question. "Should I make a call, get him busted for trespassing?"

Montgomery shook his head, watching the screen closely. "The girl had the right code or the security alarm would have gone off."

"Obviously. If you don't mind my saying so."

Montgomery shot the lawyer a quelling look. "I do mind."

"Sorry. But Bannon wasn't supposed to be there. And who is she, anyway?"

Montgomery interrupted him with a curt gesture. "Shut up. Stop it right there. On her, full face, not profile. And zoom in."

The pixels formed and reformed into mosaics, changing continually until the young woman's face filled the screen. Montgomery's cold gaze moved over the image.

"Recognize her?" Duncan wasn't following the order to shut up.

It was a while before the older man answered. There was a slight hitch in his voice when he did. "No."

CHAPTER 5

Erin's house was small, with weathered white paint that clung to what looked like hand-hewn clapboards. Bannon had said an immediate yes to her two-days-later invite and she'd met him in town. Now he went up the front steps behind her, glancing briefly at the Blue Ridge looming overhead. Where she lived was much closer to the mountains than Wainsville. The sparse woods that marked the edge of the valley thickened on the slopes, covering the rugged land in forested folds of deep blue and gray.

She took a key out of her pocket, unlocked the door, and turned to him with a slight smile. "Come on in."

Without commenting on it, Bannon noted that the lock was new. Its bright brass gleamed reassuringly in the afternoon sun. A good thing, since her house seemed to be some distance from town, if you could call the scattering of houses that. He could just make out part of the sign for the old-fashioned general store and gas station fifteen miles down the road, at the solitary stoplight they'd driven through, as he followed her in his car. He'd scoped it out—definitely the kind of joint where you could get a MoonPie and a bottle of RC Cola to wash it down, and find out where the trout were biting while you were at it.

She motioned him inside and Bannon stepped over the threshold, looking around at a large, sunny room that had been turned into a studio. "Great place. How long have you been here?"

"About three years. Actually, it belongs to a friend who moved to

Vermont to teach art at a college there. She didn't want to leave it empty and she asked me to house-sit at no charge."

"Aha. Good deal."

"Yes, it is." Erin waved toward pine plank shelves filled with art supplies and pads of paper. "It has everything I need already built in."

He nodded. There were cardboard boxes on the bottom shelves marked with the same word over and over. *Home. Home. Home.* A lot of life could get packed up in boxes that never got unpacked. He had a few in one of the condo's closets.

He counted about twenty on her shelves, different sizes. He'd guess they held mementos, maybe toys, letters, and albums. His first look around didn't catch any family pictures or photos of anything like a farmhouse. He'd sort of expected one or two of her as a knock-kneed kid on a porch, with her mom and dad.

His gaze moved next to the high windows. Their glass was old, the same type she'd admired at the barn restaurant, but the panes were thinner and more fragile. At least the thumb locks on top of each frame were turned. For what it was worth. Vintage windows were easily forced. The breeze outside, strengthening again, rattled them audibly.

Erin went to one window and pressed a hand against it to steady the frame. "I should caulk these, but I never seem to get around to it. The house is old—probably older than the Montgomery mansion, don't you think?"

He shrugged. "Could be."

"The answer is yes." She laughed. "And I feel it every time the wind blows. But my friend doesn't want to install new windows. Anyway, I love the light. It's always changing."

Bannon nodded and put his hands in his pockets, not sure where to sit, or even if he wanted to. There were a lot of things he wanted to look at without seeming nosy, beginning with a tall easel that held a thick pad of watercolor paper she'd been sketching on.

She put her things on a drop-leaf table by the door and went into the kitchen area.

"Should I start some coffee?" she called.

"Sure." They'd finished a late lunch at another out-of-the-way place, a farmhouse that doubled as a B&B and served meals on the weekends. The generous portions had made them too full for coffee afterward, but he was ready for some now.

"Want cookies? I made them."

"Hell yes. Thanks."

He moved in front of the easel, studying the large, unfinished drawing of a horse in her distinctive style, standing to one side in a vast, featureless landscape. Idly he wondered why so much of the paper had been left blank.

"I like this," he said when she came back into the room, gesturing toward the empty part of the paper. "But there's more to come, right?"

She nodded. "Good guess. It's for a book cover. The title goes here"—she ran one finger along the top of the sketchpad, then the bottom—"and the author's name goes here."

"That leaves room for a whole herd of horses in the middle."

Erin laughed. "Nope. There's only going to be one." She gestured at the paper. "They want a gorgeous sunset in the background. But it can't be more gorgeous than the hero. He's supposed to stand next to the horse, hand on the bridle. I was hoping to find a photo in this I could use." She picked up a glossy equestrian magazine and riffled the pages with a sigh before she tossed it back down. "No luck."

"Too bad." He remembered the photo he'd seen on Facebook of her working from a torn-out magazine page. "What kind of man are you looking for?" He had to laugh a little at what he'd just said. "Uh, that didn't sound right. Sorry."

Erin's pretty lips turned up at the corners. "I knew what you meant."

Bannon covered the awkward moment by saying, "Fill me in. How do you get a book cover assignment living way out here? Do you have an agent in a big city or something?"

"No. The art director for the publisher tracked me down online. Like you." There was a teasing light in her eyes.

"Wait a minute," he said with mock indignation. "You contacted me, if I remember right."

"Bannon. You said—"

"Okay, okay. I did plan to find you one way or another."

She smiled to hear that. "Anyway, I have a really good computer and scanner and all that—a friend set it up for me. So I don't really need an agent."

A friend. That term, according to his second-date interpretation, meant ex-boyfriend. They hadn't gotten around to discussing priors. He told himself he didn't care if the guy was smart or whatever. No picture of him on display, no problem.

For most of the afternoon they had both avoided discussing the case that had brought them together in the first place and he wasn't about to bring it up now. Doris hadn't found anything new and Chief Hoebel hadn't bothered her. Bannon was relieved about that.

"And here we are," Erin said.

It had been tough to wait two whole days to see her again, but he didn't want to seem too eager. He hadn't been expecting to be invited to her house that fast. He liked what he saw. It was sunny and small, the opposite of the Montgomery mansion, whose brooding atmosphere still lingered in his mind.

"I like your place. Feels friendly."

"Thanks," she said simply. "So where do you live? You never really said."

"In a condo. It's basically a big white box. Boring, huh? The painting I bought from you is the best thing in it. It's up on the mantel."

Erin seemed pleased. "Oh. I hope I get to visit. It's always interesting to see what work looks like in someone else's house," she added.

"Sure, of course. Whenever." He made a silent vow to clean up the second he got back. A forgotten beer bottle or two and tossed socks didn't count as interior decoration.

Bannon switched back to the previous subject, looking at the pad of paper on the easel again. "So, have you designed book covers before?"

Erin shook her head, studying the sketch herself. "No, this is my first. But it pays well. I'd love to do more."

"You will," he said emphatically.

"Think so? I wish the art director had been more specific—he wants the first sketches in two weeks," she said with a sigh. "If he likes what I send, then I get the job."

"Your work is really good, Erin."

Her answering smile warmed him and so did the aroma of brewing coffee. The coffeemaker beeped and Bannon walked away from the easel to follow her into the kitchen.

She took out two cups, one tall, one short, from a cabinet above the sink, stretching up with the lithe grace he'd noticed the first time he'd met her. He caught a flash of smooth skin when her movement briefly bared her waist, and his mouth went dry. He swallowed hard, looking at her hands instead.

In swift movements over the counter, she collected an old sugar bowl and spoons before she put two different saucers under the cups. "Nothing matches," she said cheerfully. "Hope you don't mind."

He shook his head. "Why would I?"

"If something breaks, I don't have to care. Life is easier that way, don't you think?" Her light, chatty tone caught him off guard for a second.

"I know what you mean," he replied. "And I don't have to answer to anyone but a cat. He hasn't complained yet."

Okay. He had officially declared himself single with no significant attachments at all, something they hadn't gotten around to talking about. He had to hand it to Erin. Somehow she had managed not to ask that important question directly, but now she had her answer.

"A cat, huh? What kind?"

"Tiger-striped. His name is Babaloo. For no good reason. But he answers to it."

"Cats are good company. Dogs too. I always had a big mutt growing up but after my parents died"—she hesitated—"I was moving around too much to take care of one."

The thought of her being alone bugged him in one way, pleased him in another. He remembered the online photo of her working and the man's shirt she'd been wearing in it. If he got a chance to check the back of the doors, he could see whether the shirt was hanging on one, look at the inside of the collar for a laundry mark with a name—no. There was no way in hell he was going to do that.

Police training was a curse sometimes.

Erin was looking at him, her china blue eyes wide and thoughtful. "Milk or cream?" she asked.

"Neither. Black is fine. And no sugar for me."

She lifted the lid of a fat, brightly striped jar and took out several irregularly shaped cookies that smelled fantastic. "Here you go. Baked yesterday."

"Sign me up."

Erin arranged everything on a tray and turned to head toward the studio. Bannon went ahead of her, assuming they would eat at the drop-leaf table, but she didn't bother to clear it off, going over to the pine shelving instead. She set down the tray on a cleared-off shelf. Resting on the floor underneath it was a steamer trunk with studded trim and leather handles. She pulled it out, unfolded two chairs, and positioned the tray on top of the trunk. "Sorry. I don't have much in the way of conventional furniture."

Bannon chuckled. "This works fine for me. Hand over the cookies and nobody gets hurt."

She settled herself gracefully and picked up the plate, extending it to him.

They ate a few, then sipped their coffee. He was having a hard time reading her, and he was usually pretty good at it. Still, it had been a while since he'd been this close to a beautiful woman. Bannon hardly knew what to say, and he was glad she'd given him the tall cup with the extra coffee so he could stall for time with it.

She finished hers and set it down with a satisfied sigh. "I needed that."

He murmured agreement as he looked at her over the rim of his cup, riveted for a fraction of a second by the absentminded but sexy way she patted her lips with a napkin.

Erin folded her hands over her crossed knees, looking thoughtful. "Hey, I meant to ask you if there were any more leads on the Montgomery case. We didn't talk about it. Unless you don't want to."

He set down his cup, empty at last. "No, it's okay. The answer is nothing much. But I have to check in with my contact at the TV station. I know they got thousands of e-mails—my guess would be that they're still sorting them out."

Erin had seen the segment, of course, but she knew nothing about Kelly Johns. And Bannon wanted to keep it that way.

"I wonder if they plan to film the Montgomery mansion," she mused. "Would you know?"

"Ah—no, I don't. But they might. With that level of interest, they're likely to keep the story on the front burner."

Erin nodded, thinking it over before she spoke again. "Was that your plan?"

Bannon was taken aback by the blunt question. She had a knack for getting to the point sometimes. He hadn't told her much of anything about the reasons for his decision to bring the cold case back into the public eye. "More or less," he hedged. "It was kind of a fluke that I saw the Montgomery files in the first place. I got interested from page one."

"Why? You never did say."

He took a deep breath. Maybe he shouldn't explain, but he trusted her. "Because it was headline news for months back then and never solved," he said finally. "It seemed to me that the case shouldn't be declared cold, and it was about to be. Forensic techniques have changed a lot since then. We can pick up a lot of information we used to miss. I thought it was worth a try."

Erin nodded. "You're not the only one working on it, are you?"

"No. Technically, I'm on official leave anyway. So a colleague at headquarters is doing the research for now." He couldn't tell her everything.

"I didn't realize that."

Somehow he'd assumed that she would automatically look him up online, find out the particulars of his background if she could. Didn't everyone do that these days? Not her, apparently.

"Once I stumbled on it, I realized a case like this could get me up to speed again. So I took it on."

Erin nodded. "Why exactly were you on leave?"

Bannon took a deep breath. A few minutes of life-threatening terror and two years of numb despair didn't add up to much. *Keep it simple*, he told himself.

"A drug bust went wrong, and it was me or the dealer's two little boys. So I put my hands up and played target dummy. He blew a few holes in me. Took a while to recover."

"What happened to the boys?"

"They lived," he said shortly. "He escaped with them. I don't know where they are now."

Erin smiled. "You're a hero."

"Sort of. I could have done better." He was in the hot seat. Bannon hated to talk about himself in those terms. His back chose that moment to twinge painfully but he kept his expression impassive. "They were just kids. I still feel responsible."

She looked at him for a long moment, her china blue eyes unfathomable. "I'm not going to argue with you. You were there. I wasn't." Then she rose to take the tray and cups back to the kitchen. He watched her walk away, her skirt swishing against her bare, shapely legs, and felt an agonizing pang of desire.

This is a second date. Take it slow, he told himself. But he couldn't really call their tour of the Montgomery mansion a first date. It had been more like an excuse for making a connection with her. That, and necessary research on the case. He should have accomplished something in the way of following up by now, whether or not Doris's clandestine investigating had stalled.

Mindful of his injury, Bannon got up while he could do it without Erin looking. He rubbed his clenched fist against the tense muscles of his lower back, then stretched, listening to the clatter of cups and spoons. He was standing straight, looking out of one of the tall windows by the time she returned, his gaze narrowed.

He was on full alert. Someone or something had moved deep within the lengthening shadows on the slopes and caught his eye. But it was gone now. No reason to scare her over nothing.

"Like the view?" she said lightly.

He nodded slowly. "Yeah. But who owns all that land?" Bannon pointed to where he had seen the movement.

"The state. There are trails through it. You can't really see them from here."

"Oh. There must be hikers, then."

Erin smiled. "And the occasional bear. It's a wilderness area."

Bannon scanned the forested slopes again, seeing only trees. The wayward breeze that had rattled her windows didn't move them, since they had no leaves yet to speak of. He blinked before checking one last time, and leaned on his bent arm against the window frame to brace himself.

"Hold it right there," Erin said.

He turned to her, startled. "What?"

"No, don't look at me. Go back the way you were. I want to draw you for the cover."

He darted a glance at the empty space on the pad of paper. "Are you kidding?"

"No."

Bannon was speechless for a couple of seconds. "Uh, what kind of a book is it again?"

"Contemporary fiction. You don't have to wear a kilt or armor or anything like that."

"Oh, good. The guys at the station would never let me live it down."

"It's only a preliminary sketch," she promised. "No one will recognize you, ever. Please?"

"Ah—okay." What else could he say? Bannon had never had a formal portrait done in his life. Hating to have his picture taken, he had deliberately screwed up his features for every school portrait from elementary school on, and even his cop ID photo didn't look much like him.

He told himself he had nothing to be nervous about. This was no big deal. A sketch. So what?

He stayed standing the way he was but he could feel his body tense the second she picked up her pencil and moved to the easel. Once there she paused. Silent seconds passed. Just knowing she was looking him up and down, even professionally, pretty much blew his mind.

"Relax," she said softly.

"Got it. Anything for art." Bannon wished he'd known she was going to ask him to do this, but her request hadn't been planned. Of course, he could have laughed it off and refused. He hadn't.

He took a deep breath, thinking that a shot of whiskey would help. That tall cup of coffee had his pulse banging. How long was this going to take? He had to will himself to relax.

"That's better," she said. "Take it easy. I guess you've never modeled."

"No, I haven't." He suppressed a laugh and held the pose. "Not a lot of call for it around the Wainsville headquarters. Except when they need an extra guy for a lineup."

"Um, you moved," she said. "Hold still."

"Sorry. Guess I should think about something else," he joked. "Like my horse." He almost turned to glance at the empty part of the paper where he was going to be, then stopped himself.

"Just don't look at me. Don't think about anything much, okay?"

As if. Her gaze made him self-conscious, but there was no way he was going to admit it. He stared out the window, finding geographical features in the landscape and putting them in an order he could remember. Standard recon drill.

"Very good. Stay like that. You're doing great."

"At least you work fast," he muttered, trying not to smile. He could hear the faint sound of the pencil strokes as her hand brushed over the paper.

"Almost done," she whispered absently.

Two words, two ordinary words, but the alluring softness of her voice as she said them was impossible to ignore. He fought a warm sensation of arousal throughout his body. She was standing at her easel and he was several feet away, but the feeling of sudden closeness between them was overwhelming.

Look outside, he told himself. *Look hard*.

He stiffened.

There it was again. Something moved. He caught a hard glint of light on metal. A gun? At this distance he couldn't tell. Without thinking he dropped his arm and stood up completely straight.

Something—someone—had to be out there. *Think it through*, he told himself. The way the rays of afternoon sun slanted, someone could see into the windows of Erin's house better than Bannon could see out. If they wanted to. If they were looking.

His arousal was instantly replaced by an uneasiness that raised invisible hairs on the back of his neck.

"What's the matter?" She picked up a pencil sharpener and began making a fresh point. The thin, scraping sound put him on edge. She didn't have to know why.

"Nothing." He rubbed a hand over his jaw to get rid of the tension that had clenched it.

"Want to see?"

She meant the drawing. What he really wanted to do was blast out the back door and see if he could catch—what, a figment of his imagination?

He didn't think so. A bear didn't move that fast, not in spring. A burdened hiker didn't either. The glint of light had lasted a microsecond, but his every instinct told him it could have reflected off the lens of a rifle scope. Or a gun. Drawn and swiftly covered.

Someone was out there.

Give chase? No way. He couldn't leave Erin alone if he was right. Explaining what had triggered his trained sense of being watched would scare her and make him sound paranoid. Was he?

After the shooting, a well-meaning shrink had told him he might experience flashbacks. He never had. He didn't think this was one.

He took one last look out there, spotted nothing, and turned around to answer her. "Of course I want to see it." Bannon went over to her and studied the drawing, forcing his mind to focus.

Her addition of a male figure had been done with skill. The face was in shadow, sketched in no more than three or four lines.

"Do you like it?"

"It's excellent," he said honestly. "I'm impressed." The pencil outline of him standing had been completed with assurance and speed. The arm he'd rested on the window frame was now magically resting on the sketched neck of the horse.

She hadn't tried to capture his actual likeness. Not as far as his features, anyway. The tense muscles, the animal alertness and thousand-yard stare—he would have to agree that was probably exactly what he'd looked like to her, without her knowing why.

Bannon stepped back, aware that she was gazing at the drawing again and not at him.

Erin frowned abstractedly and began to lightly sketch clouds into the background. Then she curled her hand into a fist and smudged the lines with the side of her hand, not caring that she smudged her skin into the bargain. The clouds turned into something soft and otherworldly, floating under her touch.

What a hell of a gift, he thought suddenly, to be able to create beauty out of blank nothing. Something told him that she saw the world that way more often than not.

He noticed a sunset same as anyone else, but what he looked for was danger. Staring down the barrel of a gun two years ago had marked his mind forever. He pushed the thought away as hard as it had hit him.

"Thanks for being a good sport, by the way." Her remark was polite, but he picked up on the hint of flirtatiousness in her tone—and then he saw something else he hadn't expected. There was a look of admiration in her eyes. For him. He suspected that art had nothing to do with it.

"If all you want me to do is stand still—" He broke off. Bannon realized she'd liked getting a really good look at him while she drew, liked it a lot. The thought erased everything.

He had a strong feeling she wanted more from him than just standing still. Much more.

He wouldn't say no to anything Erin wanted him to do for her. Acting on an impulse he was compelled to obey, he put his fingertips under her chin and tilted her face up to his. Jesus, what eyes. They were a thousand shades of blue this close. He had only a second to be dazzled by them before they closed and her lips parted. The little breath she drew stole his own.

Bannon moved his mouth over hers and kissed her, stroking her arms, her waist—stopping there unwillingly.

With an almost inaudible moan, she gave in, her hands moving around his back to hold him. Not closely. Her high breasts just brushed his chest. He wanted to pull her against him with all his strength. He didn't.

Her lips were soft and tender, responsive to his searching mouth, demanding silently that he deepen the kiss.

That much he would do, but no more. And not for much longer. Bannon drew in his breath and lifted his head. Her eyes fluttered open, but not all the way. The dreamy look she gave him did something to his heart.

He didn't dare kiss her again. Not now, anyway. But he couldn't go, not if it meant leaving her alone.

"What's the matter?" Her voice seemed far away, even though there was nothing between them now but the clothes they had on. Her body was warm and pliant against his. His protectiveness warred with his arousal.

"That's hard to say." He rubbed his cheek against her silky hair, looking out over her head through the window. "But I don't think you're safe here."

CHAPTER 6

Spreadsheets. Fiscal-year breakdowns. Audit inquiries. Registered letters from investors and creditors, and lawyers for both, never opened. Montgomery wished he could crumple up every single piece of paper on his desk and throw it into the fireplace. The blaze had died down—his problems hadn't. Over the last several years, he had amassed hundreds of millions in wealth for his hedge-fund clients and himself. In a few short months, it had dwindled to nearly nothing as one sure thing after another fizzled.

He barely slept. Couldn't eat. His thoughts drifted and whirled for hours these days. His head felt hollow. And then he had been blindsided by the reopening of Ann's case, forced to dodge the media with help from Ollie Duncan. At least his lawyer and the reporters didn't know that his empire had effectively vanished.

Yet.

The hall leading away from his luxuriously appointed study echoed with the precise click of Caroline's high heels, walking away after another quarrel. This one had been about the household bills. She was outraged by his questions about them.

He looked around his study, redecorated last year in grand plantation style, with an extravagant price tag to match. She'd had antiques shipped in from all over the South, snapping up what she called bargains and adding custom details that cost a fortune.

Wine red striped damask covered the walls, topped with elaborate molding. Hand-carved, of course. The immense cream-colored sofa with the walnut frame had been carried into the room by a team of movers and positioned on the expensive carpet, immovable. Two gigantic armchairs in a coordinating shade of silk flanked it and an inlaid-marble coffee table that picked up both the cream and wine shades took up the center of the seating area. Behind him, the room's walls were divided by floor-to-ceiling windows that met at the corner, gorgeously swagged and draped to shut out the sunlight that bothered him more and more.

Even the extremely faint hum of the computer on a small table to his left bothered him. It was on, but the screen was dark. Not that it mattered.

He sat at a partner's desk, a massive old piece placed on the diagonal so he could face the door. He'd essentially founded Montgomery Holdings from it years ago, landing his first investors on the strength of his name and reputation as a breeder of champion racehorses, using his operation as collateral at first, then expanding that. Selling million-dollar shares of winning Thoroughbreds put out to stud had been one scheme among many.

Caroline hated the Victorian ugliness and sheer size of the desk, but she had given up the struggle to get rid of it. Montgomery never would. Every man needed a last retreat, and the desk was his.

Crafted for two lawyers, country gentlemen in private practice, it could be used from either side. The antiques dealer had proudly shown off a hidden recess under the top nearly as wide as the desk itself, empty at the time, but undoubtedly intended for quick concealment of documents in the event of an unexpected visitor. And he'd shown Montgomery another ingenious feature: The corner legs on either side of the desk had been fashioned to hold small silver flasks in case the gentlemen felt the need for a restoring nip of whiskey.

The flasks were long gone, but Montgomery had improved on the hiding places. The recess now held a large-screen laptop, whose power cord ran through one hollow leg and under the carpet, connected to the Internet by a wireless router in a cabinet. He had just checked the thing, reassured by the row of tiny, unblinking lights indicating connection with an encrypted network that was his alone.

State of the art. Invisible. Anything but antique. Outside of the desk, he didn't share Caroline's enthusiasm for them. Besides the study, the only room where he felt at peace wasn't really a room, but a solarium filled with plants. Other than there, she didn't allow anything living in the house. Cut flowers and forced shrubs only. And above all, no pets. To him, the house was a lifeless showplace. It was practically new—he had bought it at her urging five years ago. For cash. Her name wasn't on the deed, and that had allowed him to keep full control. It was mortgaged to the hilt now.

And close to foreclosure.

The mansion that had been entrusted to the historical society was not strictly his. That at least had been a home to generations of Montgomerys, the happily married and those who strayed, fortune-builders and wastrels, successes and the occasional suicide, along with children and cousins and servants by the score.

He had never returned to it once Ann's grieving mother insisted they get out. Another failure of nerve on his part. At the time he had been inclined to wait, believing, irrationally, that whoever had taken his only child might bring her back and claim the reward.

But he had eventually resigned himself to the fact of Ann's death and closed the door on the past. The case drifted out of the headlines, though some local people had kept talking about it. Years went by before they stopped.

And now RJ Bannon had walked over a few graves and it was news again. Montgomery didn't know why anyone cared. Well, yes, he did—the reward money was mentioned in the broadcast.

He couldn't figure Bannon out. Hero cop or not, he was tough, young, and an adversary to reckon with. Obviously intelligent. But what the hell did he stand to gain by reopening the case? If it was the reward he was after, he was walking into a bear trap.

Ollie Duncan had seen to that, even if his bills hadn't been paid for months. The lawyer hadn't gotten any information out of Bannon, though. Called on the carpet, the police chief had no explanation for the broadcast. Hoebel owed them that and hadn't delivered.

But that score was lopsided. Montgomery owed Hoebel money, a lot of it. A year ago, their relationship had been straightforward enough: Hoebel was paid a flat monthly fee in the low thousands to keep Montgomery in the loop on things that wealthy people would rather keep hidden. It was a snap to find out who was facing fore-closure and eviction from a multimillion-dollar home, whose tro-phy wife had left with a black eye and a vow to get even in court, and which spoiled rich kid had run amok and stuck his parents with a hellishly expensive lawsuit. Montgomery preferred solid-gold investors with no dirty secrets and no liabilities. Hoebel had helped him filter out the undesirables.

But the tanking economy meant Montgomery had to lower his standards in more ways than one. And, unfortunately, the chief had found out that Montgomery's business affairs had come under the scrutiny of a federal agency. Montgomery regretted explaining the creative accounting that allowed hedge funds to post returns of twenty percent or more, though he had been careful not to admit to doing any of that himself.

But he hadn't reckoned on the chief's resentment. Apparently Hoebel had expected to get a chance to profit from the money ma-chine while it was going strong. However, Montgomery's fund had an ironclad requirement of one million to buy in, and Hoebel didn't have it, not on a civil servant's salary. Make that a crooked civil ser-vant.

The economy got worse and the monthly payments got smaller. A lot smaller. Last month Hoebel hadn't been paid at all. Distracted by the need to find new investors and gain their confidence, Mont-gomery hadn't been careful. Hoebel had pointed out that he'd left a paper trail of incriminating records, unshredded, that could speed up the SEC's case against him. Trust a cop to look into trash cans.

The chief saw nothing wrong with asking for money to keep his mouth shut. He didn't call it blackmail. But that's what it was. And he wasn't acting alone. Hoebel had called in a friend of his. A man named Cutt, a rogue cop who'd done time. Both men showed up on payday. Montgomery handed over what he could in cash.

Things were getting complicated.

Montgomery looked down at the papers on his desktop. The fig-ures blurred and swam. He sank his head into his hands.

He craved sleep. The pills he had once taken had lost their effectiveness and his stash was dwindling. Nightmares woke him repeatedly once the shock of the broadcast had worn off a little.

He was plagued with dream visions of Ann as a child. Alive again. Her face seemed to be watching him from the depths of his memory, sensitive and silent. In the last few days, he'd found himself gasping for breath, his heart half stopping at unexpected times.

His reason had been affected to the point of imagining a resemblance between Ann and the young woman who'd gone with Bannon to the family mansion, imagining that she looked like Luanne too. Something subtle kept nagging at him—the way she tilted her head to look at things—it was driving him crazy.

Compulsively, he'd reviewed the security footage in secret, over and over. It was all too easy to click it open, study it again. Looking for . . . he didn't know what he was looking for. Last night he had been nearly hypnotized by audio of the young woman's soft voice and Bannon's answering drawl, and their endless back-and-forth about Ann. When they had entered his daughter's room—and looked at her portrait—he'd wanted to smash the laptop screen. Smash them.

Ann was dead. Something inside him had died with her. And the place where his heart had been was still empty. He had given up on everything but making money long ago.

Montgomery's abstracted gaze moved over the framed photos on the wall. The largest and most recent showed Caroline at the Hunt Ball last February, the center of all eyes, escorted by her father into a vast, chandeliered room crowded with the Virginia horses-and-hounds set, dressed to the nines. Caro was decked out in a strapless black satin evening gown and long black gloves.

A strategic choice to conceal her lack of an engagement ring.

Her slender fingers clutched her father's sleeve. Caroline was desperate to marry and have a child. Montgomery's child. They'd had a spectacular fight about both only an hour before the glamorous photo had been taken. Her flawless makeup covered every trace of her tears and red-faced shrieking. He'd been more than happy that night to hand her over to her father, Hamp Loudon, and let the old man do the honors. He himself was nowhere to be seen in the picture.

He should never have allowed a woman that young—thirty-two to his sixty-seven—into his life, let alone his house. She would have been a fool not to try to cement her social and financial position by marrying him, and Caro Loudon was not a fool. As she saw it, she was entitled to an answer one way or another, and soon. Montgomery had put her off too long. Even certain members of her family, stalwarts of Old Dominion society, were dropping hints and asking pointed questions about his intentions. Evidently they assumed he was rich, so rich he ought to rescue them, starting with their only daughter.

The thought made him want to laugh. He could have told them long ago that old money was just as easy to squander as the new kind. The Loudon fortune had been frittered away in one ill-advised investment after another.

At least someone else had done that. Montgomery didn't have her family's financial ruin on his conscience. Caro would never be upgraded from girlfriend to fiancée, but it wasn't because she was penniless. In any case, she never admitted that. And for some reason, she seemed to think he didn't know that old Hamp Loudon's money was long gone. He knew.

He looked at the photo again. She was utterly beautiful, pale blond hair upswept, her slender neck encircled by diamond-clasped pearls, and her body on full display in that simple but sexy black strapless gown.

That kind of simplicity didn't come cheap. He'd paid the couturier's staggeringly expensive bill from one of his personal accounts. The other accounts, U.S. and offshore, were emptying faster than his best efforts to refill them.

Montgomery straightened up in his chair, shuffling through the papers in front of him in a futile way. Going through the motions. Just last night he had chatted up a few potential clients at the party after the horse auction. What a waste of time. Hedge funds were falling out of fashion, it seemed. Heirs and heiresses and even the nouveau riche kept a tight grip on their money these days.

He'd had better luck at that Hunt Ball. It was the social event of the season in this part of Virginia, and he'd had to put on a good show. Neither he nor Caro could afford to look shabby.

That was the price of success—his accountant's turn of phrase. The words haunted him.

He frowned when he heard Caroline's footsteps click back toward the study, louder and louder. Her voice floated his way. "Honey? Want to kiss and make up?"

Montgomery didn't answer. He pressed a hidden spring under the desktop and the recess appeared under it. He whisked most of the paper and envelopes in, covering the laptop. A half-completed form from his bank went in last. Caroline didn't need to know that he was removing his lost daughter as beneficiary of the trust. Or that the two million in it would automatically revert to him.

He wasn't going to use it to pay anyone back. Or marry her. It was small change compared to what he'd had not long ago, but it was all he had left in liquid assets.

"Monty? Honey? Are you in there?" There was an anxious note in her question.

"Yes," he answered irritably. His hands paused on the papers he'd left on the desktop. For show. Like the computer to his left. He tapped a key to bring its screen back.

"I just wanted to say I'm sorry." She paused in the open doorway, her striking curves silhouetted in the light from the hall beyond as she raised one slender arm to smooth her hair, the bracelet on her arm jingling faintly. Her white cashmere sweater clung to her body, rising up just a little over skintight designer jeans that looked anything but casual. "I started that fight, I guess."

"It doesn't matter. It's over." He forced his voice to stay steady.

She entered the room, looking at him, then at the desk.

"What are you doing?"

"Routine paperwork. It has nothing to do with you. Not bills."

"Oh." A mix of relief and resentment glittered in her beautiful eyes as she tried to make out the paper under his hand. She pouted. "That looks sort of like a bill."

"It's part of a financial report. Go ahead and read it. I don't care." He turned the paper around and pushed it toward her.

She changed her mind when she glanced at it. "Never mind. It's all numbers and percentages. I can't make head or tail of that stuff."

"Really? I would have thought otherwise."

She walked into the room and flung herself down on the sofa, arranging herself as if she were modeling for *Town & Country*, a habit of hers that used to amuse him. Now it grated.

"You should teach me," she said coaxingly. "Why do you keep all the desk drawers locked, anyway?"

He raised a steel gray eyebrow. "What an old-fashioned question. Suspicious women snoop online these days. Not in desks."

"You didn't answer my question, Monty." Her wheedling voice went up a notch.

He got up and took a small key from a glass dish on the mantel. "Don't tell me you didn't know where this was."

"I didn't. Honestly."

He beckoned to her and she rose from the sofa and sauntered to his side. One by one he unlocked the drawers, watching her face as she looked down at neat arrangements of pens and pencils and paper clips, legal pads and steel-engraved stationery.

Caroline stooped a little to take a monogrammed envelope from the drawer, her charm bracelet jingling again as she ran a fingertip over the engraved *M* on the flap. "Do you use these?"

"Not often."

"I would. How does Caroline Montgomery sound to you?" she asked softly. "I'm ready."

That was a sentiment he didn't share. "You'll have to wait," he replied.

Her lips thinned with disappointment. "I've been waiting. For quite a while. Daddy says—"

"Once and for all, Caroline, I don't care what your father thinks. You're a big girl. Make up your own mind."

She tossed the envelope back in the drawer. "I think I have."

He got up, towering over her. To Caroline's credit, she didn't shrink back. "Are you going to leave me?" he asked.

"Maybe."

"Answer me, Caro. Yes or no." Montgomery came around the huge desk and took her in his arms. But there was nothing affectionate in the embrace. She struggled, pushing against his chest, staring up into his cold eyes.

"What's the matter with you?" she cried.

"Nothing," he said calmly. "Nothing at all."

She broke free and ran from the room.

Montgomery stayed standing until her footsteps clattered down the double staircase and the massive front door slammed behind her. He heard the engine of her sports car screech as she threw it into gear and backed out and away.

Then he closed the study door and slid the brass bolt through its latch, locking himself in.

He went back to his desk and took out the laptop, brushing away the papers that covered it. He opened it, mechanically going through the process of starting it up, staring unseeingly at the icons popping up on the flowing screen one by one.

A round disc appeared. Montgomery House Security. He clicked on it.

Once more Bannon and the young woman walked through the house he'd grown up in, moving in and out of rooms he could never forget. She turned and looked up at a camera she didn't know was there and Montgomery hit Pause.

Then he zoomed in on her face. Closer and closer, until she was nothing but eyes. Blue eyes. Beautiful and vulnerable. Just like Luanne's. But that was a coincidence.

Montgomery stared into those eyes. He clenched his fist, not really aware that he had done so until a savage spasm tightened his fingers to the point of pain. His nails sank into his palm and he felt the wet heat of welling blood. Opening his hand with a start, he looked at the scratch, small but deep. He pressed his hand down hard on a piece of paper and held it there to stop the bleeding.

The eyes on the screen looked at him reproachfully. He stared back. It couldn't be.

A Bible phrase, half-remembered, came to him: *Blood of my blood. Flesh of my flesh*. The exact words escaped him.

Was he losing his mind? He clicked out of the screen and away from the young woman's haunting gaze.

Getting and spending had consumed him for too many years. He forced himself to return to business. Somehow, he had to repay his investors and get the hell out of this shell game. He could wangle a mega-loan, use the Montgomery stud farm and stables for collateral, and see that every damn one of them got their money, and a little extra. Maybe not at the rate of interest they'd hoped for, but they had been advised of market variability beforehand.

Numbers. Money. Move it here, hide it there. Keeping the shell game going was never easy.

Two hours later, the files Montgomery was looking at on his laptop appeared on another screen fifty miles away. Someone else's eyes, nearly colorless, blinked behind round lenses that reflected the details of Montgomery's business yet again.

Far away in his ornate study, the router's tiny lights flickered, delivering stolen data to the featureless room where three men sat staring into a single screen. Distantly, new numbers were entered by Montgomery into the grid. The totals on both sides automatically adjusted.

A little bloodshot by now, the colorless eyes widened. The hacker, a slouched, scruffy-haired kid in a college sweatshirt, spoke. "This guy is bleeding money."

Hoebel, not in uniform, growled, "Tell me something I don't know."

Paul blinked at him. "So what do you want me to do?"

"Figure out how to siphon some off. He might run. What do you think, Cutt?"

The third man, a lanky six-five, stretched out his legs and cursed when his sneakered foot connected with a metal chair. "For sure he's gonna run. The only question is when. I got a GPS tracker on his car. I can do an intercept before he gets to the airport."

Hoebel turned to him. "Don't bother. He's going to move the money electronically."

"He can't do that until he has it," the hacker reminded him. Fast fingers jabbed at his keyboard. "Right now—hello, bank bot—it's still in the trust account." He pulled up a screen and turned the laptop around so Hoebel could view it. "Take a look."

"Interesting. How'd you get in there?" the chief asked.

Paul pulled the laptop back in front of him. "I had a temp job at his bank my junior year. They told me it was a golden opportunity and they were right. I picked up a bunch of passwords and codes for my collection. They come in handy."

Hoebel snorted. "When I was your age, I collected baseball caps."

"Uh-huh." Paul hummed to himself as he opened electronic files at top speed. "Just so you know, bank security is lame. Once you get past their firewalls, you can find out a lot. Anything else you need to know?"

Hoebel exchanged a look with Cutt before he replied to Paul's question. "Yeah, kid. Do you keep your money in a bank?"

"No. Dude, my clients pay cash. Unmarked bills, low denominations—works for me. The side gig with Montgomery's accountant makes me look legit. He takes out taxes and all that."

Hoebel scowled. "C'mon, get out of there before the bank bot or whatever you called it sets off a warning. I don't want this hack session traced back."

Paul smirked. "It won't be. I know what I'm doing." He took off his glasses after he keyed up Montgomery's screen again, polishing them before he peered at the spreadsheet. "No change. He must be having a beer."

Hoebel grunted. "Hugh Montgomery? A shot of sixty-year-old single malt would be more like it."

The hacker didn't seem impressed. "Whatever. Want a screen grab of this?"

"Yeah. Get everything. And print it out."

"Okay, boss." In a few minutes a new grid appeared and Paul studied it as the two older men looked on, doing a screen grab before it vanished. A form replaced it. "Got a pdf now. Looks like a bank document."

"I told you to get out of the bank's computers."

"Duh. I did," Paul answered. He scanned the form. "It's a trust kind of thing." He read aloud. "'Designated beneficiary: Ann Montgomery.' Hey, he's changing that line. Now it's blank."

Hoebel leaned over his shoulder. "His daughter. That must be the reward he had out for her. It was held in a revocable trust. He can change it whenever he wants to."

"Hold on. He clicked Undo." The hacker zoomed in on the upper part of the form on his screen. "She's the beneficiary again. What's up with that? Isn't she dead or something?"

"She'd better be," Hoebel said in a low voice.

CHAPTER 7

Bannon settled himself into the sofa with his morning coffee. The cat was curled up in the corner of it—Babaloo hadn't moved a muscle since late last night.

He wished he'd slept that easy. He hadn't wanted to leave Erin last night, though she didn't seem to be in immediate danger. On his way to his car, after she'd gone back inside, he'd taken a quick but thorough look around the outside of her house, out of habit. He didn't know what he was looking for. She'd been nice enough to call him a half hour ago, just to check in. He hadn't wanted to scare her and she hadn't seemed scared.

That kiss they'd shared had been mind-melting. He would have to get that aspect of their budding relationship under strict control until he could ensure her safety.

He'd run through everything that happened yesterday, putting it through a reality filter. They might have been followed from the restaurant. He'd been too busy looking at her to remember much about that part of their afternoon. What had happened later—that was clear in his mind. He had seen something.

The Montgomery case had been complicated to begin with, and he'd only begun to work with what little he knew so far. He'd left a couple of messages for Doris, but he knew she wasn't likely to call him back from work and she was probably on her way there now.

First things first. Erin lived alone and she needed protection. A solution to that problem had occurred to him. His brother Linc could probably help him out.

To reach him, he punched in a set of numbers he knew by heart and put a call through systems that weren't public.

"Bannon?" his brother asked when he heard his voice.

"Yeah. It's me."

"Aww, you remembered my code. I'm so touched."

"I bet."

Linc didn't bother with small talk. He never had. "What's up?"

"Linc, I need a dog for a while. You know some K-9 handlers for the feds, right?"

"Yeah, I do." His brother chuckled. "But that cat of yours can beat up any dog on earth. I should know, I gave him to you."

"It's not for me. It's for a girl."

There was a pause. "Oh. Then you want something fluffy and yappy. You know, a Handbagese. Go to a pet store. The people I know train big dogs."

Bannon blew out an exasperated breath. "Linc, for cryin' out loud, knock it off. I'm looking for a big dog that's trained. A loaner. There's a situation developing and she's right in the middle of it—I kind of put her there. I have an obligation to protect her."

"Does she have a name? Is she pretty?"

"Erin. She's beautiful. Can we stick to the subject?"

His brother pretended to think that over. "Okay. But why do you need a dog? Can't you just follow her around with a gun like a real man? Or hide her in your bed?"

"I thought about both," he said wryly. "I don't know her that well."

"Tell me more," Linc said with a resigned sigh.

"It has to do with the Montgomery kidnapping. Erin is an artist who did some paintings of the house where it happened and she contacted me on Facebook when she saw the interview on TV. She took me there to see the inside and now I think she's being followed. I'm sure I am."

"Why? Isn't it a cold case?"

"Not that cold. There's money at stake."

"How much?"

"A couple mil. A reward, held in a trust that's about to be dissolved."

"And you think someone suspects she saw something or found

something while she was in the old house. Am I making myself clear?"

"No."

"Okay, your turn."

Bannon kept his reply to the point. "I got famous for fifteen minutes and Montgomery and his lawyer warned me to stay the hell out of the case, but not in so many words. Anyway, she lives way out near the Blue Ridge, no other house for miles. I went to her house on a second date and I got the feeling we were being watched. From a distance, but watched. I hated the idea of leaving her alone, but what could I do?"

"Huh."

That was Linc's signal word for being deep in thought. Bannon heard the clicking of a laptop keyboard.

"So you want to give her a dog to make some noise in case someone comes skulking around. I got it. Is she okay with that?"

"I think I can persuade her."

Linc laughed. "Don't tell me how. Okay. I just sent some e-mails and I'll make some calls. Let me see what I can do. You at home?"

"Yeah."

Two hours later, his doorbell gave three short rings. Linc had said that it would. Bannon got up and put the cat out the back door, then walked through the condo to open the front door.

A petite brunette smiled up at him, a leash looped around her hand. Beside her sat a big, mixed-breed dog with pricked shepherd ears and a black Lab coat.

"Hi," she said. "This is Charlie. And you can call me, uh, Karen Michaels."

He nodded. That wasn't her name and she wasn't supposed to be there and neither was the dog. Bannon pegged her for career army, special forces, division unknown. She looked strong for her size, wearing a T-shirt and jeans that hinted at sleek, feminine muscle beneath. Good going, Linc.

"I'm Bannon. Want to come in?"

She shook her head. "I gotta get back." She handed him her end of the leash. Charlie rose from his sitting position and trotted in.

"You don't need an instruction manual for this guy. He knows what to do. Should work out fine. He was raised by a woman handler, by the way."

"You?"

She smiled. "No."

"When do you need him back?"

"There's no set time. You can stay in touch with me through Linc."

Bannon looked down at Charlie, whose nose was twitching in the direction of the sofa where Babaloo had been sleeping. "How does he feel about cats?"

She bent down to give the dog a farewell pat. "Like I said, he's trained. There won't be any problem. But he's not staying with you, right?"

"Ah—no."

The brunette straightened and turned to go. "Bye, Charlie. Be good."

"I really appreciate this. Thanks, Karen."

She remembered her name just in time, and gave him a very fetching wink. "No problem. Take care."

He watched her walk quickly down the hall, thinking of a few good questions to ask his brother next time they spoke. Then he closed the door and went back inside his condo with Charlie.

Bannon observed him sniffing around, and put him through a few commands. True to his training, the dog obeyed perfectly.

"You've got all four feet on the ground, pal." Bannon stroked the dog's strong neck. Add power and speed to that. He could feel both under the soft fur.

He would cook up some story about Charlie belonging to his brother—make that his deployed brother, while he was lying through his teeth—and throw in condo rules against dogs. Would Erin mind . . . ? Just for a few weeks. His instincts told him she was going to say yes.

"Okay. Don't get used to my place," he told the dog. "You're going to be a country dog for a few weeks. Maybe longer."

He picked up the leash and scooped up his car keys, then heard his cat yowling faintly at the back door. Bannon sighed, slid the leash handle over the doorkob, and went back to let Babaloo in. Nonchalant as usual, the cat strolled in, then spotted Charlie. His golden eyes narrowed, communicating feline contempt, and the tip of his tail twitched ever so slightly, something he generally did before launching a claws-out attack.

"Chill," Bannon said to the cat. "He isn't staying." He left with the dog, who trotted obediently and silently at his side on his enormous paws.

They made one stop on the drive out to Erin's, for dog food. Bannon surveyed the bulging bags on the shelves and selected a five-pound one. It might look a little too calculated if he showed up with the jumbo size.

Not that she couldn't figure out what he was up to. He could bring a big bag over later, once she'd said yes.

Fifteen minutes later, he was walking through the parking lot of the supermarket with a sack of dog food in one hand and his cell phone in the other. He punched in a single number with his thumb. He'd had her on speed dial from the second she'd given him her number. Why fool around?

After three rings, Erin picked up.

"Hello?"

Bannon felt a surge of warm energy at the sound of her low, sweet voice. "Hey, Erin," he said casually, "it's me."

"I recognized your voice," she said with laughter in hers. "What's up?"

She didn't seem at all annoyed that they were talking for the second time in the same day. In fact, she seemed happy.

"I was wondering—I was kind of out and around—would it be okay if I stopped by? Are you busy?"

"Sure, that's fine. And the answer to your second question is no."

The dog was looking out of the car window, then back at him when he replied. "That's great. Need anything from the store? I'm here already—I just stopped in to get a few things."

"Oh." Erin thought for a minute. "A quart of milk, I guess. Two percent, if they have it."

Wow. What a domestic moment. He felt ridiculously exultant. He wanted to be the guy who brought home milk and eggs and every other damn thing in the world she might need. He grinned at the dog, who seemed to sense that good things were going on.

"Two percent," he repeated. "No problem. See you in about half an hour."

"That's great. Thanks."

He opened the trunk and slung the sack of dog food in it, then went back to the store for the milk. If they didn't have two percent, he would hit every supermarket and gas station quick shop in a twenty-five-mile radius until he found it.

He slid open the door to the dairy case and checked the rows of square plastic jugs. Yup, they had it. After completing that transaction—the bored clerk didn't seem to remember him from two minutes ago—Bannon went back to the car and drove off.

Charlie seemed content to survey the scenery as the road became more rural, and Bannon cracked the window so the dog could get his whiffs in too. It wasn't long before he spotted the sign for the turnoff to Erin's house.

The narrow road had no oncoming vehicles and there was no one behind him. He drove with one hand on the wheel, ruffling Charlie's fur with the other. "You're gonna like her. I hope she likes you."

They went another couple of miles and he saw the small white house.

Erin had heard him coming, evidently, because she was waiting on the porch. Her dress, made of some light material, floated around her and showed her figure, even though she wore a sweater over it. Her arms were folded around her middle—it wasn't all that warm out, although the sun was shining. Bannon took in the fine sight of her waiting for him as he slowed and pulled up to the side of the house.

Charlie stayed in the car when he opened the driver's side door and got out with the plastic bag containing the quart of milk. "Here you go."

"Thanks." She noticed the big black dog. "You've got company."

Bannon half turned. "Yeah, that's Charlie."

"I thought you said you had a cat."

"I do." He walked the short distance from his car to her porch. "Charlie is on loan." He mumbled something about his brother, intentionally not making that point clear.

"Oh." She rubbed her arms. "It's fine with me if he comes along."

"All right." Bannon called the dog and Charlie bounded out, sniffing the ground before he looked alertly around. "He won't knock over your easel or anything, I promise. He has better manners than I do."

Erin smiled at both of them. "Bring him inside."

Bannon snapped his fingers. "Let's go, boy."

She reached out to take the plastic bag with the jug of milk in it and their hands touched. The simple action seemed like something they'd done every day, but the friendliness of it touched a flash of deeper feeling in him.

"Thanks. You saved me a trip. Come on, Charlie."

The dog looked at Bannon, got a silent okay, and went to Erin's side, accepting the gentle hand that patted him briefly as he walked beside her into the house.

Way to go, Bannon thought with delight. He entered two steps behind both of them and stopped before he got to the kitchen, looking at the art on the easel. She'd done more work on it, without finishing it. "This is looking good," he called.

"The trick is knowing when to stop," she said, turning to him. "If I finish it, they might ask for changes. I'm happy with it, though. Now let's see if I get the job. I really need the money."

"You will," Bannon said.

"What do you think?" She glanced down at the dog. "Are you an art lover, Charlie?" He wagged his tail.

Not a crazy-happy wag, because the animal was too well-trained for that. But the dog clearly felt at home.

"Guess so." Erin laughed. "I wish I had a treat for you. But I wasn't expecting you." She patted him again, thoroughly. Charlie was loving the attention.

"Not a problem," Bannon hastened to assure her. "I mean, I have dog food in the trunk. Besides, does he look like he's starving?"

Erin caressed Charlie's muscular sides and gave him an affectionate thump or two. "No." She chuckled. "I'd say he's healthy. These mixed breeds are great dogs." There was a pause before she asked, "Is he staying with you for a while?"

"Actually, no." Bannon took a deep breath and rubbed the back of his neck. "What happened was—well, my brother—he's special forces, don't know if I told you that—anyway, he was deployed in kind of a hurry and he dropped off Charlie late last night. But he forgot that my condo doesn't allow dogs." He rushed the answer, maybe a little too much.

"Really." He saw a twinkle in her eye, but forged on anyway.

"So if you don't mind my asking—"

"Not at all." She laughed. "It seems I need protection, according to you, even though yesterday you couldn't say why, and today you happen to have this dog. What a coincidence."

He gave her a sheepish grin. "Busted."

"Yes, you are. Where did you get him?"

"Through my brother," Bannon replied. "Even though he doesn't actually belong to Linc, Charlie works with his, um, team. He comes highly recommended."

"Glad to hear it," she said impishly. "So how big is that bag of dog food in the trunk?"

His grin widened. "Five pounds. I could go get more. He can stay with you for as long as you want."

"Why don't you do that? I'll make us a late lunch while you're gone."

Bannon hesitated for only a second. "Deal."

Then he left, thinking to himself how cool it was that she didn't kick up a fuss about not knowing absolutely everything. Clearly, when Erin Randall wanted something, she went for it.

It took longer than he thought to find a jumbo bag of dog food, and he ended up backtracking to the supermarket where he'd gotten the milk. By the time he returned to the house, Charlie was sacked out in front of the wood stove on a folded blanket. Erin was kneeling in front of it, adding a split log to a pretty good little blaze.

"Hey. Welcome back. Just thought I'd take the chill off the afternoon," she said as she got to her feet and straightened up.

"Looks like Charlie appreciates it." Bannon laughed.

Erin glanced down at the dog, who raised his head and half

opened his eyes at the sound of Bannon's voice. Then he settled down again. "We went out for a long walk. I swear he sniffed every blade of grass and molecule of air between here and the mountain. And he stayed by my side the whole time."

"Smart dog." Bannon was pleased. "Good. I don't want to worry about you."

Erin tucked a wayward lock of hair behind her ear, an unconscious gesture that made him want to take her in his arms. "That's nice of you. I mean it, Bannon. Even though I think you're overreacting."

He took a deep breath before replying, damned if he would scare her unnecessarily. "Maybe I am. But the Montgomery case has a lot of twists and turns, and I'm only at the beginning of it. I'm not sure if I'm always alone, let's put it that way. And you've been seen with me. What I'm getting at is—well, this house is a little isolated."

"I'm fine here," she reassured him. "But thanks for bringing Charlie out. Keeping him for a while isn't going to be a problem. We hit it off right away."

He felt a little awkward for not telling her the entire truth, not that he could, but her sincere reply eased his mind on that score. Still, he wished he knew who had been out there yesterday. He knew Charlie could track the watcher in the woods if the dog ever picked up a scent trail on him.

"Are you hungry?" she asked. "I found some stuff. Mostly nibbles. Right this way."

She reached out to him and he took her hand. Her slender fingers were warm and strong. All he wanted to do was pull her against him and start kissing her again.

Jesus, maybe it was him she wasn't safe from. He restrained himself. "Lead on."

This time the tray was set up on an old pine table in an alcove off the kitchen area. "I didn't see this yesterday."

"Yes, you did. But it was covered with a tablecloth and a mountain of folded laundry on top of that. I put it all away. We don't have to eat off that old trunk."

She'd set out a bottle of wine and two glasses. On the tray were different kinds of cheese, crackers, and slices of apple in a bowl.

The kind of food they could feed each other if they felt so inclined. Nibble by nibble.

The thought was irresistible. The meal was impromptu but he got the feeling she was sending a message by adding wine to it. He didn't have to be that restrained. After they ate, talked, hung out, whatever—he could allow himself to claim another kiss. No harm in that.

"I opened the bottle," she said, letting go of his hand. "You're supposed to let it breathe, right? Whatever that means."

Something that Bannon was having difficulty doing at the moment, and not because the fire she'd built was doing an excellent job of warming the whole house. No, it was because she'd picked up a slice of apple and bitten into it. There was a trace of slick juice on her lower lip.

"I don't actually know myself." He wrapped a hand around the thick green glass of the bottle and picked it up, examining the label. "Hey, this is the good stuff. Am I worth it?"

"Of course you are."

He grinned at her, but waited to pour. "How much do you want?"

Erin finished her bite of apple and inclined her head. "Half a glass is fine."

They both sat down to the light meal. The first several sips of wine relaxed him. There was an easy intimacy between them. It made him think how long it had been since—

Never. There was no comparison to be made between her and any other woman he'd been with. Erin was one of a kind. Here they were on what could be defined as Date Three, and he was in . . . in something with her. It was too soon to call it love.

"By the way," she said suddenly, putting down her cheese-topped cracker, "I found Pinky." His confused look made her smile. "The bear you were asking about."

That was the last thing he wanted to talk about at the moment. "Oh, right," he said politely. "I forgot his name."

"Her name," she corrected. "Pinky is female."

Bannon nodded. "I'll try to remember that." He took another swallow of wine, a big one.

Erin got up, brushing a few crumbs from her dress, and went over to the pine shelves in the studio area that held the boxes marked *Home*. "She was in this one—whoops, no." Cardboard flapped and squeaked a little as she investigated. "Wrong box. This one."

She dragged out the right box and Bannon immediately rose halfway to help her before she forestalled him with a wave of her hand.

"Don't get up. It's light."

He sat back down again and moved the tray and both wine-glasses to one side. But she put the box on the floor before she sat down herself.

Erin reached in and pulled out a cloth bear that looked hand-made, just as she'd said. Glancing at it snapped him out of his amorous thoughts—it seemed the same as the one in the photo of Ann Montgomery as a child, which he'd given back to Doris along with all the other visual evidence.

He had to hope she was staying one step ahead of Chief Hoebel, and wished he'd been able to check in with her that morning.

Erin gave the bear a dusting-off and a couple of affectionate little squeezes to plump it, then propped it against the wine bottle. "Sit up, Pinky."

The bear toppled over and Bannon nudged it upright with a fin-ger. Women sure saved a lot of odd stuff.

"And I found something else I'd been looking for." Giving him a bemused smile, she reached down into the box of clutter again. "Plus some junk, of course." She used both hands to show off a cracked but handpainted flowerpot broken into two pieces. "Fabu-lous, huh? Why did I keep this?"

He shrugged. "I have a high school bowling trophy that would go great with it. The bowling ball bit fell off, though."

Erin tossed the pieces of flowerpot into a nearby wastebasket. "Bye-bye." She dove into the box again and came up with an old scrapbook. "This is it. My whole childhood is in here. My mother started it. She could be a little obsessive about memories and stuff. Sometimes my dad added things. He kept all my drawings. He told me now and then that I was going to be a great artist."

Bannon was definitely interested. "He was right."

"Oh, I don't know about the great part," she said softly. "I'm just happy to be doing what I love."

Without looking at him, she opened the scrapbook, which was crammed with stiff-looking pages sheathed in clear but yellowing plastic. Erin slid a finger under the plastic of one and adjusted the crooked document inside, moving it over a duplicate beneath until the edges lined up.

"This book got a little knocked around. But here's my birth certificate. Two copies. My dad was a great one for documenting everything." She pointed to a box in the middle of the document. "Look at those teeny-weeny footprints. Boy, things have changed. I don't think that hospital even exists anymore."

She was lucky to have the certificate, if so. Then he noticed that it had been typed on a really old machine, probably not even electric. Letters hopped the lines here and there. A couple of number keys hadn't even hit the paper, and the exact time of birth and her weight weren't clear. But her name and her parents' names had been carefully entered above the small footprints.

Name of child: Erin Randall.
Sex: female. Born living.
Names of parents: Ernest and Ina Randall.

Suddenly he got it. "Your name is a blend of their first names."

She seemed impressed. "That's right. Good guess. I was their one and only."

He looked again at the footprints. It seemed wrong somehow, to ink an innocent newborn for an ID, but infants did get snatched now and then, sometimes right from a maternity ward, sometimes from a home. Not that he'd ever worked a case like that, but a buddy had.

He glanced at the embossed state seal that gleamed dull gold in the light. "So where's the official hospital picture of you as a newborn?"

"Gone. If it ever existed," she said absently. "My mom said all my baby pictures were lost when we moved."

"Oh. When was that?"

"I think I was about three. I don't remember anything about the first place we lived."

An alarm went off deep in his mind. Losing baby pictures didn't fit with documenting everything and being obsessive about memories. Bannon made a mental note of the inconsistency but didn't comment on it. He watched her turn several more pages.

"Then who's that?" He pointed to a slightly blurred black-and-white photo of a baby. Not a newborn.

"My brother."

Something she'd said the first time they'd had lunch came back to him. He should have thought of it before. "Didn't you say—"

"That I was the one and only. Well, I was, after him, that is. He died before I came along, my parents said."

Bannon took a closer look at the photo. The baby boy was less than a year old, and he didn't resemble Erin at all.

"Can I see that?"

"Sure."

She turned the scrapbook his way and he took the opportunity to study the whole page. There was a faint handwritten caption below the baby's photo. *Our little boy. Henry Adam Randall, age 9 months.*

He turned it back toward Erin. "What happened to him? If you don't mind my asking."

She shook her head. "They never really said. I got the idea it was some kind of illness. Not an accident or anything. But I didn't ask."

"Not even when you were grown up?"

Erin pressed her lips together. "They didn't like talking about sad things. And by the time I turned twenty-six, they weren't around to ask."

"I'm sorry. I guess I shouldn't have pried," Bannon said quickly. She seemed distant all of a sudden—so much for the mood of intimacy that he'd been enjoying. Nothing much he could do about recapturing that. The scrapbook held poignant memories of a family she no longer had.

"It's all right. Really." She turned more pages, looking thoughtfully at photos and pasted-in drawings here and there, signed by her in painstaking capitals.

There were no school portraits, but then she'd said she'd been homeschooled. The photos of her were shadowed or with her facing away from the camera. She stopped at one that showed her with braids down her back, in her father's workshop, standing by him.

Bannon did an automatic inventory.

Ernest Randall was ordinary looking, with no distinguishing features. Thick hair, sandy colored. Light eyes. Medium height. Older, somehow, than Bannon had expected, even though Erin had said she'd come along late in life for them.

He could make out shop equipment in the background of the photo, but he didn't know what all of it was. Tool-and-die gear, maybe. Machines for metalworking. He recognized a couple of different types of table saws, not like the heavy-duty one his own father had used. His mother still kept it in her basement.

Erin tapped the photo. "He never let me touch the shop stuff but he used to make puzzles for me on this one. Jigsaws, really complicated. Later on we did word and math puzzles. He tried to teach me geometry and a little bit of engineering. It did kind of help me with drawing."

"How so?"

"If you know how things work, you can see how they should fit together." She made a funny little face. "And then you can draw them without too much thinking. It's hard to explain."

"I think I understand. And it sounds like he did too. Didn't you tell me he was an inventor?"

Her pleased smile told Bannon he'd remembered right. "Yes. And a tinkerer. I used to think there was nothing he didn't know how to do. He developed all those photos himself because he didn't trust the drugstore."

"Now that's going pretty far into do-it-yourself territory."

Erin waved a hand to indicate just how far. "He had a darkroom set up and rinsed the prints in an old bathtub and everything." She wrinkled her nose. "I remember hating the smell of the developer chemicals."

"How about your mother? What did she do?"

"She taught elementary school for a while. But not after my brother died. So she was always home for me." Erin turned another page and showed him a photo of an older woman, thin, with a sad face, wearing a dress with a frayed collar. "That's her and me, of course, next to her. We're working on this scrapbook."

"How about that." The photo was faded but it was clear that the scrapbook was new. "I can't see your face, though."

She gave a little laugh. "No, I was always looking down. I didn't like having my picture taken and they never told me to look at the birdie or anything like that."

Bannon reached over on an impulse and tipped her chin up so she had to look at him. "Too bad. You must have been a pretty kid."

She moved uncomfortably and he relinquished his light hold. "I didn't know it if I was. My parents didn't set much store on appearances or fancy things."

He nodded. What walls he'd seen in the photos had been bare. "Hmm." Maybe that was par for an old farmhouse way out in the country. It occurred to him that there hadn't been a single picture of the house from the outside or the land around the house in the scrapbook.

Erin closed the scrapbook and a card fell out of it onto the floor. He bent to pick it up, looking at the cut-out paper flowers that decorated it, underneath words written in flowing script.

To my girl of gold . . .

Looked like something her mother would have made. He handed the card to her, but she didn't even glance at it, just slipped it back inside the scrapbook, which she quickly put back in the box.

"Sorry," she said in a controlled voice. "Last time I looked at that scrapbook was a few years ago. I don't remember it being so depressing."

"Not to me." He couldn't argue with her statement. "But I know what you mean. I don't go down Memory Lane too often myself."

A chill had fallen over the room and both of them felt it—as well as the silent tension that sprang up between them. Fortunately, it was broken by the sound of clicking nails coming their way. They both turned, not startled, when a large dark shape loomed in the kitchen. Charlie stood there, looking from Bannon to Erin, his ears pricked.

"Enjoy your nap?" Bannon asked, holding out a hand to the dog. "Bet you're ready for a head scratch. I'll throw in a belly rub if you put another log on the fire."

But the dog went to Erin, not him, sitting on his haunches and looking up at her adoringly.

"Look at that. I'm insulted," he joked.

Erin smoothed and petted the fur on Charlie's back, sinking her fingers into the thick dark ruff around his neck. "Maybe we should take him out. It's getting a little late."

"Good idea." Bannon finished the wine in his glass and stood, helping himself to a last cracker and a chunk of cheese. "Not for you, traitor," he said cheerfully to the dog. He was beyond glad that Charlie and Erin had bonded so fast.

Charlie blinked and scrambled to his feet when Erin got up. "Did I tell you that he stayed right at my side without a leash?"

"No. That's great. I wouldn't want to chase him. Especially in the dark."

"Definitely not with his black coat. Speaking of that, I'm going to need something warmer than this sweater. Hang on while I change."

She left him with Charlie and went off into a room he assumed was her bedroom, not giving him a glimpse of it when she ducked quickly through the door. Just as well. His imagination had gone off on too many sensual tangents as it was.

He kneeled and ran his hands over the dog's neck and back, amused by the way Charlie let his tongue loll out. "You're gonna get spoiled," he murmured.

Bannon heard Erin come out and stood up, breaking into a big grin when he saw her. She'd put on jeans under her dress and added a short shearling jacket over the sweater. On her slender body, the oddball mix had its own charm.

"Okay. Let's go before I get too hot," she said.

"You bet. I like the outfit."

Erin shook her head as if she didn't believe him and didn't care whether he liked it or not. Then she smiled. "C'mon, boy," she said to Charlie.

The three of them went out the back door and paused for a minute on the much smaller porch attached to that side of the house. Twilight blue was stealing from the sky the warm colors of sunset, but a couple of last rays hung in there, bringing out lighter glints in Erin's chestnut hair.

Girl of gold. The words still suited her.

She turned up her shearling collar and nestled into it. "Everybody ready?" Without waiting for an answer, she went down the steps, followed by him and Charlie. "There's a trail that begins over that rise."

He caught up to her with a couple of long strides and walked beside her, catching her hand and giving it a squeeze before he let go. He could sense the energy she wanted to walk off. Once they were on the trail proper, he probably would have to fall back and let her lead. But he liked that view too.

Erin broke into a run and reached the top of the rise before he did, turning around to face him, her eyes and cheeks glowing from the fresh air. The ground they'd traversed must have once been farmland, left fallow for some time, but it still gave off a rich, loamy smell. The sun dipped below the horizon and the last rays vanished, but there was plenty of light to walk by for the next hour or so.

Bannon took in the sight of her. There was only one word to describe her. Make it two. Absolutely beautiful.

"What are you waiting for?" she teased him.

"I wish I knew." Bannon laughed.

The big dog kept up with ease as they walked over the low, rolling land, talking and challenging each other now and then as playfully as a couple of kids. Then, suddenly, she stopped again on another rise, looking back at her house. So did Bannon. It seemed even smaller from this distance, and very alone.

"My borrowed home." She sighed. "One of these days I'm going to drag my easel all the way out here and paint it."

"Bring Charlie."

Erin studied his expression for a moment, then nodded. "Scared of bears? Or whatever it was?"

"Not right now." His gaze flicked over the countryside. He wasn't lying. But seeing nothing didn't mean much. Still, he had no reason to issue a warning or offer grim advice, not when she was happy again. Besides, he knew without asking that she'd take Charlie with her from now on. The big dog would protect her when he couldn't.

"Let's go back," she said quietly.

She was nowhere near as bouncy on the return trip, slipping her ungloved hand into his as they walked. She gave his fingers a squeeze this time around. The contact was innocent enough for a church picnic, but it thrilled Bannon way down deep. He was going to claim another kiss tonight, that was for damn sure. When she wasn't wearing quite so many layers.

Maybe she was thinking the same thing. Erin just about tugged him up the back porch steps and he almost stumbled. They were laughing when they got inside, glad to be back inside the warmth. The dying fire was still heating up the old house, but not uncomfortably so. It felt right to him, to be with her this way. Like coming home.

The sharp ring of the phone broke the mood.

Erin scowled at it. "Who is that? Go away."

The phone kept ringing.

"Probably easier to answer it," Bannon said resignedly. "You know how it is. Wrong numbers keep calling."

She gave a sigh of annoyance. "Maybe." Then she picked up, softening her voice. "Hello?"

Bannon watched with curiosity as her expression immediately softened too.

"Oh, hi. I'm fine, Mrs. Meriweather. How are you?"

He ran the name through his mind. It clicked. The director of the Wainsville historical society. The woman who knew his mother.

"Wow," Erin was saying. "Really? That would be fantastic."

Sounded like something big and good was about to happen. Bannon didn't want to stand there as if he was listening to every word, so he moved into the next room. To listen to every word.

But she didn't talk for much longer. He heard her hang up and come looking for him.

"Guess what?" she asked eagerly.

"Must be happy news. Tell me."

"That was Mrs. Meriweather from the historical society. She snagged a commission for me—from Hugh Montgomery—she recommended me," Erin said breathlessly. "He wants a portrait of the best Thoroughbred in his stable, something impressive. Done in oils. He's prepared to pay me thirty thousand. I could live on that for a year, Bannon!"

"Oh."

She seemed a little crestfallen. "You don't sound thrilled."

"I'm not," he said without thinking. He looked at her face and instantly regretted his blunt words.

But he hadn't forgotten his glimpse of Montgomery's collapsing financial empire. There was no way the guy could spare thirty thousand for a picture of a pony—and there was no way he could tell Erin that. Only Doris knew that he'd gone over those confidential files. All the same, he was sorely tempted to tell Erin to collect her fee in cash, up front. Except that she would want to know why.

Hell. He'd put himself in a corner. From what he'd seen of Montgomery's wheelings and dealings, he ought to tell her to get payment in unmarked bills while he was at it. And lend her a black briefcase from the evidence locker to take the loot to the bank. Montgomery might get a kick out of that.

He just did not trust the guy. Not for a single second.

Finally he spoke. "Sorry. I don't know why I said that. Just be careful."

"About what? It's a plum assignment. I don't really know him, but that doesn't mean I can't sell a painting to him."

Bannon nodded as if he agreed completely. "Right. Make sure you get the commission agreement in writing, though. And specify half payment in advance."

Oops. Looked like the know-it-all approach ruffled Erin. She frowned at him and crossed her arms over her chest.

"Thanks for the advice." There was a trace of annoyance in her voice. "But it's unnecessary."

He had to cover his remark. "Am I wrong?"

"You happen to be right," she conceded. "But I'm not sure why you're telling me things I already know."

"Double-check and think twice. That's cop training."

She didn't seem to buy that hasty nonexplanation. He had to give her a lot of credit for reading between the lines.

"Calm down, Hector Protector." She gave him a look he couldn't quite read. "I can take care of myself. Now let's start over. Pretend you're not a cop."

"Okay." He had to go along with that. In a way, he wasn't—not officially.

Charlie came up to Erin and sat down by her side. *Two against one*, he thought.

"A real commission for a big fee. That's a first for me. I'm very grateful that Mrs. Meriweather recommended me," she said calmly.

"I can see that."

"And I need the money."

"I guess you do."

Erin mused for a few seconds. "I owe her. I should make a donation to the historical society."

Bannon couldn't help saying, "You don't have the money yet."

"But when I get it—"

"If you get it." Back to the minefield. He'd jumped in with both feet this time.

Erin stared at him. "Would you mind telling me exactly what you're getting at?" she asked after a beat.

"Ah . . ." His mind raced. Maybe he was wrong. The stables and stud farm—horses, bloodlines, land, traditions—had been handed down through generations, and that had to mean something to Montgomery. Maybe the old man could pay for the painting if he hocked some of his heritage.

Unlikely. He was on the verge of ruin and could be headed straight for a federal pen for fraud—Montgomery had to know it. So why all of a sudden was he planning to blow thirty thousand on a painting of a horse?

For some reason, he was trying to get close to Erin. Why? Bannon might have to talk to him personally. Very personally. Not in the lawyer's office.

"I'm waiting," Erin said impatiently.

"Look, I'm sorry if I said anything out of line," Bannon finally replied. "I guess I was just kind of surprised—I mean, Montgomery doesn't know you."

He wanted to put his hands around her waist, bring her to him, reassure her with caresses and not words. Talking like this was getting him nowhere with her. But her mulish expression made him hesitate.

"He knows my work. Mrs. Meriweather said he particularly liked my watercolor studies of his house. She showed him all the others and he liked those too."

Bannon held up his hands in a peacemaking gesture. "Can we just say that I overreacted? That's not a crime, is it?"

"No," she said softly. The merest ghost of a smile flickered across her set features.

He took courage from that. "Okay. Now that we discussed it, the commission sounds more and more like a great opportunity. Go for it."

If it was possible to die of insincerity, he was a goner.

Erin unfolded her crossed arms and sighed. "I can't figure you out, Bannon."

He grinned. "Just as well."

She made a growly noise at him, a girl-type growl of frustration, and Charlie looked up at her, surprised by it. "And what do you mean by that?"

"Nothing important." He took a step toward her but she took a step back.

"Whoa. Mrs. Meriweather said to meet her at the Montgomery house, the new one, first thing tomorrow morning. Apparently he gets up with the sun. So will I."

Ouch. He got the message: He was about to be kicked out, nicely enough. It happened. Not the end of the world. He hadn't expected that phone call any more than she had.

"Which means I have to get ready tonight." She sighed.

Before he could disagree with that statement, she turned around and went into her bedroom—to take off her jacket and jeans, he assumed. The door closed behind her with a firm click.

He felt a little like Montgomery had deliberately come between him and Erin. It occurred to him that someone might have tipped the old man off to his presence in her house, but he decided he'd done enough overreacting for one day.

Bannon went over to the window and looked out at nothing, vaguely hearing the sound of running water. He saw her reflection in the window when she came back out from her bedroom—she was walking slowly, brushing the windblown tangles out of her long hair until it shone.

Double hell. He loved to watch a woman doing that. It soothed his soul and made him hot at the same time.

Forget it, he told himself. But he couldn't take his eyes off her. Erin stopped when she noticed he was watching her in the glass.

He turned around. He pretty much knew what she was going to say before she said it.

"I set my alarm and the shower's heating up. It's been really nice, Bannon. Thanks for stopping by."

Her tone was cool. But she stretched up on tiptoe and planted a sweet little kiss on his cheek.

"You sure you want me to go?" In a split second, he had himself an armful of warm girl and he was kissing her. It was Erin who stopped it, pulling back, but with her arms twined around his neck and a smile on her lips.

"Yes," she replied.

Bannon was disappointed, but he didn't argue. "Okay, angel," was all he said.

CHAPTER 8

A beautifully manicured hand brushed over prescription pill bottles set in rows inside a mirrored bathroom cabinet, picking up one and then another to examine their labels, then returning them to the shelf.

"Aha." Caroline found the one she'd been looking for. She peered at the label to make sure and rattled it. "Almost full," she whispered angrily.

She'd had a feeling Monty hadn't been taking these. This prescription was the important one, meant to lower his high blood pressure and lower the risk of stroke, but he grumbled about the side effects, even though they were mild.

The other bottles held a few tablets each—she'd been helping herself now and then—sedatives, muscle relaxants, and sleeping pills. Nothing very strong; nothing that could cause addiction. But then Hugh Montgomery wasn't the type to get addicted to anything or admit he even needed medicine of any kind. He seemed to be able to keep going on pure strength of will.

Caroline held the bottle between her forefinger and thumb, looking at the small pills through the amber plastic as if she was counting them. How to get him to take these—and take his declining health seriously—she didn't know.

She was enormously afraid of missing out on everything she'd been hoping for since the day she'd set her mind on bedding and wedding the last of the Montgomery men. An extravagant ceremony at the church. A baby she could dress up and show off. A secure position in Virginia society. Bolstered, of course, by the Montgomery fortune.

Admittedly, Monty was old enough to be her father. But men of his generation produced second and third families all the time nowadays, she thought irritably. With a little luck, a young wife could provide living proof of her aging husband's virility. One bouncing baby was enough. There was no need for a second set of stretch marks.

And when overindulgence in bourbon and cigars and marbled beef finally caught up with said husband, a wife could inherit everything and enjoy it—and hand over the baby to a nanny.

But Caroline wasn't his wife, wasn't even close to being engaged to him. Age had made him cautious and a surprise pregnancy wasn't going to happen. He swore he didn't want more children anyway. The romance had long since fizzled, but they had a . . . relationship of sorts.

And now there was an added problem: the little girl from his first marriage. Long gone, never found. But Caro had a feeling that deep down he still had hope. The TV newscast and all the Web buzz had gotten to him, whether or not he wanted to admit it.

She rattled the bottle again. If he didn't take his medicine, he would be dead before she could persuade him to make her the second Mrs. Montgomery. Once in a blue moon Caro wondered what had happened to the first, the mother of the little girl, but she never dared to ask.

Probably living quietly somewhere far away. Bought off, no doubt. That was Monty's favorite tactic.

She would almost settle for that herself at this point, if the severance package was attractive enough.

Living with him had its perks, but oodles of cash to spend wasn't one. He was actually fairly stingy and it seemed to be getting worse as he got older. Caroline had no idea of his actual wealth, though. Or whether she was mentioned in his will.

It would be a nice gesture if he didn't plan to marry her. She was farther from that goal now than she had ever been, fighting the first signs of middle age, which had made an unwelcome appearance when she'd turned thirty. Now, two years later, her porcelain skin was looking a little . . . cracked. And the best plastic surgeon in Virginia had told her she was too young for a face-lift.

Shots and wrinkle creams could only do so much. Sometimes she wondered why she bothered with either. Monty probably hadn't noticed the frown line between her graceful eyebrows before her dermatologist zapped it with a needle full of magic. She gazed into the mirror on the cabinet door, willing her features into a calm mask.

The veined black marble tiles on the walls of Monty's bathroom didn't flatter her skin. There were gray hollows under her eyes that expensive concealer didn't hide anymore. Her salon stylist was staying ahead of the gray in her hair—the woman was always telling her to put on a happy face to brighten up the pale blond shade. As if smiling would help turn back time. Caroline's lips, recently plumped with injected collagen, curved in a stiff smile at her reflection.

From a distance, she was gorgeous. Up close, the maintenance showed.

Caroline put the bottle of blood pressure medication back among the others and closed the cabinet door almost noiselessly. She wanted to slam it. But the housekeeper might hear and come running.

She walked out of Monty's bathroom, through his bedroom and past the immense bed, upholstered in masculine and pricey dark charcoal fabric. The side of the bed where she should have slept, summoned from her peach-hued chamber when he felt like it, was pulled tight, undisturbed. It had come to that.

Caroline lifted her head as she walked past the stocky older woman starting to vacuum the carpet in the upper hall. Her high heels caught the vacuum's power cord and she kicked it viciously out of her way, not stopping to listen to the woman's apology for being in the way.

Ahead was another room that faced the back garden of the house and a sheltered area for Monty's collector cars. Monty knew how to spend his money. On his non-human toys, anyway. The expensive vehicles were kept polished and in perfect working order. Lucky for them, they didn't wrinkle. She herself had gone from being adored to ignored in the last couple of years.

The room was undecorated and nearly empty, except for a telephone on a small table and an ugly armchair next to that. She could slam the door, now that the vacuum was going full blast and droning monotonously, and sit there as long as she liked.

Caroline stalked inside, flung herself down into the chair, and looked out the window.

Well, well. Monty was going somewhere. He hadn't told her about it. She scrambled to her feet and made sure of which way he was driving before she raced down the back stairs to her own car, parked close to the house. There was only one road in that direction and it led to the Montgomery stables and stud farm, twenty-seven miles away.

The morning mist was burning off, floating away through the white-painted rails of the paddocks and exercise areas. Its departure revealed the springy dark ground inside the working areas, and the close-clipped grass outside them, emerald green and flawless.

Trying to stay out of sight, Caroline squinted at the back of a man walking toward the stables until Monty came into focus. Bifocals were the next humiliation she would have to endure, she supposed. She ought to have recognized him just by his clothes. He wore the same patrician and deliberately shabby riding jacket he'd sported for decades—rich people could be so strangely cheap about things like that—buff-colored breeches, and riding boots. He turned to speak to someone following him whom she couldn't see yet.

Caroline drew back into the doorway of a small, remodeled house that served riders and trainers as a hangout and a place to change. It was never locked. She tried the door and ventured a look inside. Not a sound, not a soul around. Thank God. She dashed inside and upstairs, positive he hadn't seen her.

From an upstairs room with sloping eaves, she listened to Montgomery from behind a window with a cracked pane and blowing curtains.

His voice was low, with a courteous note in it she knew, although it had been a while since he'd spoken to her that pleasantly. Feminine instinct told her that he was with a woman, and that instinct had claws.

Still listening, she extended her red nails and examined them. Made for scratching. But she was a Loudon, and she had never indulged herself in a catfight.

However, there was a first time for everything.

Caroline waited, dragging in breaths that hurt. Monty had paused. She pushed aside a section of curtain and peeked out. A smile, something she hadn't seen on his face in longer than she could remember, eased the lines of age and strain on his face.

The woman came into view. She seemed awfully young to Caroline, with long, shining chestnut hair that flowed freely down her back. Slender. Wearing jeans and a short shearling jacket, unbuttoned.

Was Monty hiring her as an exercise rider? She didn't look like a jockey, and no female jockey had ever worn Montgomery silks. But he'd hired a few women to exercise his horses.

That had been forever ago, during a time she referred to as B.C., as in Before Caroline. She hadn't wasted any time in easing them off the payroll and out of the stables.

She desperately wanted to move closer to the window, even open it slightly so she could hear better. But the two people below might hear her do it. She stayed behind the curtain, her hands keeping it from blowing around too much. She clutched the plain material when the woman in jeans turned around. Caroline studied her face intently. Whoever she was, she looked young enough to be his daughter. The thought made Caro want to gag.

It hadn't been that long ago that she got taken for his daughter. As compliments went, it was on the creepy side, but she'd laughed it off. Monty never had, now that she thought of it.

Her eyebrows went up when a second woman joined the twosome. Was she the mother of the first? Probably not. She was older than Montgomery, by the looks of her. Her pure white curls bobbed as she spoke to both of them in a fluty voice that sounded vaguely familiar to Caroline.

The right name came to mind in a few seconds: Mrs. Meriweather. From the historical society. But what was she doing out here at this hour of the morning? Had the roof fallen in at his ancestral manse? Or was she hustling Monty for more money for that dusty little museum of hers? Maybe she was reminding him that she hoped he'd write a history of the Montgomery clan. He'd never even gotten around to opening the accordion files of family papers and documents someone had organized for him years ago. *Good luck with that*, Caroline thought sourly.

If that old house collapsed, good riddance. For no particular reason, Caroline hated that place. He should have given it outright to the society, not just used it for a tax deduction. She'd overheard a couple of phone calls on that subject, understood that he would need more and more deductions to offset his quarterly somethings. What she didn't understand was why the well of cash seemed to be drying up. She would give anything to find out, but Monty didn't talk about his financial affairs.

Caroline just might have to hire someone to sleuth for her. She'd only stayed with him for the payoff, after all. And if there wasn't going to be one, then it was back to Daddy's house for her.

The group below moved out of her line of vision and into the stables. She leaned against the window frame, waiting to see if they would come back out, but no one did. Caroline moved the curtain, staring out boldly this time.

Erin was several feet behind Montgomery and Mrs. Meriweather, standing just inside the sliding doors of the stables. Then something made her look back at the tiny house opposite. She realized a trick of the light rendered her invisible to the pale blonde she glimpsed at an upstairs window.

Looking angry, the other woman stood there for only a second, long enough for Erin to notice that she dressed well and wore a lot of makeup. The haughty tilt of her chin said socialite, but that was a guess and nothing more. She did seem to belong here somehow. Suddenly she whirled around and disappeared into the dark recess of the room behind her.

Who was she?

Erin glanced at Hugh Montgomery, deep in conversation with

Mrs. Meriweather, who was singing Erin's praises as an artist. Interrupting them to ask if the woman she'd just seen was his wife didn't seem tactful or wise.

Mrs. Meriweather, chatting a mile a minute in the car while Erin drove, had mentioned that Hugh Montgomery lived with a much younger blonde named Caroline, but not whether they were married or engaged or what. Erin didn't think the woman at the window had been wearing a diamond ring or any rings on her fingers—the light would have caught it. For what it was worth, Erin had noticed that Montgomery didn't wear a wedding ring. But a lot of men didn't.

She hoped and prayed he wasn't going to make a wrong move. Bannon's uneasiness and oblique comments after last night's phone call came back to her. What did he know that she didn't? She hadn't wanted to listen.

Montgomery kept right on talking to Mrs. Meriweather, who was so much shorter than he that she didn't seem to notice him looking at Erin and not her.

His gaze stayed mostly on her and an inexplicable feeling of being under a microscope made her tense up every time he caught her eye. Accompanying it was a very strange sense of déjà vu. Yet she was sure she'd never met Hugh Montgomery before.

Wait, she told herself. In a way she had. There was the portrait at the old house, done when he'd been much younger. She had been struck by the sadness behind the authoritative face in the painting. At this late stage of his life, the second quality was even more evident.

"The cost is no object," he was saying to Mrs. Meriweather. "So long as I get what I want."

Erin cringed inwardly. What a way to put it. Well, there was nothing in writing. She could back out. One thing for sure, she suddenly didn't like the idea of being alone with him. If—and it was getting to be a big if—she took this project on, she would make sure she never was. Fortunately, a stable of this size and complexity was a busy place, with grooms and riders coming and going with horses often.

She wondered if he was going to talk to her directly at some point. Maybe not. Some rich people delegated everything, including relationships.

But the way he looked at her and the unhappy woman she'd seen at the window turned the fresh mood of the morning into something off-kilter. She no longer wanted to be there. However, it wasn't as if she could walk out and leave Mrs. Meriweather.

To distract herself, she walked down the paved center of the stable between the stalls. Tack and saddles were hung up in designated places on board walls and the floors were clean, with fresh straw carefully strewn about in wet spots.

She took a small notepad out of a jacket pocket and opened it, sketching details at random for later reference. Not the horses. She was concentrating on the setting. A mare stretched her neck and looked at Erin curiously, flaring velvety nostrils to get a whiff of the newcomer to the stables.

Erin scribbled a note to herself: *Bring carrots.*

She put the pad back in her pocket and walked on. Mrs. Meriweather had followed Montgomery into an office that had a wide interior window set into a wall so the stables could be viewed from it. He was pointing to framed photos on the wall. Erin could just see a row of trophies and silver cups in a glass-doored cabinet, show ribbons pinned to its back.

But she couldn't hear them. Fine with her. Erin wandered on. She found a rough wooden bench in a quiet part of the stables and sat down. Thinking about the painting he wanted her to do was easier than thinking about the man who'd commissioned it.

What was he expecting?

A lot of horse portraits were just heads against plain, dark backgrounds—an Elvis-on-velvet look that she hoped he wouldn't ask for. Horses looking over stall doors were popular too. Neither interested her very much. She'd much rather portray Montgomery's champion racehorse at liberty.

Granted, a horse worth millions wasn't going to be let loose just because she wanted to see it gallop around. Just painting the head would be a lot easier. But what if it ended up looking like an ad for equine grooming products, all lustrous mane and sparkling eyes?

She would have to start over.

Erin told herself to stop obsessing over things that hadn't happened yet. She sighed and closed her eyes, stretching out her legs and relaxing, lulled by the sounds of the place. A stable had its own symphony. The muted clip-clop of hooves over compacted straw. The clang of metal pails and the whoosh of feed being poured. Soft snorts and whinnies. The low voices of men and women who worked with horses, talking to the animals and to each other.

"Erin! Yoo-hoo!" Mrs. Meriweather waved her over. They had come out of the office and were walking to her.

She scrambled up and met them halfway.

"Mr. Montgomery wants to know when you can begin."

Erin avoided his unnerving gaze by looking at the older woman as she answered. Mrs. Meriweather's kind eyes met hers. "Ah— soon."

"I need an exact date and time. The stables run on a strict schedule." The deep voice sounded accustomed to giving orders.

"Tomorrow?" She took out her small notepad and flipped to the back, which had a calendar. Had he heard the slight quaver in her voice? Montgomery was intimidating.

"That can be arranged."

Erin practically expected to hear a whip flick. But he wasn't carrying a whip. Other than that, he looked like the horseman he was, in riding attire that had seen hard use. His boots had a high polish, though.

Well, she couldn't look down forever or dodge the commanding gaze that reinforced his aura of power. The closer she got to him, the stronger the sensation of déjà vu became.

If only Bannon was here. That wasn't going to happen, though.

He disliked Montgomery—that much was crystal clear. But it wasn't as if the older man was a criminal. Yet Bannon had avoided explaining the reasons for his antipathy.

Unable to avoid it, she raised her eyes to Montgomery's. Her breath hitched in her throat. There was something wounded and raw in the depths of his gaze that pinned her to the spot where she stood.

Erin almost panicked. Was he a little crazy? For whatever reason, she felt a sensation of something like pity for him.

Mrs. Meriweather gave her a kindly, unruffled smile. Evidently she hadn't seen what Erin was seeing in the old man's eyes. Or else she was willing to give him the benefit of the doubt. Mrs. Meriweather had said in a quiet aside on their way here that the loss of his daughter had broken Montgomery's heart forever.

Erin racked her brain for something to say, forcing herself to discuss the painting.

"Can you give me some idea of what you had in mind, Mr. Montgomery? I could do some preliminary sketches."

"All right." Montgomery walked away from both women, his large hands clasped behind his back.

"Are we supposed to follow him?" she whispered to Mrs. Meriweather.

"I think so," the older woman whispered back with frustration. "He's behaving very strangely, Erin. He rambles on and then stops—"

"But I can hear." He turned around to deliver the sarcastic remark. Mrs. Meriweather blushed to the roots of her white hair. "The horse is in the adjoining building. Please follow me."

His stride was long and the two women lagged behind. But they caught up with him when they turned the corner.

He was still ahead but he wasn't alone. The blond woman Erin had seen at the window was facing him, saying something in a murmur. She broke off when she saw them, her gaze zeroing in on Erin.

Montgomery turned around. "Mrs. Meriweather, you know Caroline. But Erin doesn't." He turned to Caroline. "My dear, allow me to introduce Erin Randall."

The blonde's blue eyes blazed with jealousy. "It's a pleasure," she said in a tight voice. She didn't hold out a hand or make any other welcoming gesture.

"Erin is a very talented painter," Montgomery continued smoothly. "She will be working on a portrait of Take All."

"I see." The words were snapped out. Caroline looked Erin up and down as if she didn't see at all.

"The three of us are going to his stall." His frosty tone automatically excluded her.

"Have fun. I'm going the other way," Caroline replied angrily.

She didn't bother to say a single word to Mrs. Meriweather, who was too well-mannered to comment on the deliberate slight in public.

Caroline's high heels clicked angrily down the paved center of the stable. Montgomery didn't look back.

Erin dropped Mrs. Meriweather off at her house with a sigh of relief, glad the morning was over. The first thing she wanted to do was get her hands around a tall takeout cup of coffee and drink it down, and the second thing was to call Bannon.

She had pulled over and parked outside a fancy place and taken her time to read the chalked menu with its daily selections. Decaf would do it. Meeting Montgomery had left her jumpy, and Caroline—well, the blonde was a piece of work. At least Erin had her pegged correctly now. Mrs. Meriweather had offered a polite explanation of Caroline's relationship with Montgomery.

After several years with no promise of marriage, his blond mistress was apparently fed up. Mrs. Meriweather added that Caroline complained to whoever would listen that Montgomery's horse Take All was a lot more important to him than she was.

The horse was a gorgeous animal that seemed to know it was a star. Take All's trainer had shown him off with great pride.

Once Erin realized that she would be dealing with that man and not Montgomery for the portrait, she'd set aside her misgivings.

Tall cup in hand, she went back to her car, wanting to drink her coffee where it was quiet. The coffee bar wasn't. She checked the little window of the parking meter—the needle was safely in the black zone. There was plenty of time to enjoy her coffee.

She unlocked the door on the passenger side and slid in, setting the cup in the holder between the seats. Erin looked in her purse for her cell phone. She wanted to hear Bannon's voice. The urge was so strong that it made her wonder about what she was beginning to feel for him.

He'd seemed so at home in her place. She'd been amused by the way he'd looked around so carefully, being protective while trying to seem casual. Deciding to use him as a model had been a stroke of genius, she thought smugly. What a perfect way to admire all that muscle and chiseled scruffiness for as long as she'd wanted to.

And he'd kept the male territorial stuff under control, except when she explained that a friend had helped her with the computer setup. Obviously Bannon had been dying to ask more but he didn't have to know about her ex, who wasn't all that important to her. Gerry, a software engineer, had taken off for greener pastures and a big job in Seattle, although Virginia had plenty of tech businesses and opportunities.

Anyway, so long, been nice to know you, she thought idly. Bannon made all thoughts of other men, past and future, vanish. It was easy to imagine him being a part of her life. *Slow down,* she told herself. *Just enjoy him. And make sure no one else has that privilege*, added a possessive little voice. Erin smiled to herself.

He finally answered, and she smiled at the sound of his husky hello.

"Hey. It's Erin."

"Hi." The obvious pleasure in his voice warmed her all over. "Nice to hear from you."

She chuckled. "I just saw you yesterday."

"Yeah, well—"

"And we're going to see each other soon." Erin interrupted him before he could say anything about one kiss not being enough. Truth be told, it hadn't been enough for her, either, but she saw nothing wrong with the two of them taking their time. Jumping into bed by the third or fourth date wasn't something she wanted to do.

"When?"

Erin touched the coffee cup to see if it had cooled a little, then fiddled with the takeout lid so she could sip and talk. "Let me check with my social secretary. I'll get back to you."

Bannon laughed. "Where are you?"

"In my car. In town. Drinking coffee." She took a long sip. "And yes, I'm parked."

"Good. So did you visit the legendary Montgomery stables and stud farm?"

"I sure did. I met the horse."

"What about the old man?"

Thinking about that required two more sips. "Him too. And his girlfriend Caroline. She didn't seem too happy to see us."

"Oh. Why was that?"

"She didn't give a reason," Erin said dryly. "She didn't seem inclined to talk to any of us. And she was downright rude to Mrs. Meriweather."

"Hmm."

Erin filled him in on more details of the morning, but she left out the way Montgomery had stared at her, and her feelings of nervousness. There was no sense in triggering Bannon's protective reflex. He meant well, but she suspected he was apt to go overboard.

"So how's Charlie?" he asked.

"He slept right by my bed on my mom's old hooked rug. When I woke up I had to pull my slippers out from underneath him. They were nice and warm." She laughed.

"That's great."

"We went for a morning walk and I threw a stick for him to get him to run. Otherwise he stays right by me the whole time."

"He's supposed to."

Erin gave a mock sigh. "He doesn't have to."

Bannon apparently decided not to argue the point. Not a problem. She really liked the dog, and that was going to work out fine.

He switched the subject. "So did you get started on the commission?"

"Mmm-hmm." She finished up the coffee. "I did some sketches and then we went into the stable offices and I signed on the dotted line."

"Okay."

The nonchalant reply made her smile to herself. Apparently he'd decided not to be bossy. He had been right about the terms, though. She'd asked for what he said. Well, she would have in any case.

"I got half the fee in advance, and the other half I get when I'm done. Mrs. Meriweather made sure I understood the fine print, not that there was much."

"Excellent." There was a pause. "Did I understand you right? You actually received the fee?"

"Yes. The envelope, please." She set the cell phone inside her purse and found an already torn envelope to rip so he would hear it. Then she put the phone to her ear and spoke to him again. "Holy cow! I'm looking at a cashier's check for fifteen thousand dollars!"

"Really?" His voice was incredulous.

Erin burst out laughing. "No. That was just a sound effect. Actually, I already deposited the check. Why wait, right?"

He joined in the laughter. "Spoken like a starving artist. Good for you, Erin. I'm glad it all went well."

"Me too."

She heard a doorbell ring on his side of the call.

"That's Doris," Bannon told her. "A colleague from the station. Nice lady, you'll like her. And now for the sound effects of me walking to the door. . . ." She heard the knocking this time and then his footsteps, very faint, and the sound of a door opening. "Don't break it down, Doris. I'm talking to someone."

Erin frowned a little.

The other woman wanted to know who.

"The artist who did that little painting of a horse I bought for you," Bannon said. "Erin Randall."

"Oh! The pretty one? She must be the reason you've been so damn busy all of a sudden," Doris said cheerfully.

Erin smiled.

"Uh, yeah—"

"Hi, Erin!" Doris yelled into the phone, over the rest of Bannon's answer. "I love the painting!"

Bannon laughed and then moved away from his visitor, by Erin's guess.

"You see what I have to put up with," he told her.

"She does sound nice," Erin said.

"We're going to go over some new stuff relating to the case. So that's what I'm doing today."

"Okay. I'll be drawing horses."

"Looking forward to seeing the sketches," he said.

Erin groaned. "The first ones are always terrible. It's like the first pancakes. You throw them away."

"Don't," Bannon chided her. "You never know. You could sell those to Montgomery too."

"You're funny."

"Glad you think so." He hesitated but not for long. "When can I see you again?"

"Let's talk tonight."

"Okay, but—"

She heard Doris scoff at him for sounding like a lovesick teenager and said a laughing good-bye.

CHAPTER 9

Bannon snapped his cell phone shut and turned to his visitor. "So what's all this?"

Doris had opened the flap of an over-the-shoulder bag to show him a jumble of files. "Tons of stuff."

"From the storage warehouse? That could get back to Hoebel."

She shook her head. "I'm not making that long drive again. I got all this from the evidence locker. His son-in-law has a habit of leaving the key around and taking long lunches."

"Lucky for us that Petey Hayes is totally incompetent."

"The chief doesn't think so."

Bannon shrugged. "What else is new at the station?"

"Too many cases, not enough officers. Hoebel works off the tension by hitting on Jolene."

"Really?" Bannon said. "He's married, right?"

"Not happily. I can't blame Mrs. Hoebel. Anyway, Jolene won't have anything to do with him. She was asking me what to do if he got too close to her. I said to tar and feather him and ride him out of town on a rail."

"You could put together a whole damn posse to do that if you wanted to. The man rubs a lot of people the wrong way."

She laughed but without much humor. "Let's not talk about him. I have to deal with him most every day, you don't." She walked over a few steps to look at Erin's painting of wild horses. "Wow. You didn't show me this one."

"It was all wrapped up in brown paper. And it was raining that day, remember?"

"Vaguely."

He went over to where she was. "She got the inspiration for this at Chincoteague, but she painted it from memory. Sometimes she does preliminary sketches, sometimes not."

"My, my. You have been getting to know her." Doris gave him a friendly little punch on the shoulder.

"Why not?" he retorted. "She took me out to the Montgomery house, the old one, after she saw me on TV. And I got to see her studio setup at her home. She has a great little place out in the country."

"I bet."

Bannon suddenly wanted to change the subject. "Okay. What do you have? I want to see it all."

Doris gave him an irritated look as she set the bag down on the coffee table. "Don't be a brat. Coffee first. Treats after that. Here, take my coat." She wriggled out of it and tossed it at him.

"Yes, ma'am." He took care of hanging it up for her and got busy in the kitchen as she settled herself on the long sofa.

"Am I going to be covered in cat hair by the time I leave?" she called to him.

"Do you want to be?"

"Yes. Now where is that big kitty? Here, kitty. Kitty kitty kitty . . ."

Bannon heard a soft thump. Babaloo had made a four-footed landing from some high hiding place in the living room.

"There you are," Doris said happily. "Come give me some love. Oh yes. Yes yes yes."

He laughed and went in to see, noticing first that she'd removed the file folders and papers from the bag and fanned them out on the coffee table. The cat was rubbing his cheek against Doris's and gently stamping his paws on her lap.

"If I ever have to go out of town, you can babysit the Whisker Dude," he offered.

"You know I would. But not here," she said. "My place or no place."

"Deal." He went back into the kitchen. The coffee was close to done. He took down two cups and threw some sugar packets onto a tray, adding a couple of spoons and paper napkins. Then he checked the fridge for milk—none.

He cursed under his breath, not that Doris would hear him, what with all her cooing at the cat.

Then he remembered a foil-box container of milk shoved back in the cabinet above the coffeemaker. Bannon stretched to retrieve it, checking the expiration date when it was in his hand. Whew. Under the limit.

He put it on the tray, filled the cups, and carried the whole business out.

"Aren't you domestic," Doris teased him.

"I try." Bannon pushed the pile of papers to one side with one hand and set down the tray in front of her with the other.

"And dexterous too."

"I was a waiter in college. Worst job I ever had." He peeled open the serving slot on the box, flicking the tiny curl of foil onto the tray.

She wrinkled her nose. "What is that?"

"You know what it is. Milk in a box. The bachelor's friend."

"Okay. I can't complain. I'll do anything for free coffee."

Babaloo turned his head in the direction of the opened milk box, sniffed, and shot Bannon a disgusted look. Then he jumped off Doris's lap, disappearing again.

Without an inquisitive cat to get in the way, she dosed her coffee to her satisfaction, using all the sugar packets and just a splash of the milk, then stirring briskly.

"Mmm," she said after the first sip. "Tastes boxy."

"Give me a break, Doris." Bannon was letting his coffee cool. He wanted to get into the files, bad. The messy writing on the folder tabs was hard to read. "Anything new here?"

"I think so. Looks like Petey put it all into random folders and threw them into a box. He didn't bother with the old A to Z. The alphabet is not his strong suit."

"How did you find it again?"

"Kind of by chance. I happened to see the box through the wire.

Near the door, like it was going to get shipped out. The lid was half off." She pointed to a file marked *Montg'ry*. "And that one was on top. So I scored the cage key when Petey was out hunting chili dogs and took a look at what was in it."

"Good going. And you didn't leave the box empty."

"No, of course not. I was getting to that." Doris finished her coffee. "Do you have any cookies?"

"I will find some." Bannon got up and rummaged in the kitchen cabinets again. "You will talk." He returned with a small plate.

Doris selected a gingersnap and nibbled on it. "Thanks."

"You're welcome."

She leaned back into the cushions. "Anyway, I took out what was in the files and stuck the papers I copied for you back in."

"How's that again?"

"I made a second set that day," she explained. "After you left. Call me compulsive."

"Never."

"When I was done, the box looked pretty much the same. Except for that folder"—she nodded at the *Montg'ry* file—"which I swiped."

"You took a risk."

Doris sniffed. "You don't know Petey like I know Petey. He won't notice."

"Someone else might."

She glared at him. "I did the best I can. Do you want the stuff or not?"

"Hell yes. But I want you to stay out of the line of fire."

Doris sat up and began to organize the fanned-out folders. "Don't worry about me."

"Someone has to."

"I can take care of myself, Bannon."

"You sound like someone else I know."

"And who would that be?" she asked. "Your mom? Give her my regards."

He promised to do that, then watched her make stacks and piles out of the jumble of paper. Doris had her methods.

When she was done, he started in on the pile nearest to him.

There were duplicates of material he'd seen, and a lot of other stuff, none of it compelling. After about twenty minutes, he yawned hugely, not able to stop.

"Cover your mouth," she chided him. "Do you need another cup of coffee?"

"No, I don't think so. There just doesn't seem to be anything much here."

She selected a folder he hadn't looked at. "Try this one. It has a few more letters from Ann Montgomery's so-called new mother. Remember that one I found out at the storage warehouse?"

"Yeah. You said you copied it by hand. Did you bring that?"

"No. But I will."

Bannon sat up straight. "Now you're talking." He opened the folder and glanced at the first few letters, which were photocopies. "No originals?"

"Dunno. I didn't get a chance to get through everything in the box."

He nodded. "I understand. But we all know that photocopies don't cut it for a handwriting comparison."

"What are you getting at? Are we preparing evidence for court?"

"Not yet. I'm just trying to think like a detective, I guess."

"Go for it, Sherlock," she said jokingly. "This case needs one." Doris set aside another folder as he read through the photocopied letters in the one he held. "I forgot to ask what's happening with the news show. Did they send you any more leads?"

"I have to call Kelly." He gestured vaguely to the mountain of printouts from the TV station he'd left in the corner. "They sent over all that the day after the broadcast. I waded through it. Mostly—"

"You don't have to tell me. Lunatics and busybodies. Half the reports in the Wainsville PD files are interviews with nut jobs." She sighed. "Big waste of everybody's time."

Bannon gave a curt nod of agreement as he read through the new-mother letters. They were short, no more than two or three paragraphs each. No salutation. Undated. It struck him that the tone varied wildly, from guilty to gloating. "Hmm. Whoever wrote these was all over the map, emotionally speaking." He laid out several on the table. "I wish we had a way to put them into a time frame."

Doris flipped one over. "There's a PD date stamp on the back that says when each came in."

Bannon countered that with a dismissive wave. "That indicates when they were received and entered into evidence at the police department. But they were sent to Montgomery, right? Or his wife? No telling when they got them."

Doris went through the other piles. "I don't really know. Maybe there are envelopes in here." He read on as she combed through the stacks for several minutes. "Nope. Either they got tossed or they're clipped to the originals. And God knows where those are."

Bannon snorted. "That's a grand old Wainsville PD tradition. Rubber-stamp everything and lose it fast. No wonder some of our cases never get to trial."

He moved to another folder and a greeting card slipped out. The illustration showed a bird singing on a branch. Little musical notes floated around it. "This isn't a photocopy."

Doris looked at it curiously. "I didn't see that."

He opened it and looked inside at a poem, four lines of flowing script that leaned to the right. His mind searched for the right word for the style and suddenly it came to him—calligraphic. But the card was printed. He read it silently.

> *Of all the joys there are on earth*
> *The gift of love has greatest worth*
> *A little angel is ours to hold*
> *And cherish forever, a girl of gold.*

The last three words rang a bell. Then he remembered—the same words had appeared on that scrapbook card at Erin's. But that had been handmade ·by her mother. This card looked standard, the kind of thing that sold in the millions. He handed the card to Doris, who read it aloud, then examined it front and back.

"Looks almost new," she said. "No signature or anything. Do you think the kidnapper sent it to the Montgomerys? That is sick."

"I guess so, if it's in the box. It was probably bought from a drugstore card rack twenty-some years ago. There's no way to trace it now."

She closed the card and looked at the floating musical notes. "Wasn't there a song like that, way back when? 'Girl of Gold'?"

"Could be. I'll ask my mom. She knows all the old tunes."

And that was because she and his father used to go dancing every Saturday night until the week before he died. The thought made his heart constrict. He would definitely call her when Doris went home.

He set the card aside. "Mind if I keep it?"

"No. Eventually I'll switch everything back the way it was. But I think I'll copy these copies on my home printer-copier thingy." She paused and gave him a worried look. "Am I getting paranoid?"

"You're smart. I was going to suggest that myself."

Doris leaned back into the cushions when Babaloo made a stealthy foray along the top of the couch toward her, his paws pressing silently into the black leather. "Here, kitty kitty," she cooed. The cat took over her lap and another purr-o-rama began.

Bannon concentrated on the folders and let Doris have her feline fix. He read silently through most of the material for half an hour, then set a few other papers aside with the odd letters. "Copy these for me, okay?"

"Sure." Doris reached out to put them into an empty folder and the cat jumped down to the floor. She took the opportunity to slide everything else back into the bag. "I gotta go. Let me know what's going on with the TV station. Just so I can stay out of Hoebel's way."

"I take it he didn't approve."

"He's always ranting about something." Doris raised an eyebrow. "And he was fuming about you going public from the second you were on the air. If you do it again—are you going to do it again?"

"Like I said, I gotta talk to Kelly."

"Oh, right." She used both hands to push her slim self up from the couch. Bannon was on his feet before her, going to get her coat.

He helped her into it sleeve by sleeve. Then she looked into his mirror to adjust the collar. "Thanks for the coffee, RJ. We shall confabulate in the near future. If I can find my keys. May I have a cookie for the road?"

He offered her the plate again and she took one, holding it in her teeth when she began to head out, the bag full of files over one shoulder. Her hands were rummaging through her coat pockets. A few seconds later, she held up her car keys.

"Got'm. G'bye, Ban'n."

He clapped her on the back. "See you around. Thanks for stopping by."

Bannon took a break and made himself a plate of food, nothing special, but it was hot and filling.

When he'd finished it, he called his mother. It was good to hear Sheila Bannon's fond voice asking the usual nosy questions about his health and how he was otherwise. They chatted in a desultory way as he wandered in and out of the kitchen. He finally got around to asking her about the song when he spotted the card where he'd left it on the coffee table.

"Mom—remember when you and Dad used to go dancing?"

"Yes, I do. Those were the days." Her voice was soft.

"I was wondering. Was there ever a song called 'Girl of Gold'?" He brought the card into the kitchen and flipped on the overhead fluorescents, which were painfully bright. "It has to do with a case—"

"The Montgomery case?"

"Yeah. Gee whiz, you could be a detective."

His mother laughed a little. "It's the only case you're working on, honey. And you're not even officially reinstated."

"Don't remind me."

"Okay, let me think." He was silent while she pondered, still studying the card in his hand. He squinted at it.

Was he seeing things?

Beneath the bright light, he would swear there were faint pencil lines under the calligraphy of the poem. He squinted harder. The lines, if they had been there, went away. Then he looked at the back of the card. There was a familiar card-company logo. It definitely wasn't handmade.

"Bannon?"

"Yeah?"

"I was talking to you."

"Sorry. I got distracted for a sec."

"I can't think of a song by that name. Or lyrics. I guess you could look it up online. Is it important?"

"Maybe. That's what I'll do."

After another minute or two, they exchanged affectionate good-byes and Bannon examined the inside of the card one more time, which was easier to do when he wasn't cradling a tiny cell phone between his shoulder and his ear.

There were pencil lines. Very faint. But definitely there.

Bannon found his laptop and fired it up, ignoring the antivirus pop-up reminders and others that pointed out the obvious fact that his computer was connected. He clicked on the Internet icon and searched for the phrase "girl of gold."

Not a song title. Not lyrics. Nothing was just like it. There were some near misses, though, phrased differently, for a great old spy movie and a classic TV comedy series. But it wasn't a catchphrase. The card was one of a kind.

Okay. He wanted a really close look at it.

He got up and went into his bedroom, dragging a wheeled box full of electronic gear, freebies from his brothers, out from under the bed. Bannon separated coaxial cables from game consoles and other gadgets, swearing at the tangle of stuff until he found what he was looking for: a small digital microscope that connected to a USB port.

"Gotcha."

Deke had given it to him, saying the high-res screen display oughta come in handy for a detective, but Bannon had never had a reason to use it, although he'd installed the software for it. He went back to his laptop and plugged it in, waiting for his hard drive to find the relevant program to run it. Then he switched the microscope on and slid the card under the lens, positioning the lettered part in a small circle of light and looking at his screen.

Bingo.

The lowest magnification clearly showed that the calligraphy wasn't printed but had been done by hand. Using the touch pad on the laptop, he cranked up the dial icon to increase the magnification as high as it would go. Now he could see the way the ink had flowed out of the pen. He took a few screen shots at both levels of magnification and saved them in a folder. Then he shut off the microscope and leaned back in his chair.

Girl of gold.

He wanted to get another look at Erin's handmade card. Not that he could verify a connection between that card and this one, but he couldn't rule it out either.

But how to take it and bring it back without her freaking out was going to take some thought.

His cell phone rang in his shirt pocket, startling him. Bannon stared blankly at the number on the little blue screen, not recognizing it. What the heck? He flipped it open.

"Hello."

"Bannon. Kelly here. How are you?" Her tone of voice was smooth and seductive.

What did she want? Give it three seconds. No, two. She didn't waste time. "Doing fine. You?"

"Pretty good."

"Believe it or not, I was just about to call you."

She laughed, a silvery sound. "What about?"

"Oh, I figured you could update me on the website response. Still getting a lot of hits or what?"

"Some. Snail mail too—enough to fill up a couple of big boxes for you. But it's been dropping. Dramatically. We were wondering," she purred, "if you'd like to do another. The producer of the segment would rather put you front and center. A high percentage of our female demographic thought you were hot."

"Really."

"Well, you are, Bannon."

He was glad she couldn't see him smirk. Kelly would have teased him unmercifully for it.

"I wouldn't know," he replied.

"What do you say? Want to come in again?"

He took his time answering. Montgomery and his oily lawyer might blow a gasket if they saw him on the news a second time. Not that he cared. So would Hoebel, though. Bannon did plan to badge up and go back to work. Someday.

And then there was Erin. Whoever was watching him was watching her too. No, he really didn't want to get his face on TV again. Not just now.

It was best to stall.

"Same deal? Scripted questions? No control over the final result?"

Kelly laughed again. "Let's talk."

"When?"

"My, my," she mocked. "What a lot of questions you're asking. Mmm, before I forget, I have one for you. Your brother Deke—do you have a contact number for him?"

"I can give him your number if you like. He's on assignment."

She pretended to sound blasé. "Oh, okay. No big rush. I had an idea for a series—something focusing on the secrets behind the news, if you know what I mean."

Bannon didn't, but he mumbled something affirmative.

She forged on. "As in super secret. I want authentic stories of real undercover agents and special forces types. Men who risk all. Dangerous dudes."

That would be his two brothers. But he thought of the lady Linc had sent over, Karen Michaels, feminine and, in a subtle way, fierce. He decided to give Kelly a jab. "No women?"

She didn't miss a beat. "Do you know any who qualify? I'd love to feature them. We could double our ratings if we get both guys and girls watching."

"Ah—no. Not offhand." Karen Michaels, or whatever her real name might be, was connected to Linc in some very personal way, and Bannon had no idea if the relationship was even allowed under the ever-changing rules of the military.

Again he heard silvery laughter. "You're lying."

"Good guess." He got off the phone after some small talk, making no promises other than to pass her number along. Let Deke deal with her. Kelly was only a couple of years older than his youngest brother. They could be great for each other.

Bannon picked up the card with the bird on it and read the poem inside again.

He might have stumbled on the first clue. Three little words. Sometimes that was all it took.

CHAPTER 10

Montgomery sat at a grand piano picking out tunes with one hand. The other hand felt oddly sluggish and he rested it on his thigh. His hard pull yesterday on the reins of a recalcitrant horse had most likely strained the tendons.

The melody line was all he could play of some old song—it was older than he was, he thought morosely. The plaintive notes sounded through the empty house.

No servants, as far as he knew. No guests. No business associates. No Caroline. That suited him just fine.

He had no idea where she had gone. The late-morning sun slanted through the windows, laying down stripes of light on the antique carpet, a treasure of intricate silk that no one was allowed to set foot on. Except for him. She could not refuse him everything. Monty stopped and rose from the piano bench, taking pleasure in walking on what was essentially his money, even if she was the one to spend it.

Not for much longer. The way things were going, he might have to close her charge accounts and take away her credit cards. She seemed to have forgotten that the bills landed on his desk.

Caro's acquisitiveness had amused him when he'd been able to indulge it. Now it sparked fights. Lately he could barely summon up the energy to withstand her outbursts, but somehow, he did. He had to force himself to think straight and pierce the cloudiness in his mind. Montgomery knew that something was the matter with him, but he was damned if he would see a new doctor or endure more inconclusive tests.

The result would be the same. Another prescription. Different side effects. Sleepless nights and a stream of bills. To hell with all of it.

Caroline would pretend to care. She was rather good at that, but her sympathy was edged with desperation that gave her away.

He wasn't going to give her what she wanted. The slow, bitter unraveling of their relationship was following a course that was familiar to him. He had an inkling that she hoped to become his widow more than she hoped to become his wife—if he would be so kind as to marry her and immediately drop dead of natural causes.

Montgomery smiled faintly. She had probably imagined herself in a dramatic but chic black veil and fitted black suit, a bereaved but lovely young woman. Standing by his grave and brushing away a single tear.

He'd always believed that animals could sense the approach of death. Perhaps Caroline's instincts were accurate.

His morbid thoughts grew darker and a heavy sense of foreboding weighed on his mind.

Let it be easy. No fuss. He wanted to be cremated and his ashes scattered where no one could walk on them. No memorial. He had specified both in a letter of intent that was separate from his will. That lengthy document left her a reasonable sum, invested safely but nowhere near as much as she probably hoped for. As far as his obituary, she would have nothing to preen about. She would be listed only as his companion, Caroline Loudon.

The newspapers and media would add a tactful line stating that his long-ago marriage had ended in divorce and name his ex-wife— that was routine. But they would not disclose where Luanne lived now.

No one knew that but him, his lawyer, and a trusted relative who had been paid well to keep certain secrets.

And then there was Ann. Given the recent coverage, the polite conventions of obituary writing would be set aside to include a line or two about the unsolved kidnapping. That and only that would make his death newsworthy enough to be featured online and on television with a photo and a brief bio. And images of her.

If she had survived, as he wanted to believe she had, would she make the connection? She did not resemble him.

There were things he could do to ensure that she had that chance. His lineage would be his ultimate legacy. If Ann required DNA testing to prove that she was his child and only survivor, he would arrange for his own genetic profile to be done—and the results safely hidden from Caroline.

He looked around the pretentious room and sighed.

Once upon a time, precious objects and valuable furniture had mattered to him. As the last of the Montgomerys, he had felt duty-bound to keep up appearances and play the role of a Southern aristocrat. Not to mention carrying on traditions that had lost their meaning.

No more.

He heard a car door slam, and a minute later, the front door eased open. Caroline entered, clutching the handles of shopping bags printed with the names of expensive stores. She didn't see him as she walked briskly to the bottom of the stairs, going up them fast.

Hiding her purchases, he thought. He went back to the piano and waited five minutes before he sat down and began to play again, just to let her know that he was in the house.

The notes were jumbled this time and the melody unrecognizable. But he didn't notice.

Caroline came downstairs an hour later, much more quietly, smoothing her hair as she entered the room. "Hello, Monty." She walked over to the piano. "Are you improvising?"

He rested the hand he'd been playing with on the side scroll, tapping his fingers on the glossy black wood. "Just playing an old song."

"Oh." She looked down at him but he didn't glance up. The scowl on his mouth showed, though. It was going to be another long evening, she thought. Caroline went over to a set of crystal decanters filled with liquor, pulled the stopper from one, and poured herself a stiff drink.

There wasn't any ice and she decided to have the liquor straight up rather than trek to the kitchen.

"Did you send the servants home?"

The butler and housekeeper lived in, but the others didn't. Lately he had been dismissing the day staff by late afternoon, forcing her to fend for herself around the house.

"Yes. They make too much noise."

"Well, they do have work to do," she said lightly.

He only shrugged. "My head was aching." Before she could give him advice he didn't want, he added, "I took something for it."

"Oh, good," she replied, going over to him and holding up her glass. "Cheers."

Monty closed the long lid over the piano keys.

"Don't stop," she said in a wheedling voice. "I was hoping you'd play our song."

He looked at her with dull eyes. "What was it again? I don't remember."

"Monty, is something the matter?" She put a hand on his forehead and he pushed it away. "Sorry. I thought you might have a fever or something."

"I'm fine."

Caroline took a big swallow from the drink in her hand. "You don't look fine."

"Leave me alone."

She was taken aback by the roughness in his tone, and then insulted.

"Okay with me," she snapped, downing the rest of the liquor in her glass and setting it on top of the piano, knowing it would make him angry if it left a ring.

The spiteful gesture worked. Monty got up so fast the piano bench fell over behind him.

"Damn it, Caroline!" He swept the empty glass to the floor, where it shattered.

Caroline fled. She didn't hear his footsteps coming after her.

Midway up the stairs to the second floor, she halted and turned around, bending to peer into the room where the piano was, looking for Monty.

He was stretched out on the couch, motionless, with one arm flung over his eyes. Maybe he did have a headache. Maybe he was drunk. She didn't care. She hoped he was out cold, because she had a little snooping she wanted to do.

She went the rest of the way up the stairs on the balls of her feet and when she reached the top, she slipped off her shoes to go down the hall and into his study. That was directly above the room she'd left him in.

Caroline turned the doorknob and paused on the threshold, half expecting him to come running up the grand staircase after her to prevent her from entering his sanctuary. It was a good thing the servants were gone. The house was so quiet she could hear the ticking of clocks behind closed doors. But there was one other sound . . . she listened hard to the faint noise and then she smiled.

Monty was snoring down below.

He never took naps—he had to be unwell. But she didn't care. She needed a little extra time.

She went in, not closing the door. She wanted to be able to hear him coming if he woke up.

Caroline went over to the gigantic antique partner's desk, moving past it to get to the computer on a much smaller, jarringly modern table next to it.

She was not exactly a tech type, but she did know what a USB port was. Caroline located it around the back and then found the on switch.

The computer hummed to life. A box on the glowing blue screen asked for a password, which she carefully keyed in.

She'd watched Monty type the same one many times when he thought she wasn't paying attention. Memorizing it had seemed like a good idea, and she was glad she had. Eventually he'd begun to order her out when he was working in here. She hoped and prayed he hadn't changed the password.

The monitor shimmered as another screen replaced the first,

with rows of icons. Excellent. This was going to be effortless and fast.

Caroline reached between her bra cups and pulled out a flash drive she'd tucked there. It was a pretty little gizmo, a promotional item from Monty's accountant. His name and title—Sidney Merritt, CPA—were printed on its red lacquer shell, a color that happened to match her fingernails.

In less than five minutes, she'd downloaded as many financial files as she could find onto the flash drive. She closed them all and went through the short rigamarole of safely removing the drive from the USB port. Back it went into her bra. Caroline ran her hands over her breasts, just in case the two-inch-long thingy made a visible lump.

No. Mission accomplished. The drive was snugly tucked deep into her cleavage. She turned to the monitor and keyboard, and shut down the computer. To her annoyance, it promptly started up again but without the rows of icons. Only the box asking for a password appeared.

Caroline exhaled a nervous sigh, then listened again. The silence was oppressive.

She no longer heard snoring, but then she'd moved to the far corner of the room. She began to investigate the partner's desk, sure he hadn't shown her everything that was in it. But pulling out the small drawers revealed the same assortment of office supplies and cache of stationery she'd seen before, orderly and neat.

There were some papers on top of the desk. Mostly bills, she noticed, and mostly from boutiques. She riffled through them, flushing with anger at rude scribbled comments not meant for her to read.

And underneath those was a carbon copy of a cashier's check. Caroline made a mental note of which bill it was under so she could replace it exactly where it had been. Then she studied it under the lamp.

The check part, gone, had been made out in his handwriting to Erin Randall. For fifteen thousand dollars. The lower left corner specified in a few brief words that it was an advance on a commissioned portrait of Take All, and that the total fee was thirty thousand.

She drew in her breath with a hiss. The bastard. He'd lied through his teeth when she'd asked him how much he was paying that girl. Told her oh-so-casually that an unknown artist like Erin only charged fifteen hundred for a painting like that. He considered it a steal.

Caroline had been willing to let that pass with a couple of sarcastic remarks. She had no idea why she'd believed him.

Fifteen thousand would have bought a decent diamond ring—thirty thousand would have bought something worth showing off. But he had other priorities. She had suspected the girl was a potential rival and now she was sure of it. More than ever, Caro knew where she stood with Hugh Montgomery. The hand holding the check carbon shook and the thin paper fluttered.

Furious, Caroline slammed the carbon down on the desk under her flattened palm, then shoved it back into the pile of bills, not caring if it was in the right place. She was going to try to catch him out in his lie; then she would wave it under his nose.

She straightened up and turned—and saw Monty standing in the door.

"Ah—hello." She controlled her anger—barely. Let him make a fool of himself. "Did you have a nice nap?"

"It was short. But refreshing." His voice was strong and clear. "I feel better." Then he held up her discarded shoes.

"Did you have fun sneaking around?" He waved the shoes at the computer, which she hadn't turned off. "Were you in my files?"

"I don't know your password."

"Really? I didn't leave the computer on."

Caroline threw him a blazing look. "It just came on. Maybe I touched a key by accident."

He tossed her shoes to one side and came closer. She saw that he wasn't wearing his, just socks. No wonder she hadn't heard him.

"Find anything interesting on my desk?" The question was sharp. Whatever had made him unfocused and irritable had been cured by his nap. Caroline silently cursed herself for not being quicker at her task.

"Yes." She might as well admit to the lesser of her sins. It would distract him from the issue of the computer. The check carbon had been on top of the desk, if not on top of the boutique bills, but it was fair game. Not private, not in the way password-protected files were. Reminding herself that it wasn't as if she'd done anything wrong. Caroline searched for the carbon under everything else. "Fifteen thousand in advance for a painting by Miss Nobody? Are you crazy?"

"Erin Randall is a talented young woman and I got a bargain."

"You lied to me!"

"So I did. To keep the peace. But you aren't entitled to question any expenditure I choose to make."

"That much money would buy—"

"Oh, here we go again." Montgomery looked mad enough to break something big. "Shut up. Just shut up."

"I want a ring!" she burst out. "That's not too much to ask for! Not after all this time!"

"You sound like a little girl," he said contemptuously. "Go on back home to daddy. If he hasn't rented out your room."

"What?" she shrieked. "Are you trying to insult me or my father? He's worth ten of you!"

She sank her red nails into the upholstered back of one of the gigantic armchairs, clutching it so as not to fling herself at him. Monty thrust his hands into his pockets and stood his ground.

"Is he? Maybe not," he said calmly. "But I take back the remark about him renting out your room. That wasn't nice."

She took a heaving breath. "Don't do me any favors."

"He can't, Caro. The Loudon house and the land it stands on are in foreclosure. The sign went up on the front lawn this morning. It's hard to see across two acres of grass, but it's there."

"What?"

Montgomery took a step toward her. "You don't have anywhere to go at the moment. But I won't bother you."

She stared at him in shock.

"I think it's fair to say that what we had is over, don't you? And by the way, I don't want to hurt you."

"Monty—" She said his name in a cracking whisper.

"I'm sure you have a lot of things to think about, Caroline. I certainly do. In the meantime, leave me alone."

He took a step forward in the direction of the partner's desk, and for the second time that day, she fled from him.

Montgomery listened until the sound of her running footsteps diminished. A door slammed far away. He went to his desk and bent down a little to run a hand over the concealed latch. It hadn't been tripped. His laptop was safe and so were the hidden papers in the recess.

Then he sat and turned to the computer she'd gotten into. It was a top-of-the-line model, fully functioning, but essentially a decoy, loaded with dummy files set up to fool someone who was financially unsophisticated and didn't know much about computers.

Caroline was both. He had to keep her away from the real secrets.

The phone on the desk rang and Montgomery answered, rubbing his temple. His headache was back and somewhat worse.

"Hello."

"Good afternoon, Mr. Montgomery."

"Hello, Sidney."

He knew exactly why his accountant was calling and fiddled with a pencil while he listened.

"We got an alert five minutes ago. Miss Loudon took the bait. And we got her doing it on the PC's webcam if she says she didn't."

His reply was weary. "She was cornered. What else would she say?"

Sidney was too tactful to ask what was going on. He stuck to the facts. "And just so you know, the records of the file downloads she made are in our encrypted files and copied to a backup hard drive."

"Overkill," Montgomery said. "There isn't anything on them she can use, right?"

"No, nothing at all," Sidney assured him. "Paul created a fun little fake company for you. For a college kid, he gets an amazing amount done. Stays late, works cheap—my kind of assistant."

"Congratulations." Montgomery wanted to get off the phone and lie down. "At least Caroline has something to do now. Besides shopping. And screaming at me."

"Ha ha." Sidney chuckled dutifully. "Is there anything else you need me or Paul to do for you at this point, sir?"

"No."

It was after midnight when Montgomery reviewed the cover layout for the hedge fund's quarterly report. His investors expected something classy, and they would get it. The understated but strong design featured a small, stylized image of a racehorse above the company name. He took out a fountain pen and signed the layout in an unsteady scrawl. It would be picked up by a courier tomorrow.

Last year, he'd had two assistants to take care of all that. His short, glowing letter to investors was his sole contribution, followed by pages of carefully phrased double-talk written by a business marketer, backed up with graphs and charts. The whole thing had been close to fiction. The numbers had begun their downward trend even then. And now it was nothing more than lies. There was a limit to how well he could do that when cold, hard numbers contradicted every word.

He booted up the laptop from the partner's desk and pulled up a private feed from the day's stock markets. From it, he entered figures rapidly in his fund file, doing calculations in his head that seemed right at first—he was good at mental math—but were wrong when he checked them. He entered the corrections, cursing under his breath. No matter how he juggled the sums, the fund was in free fall, and the rate of loss was accelerating.

Without saving his work, Monty clicked out of the fund file. He felt too numb to care.

He struggled to think for a minute, his head in his hands. Then he lifted it and opened another file, moving fifteen thousand dollars to cover the withdrawal for the painting. Transaction completed, he rose, bracing himself on his chair before he nearly lost his balance.

Keep moving. Always moving . . .

Had he said the words aloud or was he hearing them? Monty had no way of knowing. He forced himself to focus as he returned the laptop to the hidden recess. Then he walked unsteadily to the couch and lay down, staring at the ceiling.

Fifty miles away, the file he'd worked on was still open.

Colorless eyes looked over the latest entries. Paul hummed to himself.

"Stop that," Hoebel said irritably. He was slouched in a chair, looking tired. Cutt hadn't showed. "You're making me sleepy."

The hacker glanced his way. "This is a waiting game. Go home," Paul said. "Get some sleep. Digest your pizza." The air in the windowless room smelled of the fast food they'd both eaten, the box tossed on the floor.

"Just tell me if the big bucks got moved."

Paul's fingers clicked on the keyboard. "Okay, I'm looking through everything this time."

"Don't work too hard."

The younger man ignored the sarcasm. "And it looks like . . . hey, fifteen thousand bucks played hopscotch this evening. Want the details?"

"Yes."

Paul nodded. "I'm going into Notes—Montgomery likes to make notes, doesn't he? Looks like the deposit was made to cover a payment via cashier's check—"

"Who was that for?"

Paul poked around in the distant hard drive. "You know, considering he's ancient, Montgomery is pretty good with computers. But he's got more nasty holes in his encryption than I do in my socks."

Hoebel glanced down at the hacker's unlaced, graffiti-print high tops. "Don't show me."

"I wasn't going to." Paul stopped and peered into the screen. "Got it. He listed the payee as Erin Randall. Whoops—I tagged that name." He waited for a beat. "And there she is." He tapped on the screen. "I showed you this. It was downloaded from a security vidcam onto Montgomery's laptop. Who's the guy?"

Hoebel frowned. "A detective. RJ Bannon. He's one of my officers, actually. Benched for months, nothing to do but stir up trouble with an old case. You know, the unsolved Montgomery kidnapping."

"Never heard of it."

Hoebel winced. "I have a feeling your mother wasn't even born when it happened. Let alone you."

"So what's the big deal?" Paul asked without much interest.

"I guess you missed the newscast."

"Dude, please. I don't even own a TV."

"It was on the station website. Guess you missed that too."

"I'm busy." Paul rolled his eyes to emphasize that point. "College classes plus this—I mean, I love getting paid, don't get me wrong. And it's kind of a hoot to hack the accounts of a crooked rich guy, but that doesn't mean I want to know everything about him, outside of that he owes you some money."

"He owes me a lot of money," Hoebel growled.

"You know, I never asked. What do you do for him, collect debts?" Paul asked in a breezy tone. "Break heads?"

Hoebel glared at him. "Rewind that."

"Huh?"

The kid was young enough never to have seen an actual, rewindable videotape in a black plastic box. Hoebel felt like a dinosaur. "Go back to the part where you never asked," he snapped. "And remember it."

Something menacing in the older man's tone got a little respect from Paul. "Okay." He put up his hands in a gesture of mock surrender. "Whatever you say."

"And let me see that security tape again."

Paul opened it in a media program and Hoebel watched in silence. Something about Bannon's watchfulness made him uneasy. The guy was a pain in the ass, but he was a good detective and no fool. However, Bannon hadn't been able to spot the hidden vidcams. The chief knew Bannon would've avoided them or covered them if at all possible.

"Are we done with this?" Paul asked, faking politeness.

"Yeah, but can you copy it from his computer?"

A few clicks and the video file was invisibly stolen and transferred to a file on the hacker's laptop.

"I don't think I need it, but you never know. She had a legit reason to be there, and she had the key," he said. "Erin Randall is an artist—she did a painting of the old mansion. So that's what the fifteen thousand was for, I guess. He commissioned something new."

"His note has it as an advance on a painting of a horse."

"Take All?"

Paul peered into the screen. "That's the name. Why would anyone pay that much money for a painting of a horse?"

The chief shrugged. "People do. Montgomery can afford it."

"Not really."

Hoebel blew out an exasperated breath. "Fifteen thousand is still small change to him. Just do what I pay you for and keep looking."

"You bet," Paul said. "I'm on it. Let's start with the reward money in trust and check again. Looks like—hmm. Nope. It's all still there. Two million and change." He snooped through an activity log in a hidden directory. "Montgomery's been into the trust files, though, every day. But all he does is change the name of the beneficiary."

Hoebel suddenly looked a lot more alert. "Who is the beneficiary now?"

"Not anybody," the hacker amended his statement. "He just deletes Ann Montgomery. Then the space is blank for, like, an hour, then he types her name back in again. According to the activity log, he's been doing it over and over for a couple of days, off and on. Like he can't make up his mind."

"If he's in the reward files that often, we can't make a grab. He'll know right away."

"Well, we could, if I write fake code that would make it look like the dough was still there when it's really in your account," Paul offered. "But you'd have major explaining to do to the IRS and your bank." He laughed under his breath. "They'll think you're a freakin' drug lord or something with a money transfer that big."

"Count on it. But I plan to be in a country with no extradition treaty when we do the deed."

"When I do the deed, you mean." The hacker smirked at him. "You tired of fighting crime?"

"Yeah," Hoebel said. "It doesn't pay too well. No matter what they say."

Paul began to hum tunelessly again. "So long as you don't get caught."

Hoebel's eyes narrowed. It had occurred to him that the kid might be setting him up for a sting. Paul seemed awfully casual about everything he was doing. "Don't you worry about that?"

"Nah." Paul stopped typing on the keyboard and leaned way back in his swivel chair. "I'm working for a real police chief. Hey, do I get a toy badge? Or a tour of the station?"

"No."

"That's not fair. You law enforcement types have extremely cool software and databases. How about some free downloads?"

"Absolutely not."

The hacker sighed and ran his fingers through his scruffy hair, making it look worse. "I guess I'll live. But pay me what you owe me."

Hoebel grunted and reached into his pocket, peeling off several hundreds. Paul took them without counting them and stuffed them into the front pocket of his oversized hoodie. "Thanks. Throw in some overtime once in a while. These late hours are killing me."

The chief looked at him and something else crossed his mind. "If you're not watching him, what happens if he suddenly moves the money?"

The hacker went back to his endless clicking around. "Dunno. Maybe he gets a free toaster from the next bank or something."

"Get serious."

Paul turned his head away from the screen to gaze calmly at Hoebel. "I get pinged, that's what happens. I already set up automatic warnings with a line of new code. When I get one, I'll text you on the cell phone you gave me. Can I take it home when we're done with Operation Montgomery?"

Hoebel shook his head. "Don't get attached to it. I'm going to keep changing them on my side and yours, so they can't be easily traced."

"Keep spending, dude," Paul said. "It's good for the economy."

"They don't cost me anything," the chief said. "I get 'em from the evidence locker. One-stop shopping, know what I mean?"

"No, I don't. That's why I wanted a tour of the station."

Hoebel only laughed and reached for his jacket, stepping over the fast-food trash on the floor.

"You heading out?"

"Yeah. Meeting up with Cutt."

The hacker's glasses obscured the expression in his eyes. But his tone of voice made his opinion of the third man clear. "He's a scary guy."

"Sometimes."

Paul began to type again. "His brain shorts out. I can see the sparks in his eyes. What did that?"

"Prison."

"What was he in for?"

"Assault. Deadly weapon."

"And you said he used to be a cop?"

"One of the best. But he liked to break the rules." Hoebel thrust his bulging arms into his jacket sleeves. "Someone snitched on him and he went crazy, half killed the guy. He did hard time for it."

Paul didn't turn around when he heard Hoebel open the door to the room so he could leave. "Lock that behind ya," was all he said.

"You got it," Hoebel replied.

The chief went up the stairs of his favorite diner, using the large plate-glass window to check out the seated customers until he spotted a lanky man with his legs stretched out under a table. Cutt didn't seem to notice him as he walked in. He was pouring sugar from a ribbed glass dispenser into a thick mug of coffee.

Hoebel went down the main aisle to the other man's table. "Hello, Cutt."

The lanky man only grunted in response, preoccupied with what he was doing. The glass dispenser was nearly empty.

"Save some for me," Hoebel kidded.

In answer, Cutt shook the dispenser hard and the last of the sugar spilled over the table. Brushing it away, he stirred the black brew and took a slow swallow.

Hoebel grimaced. "You drink your coffee that sweet?"

"Sometimes, if I need a cheap rush. I was out drinking. Still feeling it."

Hoebel studied the other man's face. There were gray circles under Cutt's eyes and a tiny muscle jumped at the side of his jaw.

"Yeah? Stay off the hooch. Things are getting interesting." Hoebel shed his jacket and slung it over the back of a chair upholstered in red vinyl with silver-colored studs.

"What's going on? You coulda called instead of dragging me out of bed at this hour," Cutt complained in a low voice.

The chief shrugged. "I prefer talking face-to-face." He accepted a glass of water from a busboy and asked for menus.

"I don't. And I hate public places."

Hoebel folded one hand over the other and leaned across the table. "That's because your face was famous in all the wrong places for a while. Guess what. I still have an original Most Wanted poster with your mug shot on it."

The other man told him he could roll up the poster and exactly where to put it.

Hoebel chuckled. "Not unless you autograph it first."

The other man grunted again and drank the rest of his coffee, a morose expression on his face. Then he asked, "What's going on?"

The chief opened his menu without really reading it. He knew all the selections by heart. "We're doing a watch-and-wait. Nothing's happened. But Paul seems to know his stuff."

"That punk needs to show some respect."

The chief looked up from a menu photo of two perfect fried eggs in bacon parentheses. "What happened? He rub you the wrong way?"

"Yeah."

Hoebel folded his menu and noticed that Cutt hadn't even opened his. "You can't be serious. He's a college kid. You're an ex-con."

"He said something about that."

The chief narrowed his eyes. "Not in my hearing."

"That's because you pay him."

Hoebel scowled. "I'll straighten him out."

"Before I do?"

"Yeah," the chief muttered. His partner in crime could be hard to control.

"Thanks." Cutt slouched in his seat and yawned, revealing back teeth with a couple of large cavities.

The chief almost flinched. That bit of ugly wasn't on the Wanted poster, he thought, but it went with the junkyard dog look of Cutt's face. Meaner than mean.

"Okay. What are you having?" A pretty young waitress was coming their way.

Cutt answered first. "Burger. Rare. Everything else on the side."

"Sounds good. I'll have the same thing, Lily," Hoebel said to the young waitress as she took a pad out of her apron pocket.

He intercepted the nasty look she gave Cutt. What was that about? Looked like they knew each other from somewhere.

"Almost the same," he amended his order. "Just remind Betty that I like mine well-done," he said with a wink.

"Sure thing, Chief." She favored him with a dazzling smile. Hoebel smiled back, then turned to Cutt.

The other man mimicked her reply under his breath. "She likes you, Hoebel. How'd you get so lucky?"

"Excuse me?" The chief's wary reply made the pretty waitress turn around for a second. Then she kept on going toward the kitchen, suppressing a giggle. "What's it to you?"

"Leave her alone."

"Huh?"

"You're married. Don't cut in front of us single guys."

"I didn't know you were in line." Hoebel's tone revealed his irritation. His lukewarm desire for his wife had turned to ice long ago. When it came to women, he flirted with some and slept with the others, given half a chance and an overnight shift at the station. Lily was in the first category, but he was thinking of moving her to the second. Not that it was any of Cutt's business.

Cutt's reply was quiet. "Not anymore. Lily turned me down a couple of nights ago. We got to talking and some girl she was with told her where I spent the last seven years."

"That's tough." The chief smiled thinly. "But can you blame her? Doing hard time isn't a big draw with the ladies."

"Shut up, Hoebel." Cutt's voice was cold and tense. The unforgiving look in his eyes made the chief comply.

"What's gotten into you?"

Cutt didn't answer.

"There's plenty of women in the world to go around," the chief said finally.

"Not pretty ones." Cutt's tone was flat, as if he'd had the last word.

The glitter in his eyes creeped the chief out. Hoebel countered with a distraction. "Forget it. Just forget it." He looked around. No Lily, gracefully balancing a tray and swaying a little on her long legs. Not even a whiff of a burger from the kitchen. He was hungry. "Guess the grill broke down."

"Huh?"

"Never mind. What were we talking about before?"

"Paul."

He nodded. "Look, I don't need to know exactly what he said to you." Hoebel had no wish to set off Cutt's hair-trigger temper.

The other man's eyes darkened. He took several seconds to respond.

"I don't trust him. A punk like that could be on anyone's side. In prison, they caused the most trouble."

"Yeah, well, you're not in prison," the chief said. "And he gets damn good pay for being on our side."

"That doesn't mean anything, Hoebel. Someone else could be paying him more."

"Like who?"

"Old man Montgomery."

Hoebel wished he could laugh that idea away, but he couldn't bring himself to do it. "I don't think so," was all he said. "He doesn't even have the cash to pay me. Basically, he's a rat in a trap."

"Set by you? Or by Bannon and the girl?"

Hoebel glared at the other man. "What are you talking about?"

"Like you don't know. The girl in the security tape you showed me—the one that lawyer, Duncan, gave you behind the old man's back."

"Yeah. I had Paul download it again just to keep an extra copy on his laptop. You never know when you're gonna get subpoenaed. They take your stuff." He looked at Cutt's stony expression. "That was a joke."

"I was thinking that you wanted to look at her wherever you were. You even told me her name. She's pretty. Prettier than Lily," he added with a flash of contempt.

The chief didn't know what to say to that. He was beginning to trust Cutt less than he trusted Paul.

"Get to the point," he snapped.

Cutt sat up straight, like the cop he'd been once, reminding the chief of an animal run wild that hadn't forgotten how to act tame.

"She could get in the way, Hoebel. You said so."

"Maybe." He had, unfortunately. So sue him—he liked to juice up stories. It made them more interesting for his audience, which was usually rookie cops and wet-behind-the-ears media types and cute waitresses. Not men like Cutt.

"I did a little investigating—on my own. I followed them the other day. They didn't see me. I went way up in the hills behind her house and watched them for a while." He didn't mention seeing her at the art fair for the first time way back before all this crazy crap got started. He'd found out where she lived simply by waiting and following her home. That little house Erin lived in stood out on the rolling land. Lately he'd been keeping an eye on her more and more. Binocs got him the best view, but he used a detached rifle sight sometimes. It was easier to fit in his pocket.

The chief scowled. He didn't need this. Cutt was unstable—he'd read his psychiatric file before hiring him, exploiting the fact that an ex-con didn't have a whole hell of a lot of job offers.

Two years ago, Cutt had jumped at the chance to be the muscle behind Hoebel's dirty work for Hugh Montgomery, and he'd done a damn good job.

Following Bannon and his arty girlfriend around was volunteer work that wasn't about doing good. Cutt was headed for a fall.

Maybe it was what the man wanted, the chief thought. Former

prisoners could miss the thick concrete walls that had kept them penned up, would violate parole and commit stupid crimes to get back in. They needed the box.

The craziest, like Cutt, sometimes craved solitary. Four walls. No window. Locked away, they were free to scream. No one would come.

"Why did you do that?" Hoebel asked finally.

Cutt's shadowed gaze didn't meet his. "I don't know why. I've been restless. Thinking too much, I guess. About everything."

"Don't. As far as Montgomery, we have to get paid and get out."

Their orders arrived at last, but Lily wasn't the one balancing the tray. It was a guy from the kitchen, someone in a grubby line-cook's apron. They didn't bother to say thank you.

The two men doused the grilled burgers with ketchup and forked slices of raw onion on top of that, eating without speaking.

CHAPTER 11

The question for Bannon was where to start looking. He was going more on instinct than anything at this point, with the sketchiest of clues. Three words, "girl of gold," that weren't from some old song. Words that seemed machine-printed on a store-bought card, but had been penned in ink. He'd taken screen shots from the digital microscope image, saved them on his laptop.

Bannon touched a key to bring the screen to life. He opened the folder with the screen shots and studied the calligraphy again. He was no expert on the subject, but it seemed flawless, offering no clue to the personality of the writer.

But he couldn't shake the feeling that the same person had used the same words on another card. He wanted a much closer look at the sentimental card handcrafted by Ann's mother. The photos in the scrapbook it had fallen out of might tell him something more about the lonely-looking woman in some of them. His guess: She had been an unhappy wife, married to an oddball who kept his distance from the world. One child dead, one living. Who had known them? Who remembered them now? Bannon had a hunch that the Randall family had hidden in plain sight.

And that Randall wasn't necessarily the real family name.

He'd have to hit some databases, maybe call in a couple of favors on the federal side through Linc or Deke.

Bannon sifted through the copied papers of the Montgomery files several more times, looking for something he might have missed, setting aside anything, no matter how minor, that concerned the little girl. Crimes of this type often involved crossing state lines. He and everyone else with a badge in the state of Virginia had sat through talks on the subject by federal officers and the occasional criminologist, but Bannon had listened more than most, studied up on his own time when he could. Child predators wanted sex; child abductors sometimes just wanted a child. But those lines blurred.

Before he'd made detective, he'd been schooled some by a grizzled veteran of the state police on the grim truths of crimes against children. *Sometimes the victim is killed within an hour or less. Sometimes not. Some kids are kept for years, until they forget their own names.*

What else had the man said?

Sometimes there's more than one perp, especially in abduction cases. Easier to take a kid if a woman's involved.

One trick the old guy had shared was that it could help to put yourself in the shoes of an abductor or predator. Set aside the concept of right and wrong. Adopt the twisted logic of a psychopath and think like one. Then look at the clues again with that mindset.

Bannon would try to.

He had very little to go on, but the most likely scenario was that there had been two people involved in the Montgomery kidnapping. A woman to keep the little girl from becoming too frightened and screaming. A man to take care of the rest.

But there were no details to go on. In the months the case had been headline news, virtually no physical evidence relating to Ann's disappearance had turned up. Reviewing everything spread out on the coffee table once more didn't reveal points of connection he'd missed.

But he wasn't going to dismiss his instincts. He had more digging to do, that was all, in places other than the official files. Bannon rubbed his forehead. He'd have to search county records, libraries, look through bound copies of newspaper accounts in those years—grunt work. Not thrilling. But he would do it.

He sat back into the couch cushions and closed his eyes, constructing scenarios in his mind, interweaving theme and variations, methods and motive.

A pair of child abductors had snatched a little girl from a rich family, reasons unknown. They had never asked for a ransom. The whirlwind of media attention could have panicked them into killing little Ann, most likely within a few days of taking her.

Think like them.

The idea was loathsome, but he forced himself to do it.

They hadn't wanted money. They had wanted a child young enough to forget where she came from. And they had left no trace, a sign of meticulous planning. Ann had been taken in the night, when the household was asleep.

But why would anyone assume they could get away with kidnapping the only daughter of the Montgomerys? For the perpetrators, there had to have been an element of challenge to the crime. To Bannon, that suggested a high degree of intelligence.

Ann Montgomery had been taken in a more innocent time, before nationwide Amber Alerts. The abduction had been all over the newspapers, but that didn't mean the investigation was everything it should have been.

Then and now, kids vanished without kidnappers. Off the record, the officers involved could have seen the case not as an abduction but a simple disappearance, especially without a body and or any apparent clues. A curious child wandered out of bed and out the door. It did happen. Lost in the woods. Swept away by a rising creek in a nameless gully. Trapped in the twists of a hidden cave at the back of a rock overhang.

Missing, presumed dead.

It was a routine phrase for official documents. Still, it nagged at him. It was the first thing he'd read on the Montgomery case. Had the original investigators been too quick to jump to that conclusion? Bannon had no way of knowing.

He pushed himself up and off the couch, afraid he was overthinking things. Sure, his scenario was plausible, as far as it went, but believing it instead of finding out facts wasn't going to get him anywhere. The way certain elements of Erin's story fit his theory—that could trip him up, big time.

Bannon found his cell phone and punched the speed dial key for her number as he walked to the window. It was a nice day. She might be outside. He was pleased when she answered before the last ring on his side of the call.

"Hey." She sounded happy to hear from him. "I was just going to call you."

"Yeah? Then I must be psychic."

Erin laughed warmly—the sound that did something to his heart. "Were you thinking about a big black dog?"

"Uh, no," he said honestly. "But is Charlie okay?"

"Oh, he's fine," she assured him. "But I was going to get started on the painting for Montgomery today. I can't bring Charlie to the stables and I don't know how long I'll be there. So it just occurred to me—if you happened to be driving out this way—"

"Yes," he said instantly.

Erin laughed again. "You don't even know what I was going to ask."

"I don't care. I just like saying yes to you."

"Be careful, Bannon. I might take advantage of you."

"Please do. Whenever. So you want me to walk the dog? No problem. Over the hills and through the woods. I'll even check him for ticks afterward."

"Charlie, did you hear that?" Her voice was distant for a few seconds as she spoke to the dog. "Bannon's a good guy."

"I try," he said. He felt a little guilty for not asking her if he could look at the card she'd tucked back into the scrapbook. He was just going to do it. "When are you leaving?" he asked.

"In fifteen minutes."

He frowned. That was sooner than he could get there. "Okay. I'll be out there in half an hour."

"Sorry to miss you." Her voice held a seductive, faintly teasing note.

"Yeah. Well, I have a lot of things to do. Another time, right?"

"You bet. I'll make dinner."

Bannon grinned. "Sounds great. Tell me when."

"As soon as I go food shopping. We'll figure it out. Oh, by the way, before I forget, the key will be under the mat."

"You might as well leave the door wide open," he said wryly.

"Okay, it's dumb, but I can't think of a better place."

"Then maybe I can get out there a little sooner." He could practically hear her sigh.

"I'll be gone. Thanks again, Bannon. I really appreciate it. And so does Charlie."

She hung up and Bannon grabbed his car keys and a jacket. It had been years since he'd gotten a speeding ticket. If he got pulled over, he'd flash his badge at the highway patrol officer, say he was on a case. If the guy didn't buy it, so what? Keeping Erin safe was worth a few points on his license.

Her car was nowhere in sight as he drove up to the house. What he'd expected, but he felt a pang knowing she was gone, even though he'd have the house to himself.

Charlie's deep bark came to his ears as he got out and slammed the car door. It was a good sound. Intimidating.

He glanced through the driver-side window, remembering the laptop he'd strapped to the passenger seat so it wouldn't bounce around on the road. Bannon opened the door again and moved the laptop to the footwell, and then locked the door. You never knew.

He saw the dog move from window to window inside the house as he walked around outside, doing a perimeter check for the hell of it. Everything looked okay.

Charlie must have caught a whiff of his scent through the rattle-trap windows, because he stopped barking by the time Bannon got to the rear windows. From where he was, about fifteen feet away, he could see in pretty well. The dog had his paws up on the windowsill and was grinning at him.

"Yeah, you're going for a walk," Bannon said. He gave everything a once-over and then his gaze was caught by white bits of something on the ground under the windows. He went closer to have a look-see, squatting on his haunches to touch a finger to the dirt and pick up a couple of the white bits.

They were paint flakes. He straightened and inspected the old panes and the frames, paying particular attention to where the upper window met the lower.

On the other side of the glass, Charlie followed his motions. "Down, boy," Bannon said. The dog might have pushed against the windows, loosened the old paint. Hard to tell. There were no marks on the exterior wood, nothing that showed an attempt at forced entry. He ran his fingertips over every inch of the frame that he could reach, feeling for what he might not be able to see.

A couple of places flaked under his touch and more white bits fell to the ground. Inconclusive. But it worried him. Bannon stepped back. From a distance, everything looked fine again.

He turned around and headed back to the front door, letting his gaze sweep over the surrounding land. The gently rolling acres blended into the brushstrokes of green that brightened the woods. Spring was coming on strong. Above it all the Blue Ridge loomed, gradually diminishing toward the north and south.

He came around the corner of the house, went up the porch stairs, and bent down to raise the mat and retrieve the key. Unlocked, the door swung in and there was Charlie, sitting firmly like the well-trained dog he was, ears up and alert. His tail just barely wagged.

"At ease," Bannon said jokingly. He covered the distance to the dog and gave him some solid pats. Charlie scrambled to all fours, shamelessly making the most of the unexpected attention until it stopped.

Bannon straightened and turned his head, suddenly aware of a faint, very feminine scent in the air—the sweet essence of Erin. He guessed that it was wafting from her bedroom, brought to him by a drafty window. The door of her sanctuary was slightly ajar. Maybe she had left the cap off a perfume bottle.

He could just see inside, but he forced himself not to look.

Desperately in need of a distraction, Bannon glanced around for the dog's leash. Not that he would need it for Charlie. But one thing for sure, it wasn't in her bedroom. He spotted it on a hook by the front door and grabbed it, yanking open the door. He was nothing but a hound dog himself.

He and Charlie set out in the same direction that Erin had taken him before, ambling over fields that were a little muddy, then running where it was drier. Bannon sucked in deep breaths, enjoying the freshness of the air. He stopped for a little while, warming his hands in his pockets as Charlie found something unbelievably interesting to sniff. Bannon surveyed Erin's house from this new vantage point.

His fingers found the key he'd taken along. It bothered him that she'd left it under the mat, even though she'd done it for him. Granted, she'd grown up in the country, but things had changed. There were no safe places left in the world.

Charlie brushed by his leg and Bannon realized the dog was heading back to the house. He followed, wanting to get back in himself. True to his promise, he checked the dog for ticks and found none before he opened the front door for both of them.

The big dog padded to a rug that had to be his favorite, judging by the way he thumped down on it and stretched out.

"Did I wear you out?" Bannon asked.

A heavy black tail pounded in answer. Charlie raised his head to look at Bannon.

"Lie down," he said. He was heading for the box that held the scrapbook and he didn't want to be watched by the dog. Charlie obeyed.

He found it quickly, flipping through the pages once he had the scrapbook on a table. The birth certificate and its little footprints caught his eye. Bannon paused there, reading the information on the form more closely.

Slipping a finger under the plastic, he eased the form out, remembering that there were two copies when he saw an identical one beneath the first. He inspected the embossed official seal. It would be easy to find the hospital where she'd been born so he could compare hers to her brother's, see if it all matched.

If the addresses were different, he'd have more leads and other people to talk to. Shouldn't be a problem. Flashing tin at nervous clerks had netted him a lot of useful documents in the past.

Yes, sir. Happy to help. Bow and scrape.

He didn't mind taking advantage of minor bureaucrats.

Bannon flipped through more pages, looking intently at the photos, and then finding the handcrafted card. That he took over to the light. The handwriting was wobbly, with none of the polish of the calligraphy on the store-bought card. But there were those same damn words. His brows knitted as he stared at them.

The soft sound of the dog exhaling was enough to startle him. But Charlie was asleep.

Great. No witnesses, he thought wryly. But he hated to take even scraps of paper from her without asking. His gaze moved over the shelves and settled on a row of bulky shapes surrounding her widescreen monitor. Scanner. Backup hard drive. And a printer-slash-copier, exactly what he needed.

He pressed the power button on the printer-copier. A small green light came on. Then he checked the paper tray. Almost full, good to go. He slid the birth certificate onto the glass and pressed the start button, then took it out and photocopied the card.

Doing both took less than a minute, although it didn't entirely ease his conscience. He folded the copies and tucked them into his shirt pocket. Then Bannon stepped over Charlie, heading for the table where he'd left the scrapbook. He put both originals back exactly as he'd found them, trying to make no noise with the protective plastic, and closed the book. Once it was safely back in the box and that put away, he left, pulling the door shut behind him and locking it.

Bannon squatted down to replace the key under the mat. Then he took off, not pulling over until he reached a town that was big enough for him to pick up a decent wi-fi signal in the parking lot of a new-looking strip mall. He reached into his pocket and unfolded the copies he'd made, entering the name of the hospital on the birth certificate in the search bar.

A couple of hits appeared way down on page five of the search results.

Just as he'd thought. The hospital was no longer in existence. No biggie. He clicked on a bookmarked database for paramedics and first responders and keyed in a couple of useful codes, then spent about thirty minutes figuring out where the hospital's paper records had ended up.

At yet another hospital. Not at the same location. Farther away. Bannon pulled up a map, memorized it, then shut down the laptop and headed that way

An hour later, he was walking through basement corridors that gleamed under narrow bars of fluorescent light, to the records department. He could see the door from where he was—a half door with a section of counter built in to it. The bottom part was closed and the top part had been left open.

The sound of his footsteps got someone's attention in there. A balding man in a shirt that was too large for him reached the other side of the door just as Bannon was about to knock on the counter.

"May I help you?"

"I hope so." Bannon reached for his badge and opened the flat leather case that held it, putting his thumb over the name on his ID. The clerk didn't seem to notice that little maneuver, even though his eyes widened at the sight of the badge.

"What do you need, Officer?"

Bannon gave him an amiable smile. "Nothing too difficult. I'm trying to track down a birth certificate for a baby boy."

"What kind of case is it?" the clerk asked eagerly. "I watch all the police shows. True crime too."

Bannon nodded. "It isn't anything exciting. Sorry." He reached into his shirt pocket and unfolded the photocopy of Erin's birth certificate. "The boy was her brother. He died before she was born, and that was, oh, twenty-seven years ago."

The clerk whipped a pad onto the counter and made notes as he read the information on Erin's certificate. "Male child's age at death?"

"Under two years," Bannon answered.

The clerk did a little math. "Then that would be more than thirty years ago. Goodness. That block of files is a little disorganized, but I think I can help you. May I use this for reference?" He held up Erin's birth certificate.

Couldn't the guy remember a name like Randall? For some reason, Bannon was reluctant to let go of the copy. But all he said was, "Of course."

The clerk folded it in half and pointed the pencil at him. "One more thing. Do you know the birth month of the male child?"

"No. This is just to confirm a couple of details. Like I said, nothing exciting."

"Is that all you need? I could get you a death certificate," the clerk offered. "That is, if the decedent had been admitted to the old hospital. If not, then he's not in the system. The female child will be, of course. But you have that certificate."

Male child. Female child. Decedent. Not in the system. The clerk's officiousness annoyed Bannon, who tried not to show it. The guy couldn't be making much of a living at a job like this, so maybe he had to make what he did sound important.

"You could also obtain a copy from the county bureau of records," the man was saying.

Something he hadn't thought of. It might be interesting. "Let's start with the birth certificate," Bannon replied.

The clerk pushed a pen and several forms at him that asked questions about who he was and why he was requesting the certificates. For something to do while he waited for Bannon to fill in the blanks, the clerk got busy feeding pencils into a whining electric sharpener near the counter part of the door.

The noise made Bannon grit his teeth. And the forms made him reach for his wallet. Given that he hadn't been officially reinstated, he didn't feel like answering any questions. He took out a fifty, slapped it down on the forms, and pushed them back toward the clerk.

"Ah—certainly. One copy or two?" the clerk asked, quickly scooping up the bill and putting away the forms.

"One oughta do it."

The other man gave him a conspiratorial wink and walked away.

Bannon settled into an uncomfortable plastic chair and waited. The clerk returned in twenty minutes with a photocopied birth certificate. "Here you go. I added an official seal in case you need it. And oh—here's the one you gave me." He put both certificates side by side on the counter for Bannon's inspection.

The names and sex and dates were different, but one thing was not. Bannon drew in a sharp breath. The footprints were identical on both forms. He muttered a thank-you to stall the clerk and looked again, hard, to make sure he wasn't seeing things.

He wasn't. The footprints were exactly alike. Tiny toes in the same position. Every fine crease in the same place on the soles.

There was only one explanation for that. One of the certificates had to be a forgery. The footprints of one baby had served to legitimize another, born a few years later.

Bannon's intent gaze moved over both certificates and picked up another difference, more subtle than the first. The official seals were not identical—the emblem was, but not the Latin words of the state motto. He wasn't going to give the officious clerk a reason to remember him by pointing out the discrepancy. Bannon folded Erin's document and put it into his pocket. "And thanks for the gold seal," he added offhandedly, picking up the certificate for Erin's brother and squinting at it. "What does it say? I never was too good at that state stuff—the flower, the bird, and all that."

"Do you mean the motto?"

"Yeah."

The clerk's thin chest puffed up under his shirt. He looked like a kid who had the answer to everything and was about to spout off in front of a classroom. "The official motto of the state of Virginia is *Sic Semper Tyrannis*. I believe it means 'Thus Always To Tyrants.'"

"Oh. Interesting." Bannon folded up the second photocopy and put it into his shirt pocket. He didn't know what the Latin words on Erin's seal meant, but they were different, that was for damn sure. And he was going to find a translation website the second he got home.

He drove fast, stopping only once at a drive-through place for a bucket of chicken à la grease. That got left on the kitchen counter while he booted up his laptop and found a free Latin translation site.

Bannon typed in the words that circled the seal on Erin's birth certificate. *Veritas Temporis Filia*. The thin line of the cursor blinked in the blank space for the translation.

Preoccupied, he heard the bucket of chicken move on the counter a second before it hit the kitchen floor. "Babaloo! Damn it!" He jumped up and went in to deal with the cat, whose green eyes sparked as he crouched over a deep-fried thigh, prepared to defend it tooth and claw. The rest of the chicken was scattered on the floor. Bannon cursed a blue streak and picked the pieces up with paper towels, throwing them back in the bucket and stuffing the whole mess into the metal garbage can, then slamming down the lid.

He washed his hands under the sink tap as the cat slunk off to feast somewhere else; then he returned to the living room.

The translation was waiting for him. The cursor blinked at the end of the sentence. He read it aloud.

"Truth is the daughter of time."

Bannon blew out a long, slow breath as he sat back. What the hell did that mean?

CHAPTER 12

The sunny room was too warm. Unsteadily, Montgomery sat down on the couch in his study, overwhelmed by dizziness. Attempting to summon up the strength to fight it, he told himself not to lean back and realized that he had. He tried to focus on the mantel clock when it chimed. Several seconds ticked away until the blur resolved itself into an antique face and slender hands at a right angle. Half past two.

Vaguely he thought that a man his age was allowed an afternoon nap. He stayed where he was. Cradled in soft cushions, his head seemed too heavy for him to lift. The sensation was disturbing.

Distantly, he heard Caroline's shrill voice calling him but he ignored it and let his eyes close.

The drapes were drawn when he awoke, feeling groggy. There were voices in the room and people behind him. Who? Montgomery focused on the clock's face. The slender hands had joined at six-thirty.

Silky hair brushed his cheek and a subtle fragrance stimulated his memory.

"Monty? Talk to me," Caroline said anxiously. "Dr. Ehrlich is here." She was bending over him, standing behind the couch. A middle-aged man moved into his field of vision, which seemed to have narrowed.

"Ms. Loudon asked me to stop in," he said, almost apologetically. "She said she couldn't wake you."

"I'm awake," Montgomery said.

"That's good," the doctor said. "Very good. But just to be on the safe side, I'd like to take your blood pressure."

"No need."

Caroline came around to where he could see her, with her arms folded across her chest. "Please cooperate, Monty."

"Why?" he asked dully. "You probably tried to poison me."

Her eyes widened with shock and she dropped the pose, turning to the doctor, whose gaze moved over the older man in quick assessment. Then he put a calming hand on her shoulder and guided her away from the couch.

Did they think he was deaf? He heard every word of the doctor's low reply. But the sense of it escaped him.

"Confusion is one symptom. . . . He's a little aggressive. . . . No telling what . . ."

Caroline answered the doctor in a whisper as Monty closed his eyes again. He stayed awake. He could feel their footsteps through the soles of his feet as they returned.

"It was a joke. Lunch was too heavy. There's nothing much the matter with me."

Caroline eased onto the couch beside him. "I'll be the judge of that," she said with feigned warmth. "Now that the doctor's here, I'm sure you don't want to go to the emergency room. You know how long it can take sometimes."

He'd had his share of tumbles from riding, and the occasional broken bone. The thought of being parked on a gurney until some snot-nosed intern got around to examining him roused Montgomery out of his torpor. "I suppose you're right."

Dr. Ehrlich went to the chair opposite, where he had set a large, multipocketed briefcase, its flap opened wide. He took a curled stethoscope out of one pocket and unfolded it, putting it around his neck. Then he removed a portable blood pressure monitor and came to where Montgomery was sitting.

With deft fingers, Caroline removed his cufflink and began to roll up his sleeve, stroking his bared skin as if she wanted to soothe him. He found her touch intensely irritating. Montgomery pulled his arm away and finished rolling up his sleeve himself.

A tiny frown settled between her perfect eyebrows as she gave up and moved aside. The doctor wrapped the cuff tightly around Montgomery's upper arm and held the cold disk of the stethoscope against the inside of his elbow, not saying anything as he listened and watched the readout.

Caroline was silent. Montgomery was grateful for that.

The doctor frowned when the display beeped. "I don't like that number." He lifted the stethoscope disk and took the earpieces out. "I'm afraid we need to have a little talk, Mr. Montgomery."

Montgomery ripped off the blood pressure cuff. "You're not my doctor."

"Your pressure is sky-high. Caroline told me that your cardiologist recommended medication. Have you been taking it?"

He wouldn't answer. Caroline did it for him.

"No, he hasn't."

Montgomery threw her a contemptuous look. "Did you count the pills, Caro?"

She lifted her beautiful head high. "Yes, as a matter of fact. Will you excuse me for a moment, Dr. Ehrlich?"

The doctor nodded and put away the tools of his trade, avoiding Montgomery's steady gaze. Both men heard her heels clicking and, far away, the faint sound of a cabinet door slamming. It wasn't long before she'd rejoined them. Her long fingers clutched several pill bottles. Visibly shaking, she tossed them onto the coffee table.

"I don't know what to do. He just won't take them."

The doctor glanced down at the jumble of bottles, then gave her a puzzled look. "But these are mostly empty. Someone has—" He stopped when he caught her furious glare at Montgomery.

"You dumped them," Caroline hissed.

Montgomery only shrugged.

The doctor studied his reluctant patient for a long moment. "You do know that you're flirting with disaster."

Montgomery's response was cold. "Maybe I don't care."

"You should."

Caroline gave him a pleading look. "He's right, Monty."

Making a fierce effort, Montgomery rose from the couch, refusing the helping hand the doctor extended to him.

"As you can see, I'm fine," he said in a low voice.

The doctor shook his head and packed up his briefcase. "High blood pressure is nothing to fool around with. I suggest you call your cardiologist as soon as possible."

Standing, Montgomery towered over him. "Thank you for coming." His tone was anything but grateful. "Caroline will see you out."

She pressed her lips together, saying nothing as she ushered Dr. Ehrlich into the hall. Montgomery stayed upright, bracing himself with one hand on the back of the couch. He wasn't sure he could get up again if he allowed himself the luxury of sitting back down.

In another few minutes, she stalked back in. "You made a fool out of me."

He laughed harshly. "Did I ruin your dramatic scene? I'm not sorry. You should have looked at the bottles."

"Is that my fault?" she cried. "Why did you throw the pills away? I know you did, there were lots of them yesterday!"

"To get you off my back. I knew you'd taken the bottles out of the cabinet. I had them arranged in alphabetical order. You didn't put them back right."

"This is crazy. Monty, you could die if you don't take them!"

"I feel fine." He didn't. It cost him to keep standing. His hands tightened on the back of the couch. She didn't seem to notice that his knuckles were white.

Caroline waved that away, then pointed her finger at him accusingly. "You are going to your cardiologist tomorrow if I have to drag you there!"

"You can't make me."

A frustrated scream choked in her throat. "Damn it, Monty! Stop acting like a child!"

He gazed at her calmly and kept his voice calm. It was ridiculously easy to get Caroline mad. "I think you just described yourself."

She began to pace the room, walking fast, working off her righteous anger.

"Something is the matter with you," she said at last. "I apologize for caring."

"I rather doubt you're all that interested in my health, Caroline."

She whirled around, her hands on her hips. He liked her like this—ready to fight.

"What if I hadn't found you in time?"

His shoulders moved in an indifferent shrug. "Nothing happened. Why are you carrying on like this?"

"You heard Dr. Ehrlich. He's trying to help you, but you just won't listen—or—or let anyone help or get close—"

He almost swayed where he stood, but forced himself to be still. Blood pounded in his ears. "Closeness is overrated. Someone always gets hurt."

"Monty, you can't keep pretending that you'll live forever."

"I have no such illusions," he replied grimly.

"Let me take care of you. Is that too much to ask after all this time?"

He held up a hand. "Stop it. I don't want anyone taking care of me, least of all you. We aren't going to marry. Get that through your head."

"You're behaving irrationally," she snapped. "Dr. Ehrlich said so."

"A brilliant diagnosis, considering I never met the man before today."

"He's a—a friend of a friend. And he was the only doctor who would come to the house!"

"Ah, yes. I was curious about that. Do you mind if I ask how you persuaded him? He's not your type. Not good-looking and too conscientious by half." He smiled when she shot him a hateful look. "But he will send a bill. Are you going to pay it, Caro? Because I intend to rip it up."

"Monty, you need help!"

His eyes glittered. "You can't grab the reins. Don't try."

"I'm not—"

He took a deep breath and shifted the position of his braced hands before he spoke again.

"I want you to leave, Caroline. Of your own accord."

Her beautiful eyes glowed with angry fire at the blunt challenge. "I can't."

"You mean you won't. Scared?"

She didn't answer.

"It's not that hard," he taunted her. "Open a suitcase. Fill it up. Take whichever car you like—you can keep it."

"I live here. With you." The reply was issued through gritted teeth. "It's been years, Monty."

He sighed. "Not very happy years, were they? Why did you stay?"

Tears shone in her eyes, and a few of them spilled over. She dashed at them, smearing her makeup, before she swallowed hard. "I stayed because I love you. And I still do."

Monty's expression was bland. "No, you don't. You never did."

Caroline turned her back on him and rushed out of the study.

He waited another minute, then staggered to the armchair and collapsed.

Much later, waiting up, Caroline heard him go into his bedroom. He had been unwell—they had been together long enough for her to know it for a certainty. She moved closer to his room from where she was standing at a turn in the upstairs hall, biding her time as he went through a pre-sleep ritual she couldn't see but that was as familiar to her as her own.

A brief shower, followed by a vigorous drying-off. Clothes and towels kicked to one side for the housemaid to deal with. The heavy door of his great-grandfather's mahogany wardrobe squeaked open. That was another piece of furniture she hated—it reminded her of a huge coffin. She knew he was taking out a pair of monogrammed pajamas from a built-in drawer.

Caroline could imagine his tall, still-fit frame properly clad in striped, piped flannel. All buttoned up. Safe from her, she thought angrily. She couldn't hear him ease between the covers and lay his head on the pillow, but she knew that was next. He had a habit of staring at the ceiling before he fell asleep. She'd watched him do it often enough. But it had been a long time since her body had been next to his.

No matter what he insinuated, she had never cheated on him. She regretted being so noble. Listening and waiting in the dim light of the hall, Caroline happened to catch a glimpse of her worried expression in a mirror on the wall and scowled. So much for getting her beauty sleep tonight.

His attitude toward the doctor was no surprise. Monty hated to seem weak. No matter what, he had to be in charge.

Don't grab the reins.

Her lawyer would do that for her. Caroline's lips curved in a small but triumphant smile. It was high time Monty got taken down a peg. The Loudons were his social equals, but his fortune had tipped that balance.

She had waited too long, played her game carelessly. Beauty hadn't been enough. Unfortunately, her looks were fading fast and she was obviously replaceable. Caroline didn't believe one word he said about that girl he'd hired to do a painting of his stupid horse. Erin Randall was way too pretty.

It enraged Caroline that he had been so cynical about her last-ditch declaration of love. He could have let that slide, left her a little dignity, even if he was smart enough not to believe her.

To hell with him.

Insomnia was his new best friend. Sleep, when it came, gave him troubled dreams. Lying awake was preferable. Montgomery waited until he heard Caroline head for her own bedroom and listened to her close the door with a sharp click. He turned his head and looked at the smooth, plump pillow next to his. Without emotion, he tried to remember how long it had been since Caroline's head had rested there. Quite a while.

She wouldn't come to him tonight either. But then that was the last thing he would want.

Montgomery sat up, pushing the covers away and getting to his feet. A shot of hard liquor might do him good. He kept his favorite tipple hidden in a closet, just to make sure he'd always have enough. It was handmade bourbon, aged to perfection by the son of the fellow who'd sold the same stuff to his father—and every other local squire who was willing to ride half a day into the woods to buy it from him one unlabeled bottle at a time. The original maker was an expert distiller known to all the gentlemen in the county. Just not to the government.

Montgomery went to the closet and reached in for the bottle, carefully stashed behind a jumble of decorative objects that Caroline had bought and then not liked. He pushed them aside, feeling his fingers touch the cool plaster of the interior wall. Not there—the bottle had been taken. Or moved.

Then he remembered that he had moved it himself, to the large storage cabinet in his study that held miscellaneous family papers and years of correspondence, set aside for him to write a family history someday. It was safe enough there. He knew Caroline had already pawed through the letters some time ago. She was the kind of woman who could not resist snooping and he had obligingly left the accordion folders unsealed to give her something to do.

He flicked open the latch and reassured himself that the bottle was there, moving aside a fat folder or two and circling the neck with his fingers to bring it out into the light. Excellent. There was more than enough in it for his purposes. He could sip and read something until he felt sleepy.

Montgomery looked around. The coffee table held the usual magazines, stacked with don't-touch precision, all about horses and hounds, socialites and snobs.

On impulse, he grabbed an accordion file from the storage cabinet and tossed it onto the couch. Might as well see what was in it. The date on the label was decades old, from when people prided themselves on writing intelligent letters. A few bounced out when the thing landed. No one had rewound the string around the disk that kept it closed.

Finding a glass, he poured himself a double shot and moved toward the couch with the bottle in his hand, setting it down on the floor before he sank into the richly upholstered cushions. It didn't take too long for the strange edginess that kept him awake to mellow a little.

Idly, he sipped the bourbon and cast a glance into the accordion file, picking up the letters that had fallen out and stuffing them back into the slots inside. It had been organized—who had done that? A former secretary, he supposed. He'd had several. Feeling angry that he couldn't remember, he upended the damn thing and let the contents spill out, brushing his hand over the pile to separate the papers.

Whoever had put it all in order had been wasting her time. There was never any need to keep such stuff. He picked up a letter in a little-old-ladyish handwriting that thanked him and his lovely wife most sincerely for the annual tour of their historic home. That had been Mrs. Meriweather's idea and Luanne's responsibility. After the third year of strangers traipsing through the halls, he'd put his foot down. No more tours. He crumpled the letter into a ball and tossed it on the floor.

A detailed pencil rendering of an odd mechanism caught his eye. He picked it up, admiring the draftsmanship and noting the words *Patent Pending* below the—what was it? He read the neatly lettered title. A Device for the Walking of Horses, Attaching to a Standard Halter. Montgomery took a large swallow of bourbon and looked for the inventor's name. There it was. Randall Ernest.

That rang a bell—no, it didn't. Randall was Erin's last name, that was all. This Randall Ernest was some forgotten genius. Or crackpot. He supposed the half-remembered secretary had dealt with the man. There was no way he could assign a face to that unremarkable name.

Bored but still wide awake, he studied the rendering again. The device was ingenious, if useless. Carelessly, Montgomery finished the bourbon and set the glass on the paper. The drop of liquor that ran down its side brought his own faded scrawl to life. *Not interested.*

He ought to burn these files, he thought. The ache in his head had started again. Or seal them and send them to that Bannon. Let the detective beat his brains out, while he was looking for clues and causing trouble.

A star-filled but otherwise dark sky arched over Erin as she took Charlie outside for a last, short walk. They stayed near the house. Only her bedroom window, curtains drawn, was lit from within.

The sense of peace she always got from being out in nature filled her heart. She breathed in the cool night air, keeping her hands warm in the pockets of an old, baggy jacket. Charlie sniffed the grass first, then the air, alert as usual. He returned to her side and sat down on his haunches, positioning his head directly under her hand.

Erin laughed softly as she looked down. "All right. I can take a hint." She patted his big head and rumpled the thick fur at the back of his neck.

For a few minutes longer they stayed outside, enjoying the peaceful night. Erin took one last deep breath and turned to go in. Charlie stayed by her.

She made sure the back door was locked, and then the front, before she shed the jacket and hung it up on the hook that held the leash. The lamp in her bedroom spilled warm light into the studio area, reaching as far as her easel. Erin stopped to flip through the large sketchbook she'd taken to the Montgomery stables today.

So far she was pleased with her drawings of the magnificent stallion, although none were complete. But she'd captured something of Take All in bits and pieces. The proudly arched neck and well-groomed mane. Liquid dark eyes with a touch of mischievous spirit. The strong shape of his head. She'd used quick, swooping lines of dark pencil to outline the powerful contours of his back and hindquarters.

She wished she could show them to Bannon. If only he had been here with her, walking under the stars. They could have come in together, chilled, and done some cuddling. Maybe more. She wasn't sure if her restless longing for him was emotional or physical or both.

Erin closed the sketchbook and headed to her bedroom. She undressed and slipped into bed, wondering what Bannon was doing right now. Probably the same thing. It was a little too easy to imagine him unbuttoning his shirt and tossing it aside, revealing a chest and arms that had to be pure muscle.

Sometimes it was a wonderful thing to be so visually oriented. Erin almost giggled as she settled into her pillow. She let her imagination go a little further with her vision of Bannon . . . and then she sighed. He wasn't here, so right now it was frustrating.

Charlie padded into the room, ready to sack out on the rug by her bed. She rolled over and reached out to pat him one last time. The dog settled down in a sphinx position, front legs outstretched and head up, as if he was listening to something.

"It's okay, boy," she said softly. "Settle down."

Charlie turned his head to give her a soulful look and then resumed his watchful pose. He really was a great dog, she thought. It was a pleasure having him around, especially since it looked like Bannon was available for an occasional walk during the day. She didn't want to keep Charlie cooped up if she didn't have to.

"Go to sleep," she said.

Obediently, the dog rested his head between his paws. Erin pulled up the covers under her chin and stared dreamily at the ceiling. In another few minutes, she'd drifted off.

The dog's ears pricked and turned. His head came up. But he stayed where he was.

Erin awoke with a start when she heard Charlie's deep growl. The big dog suddenly jumped at the window still shrouded by curtains, not barking, breaking the fragile old glass with the force of his leap. A man's voice cursed. Erin shrank back in terror when she glimpsed someone on the other side of the jagged shards entangled in the curtain. Someone tall. Broad-shouldered. Menacing. She couldn't see his face in the half light before dawn.

The dog's nose was bleeding but he stayed put, barking ferociously, back fur raised, looking and sounding twice as big as he was. The intruder vanished and Charlie turned to her.

Erin scrambled out of bed, switching on the light, trying to see the dog's wound. "Stay!" she whispered. In less than a second she plucked a half-inch sliver of glass from his sensitive nose, drawing a sharp breath when he flinched.

"Good dog. Good boy. I'm done."

The dog stood patiently as she wiped the blood from his nose with a corner of the bedsheet. She scrubbed her cheeks, suddenly aware of two hot tears that were rolling down them. She told herself fiercely not to cry as she took hold of Charlie's head and turned it this way and that. Eyes, ears—both uninjured. Thank God. She saw no other cuts or bits of glass.

She looked around wildly, finding jeans and a top, struggling into them. The prowler could be trying another window. Or the door.

Charlie seemed to have no interest in the window and quickly moved away on patrol—there wasn't any other word for his deliberate progress through the house.

Her heart was hammering under her ribs. Where was her cell phone? Erin couldn't remember. Damn it—the bag she'd taken with her to the stables—it had to be in there. Unless it was in the car.

She edged into the studio area step by cautious step, hugging the wall, keeping her eyes on the windows. She saw nothing outside from her vantage point but the sky, quickly growing light. Even so. The man could still be there. Erin got down on hands and knees and headed for her toolbox. There was a claw hammer in there. Better than nothing.

She had the hammer in hand when she saw her bag. On the floor, where she'd dropped it. Erin let out her breath as Charlie came over.

"Sit," she whispered. He obeyed. It occurred to her that he wasn't growling. His back wasn't up. Still, she wasn't going outside. She reached over from her position on the floor and dragged the bag to her with the hammer's claws. Then she scrabbled inside, looking for the little phone, praying that it was charged.

She flipped it open, keeping a hand on Charlie's powerful neck, more to reassure herself than him. The battery icon was low, but it had enough juice to make a call.

For a moment she hesitated. 911? The friend who'd rented her the house had warned her that it took forever to get help this far out in the sticks. The sheriff was a local joke and so were his deputies. She'd lost the number of a former boyfriend who lived about two miles away.

Erin called Bannon.

* * *

She hadn't finished telling him what had happened before he interrupted her. "Coming. Stay on. And stay down. Let Charlie tear out the sonovabitch's throat if he comes back."

"You didn't tell me Charlie did things like that," came her soft reply.

"Part of his training. Keep him with you."

He pushed the button to put his cell phone on loudspeaker so as not to lose her, grabbing his jeans from last night, belt still in the loops. One, two, legs in, three, sweatshirt yanked over his head, four, boots he didn't bother to lace. Less than five seconds had passed when he picked up the phone. "I'm outta here." He took a gun from a drawer. His own, not department hardware. A Glock.

"Okay," she whispered.

Bannon scooped up his car keys, pretty sure the rotating light to slap on the dash was under the passenger seat. If not, the hell with it. His fellow law enforcement professionals could follow him to Erin's house if they wanted to. His car could do ninety to a hundred easy on clear roads, and Wainsville didn't have a rush hour. He flung open the door and found it blocked.

The building manager, a guy who had a bad habit of starting work at dawn, was standing there with two large cardboard boxes stacked at his feet. He goggled at Bannon, just as startled as he was. "Hello there. I didn't want to knock. These came in yesterday—hey!"

Bannon swore under his breath and pushed past the boxes, then got a glimpse of the TV station logo on the cardboard and sent the top box flying inside with one swipe of his hand, kicked the bottom box inside after it, and slammed the door, not waiting to hear the click of the automatic lock.

"Didn't mean to wake you!"

Bannon swore again and ran for his car.

CHAPTER 13

Bannon drove at top speed down the narrow road to Erin's house, skidding over ruts and slick spots. Dark clouds were drifting over the Blue Ridge, spitting cold rain that hadn't been falling in Wainsville. His car bounced over a rise and slammed down again. The axles were taking a hell of a beating. He didn't care.

On the way here he'd blown right past a highway patrolman who'd pulled over a couple of lowlifes in a battered van. The officer hadn't had a chance to call him in, let alone stop him. Bannon was going that fast.

He gouged out deep ruts of his own as he came to a swerving stop on the wet ground of her front yard, positioning the passenger side parallel to the house. With luck, the car would take the first bullets if anyone had him in their sights. Bannon barely paused to draw breath as he pulled his gun and scrambled out, head down, scanning the house and the land around it through the window.

Empty.

Which didn't mean—

Erin opened the door and peered around it, holding on to Charlie's collar. Bannon lowered his gun but stood tall, even though he was ready to drop to his knees and give thanks she was alive. He'd imagined the worst.

"He's gone," she said in a shaky voice.

Bannon wasn't so sure. His reply was almost a whisper. "Do what I told you. Get back inside and stay the hell down." He gestured to Charlie. "Keep him between you and trouble."

Erin opened her mouth as if she was about to protest but thought better of it. Charlie kept his shoulder to her knee, guiding her. He was a damn good dog.

She left the door ajar. He could jump up there and slam it, or go for a walk.

Bannon walked, taking it nice and slow. Going around the first corner was no fun, but he did it. The second was easier. The third corner revealed blurry footprints in the tangled mix of grass and mud outside Erin's bedroom window. He glanced down, not squatting in case someone was planning to catch him off balance and whack him for all eternity.

The rain wasn't letting up and the blurred footprints didn't tell him much. He guessed that the prowler had long feet. That wouldn't put anybody in jail.

But then, whoever was behind this attempt to break in to Erin's house most likely would never see the inside of a jail. Because someone else was behind the lone man who'd threatened Erin— every instinct Bannon possessed told him that. He had a few ideas. Could be a cop on the take—or the chief himself. Bannon had been connecting some more dots all the way out here and the way he saw it, reporting what had happened here to the police wasn't looking like the best option.

He looked up at the windowsills of the old house. They were close to six feet above ground level. The thug was tall, if he'd been able to look in like she'd said.

There was the broken pane. Rain-spattered shards lay on the ground where the glass had exploded outward from the force of the big dog's lunge at the window.

The footprints ran out from the house, dug deep at the toe— Bannon squinted at the double line of prints until they got too small to see. The prowler had gone back the way he'd come, into the forest that clung to the looming mountains. Bannon's gaze moved back to the ground surrounding the house. The footprints closer in were well spaced and far apart. Bannon guessed the man was lanky. Maybe a long-distance runner, maybe ex-military. There was something disciplined about the evenness of the stride.

Skip it for now, Sherlock, he told himself. He could just about hear Doris's crisp voice saying the words in his mind. The fourth corner of Erin's little house was coming up.

Bannon swallowed hard and stepped around it, gun braced in both hands. No one was there.

He bounded up onto the porch, pushing the door open long enough to get inside himself, then slamming it shut and locking it.

Erin had squeezed herself and Charlie into a corner. Actually, the dog was in front of her. He looked up at Bannon but didn't move.

Bannon made a mental note to thank Linc's girlfriend ten times over. Karen, or whatever her real name was, had trained the big black dog unbelievably well. He holstered the Glock and gave Erin a hand up.

"I did a perimeter check. We're alone."

"Gee whiz. Sounds romantic." She dusted off the back of her jeans, then stuck her hands in the front pockets. Bannon looked her over. He was waiting for the shock to wear off.

Her casual tone didn't fool him. Granted, she didn't seem like the sob-and-scream type. But she would crack one way or another. Bannon wasn't going anywhere until the fear she was holding back surfaced.

His being here could trigger it. That was the reason he didn't take her in his arms and tell her something stupid like everything was going to be all right. Maybe it would be someday, but it wasn't now.

It felt strange as hell to be standing here again, as if he and the prowler had something in common. Only yesterday, sneaking a copy of her birth certificate and that card hadn't bothered him enough to stop him from doing it.

As for what he'd found out from the hospital clerk—later for that. Much later. Even if it turned out to have something to do with what had just happened.

Bannon had something to say that she wasn't going to like: She couldn't stay in this isolated little house after today. She was going home with him. Charlie too.

He had to figure out what was going on and get a chance to straighten out the bad guys. Or take them out before they found her again. And oh yeah—found him too, for starting all this. He had to have been watched the time he'd come here to walk Charlie. He'd relaxed his guard some. Maybe the watcher had tailed him to the hospital somehow, even observed his interaction with the clerk. Then seen Bannon's bribe and raised it to a hundred to find out what he was asking for after he was gone. The scenario was unlikely but not impossible—Bannon tripped up sometimes, everyone did. The most dangerous state of mind was thinking you'd gotten too good to fail. He had. He was leading someone to Erin. His hand moved to his gun. Not a problem solver. But it was there.

"It's not good, Erin," he replied. "Even though it looks like your prowler headed for the hills."

"Should I call the sheriff?"

Bannon shot her a quizzical look. "I assume there's a reason you didn't."

He could come up with one of his own: Hoebel had begun his career in a little town that was more or less in between where she lived and where he lived. There was no doubt in Bannon's mind that the chief could call in favors. There were always a few cops who were happy to do dirty work on the side, especially if it paid better than overtime.

"The friend who rented me this place didn't think too highly of him or the deputies."

"How long was she living here?"

"Seven years," Erin replied.

"Then she would know."

"I guess."

"Did you see the guy's face?" he asked after a few seconds.

"No." She moved into the kitchen, reaching for a zip-locked plastic bag and opening it, pulling out a dog biscuit. She tossed it at Charlie. "Thanks for saving my life." The big dog snapped the bone-shaped snack out of the air. "You're welcome. It's the least I can do."

Her voice was cracking.

The dog swallowed it in a couple of bites and gave Bannon a what-now look as Erin found a chair for him and one for herself. She had to do something and it didn't have to be rational. She set the chairs in the middle of the floor, like they were about to have afternoon tea at an imaginary table. He noticed how hard she gripped the wood.

Here it came. Meltdown. He'd seen it before. A female cop usually took over at this point, when there was one around.

Erin didn't sit, but went to the sink. She picked up a can of cleanser and shook half of it into the sink, running a little water over the scattered powder. Then she scrubbed. And scrubbed and scrubbed, until the sponge was in tatters. Her hands had to be raw.

Bannon stood by and let her do what she needed to do.

He wanted to go to her.

Breathing hard, she stopped her circular motions and turned on the cold faucet full blast, rinsing the powder and tiny scraps from the sponge down the drain. Then she held her hands under the water until they were red, staring fixedly into the swirling water in the sink.

He had to do something. Bannon went over and turned the faucet off, handing her a dish towel, deliberately not making eye contact. Then her legs began to buckle.

Bannon caught her before she fell, wrapping her in his arms and letting her take out her fury and fear on him. At least a minute ticked by as she hammered at his chest, and she hit hard. Bannon took the punishment for the man who'd stalked her and found her. He held her close, outwardly calm until her raging emotions began to subside. She didn't have to know that he considered himself to blame for putting her in harm's way.

He should have been here. Next time—hell. There wasn't going to be a next time. He'd keep her safe.

When she lifted her face to his gaze, his heart damn near broke. Swollen and blotchy were his new words for beautiful and strong. Bannon pressed his lips together to keep from kissing her.

"I—I guess I'm done," she murmured. "No guarantees, though."

"Punch me some more. Whatever it takes."

She managed a wan smile that didn't last long. "No. Sorry. Did I hurt you?"

"A couple of times, yeah, you actually did. You're tougher than I thought, Erin."

She shook her head. "I don't think so. But I would have gone for the guy with the hammer."

Charlie came over to her and brushed against her leg, then stayed there.

"Glad he was here. I can't tell you how glad," Bannon said flatly.

"I'm not sure I'm going to be able to give him back."

"Ah—" Bannon hesitated. "We can talk about that some other time. He's yours for as long as you need him."

She nodded and turned toward her bedroom. "That's good to know." Then she stopped and looked back toward Bannon, her blue eyes huge and vulnerable. "I can't go in there. I just can't."

"You don't have to. What do you need?"

"Clothes. I want to change," she said weakly.

"I'll bring some things out." Bannon took her by the shoulders and used a little body language to get her to sit down in one of the chairs.

"I guess I should shower first," he heard her say as he went into the bedroom. He looked over his shoulder. She'd gotten up and was pacing.

"You can do both at my place."

She waited a beat before replying with a distracted "What?"

"You're staying with me. Where else are you going to go?"

He grabbed armfuls of clean, sweet-Erin-smelling jeans and tops and socks and bras and panties from random places. Then he went back to where she was.

"Hadn't thought about it. Hey—" She came over and picked up a few items. "There's enough here for a month."

"Yeah. I'm giving you the bedroom. I'm taking the couch. Got a duffel bag or something?"

She gave him a dazed look. "Somewhere."

"Don't forget to bring your art supplies. You can pack those yourself. And don't worry about being in my place alone if I'm not there. It's secure. My brother rigged a system for me. Flip a switch, you're safe. And there are neighbors." He couldn't think of their names. Not a selling point.

"Bannon—"

She was bent over and reaching into a lower shelf. She dragged out a gigantic duffel bag that would hold everything in his arms and then some.

"One more thing. Don't argue."

Erin unzipped the bag. "I'm not sure this is the right thing to do."

"It's not permanent. But you can't stay here." He dumped the armload of clothes into the bag and she zipped it right back up, her mouth set in an unhappy line.

A short-order cook flipped the last pancake onto a plated stack and let the roadhouse waitress take it away. She brought the breakfast order to a lanky man slouched with his hands in his jacket pockets, the solitary occupant of a booth with two place settings. "Syrup?"

He nodded without looking at her. She took a couple of steps over to a condiments-and-cutlery station and got it for him.

"I guess you want to get started on that before your friend gets here."

He didn't answer, not picking up the cup of coffee she'd provided a few minutes ago, only staring at the wall opposite him.

"Let me know if you need anything." The woman walked away. This time his eyes followed her, blinking at every swish of her pleated skirt.

Cutt felt the air move when the door opened and Hoebel breezed in. The chief's heavy tread came his way and in a few seconds they were facing each other across the speckled tabletop of the booth.

"How's it hanging?" Hoebel asked, looking over his shoulder for the waitress.

The other man didn't bother to reply. He reached for the syrup jar and drenched the pancakes, then used his fork to steady the stack, sinking his knife into it until it clicked against the plate.

Hoebel turned back to him and noticed the gauze carelessly wrapped around the middle of Cutt's hand. Dark red blood was seeping around his thumb as he ate. The sight made the chief frown. "What happened to you?"

"I was fixing a window this morning. It broke."

The chief eyed him warily. "Looks like you need stitches."

"Maybe so. It won't quit bleeding." Cutt held up his hand to show his palm and a queasy look flashed over the chief's face. That side was worse. A lot worse.

"Go to Valley General. Tell 'em I sent you. You got work to do."

"Okay. Like what?"

The chief leaned over the table and lowered his voice. "Need you to follow up on some accounts. Rough up the no-pays all you want. We've got cash flow problems."

"Want a report?" Cutt tugged at the wrapped gauze, adjusting it.

"No gory details. I don't want to lie under oath if you get carried away. Just bring me the money." He took a piece of folded paper out of his jacket pocket and slid it across the table to the other man. "Here's the list."

Cutt unfolded the paper and glanced at the handwritten names underneath it. "Doesn't Montgomery owe you?"

Hoebel shrugged. "Yeah, but he's stalling me. I can't exactly shake him down hard. Think of this as a helluva fast way to raise capital on our own."

"If you say so. I'm no businessman."

The chief smirked. "You're the muscle. I'm the brains."

"Is that so." Cutt shoveled bites of pancake into his mouth one after another, hardly chewing before he swallowed. The greedy way he devoured his meal made Hoebel put a menu in front of his face.

"Just coffee for me," he told the waitress when she came over.

"Okay. Coming right up." Her voice was as sunny as her smile. But she walked away quickly when she noticed the bloody bandage on Cutt's hand.

The men left together about an hour later. Hoebel led the way to Valley General, waving Cutt onward into the parking lot as he drove off, whistling tunelessly. In another couple of minutes he was zooming up the ramp of the highway that would take him to Wainsville.

High time he put in an appearance at the station, just to let everyone know who was boss. His second-in-command might get ideas otherwise.

Seemed like a minor scandal was brewing over missing and tainted evidence. A nitpicking judge was about to flush a high-profile trial down the courthouse toilet because of Petey's lazy mistakes signing materials and folders in and out. The whole damn police department would be blamed for the lapses and a couple of felons might go free. Hoebel didn't need the bad publicity. His son-in-law had better pull up his socks and put down the girlie magazines he was always reading or Hoebel would have to fire him.

Unfortunately, Petey had no other way to provide for Hoebel's darling daughter, who didn't work. He sighed irritably, switching lanes just for something to do. No, she would come whining to him for money the second Petey got the ax. Nothing doing.

Hoebel had learned a couple of things from being married to her mother: don't share and don't play nice. The fat bonus he planned to pay himself when that punk hacker started draining Monty's accounts was going to make the blackmail money look like chump change, and it was going to be all his.

He pulled off the highway and took a two-lane back road to Wainsville to give himself more time to think. There was another problem he'd let slide.

Bannon.

The chief had no idea why Montgomery hadn't complained directly to him about the TV interview and the attendant publicity—it sure as hell wasn't because the tough old guy was intimidated or anything by having to pay him off. That was a business arrangement, nothing more. Hoebel personally didn't know what the detective was up to. Bannon had always been too improvisational, to his mind. And too damn smart for Hoebel's good. The chief pondered the situation as he drove on. Might be worth slapping a hidden GPS beacon on Bannon's car to follow his movements for a while, see if any patterns emerged.

Such as back-and-forth trips between the old Montgomery mansion and Bannon's place. The young detective had gone there once that Hoebel knew about. Return visits would mean he was looking for something. It'd be almost funny if he had something on Montgomery too.

Like what?

Hoebel pondered the question, thinking that Bannon was most likely after the reward. If so, he was following a trail gone cold decades ago. But maybe that could be it. He knew the detective was broke or close to it. His continuance-of-claim forms were clogging the in-box on Hoebel's desk, along with a thousand other things that Jolene had tagged for him to sign. He hated paperwork. The chief considered himself a man of action, and he had the aviator sunglasses to prove it. He adjusted them in the rearview mirror.

Bannon's involvement was one more reason for Hoebel to do an end run around Montgomery. The old man did seem to be nervous about the reward money, judging by the after-midnight fiddling around with his hidden accounts. But he'd be crazy to think that little Ann was still alive. More likely Montgomery just needed the dough.

Hoebel did too. And if the two million ended up with him, and sooner rather than later, it wasn't stealing per se. Montgomery hadn't settled his bill—and never would. He grinned. That was the beauty of blackmail. He wondered how the old man would react when the reward got sucked out of the trust. He'd probably have a stroke. Join the crowd, Hoebel thought cynically. Bluebloods like Montgomery were a dying breed.

Coroners' reports for the oldest family names in Virginia landed on Hoebel's desk now and then, when the circumstances of the death were ambiguous.

Cirrhosis of the liver could look like poisoning. Suicide could be faked by interested parties, including the victim, for a major insurance payoff. Then there were the riding accidents. Broken necks and not a horse in sight. Or fun with guns. Men got shot for fooling around with other men's wives. By the angry husbands. Or their own wives.

Montgomery seemed to toe that particular line. But he wasn't long for this world, in Hoebel's professional opinion. Too many secrets, too much stress. A stroke would be better than blowing his brains out, if the old man got that lucky. No one would cry.

Not Hoebel, that was for sure. No, the chief would have to skip the funeral, if it came to that.

The police station building came in sight as Hoebel mentally reviewed his plan for early retirement. Buy a beach house for cash, sock the rest away in an offshore account where his soon-to-be ex-wife couldn't get her claws on it. He'd let her pay for the divorce. Georgina wouldn't miss him much.

His thoughts turned again to his least favorite detective. Interesting that Bannon had latched on to the case just as Hoebel was in the process of making the documentation on it disappear into storage. At least the TV reporters had stopped yammering about it during the last few days. The chief guessed that their appeal to the public hadn't turned up any significant new leads. He'd left it to Jolene to sort out the letters and e-mails sent directly to the station house. Not that he'd looked at any. What for?

That little girl wasn't ever coming back. If any remains turned up, he could make 'em disappear.

He parked in his reserved slot and got out, going quickly up the steps to the front doors. When he saw his reflection, he smoothed down his hair, telling himself that it looked okay for a man on the far side of forty. Not thick. Not thin. But hanging in there, like the rest of him.

Hoebel breezed past the rookie at the front desk, whose name escaped him at the moment.

"Morning, Chief."

Hoebel nodded rather than reply. He could see Jolene from here, and he'd much rather chat with her. Even though she was on the phone right now. Probably that boyfriend again. He'd met the guy—he seemed too young for Jolene. Hoebel hooked his thumbs on either side of his belt buckle and walked to her, stopping by the side of her desk to get her to hang up.

She said good-bye in a low voice as he let go of his belt and reached across her for a stack of mail.

"Was that a personal call, Jolene?"

Her hand blocked his as she looked up. "No. I was talking to Doris. And I haven't opened that stack yet."

"Bad girl."

His teasing fell flat. "I was catching up on other things. And I wasn't sure if you were coming in." She gathered up a sheaf of pink-paper memos and a thick pile of letters stapled to the envelopes they'd arrived in. "Here's your messages and the correspondence from yesterday." She thrust all of it at him and he had to take it.

It rankled him a little that she didn't call him chief or sir, but he still felt like flirting. "Looks like I'm popular."

That got him a frosty smile. "I wouldn't know."

Exasperated, the chief opened his hands and dropped the whole mess on her desk in front of the framed picture of her boyfriend. Jolene needed to get her priorities straight.

But he wouldn't write her up for insubordination. She was wearing a short skirt, from what he could see of it. He'd ask her to come into his office to make sure.

"Open today's mail and put the important stuff on top. Bring everything to me in five minutes." Hoebel went into his office and shut the door behind him.

Jolene got busy with a sharp letter opener, slitting one envelope after another without looking up again until Doris came down the hall.

"Jolene, how come you hung up on me?"

"I had to." The younger woman cast a meaningful glance at the closed door. "He wants his mail served on a silver platter."

"Aha. So he decided to show up," Doris said in a low voice. "Big of him."

"Isn't it?" Jolene put the last of the morning's letters on top of the pile. "When I came in there were five burglaries posted on the board. In this town that counts as a crime wave. And we're getting tons of mail about the Montgomery case, not that he cares. The way he swaggers in here makes me sick."

She got up, imitating the way Hoebel walked with his thumbs behind his belt, taking several steps.

Doris laughed.

"It's not that funny," Jolene said with a small smile on her lips. "He's always hitting on me."

"File a lawsuit."

"You have to have proof and it takes years. All I want to do is quit. But I can't afford to. Nick and I want to get married and have a nice honeymoon." Jolene grabbed the letters and papers. "Be right back."

Doris parked herself on the edge of the younger woman's desk. "Leave the door open. I'll sit here where he can see me."

Jolene winked at her as she walked to Hoebel's closed door and knocked.

"Come on in. I'm ready for ya." The chief's drawled reply made Doris roll her eyes with disgust. The women exchanged a conspiratorial smile.

Turning the knob, Jolene went in, opening the door wide and flipping down the stop with her foot, to his obvious annoyance.

Doris made it worse by grinning cheerfully at him. "Hey there. We decided to go out for coffee," she announced. "Can we get some for you?"

Jolene went along with the ruse, nodding at Doris. She set the organized pile of mail on top of his messy in-box, straightening the different-sized papers before they all slid out. "I know how you like it," she purred.

"Uh—" He stopped mid-sentence when he realized he'd been had.

"Skim milk and no sugar, right?" Jolene asked. "Georgina told me you're on a diet."

"Yeah," he muttered.

Bannon unlocked the door to his condo and stepped aside to let Erin go in ahead of him. They had stopped on the way to get her some things at a big-chain drugstore. He'd tried to be unobtrusive, but she hadn't seemed to mind him hovering at the end of various aisles.

You never knew.

He'd checked his rearview mirror often enough on the way here. The roads had been largely free of traffic and no one seemed to be following them.

She had stared straight ahead, holding a sketchpad to her chest like it was a shield. The rest of her art supplies were in an old tackle box next to the large duffel bag that held her clothes.

He had that slung over his shoulder as he entered. Bannon put the duffel down on one of the boxes from the TV station, moving it with his foot to line it up with the other one. His place looked like a storage unit as it was, even without the two giant cartons by the door. Kelly had kept her part of their bargain, maybe too well. Both were probably packed with crazy letters and a gazillion printed e-mails. Too bad he'd forgotten to be careful what he wished for.

"Home sweet home," he said to Erin. "It's kind of a mess at the moment. Sorry about that."

She shook her head. "I don't care. And it's not like you were expecting me."

"No." From somewhere behind him came the almost inaudible whoosh of a furry critter moving at warp speed. He smiled to himself. Babaloo wouldn't come out from his chosen hiding place until Charlie got settled in. And the big black dog had better watch his back.

Charlie circled through the condo, his nose twitching now and then when he came across a familiar-smelling spot. He seemed to remember the place.

"Can you get a good look at that cut?" Erin asked. "I don't think I did."

Bannon sat on the couch and motioned the dog to come to him, using the circle of strong light directly under the lamp to examine Charlie's nose. "No blood. It seems to be healing. But I can call a vet. Want to take him in?"

The dog stood patiently as she came over to look for herself. "I'm not sure, Bannon. What do you think?"

"He seems fine."

Erin sighed and stroked the dog's head. "I guess we'll know if it starts bothering him."

"Yeah." He rumpled Charlie's thick neck fur and then let him wander off. The dog selected an area rug and flopped down on it. "Go ahead and get comfy, boy. We're back to square one."

The unthinking comment made Erin look sad all over again. "Are we? What exactly does that mean?" she asked him softly.

He rose from the couch and went to her. "I really don't know, Erin. Let's take it one thing at a time for now, okay? Until we can figure out what to do. Right now you're here and you're safe."

She nodded, putting the bag from the drugstore by the tackle box with her art supplies and propping the sketchpad against both.

"Did you have plans for today?"

Erin gave him a numb look, not replying for a few seconds. "Yes, but—what time is it?" she asked, looking around for a clock.

He was about to answer when her gaze stopped at the mantel and the framed watercolor he'd bought from her. That rainy day seemed awfully long ago.

"Oh," she said with surprise. "The Chincoteague horses—I'd forgotten about that painting. It looks really nice there."

"I thought so too," he said quickly, grateful to have something to talk about besides what had happened. "I am going to hang it up eventually," he added. "Just haven't decided where yet."

"You don't have to. Sometimes it's fun to move paintings around for a while. Find out where they want to be."

Bannon smiled. "I like that idea."

She smiled back but the moment of happiness faded quickly. Erin seemed too restless to sit. She stood there, rubbing her arms as if she was nervous or chilly or both, and Bannon snapped out of it.

"Do you want to lie down?" he asked. "Let me get the bedroom ready—I tore out of here the second you called."

"Don't go to any trouble."

Bannon interpreted that instantly. "Uh, I speak female. It isn't ready and I have work to do. Just make yourself at home in the meantime."

He went into the bedroom. He really did have work to do. A heap of sweatpants and socks and underwear filled a whole corner. Grubby jeans tossed in that general direction a while ago had snagged on the back of a chair on their downward trajectory. They were still hanging there. Man-type grooming products, some with no tops, were crammed into a cardboard box that had once held hiking boots. How was it that the room had never seemed messy to him until now?

Bannon grabbed empty laundry bags from the bottom of the closet and stuffed his dirty clothes into them, throwing the full bags over to the door. His dress shirts and two suits he never wore got shoved hard against one side of the closet—he took extra seconds to space out the empty hangers for her. Then he wedged the shoe-box and its contents into a dresser drawer and took a pair of clean socks out of it, slipping one over each hand and dusting like a mad-man before he peeled the socks off and stuck them in one of the laundry bags. Good enough. Fresh sheets next. He found some and whipped them on, clean and taut.

His big bed was almost ready for its beautiful occupant. He bit his lip to keep from thinking of her in it. Chestnut hair tumbled over a pillow. Those luminous blue eyes looking up at him as he . . .

Save it for your dreams. Do the right thing, he told himself.

He shook out the comforter and sailed it over the top sheet, straightening it when it settled. Then he punched the pillows into shape.

"That was fast," Erin said when he came out, a laundry bag in either hand.

"Yeah. You're set. Everything but the pillow mint." He gave her a sheepish look.

"Thanks." Her gentle voice communicated more than the single word did.

"So—um—go ahead and take your things in there. I cleared off the top of the dresser for your art supplies and personal stuff. And there's plenty of room in the closet if you want to hang up some clothes."

"I really appreciate everything you're doing, Bannon."

Her soft look melted him. He told himself to keep the conversa-tion light and keep his distance. "Yeah, well—do you want break-fast or anything? You should eat something."

She nodded. "I could manage a slice of toast. Just one. And tea would be great."

He nodded. "No problem. I have bread. And a couple of tea bags—somewhere."

He knew exactly where they were: in a drawer stuffed with Chi-nese takeout menus, soy sauce packets, and enough chopsticks to build a birdhouse.

"Not Earl Grey or anything fancy like that," he added. "Just plain tea."

Something hot to drink would do her a lot of good. She could wrap her hands around the cup. Sip slowly. Nibble on the toast. Not think.

"That's fine." She smiled faintly and walked away from him to pick up her duffel bag.

CHAPTER 14

Another damned beautiful morning. The tall magnolia tree outside the window was covered with white, waxy blossoms, big as pinwheels. But the sunlight hurt his eyes, even through the filmy chiffon of the first layer of curtains. Montgomery yanked the cord that closed the heavy drapes, plunging the study into gloom.

The locksmith installing a turnbolt on the door looked his way, surprised. "Mind if I turn on a lamp?" he asked.

"Be my guest." He sat at his desk and closed his eyes.

There was the click of a switch and then the sound of the drill the man was using. A female voice interrupted.

"What are you doing?"

Montgomery opened his eyes to see Caroline standing in the doorway, staring at the locksmith.

"He's installing a lock, Caro."

"Why?"

Montgomery sighed. "For privacy. Mine."

The locksmith didn't look at either one of them when he spoke again. "Uh, sir—I think I'm missing a part here. Could be in my truck. Back in a sec."

Montgomery waved him away and prepared himself mentally for a tirade from Caroline.

"I haven't been snooping," she said angrily, clenching her fists against her elegantly belted waist.

He didn't argue with that, but studied her instead for a long moment. Then he folded his hands on top of the antique partner's desk. "I hope that we can come to a civilized agreement. I called Ollie Duncan an hour ago and told him to contact your attorney. Shall we let them take it from here and draw up a settlement of some sort? Subject to our mutual approval, of course."

She gasped and her beautifully made-up eyes filled with tears.

"Do you know what I like about lawyers?" he asked in a conversational tone. "They don't cry. At this point in my life, I would rather be billed five hundred per hour than watch a woman weep."

Caroline grabbed up a porcelain figurine of a female nude from the nearest shelf and hurled it across the room. The head cracked neatly off and lay there among the other pieces. Montgomery surveyed the damage but seemed unfazed. "Hmm. Not worth fixing. You bought that, as I remember."

She stood there, shaking with rage. "Yes, I did. And about a thousand other things. I decorated the entire house!"

"Not with your money," he pointed out. "And I suggest you limit yourself to that one item, if you have plans to destroy anything else I paid for."

His controlled tone set her off. "How dare you talk to me like that!" she shrieked. "You can't lock me out of a room in a house I live in! You have no right—"

"Caro, don't. You know it's over." He rose and leaned stiff-armed on his desk, bracing himself with outspread fingers.

He gazed at her steadily, almost amused by how quickly she ran out of steam. Of course she had been snooping. He had no doubt that her lawyer was already reviewing the bogus files she'd taken such pains to download. However, this didn't seem like the moment to tell her that she'd been captured on webcam doing the downloading.

She swallowed a sob, then turned on her heel and stormed out. Montgomery sighed and sat back down, occupying himself with paperwork. The locksmith returned and finished the job in silence.

The day wore on. Caroline went out at some point—he heard her car drive off without noting the time or caring. The housekeeper brought in lunch on a tray after that and took it away untouched. His head ached badly. The smell of food made it worse.

Montgomery locked the door after the housekeeper and returned to the antique desk, opened the secret compartment under the top, and lifted out his laptop. He tapped a few keys, pulling up spreadsheets he'd been working on.

He checked the e-mail. No personal messages came to this address—only updates from Sidney, his accountant. Montgomery read the last one, which recommended a new type of anti-virus software. Given all their precautions, it didn't seem necessary, but he might as well install it.

The program downloaded swiftly but took much longer to sniff through his financial documents and files. Montgomery grew bored watching the box that showed the percentage of checked files, and pushed his chair back from the desk, rising unsteadily.

Dull pain throbbed in his temples. He had to lie down. He went to the sofa and stretched out full length, putting his arm over his eyes and letting his mind drift.

A beep brought him back to full consciousness.

Confused, Monty sat up partway. The room was dark, but then the heavy drapes had been pulled—he dimly remembered doing that in the morning. He listened and heard nothing.

His nap hadn't eased his headache. The dull pain was sharper now. Upstairs—there were pills he'd hidden upstairs.

Monty got to his feet and went over to the desk. His hand hovered over the laptop's keyboard, about to shut it down. But the warning on the screen flashed at him.

He blinked as he read key phrases.

Malware detected. Unable to destroy. Self-replicating virus in system, type unknown. Trojan horse installed and functional but not activated. Firewalls breached, security compromised. Extensive corruption in all directories. User files will be misdirected via . . .

Line after line of baffling code appeared. He scanned it all without comprehending it, until bracketed e-mail addresses popped up at the very end. Only one had a name he knew.

hoebel@wainsvillepd.gov

The brazen bastard. Montgomery's big hands clutched the edge of the desk for support. The screen blurred as he stared into it. He'd been hacked.

Fake company names and tax ID numbers were set up throughout the files, traps waiting to swallow the last of his money. He sat down and keyed in commands, frantically trying to remember the moves in his shell game. The accounts showed no changes other than the ones he'd made in the last several days. If he was remembering right.

The ache in his head was fiercely painful. He forced himself to stay where he was, typing in one last password.

It was the key to the trust account that held the reward money. If unknown electronic fingerprints showed up on it, Montgomery would rat Hoebel out at the highest level of the state government and tip off the feds. The blackmail would end. As for his own financial misdeeds, Montgomery had powerful friends who would arrange for immunity from prosecution, if his new plan to pay back his investors and get out worked.

But if Hoebel had gone so far as to steal the two million, Montgomery would kill him. He would.

He sat back in his chair, pressing his fingertips against eyelids that he had to close. His eyeballs seemed to be about to burst out of his head.

The weird sensation eased and he opened his eyes, seeing the same warnings on the laptop screen as before. Someone had been into the trust account. And gone out again. The money was still there. Every cent of it. And the beneficiary's name was still Ann Montgomery.

His only child wasn't dead. His obsessive review of the security tape had begun to convince him of that. And meeting Erin in person had done the rest. But Ann, his Ann—dear God, he would have to call her Erin—knew nothing of that. And he knew nothing of how she had survived, only that she had. He might be dead before she learned the truth.

Pain, flashing, uncontrollable pain, made his mouth twist on one side.

What he was about to do might be the last move in a game he'd been losing for months. Shaking, forcing himself to focus, he whisked the entire sum into another account, long since drained, held by a bank that served only private clients.

He picked up the receiver of the phone on his desk, an old model with an actual dial. Like him, it still worked well enough. He made a call to the bank's president, an old acquaintance, and steadied his uncertain voice to something resembling authority. He requested that the account be frozen unless he came in and personally authorized any changes.

Done. No questions asked.

But there was one more thing. He jotted down a codicil to his will leaving the money in the reopened account to her, fiercely aware that he had no one to witness his signature. He was in no condition to drive to a notary or wait for anyone to come to the house. Montgomery jabbed at the laptop keyboard again. The tiny light for the webcam flashed. He recorded himself reading the codicil aloud, held it up to the webcam, and put a book behind it to sign his name on camera. A few more clicks to review the result and check that the written words were legible and his voice, clear enough, came next. He saved it and, with clumsy fingers that barely obeyed him, sent the video file as an attachment to his lawyer and his accountant.

Video wills were legal and so would this be. His face, his voice, his signature, each and every word of his intention and instructions were recorded and date-stamped, and safely sent. If Caro found the laptop, she could not destroy or alter what he had done.

Ann would have something if he didn't survive. He wished it was more, far more. At least she would know that he'd given her all he had. Montgomery rose with great difficulty and staggered to the bar. He sloshed bourbon into a short glass and tossed it down without water. Gagging, sickened by the backwash into his raw throat, Montgomery made his way back to the desk.

Caro wouldn't be stopped by a mere lock on a door. He would notify his accountant of the security breach, then shut down the laptop and hide it away.

No. Not yet.

He wanted to see his daughter again.

His fingers felt oddly thick as he opened the file with the security video from the Montgomery mansion.

Bannon was following Erin Randall down the hall.

They had just left Ann's bedroom. Montgomery knew the way to it by heart, as if he had walked it yesterday. As if she were still three years old.

He paused the video on Erin's lovely face as she turned to ask Bannon something. He replied and she looked up, not seeing the electronic eye looking down at her.

Capturing her.

Alive.

Montgomery's breath caught and the pain in his head intensified to the screaming point. Slack, dragged down, his mouth gaped open. Yet he couldn't hear himself scream. A strange silence pervaded the room. Three words echoed but only in his mind.

. . . *keep* . . . *her* . . . *alive* . . .

A flicker of strength coursed through his body and into his hands. Somehow he closed the laptop and thrust it into the compartment.

It was the last thing he did before a tiny blood vessel in his brain ruptured. Montgomery jerked and fell forward onto the desk, arms outstretched as if he were drowning. His weight shut the top. Then he rocked backward in his chair and tumbled out of it to the floor.

Machines hummed. He could hear himself breathe, caught somewhere between dreaming and death in a half-lit room. There were people in the room, coming and going, not talking. An older woman bent over him and he tried to speak to her. His words made no sense. She didn't reply. Something pierced his skin and a tiny flash of pain ran up the inside of his arm. A feeling of peace replaced it. She went away and he lay there motionless.

The room dissolved around him and so did the years.

He saw his young wife walking hand in hand with a little girl— their daughter. They called to him, laughing, coming closer with every step, but they never reached his side. Luanne, he called back. Luanne. He took a step toward them and they vanished, replaced by a burst of brilliant light that dazzled him. His eyes hurt and he began to cry. Tears trickled out from under his closed lids. He didn't see the nurse return or know that she had wiped the tears away.

CHAPTER 15

Returning from his usual morning run, Bannon turned his key in the lock and pushed open the door.

Erin turned around, startled, as he stepped over the threshold, fear in her eyes. It had only been a day since the attack.

He wanted to kick himself. "Sorry," he said. "I should have knocked or coughed or something."

She shook her head. "I would have jumped, no matter what."

"With good reason. Let's decide on a signal or something. So you always know it's me."

"A secret knock? Not shave-and-a-haircut." She looked worried. "Just say your name."

"Right. That opens every door." Bannon put a hand to his bristly chin. "Speaking of shaves, I need one. Mind if I—"

"Don't be silly. This is your place."

"But I want you to be comfortable here." Bannon shut the door behind him and locked it.

It dawned on him that he'd better have another set of keys made. The last thing he wanted was for her to think she wasn't free to come and go, but she wasn't likely to ask him straight out for the keys to his place, considering that she barely knew him. The idea of her having the keys didn't bother Bannon at all. In fact, it made him happy.

"Hey, you need a set of keys. Okay with you if I run out to the hardware store?"

Erin nodded but she didn't smile. He was sure there was something she wanted to say. Finally she said it. "How long am I going to be staying here?"

That was a big question. All he could do was hold up his hands in a gesture of mock surrender. "That's not up to me. As long as you want to."

She swallowed hard. "Okay. I guess neither of us knows the answer. What now?"

"Breakfast," he suggested. "Tea and toast again?"

"Right. But I bet you want something more substantial."

"You read my mind. I can pick something up when I get the keys made. Charlie, want some sausage?"

The dog looked up at him expectantly, too well-behaved to jump up or beg.

"Do you have food for him?" Erin asked.

"I can get a small bag at the market next to the hardware store. One-stop shopping, Wainsville style."

"It seems like a nice town."

He made a face. "You didn't exactly get the scenic tour. I was going too fast for that."

"And looking in the rearview mirror every other second."

"Yeah, well—I didn't see anybody."

"Me neither. I was covering the side mirror."

He studied her for a moment. "Seriously? Good for you."

"I thought"—she hesitated—"I thought if he was following us, I might recognize him. But I really didn't see his face when he tried to break in. Just his outline."

"I wish I had been there," Bannon said with blunt honesty. He and Charlie would have made hamburger out of the guy.

She managed a tiny smile. "That's nice to know. But I'll be okay on my own for now." He hadn't left her at all the previous day.

"Yeah?" She met his searching gaze steadily enough. "All right. Then I'll head out."

"You do that." Her voice didn't waver. She went to the large sketchpad she'd brought and picked it up.

Bannon looked at her curiously. "Got work to do?"

"Always. Beats worrying."

"You're right about that."

Erin moved to the couch and sat down with the sketchpad, smiling at Charlie when the dog padded over to her and lay down halfway, his big head up and alert.

Talk about security. She was as safe as she could be with Charlie there when he wasn't. Bannon smiled inwardly. The dog was living in a fool's paradise, though. His cat still hadn't put in an appearance.

"Erin, did I tell you that I have a cat?"

She looked up at him quizzically. "Maybe."

"He's a big striped monster, just so you know, and he doesn't like dogs. Even this dog. So if Babaloo does a ninja cat death-defying leap out of nowhere—"

She stroked Charlie's head, getting a look of dopey adoration from canine brown eyes. Bannon knew exactly how the dog felt.

"Charlie, we have been warned," she said.

He grinned at both of them. "I think he can take my cat in a fair fight. Too bad the Mighty Bab doesn't fight fair."

"Got it. I'll referee."

"Erin . . ." He wanted to say something more. But she interrupted his thoughts.

"Go run your errands. We can eat together when you come back."

"You sure? I can fix you something in a flash."

"Quit hovering. I can wait."

"Okay. Back in fifteen." Bannon scooped up his car keys and headed out, making sure the door locked behind him.

He came in to see her with the sketchpad open over her lap and a pencil in her hand. With that same light touch he'd noticed when she'd used him for a model, she was making changes on a drawing of a horse. Erin sighed. "I'm not happy with this."

"Looks good from here," he said, shucking his jacket and slinging it over the boxes from the TV station. He set a sack of dog food on the floor beside them. "Can I see?"

She put the pencil to one side and lifted up the pad of paper, facing it toward him. "Montgomery's stallion. Just a preliminary sketch."

"Wow. Keep going," he said.

She flipped the pad shut. "I was thinking of getting out to the stables today. It's a peaceful place. Not too many people. But not lonely."

"Could do you good." No law said she had to stay here. Just his overprotectiveness. Bannon set down the bag with his egg-and-sausage combo. He didn't want her to leave just yet. "But I promised you breakfast."

"Better feed your cat first. He finally showed up."

He looked around. "Where is he?"

Erin pointed at the bottom of the armchair facing the couch and Bannon noticed two glowing eyes in the shadows underneath it.

"He looks too mad to eat," he chuckled.

But Babaloo wriggled out and followed him as he headed into the kitchen. The cat jumped up on the counter to eat a few morsels of kibble.

"You were right. He was hungry."

"Told you."

"Here he comes," Bannon warned her as the cat sprang down to the floor and slunk along the baseboards. "Tell Charlie to watch out."

Bannon came back with a plate and cup holding Erin's minimal meal.

"He disappeared," Erin reported. She sipped and nibbled at her toast and tea as Bannon unwrapped his breakfast and devoured it in three bites. He crumpled up the paper into a ball. "Slam dunk. Into the kitchen can. Watch this."

"From here?"

"Sure." He missed his target. "Okay. I tried."

She laughed a little and handed him her plate and cup when he got up to retrieve the paper ball from the kitchen floor. "Thanks for breakfast."

"No biggie. And I got you those keys," he called to her when he set her dishes into the sink.

Bannon went to his jacket and pulled out two keys on a split ring, jingling them. "Here you go."

"Great." Something about them triggered an emotional reaction in her. "I'm not sure I have my own keys." She shook her head as if she didn't want to think about that. "Are you going to drive me h-home so I can pick up my car?" Her voice almost cracked on the word "home." He understood why. It would be a while before the little house felt safe to her again. It might never.

"I could." They had left the hatchback where it was without thinking twice. He hesitated. "But are you sure you want to? We could rent a car for you here in Wainsville."

"That's not a bad idea," she said slowly.

Bannon didn't want her to change her mind. If someone was stalking her, driving a different car was the way to go, especially since they hadn't been followed here. There was no way of telling if the attempted break-in had been a random event or what.

Her own car was pretty good bait. But it would be a tough trap to spring. He thought for a few seconds before he spoke again. "Look, Erin, I'd like to really go over your house inside and out, see if I can pick up any clues. I was even thinking I could hide minicams in a couple of spots—it won't cost you anything. I had a couple here last time I looked—"

"Why?"

Slow down, idiot, he told himself. He didn't want her to think he was a paranoid gear freak, just because Linc and Deke were in the habit of giving him equipment they weren't using. "Uh, not set up. Just sitting in a box with other stuff from my brothers—you know. Gadgets are an occupational hazard for cops and military and special ops people—anyway, I end up with the extras."

"Oh." She really didn't seem thrilled with the idea. He took another tack.

"It's not permanent. If I have the right cams, I'd hook 'em up to your computer and we could pick up the feed here."

"And what will that accomplish?"

Bannon's expression sobered. "If the creep comes back, I'll have a visual of his face, maybe more."

She shuddered. "I don't want to see it."

"I understand. But I might be able to match him to a visual database. They can filter for a lot of things to get a positive ID. Tattoos, broken down by name, words, and gang affiliation. Broken teeth. Scars—"

Erin's troubled sigh stopped him in the middle of that explanation. She rose from the couch and paced the room, not looking at
him for a minute. Not really looking at anything.

"Besides that," he added, "I want to fix the broken window."

"You mean replace the pane? That's not easy."

"True enough. I guess I'll just board it up. If that's all right with
you."

"It'll have to do."

She bumped into the big boxes and glanced down at her stubbed
toe. "Ouch."

"Sorry. I'll get those out of your way," he offered quickly. "Someone at the TV station sent the viewer responses—"

"Oh. Right. I forgot about that interview you did," she said absently. "How's the investigation going?"

Had she forgotten about their tour of the Montgomery mansion
too? He couldn't blame her if she had. Maybe she just needed to
distract herself, but her question wasn't something he wanted to
answer.

"Okay, I guess, for such an old case," he said noncommittally.
"But I came across a couple of interesting leads. Ask me again in a
week." His sense of responsibility for putting her in danger gnawed
at him. How to tell her—he couldn't. Not yet.

She looked at the boxes again. "That's a lot of stuff. I hope someone knows something about that little girl."

He tensed all over, thinking about the faked birth certificate
he'd tracked down and the possible link between Erin's parents—if
they were her parents—and the abduction of Ann Montgomery.
There was no way in hell he was going to get into that today.

Erin was still in shock from what had happened to her. That he'd
looked at her scrapbook when he'd gone to her house to check on
Charlie, even though she'd showed it to him before—not good.
Taking it one step further and photocopying the handmade card
and what she thought was her birth certificate was totally out of
line.

He fully intended to explain everything. Just not now.

"Erin, you have other things to worry about."

"Yes."

She didn't seem to want him to explain any more than he wanted to. Her agitation came across in her body language. Erin suddenly looked like she was ready to run away. "I hope you don't mind, Bannon, but I have to get out of here."

Whoa. He hadn't expected to hear that, but it wasn't as if he could stop her. "Uh, where to?"

"A nice, quiet barn. Montgomery's will do it. Hanging around with horses is all I want to do right now. They don't talk."

"I can drive you there—wait a minute. No, I can't."

She started collecting her art stuff, looking around, he guessed, for something to carry it in. She went into the kitchen and came back with a plastic shopping bag, twisting it nervously through her hand. "You don't have to," she said. "Renting a car is fine with me."

"That's probably the best plan. I don't want to run into Montgomery at the barn. He doesn't like me."

"Whatever. Let's just go, okay? Where is the car rental place?"

"A mile away."

"I'm ready."

Charlie got up and looked at her, then at Bannon.

"Stay," he said to the dog. "I'll take you out for a run as soon as I get back."

The rental didn't take long and the clerk barely looked at them as he shoved the triplicate forms across the counter for Erin to sign. She insisted on paying for it, refusing his offer to cover the cost.

Come to think of it, he told himself, she had more money than he did at the moment. Half her advance on the painting commission, as in fifteen thousand. Whereas he was still waiting for Chief Hoebel to sign off on his continuance of claim so he could draw his pittance. But something about Erin made Bannon want to put every dime he had on the line if it would make her life easier or happier.

Yeah. He had it bad. And her vulnerability was making it worse.

He drove behind her as far as the discreetly marked private road to Montgomery's stud farm and stables. Erin turned left, waving to him, and he drove onward. No sign of the man himself. Or anyone who looked like an employee. Just a blonde in a luxury sedan, who was parked near the sign and seemed to be waiting for someone. Maybe a horse buyer or a rider from the local hunt club, he thought idly. She sort of seemed like she belonged there, but not quite.

He was miles away before it occurred to him that the blonde might be Montgomery's girlfriend Caroline. Erin hadn't liked her. He guessed that Caroline probably felt the same way.

Then he wondered whom she was waiting for.

Bannon blew out a breath and told himself to stop obsessing over every little thing that concerned Erin. As if that were possible. He already knew the way to her house well enough to drive there in the dark. The early morning rain had let up, but it was going to be another jolting trip over the rutted road to the little house. His back was aching when he finally got out of his car and looked over to hers.

Seemed the same. Before he muddied the ground by walking around, Bannon inspected it through narrowed eyes. No new footprints on this side—the ones he could see were his own, since the stalker had come and gone around the back of the house.

He reached into the car to get the gear he'd scrounged from the box of electronics under his bed. Two tiny vidcams and a motion sensor, plus a spaghetti-like snarl of connector cables, made the canvas bag he'd thrown it all into look lumpy. He'd sort it out inside the house. No doubt he was missing some key part, but he had time. He had a feeling Erin was going to be gone for the better part of the day.

He'd asked her to call him when she was done so he could escort her home. She hadn't seemed to mind.

Bannon tried to stay on the grass as he approached the porch, just in case there was a partial imprint in the mud. Nothing. And the steps showed only his footprints and Erin's. He went up them, taking out the key she'd given him—fortunately, she had brought it with her after all—and unlocking the door.

Inside there was that same faint, sweet smell that he remembered. This time it came to him courtesy of the draft from the broken window. Bannon found some heavy brown paper in her studio area, noticing that it was the same type she'd used to wrap up the painting of the Chincoteague horses he'd bought on another rainy morning.

He went into her bedroom, laying the paper down on the rug and tearing off a piece to pick up the shattered glass and put it into the center of the paper, then folding it up carefully. No telling if the dog or the intruder had touched it first. Old and fragile to begin with, the pane had shattered in both directions. But he would dust it for fingerprints when he got home.

Bannon did a walk-through, grateful for the opportunity to really examine things closely. He forced himself to stay away from the box that held the scrapbook, though. But something else caught his eye.

That pink stuffed bear. The one that looked like Ann Montgomery's. Worth a closer look, too, with the digital microscope he could plug into his laptop. He would do that when she wasn't around. And he wouldn't have to explain to her why he'd brought it back. Women kept stuffed animals from childhood—most likely she'd figure that he was just trying to comfort her somehow.

He hauled the vidcams and cables out of the bag he'd brought and put the pink bear in it.

It took a lot of ingenuity to get it all connected and plugged in. The vidcams had power—a tiny light glowed inconspicuously on the back side of each one. Whether the image feed from her computer would happen and whether they would be able to pick it up from his place were two very big questions.

Nothing ventured, nothing gained.

With a sinking feeling he realized that he hadn't asked Erin for her password. Bannon swore under his breath. He touched a key, hoping she'd left everything on, ready to go, and not password-protected.

She had.

He fiddled with the vidcams, then turned to her computer and prayed their icons would show up.

They did.

He set about hiding them in the applications folder, just in case the stalker went looking for them too.

*   *   *

Caroline stared straight ahead through her windshield. Her lawyer had been kind enough to drive out to the stables and meet her by the entrance to the private road. Then he'd followed her to this secluded pull-off. She hadn't wanted to invite him into the house, or start any rumors by visiting his offices so soon after Monty's stroke.

Once they'd parked side by side, she let him into her car. Jeffrey Burney was a typical middle-aged male with a midlife-crisis-sized sports car, and she wasn't getting into it. Seats that low-slung made skirts ride up, which she supposed was the idea.

Anyway, she doubted that the luxury sedan was bugged. It was Monty's preferred car, and even Monty wouldn't bug his own vehicle.

Jeffrey Burney was looking through papers in his briefcase on his lap, not talking at the moment.

"So did you get a chance to look at the files on the flash drive?" she asked.

"No."

"Jeffrey—I gave it to you two days ago," she chided him.

He found the papers he was looking for and handed several to her. Caroline stared at printed code that made no sense at all. Random letters were interspersed with little squares and arrows and blips. "What the hell is this?"

"The files. What you saw wasn't what you got."

"Don't confuse me."

"Caroline, you were looking at what you thought were financial files on Montgomery's computer."

"I didn't think so. That's what they were," she insisted.

"He or someone he hired fooled you but good. The files were programmed to self-destruct once they were saved to the flash drive you used. The information on them was probably bogus to begin with. And now, as you can see, it's pure gibberish."

Caroline's eyes widened and her hands clutched, about to tear the pages when the lawyer took them back. "Don't. These might come in handy as evidence. I'd like to hire a forensic accountant."

She cursed violently. "How much is that going to cost me?"

"All fees will come out of the final settlement."

"And what are my chances of getting one?"

Burney permitted himself a wry smile. "Not too bad. His having a stroke does complicate matters. I would advise patience."

"Like I have a choice?"

He folded the printouts and slipped them back into his brief-case, closing it with a dignified-sounding snap.

"You can make a better case if you stay with him for now. Do everything a wife would do, see to his needs, run the household, that kind of thing."

"He never let me do any of that."

Jeffrey cleared his throat. "He may not have a choice. From what you've told me, he's partially incapacitated and his prognosis is un-certain."

"He might make a full recovery," she grumbled. "His doctors wouldn't say one way or another. It was a hem-something kind of stroke. Hemorrhagic. Not that common."

"I see. Well, whatever kind it was, you do have a second chance here."

Caroline fumed. "Are you sure?"

The lawyer shrugged. "Judges have a lot of discretion for plain-tiffs like you. The more you seem to be married, the stronger your case for a settlement payout becomes."

She drummed her fingers on the steering wheel. "All right. I guess I can fake it a while longer. I've been doing it for years."

Burney slid her a sidelong glance. "Just remember not to lose your temper, my dear. Or take advantage of his weakness. There are servants in the house and I imagine relatives will be visiting—"

"He doesn't have any. Even if he doesn't think so, that daughter of his that got kidnapped is dead."

"Are you talking about the little girl who was on the news?"

"Yes."

"How do you know she's dead?" he asked.

"She has to be after all this time," Caroline snapped.

The lawyer frowned. "This conversation is between us, of course, but I wouldn't go around blurting out remarks like that if I were you. It seems—uncharitable."

"Jeffrey, I'm a realist."

He shook his head. "Ultimately, how you present yourself to a judge isn't going to have a lot to do with reality. Think of yourself as a loving young wife and act the part. Day and night."

She heaved a sigh. "I'll try. That's all I can promise."

"When is he coming home?"

Caroline looked out the window. "Soon. In a few days. A physical therapist called me today to go over all the stuff he's going to need. An adjustable bed. A walker. Gizmos to pick up things. Pill organizers. I hope I die before I get old."

Burney looked out the window rather than at his client. "Don't talk like that," was all he said.

Bannon pulled in at the entrance to Montgomery's private road hours later, driving fast. Erin's call had come in just as he was putting a few final touches on the vidcam hookup at her house. He'd left it as it was. If it worked, fine. If not, he would go back tomorrow and adjust it. The whole business was a long shot anyway.

The stalker wasn't likely to stick around if she wasn't there. Or so Bannon hoped.

He'd boarded up the broken window and reinforced all the others with screws drilled into the frames, for what it was worth. He hoped her friend in Vermont wouldn't mind.

Bannon turned on the radio and picked up a station featuring a neo-bluegrass band he liked. He listened, content to wait, and then he saw the car she'd rented. He waved to her and she waved back, her expression serious.

To be expected. He was going to take her out or let her order in, whatever she wanted. Long day for both of them—and he suddenly thought of Charlie.

Damn it. Good thing she accelerated as she led him out and kept the pedal to the metal all the way home.

She pulled in first, taking a slot next to the one he considered his, though none of them were assigned by the condo management.

When he got out and went to her, he saw that her expression was not so much serious as sad.

"Hey, Erin. How'd it go?"

She only shrugged, reaching inside her car for the plastic bag of art supplies and her sketchpad.

"Is something the matter?" he asked, catching himself. "Okay, stupid question. Besides what happened this morning, I mean."

"I'm okay," she said. "Let's get inside."

She led and he followed, curious and uneasy. Once he'd unlocked the door, his guilty conscience made him take the dog out at once. When she was ready, she'd tell him what was on her mind.

He heard her in his bedroom, moving around, putting her things into some kind of order, maybe. Erin came back out and sat on the couch.

"Want to talk?" he asked. "You don't have to and I'm not going to bug you if you don't."

"It's Montgomery," she said.

"Oh. I hope he didn't—"

She came right out with it. "He didn't do anything. I was off by myself for hours at first. And then one of the horse trainers happened to come by."

"And?" There had to be more.

"He told me Montgomery had a stroke and was in the hospital. Other than that, the trainer didn't know much. And then Montgomery's bitchy girlfriend—Caroline, I told you about her—well, she came looking for trouble and told me to pack up my stuff and get out."

Bannon absorbed the information. "I'm sorry to hear that about Montgomery. I wouldn't wish a stroke on my worst enemy. But it's a good thing you cashed the check," he said bluntly.

"Caroline didn't seem to think so. Can you believe she had the nerve to even ask me about it? It's not like she could stop payment on it. She didn't sign it. Montgomery did. I feel bad for him if she's all he has to come home to."

He thought back on the blonde he'd seen waiting in the car at the road to the stud farm and stables, trying to remember his impression of her. It had been fleeting, but telling, given what Erin had just said.

That the woman didn't quite belong where she was.

CHAPTER 16

"It's a miracle he can walk," the housekeeper said quietly. She and the butler were looking through a downstairs window that faced the circular drive as Montgomery was assisted out of the rear seat of his car by a strong-looking young woman wearing a scrub top over jeans. Her thick-soled white shoes were the other clue to her occupation: private-duty nurse.

"The doctors try to get patients up and about now. Not like the old days. He didn't spend more than a week in the hospital."

"It's a good thing he can afford help," she said. "If she broke a nail, then where would Mr. Montgomery be?"

The butler knew which woman the housekeeper referred to. "Miss Caroline arranged for twenty-four-hour nursing care in shifts. Someone will be here around the clock."

They watched in silence as Montgomery stood on his own, flanked by Caroline, somewhat overdressed in designer tweeds, and the capable young nurse.

The driver got out on the other side of the car and so did another man, who immediately went over to Monty.

"Is that the doctor?" the housekeeper asked.

"I think so."

"Why is he here?"

"You can thank Miss Caroline. She wants him to brief us on Montgomery's needs. A lot of things will have to change around here."

The housekeeper's frown cut two deep lines on either side of her mouth. "And not for the better, I expect," she muttered.

"We shall see," was the man's curt reply. He went to the door to open it for his employer and the people with him.

It took a while for Montgomery to get up the stairs. He climbed them slowly, clutching the banister as if his life depended on it, holding the arm of the private-duty nurse. But he didn't falter. Caroline waited at the landing with the doctor, who observed the step-by-step progress of his patient with approval.

"Vernette is a gem. She came highly recommended. He's doing well, considering," Dr. Xavier murmured.

Caroline smiled thinly. "I'm glad."

"You might want to think about getting a stair elevator installed, though," he added.

"I've called a few companies. Thank you for the reminder."

She locked eyes with Montgomery when he paused to rest halfway up. His face expressed grim determination—and unhappiness.

He took a deep breath and continued his arduous journey to where she stood.

In another twenty minutes, Vernette had Montgomery comfortably settled on the couch in his study. Caroline perched on it also, but a few feet away. She pulled down her tweed skirt and crossed her slender ankles, putting on an expression of concern.

"Well, here we are," Dr. Xavier said cheerfully, glancing around at the others. The housekeeper, the butler, the driver and some of the day servants, and the nurse looked back at him. "I'm going to call you guys Team Montgomery. He's making a remarkable recovery so far and there are just a few things that I want to discuss with you." He caught Montgomery's glare. "Sir, I don't mean to talk about you as if you can't hear or speak. I'm just addressing everyone here in a general way."

"Then get to the point." Montgomery's growl was somewhat subdued but still very much his own.

"Will do. And I'll try not to be too technical." He turned as if he were addressing a class. "Okay. As most of you know, Mr. Montgomery had a type of brain event called a hemorrhagic stroke. It can be devastating, but he was lucky. Very lucky. He was brought into the ICU not long after his wife found him unresponsive—"

"I'm not his wife," Caroline interrupted him. "And Finch was the one who found him."

The butler wished he could rub his stiff shoulder, which still hurt. He'd broken down the study door to get to Montgomery. The housekeeper had asked him to, worried when the old man hadn't come down to breakfast. Caroline had nothing to do with it. But at least she was being honest with the doctor. For what that was worth.

"Ah—sorry." The doctor gave her an awkward nod. "Moving on, then. We opted for constant monitoring and conservative care, as the MRI revealed no significant bleeding into areas of the brain where you just don't want to have bleeding. Meaning no surgery and no stents. And we're going to continue that approach with the help of Vernette and the other private-duty nurses. And all of you."

He continued to outline practical tips for post-stroke patient care. Caroline listened with half an ear. She was watching Monty, whose gaze was moving around the room, touching on every face but hers. He seemed to be taking in familiar details of the room where he'd spent so much time. Like that ridiculously large antique desk of his. And the computer beside it, which he'd used to bait her, she thought angrily.

Monty still seemed to have all his faculties, unfortunately. But she had an inkling he wasn't as focused. She shifted her ladylike position to avoid contact with him when he sat up a little straighter, suddenly looking intently at the door.

His fierce scowl made her smile with satisfaction. She'd had the new lock removed first thing. For his safety, of course. The drilled holes had been filled in and the marred wood repainted almost perfectly. She could come and go again, not that it mattered. The files on the computer were completely corrupted. She had no reason to sneak in and download things anymore. But she did want to keep an eye on him.

The doctor was discussing the importance of keeping clear pathways in every room to minimize accidents. No scatter rugs, no bric-a-brac, no excess furniture, and so on. Caroline looked again at the antique partner's desk. If she had her way, it would be the first thing to go.

Monty signaled the nurse with a wave of his hand, not caring that he was interrupting the doctor.

"Yes, Mr. Montgomery? Can I get you something?"

"Get me up," he said, adding as an afterthought, "please."

Caroline was surprised. That was a new word for Monty. She stretched out a hand to help as the nurse helped him rise, but he brushed her away.

Leaning on Vernette's arm, he nodded at the desk. "I'd rather sit there," he said. "But I was listening. I'd like to take notes."

The doctor nodded briskly. "That's great. If you can get back to your normal routine without stressing too much, that is definitely what you want to do."

Monty seemed a little annoyed by the other man's relentless cheerfulness but he didn't sneer at it. He took his rightful place in his chair behind the desk.

Dr. Xavier chuckled. "There you go. Back on the throne. How does that feel?"

"Not bad." Montgomery opened one of the side drawers and took out a pen and paper. "Go on, Doctor."

Xavier began to advise the others what to watch for in terms of recurring symptoms. He glanced down once, unable to pass up the chance to assess his patient's handwriting, but that didn't stop Montgomery. He took notes now and then, writing slowly and keeping his hand steady by resting it on the smooth paper.

Montgomery didn't look up when Caroline came over and stood behind him. She put a hand on the back of his chair and leaned down to read his notes, which were close to perfect. Not as forceful as his handwriting generally was, but there was no trace of shakiness. "Look at that. You're doing great," she said reassuringly.

She gave him a half hug, draping her arm over his shoulders as she tapped the paper with a manicured fingernail. "I'm so proud of you, Monty." She pressed her cheek to his in a show of affection. Then he wrote a few more words for her eyes only.

Leave me alone.

Caroline straightened, fixing a smile on her face for the benefit of everyone else.

She had to sleep sometime. He knew his homecoming must be a strain on her and once her audience had departed, Caro disappeared, going into her own room around nine o'clock without saying good night. Really no different from their previous routine. She hadn't shared his bed for months.

Montgomery settled into an armchair and stayed up with a book he wasn't reading, watched discreetly by the next nurse in the shift rotation from the screened area set aside for her in his room.

He dodged her attempts to chat and eventually the late hours and quietness got to her. In a little while she dozed off. The woman lacked Vernette's energy, but that was a good thing. The night nurse had sunk down into her armchair, sleeping heavily, her mouth open.

He was already feeling somewhat better. It might be worth his while to retain Vernette, just as a buffer between him and Caroline. When he was recovered, he would definitely fire the others—and find out who'd hired them in the first place. No one had power of attorney over his medical care, not even Ollie Duncan, but Caroline was acting as if she did. She seemed so confident. Had she wangled money out of his lawyer somehow?

Keeping an eye on the sleeping nurse, he set aside the book and rose from his chair, making his way slowly but surely back to his study.

One hand touched the place where the lock had been removed from the door, before he lowered it to turn the doorknob. That morning he'd half expected to find that Caroline had made good on her threats to sell his favorite desk. Perhaps she'd been afraid of seeming overly bossy in front of Dr. Xavier or the servants.

He crossed the room and sat behind the desk once more, tired by his brief journey to it. Montgomery rubbed his eyes, feeling irritable and unfocused. He'd had a reason for coming in here, but it had floated out of his conscious mind.

Par for the course, he supposed. His legendary willpower was going to have to see him through this.

The renowned neurologist at the hospital who'd consulted on his case had taken the trouble to personally explain that he might have memory lapses at unexpected times, especially if he was under stress.

Besides the MRI and CAT scan, the bloodwork and drug regimen and constant observation, Montgomery had been subjected to some ridiculously simple tests over and over again. His team of doctors seemed pleased by his curt answers. Who is the president? Very good. How old are you? Right again. What day comes after Tuesday? That's correct.

Maybe at his age they didn't expect much. All Montgomery had wanted was to get out of there.

The neurologist had added that there would be good days and bad days, and topped off that trite comment with the inevitable advice to take them all one day at a time. Almost as an aside, the man warned him about mood swings and senior moments before scribbling a bunch of useless prescriptions that supposedly would cure them.

Caroline would have them filled—more little bottles for her to obsess over. He wouldn't take them.

Montgomery lifted the lid of the desk and withdrew the laptop as he remembered why he was there. He always checked his accounts late at night. It had been too long. His sense of time seemed altered by his hospital stay, and looking at a calendar made him uneasy. Many days had gone by, shadowy and lost, because of the heavy medication he'd been given. He could still hear faint echoes of disturbing dreams.

Luanne had come to him. And so had his lost daughter. Both were gone from his life forever, but they had seemed so real in his drugged visions that their laughter lightened his burden.

Until he woke up to computerized machines and the peering eyes of strangers and loneliness that swallowed his soul.

He forced himself to pay attention as the screen came to life. He had to get back on track. Financial companies didn't run themselves into the ground on their own, he thought bitterly. The frantic effort to stave off the inevitable collapse and its consequences had probably been enough to burst a blood vessel in his brain. He was still a CEO of . . . whatever was left. The thought made his mouth twist sourly.

Montgomery looked at the system configuration, just to reassure himself that the extra memory he'd had installed was still there and still available. He'd come close to maxing out what a laptop could hold. But using that memory was the only way he'd be able to fill in the gaps in his own.

He was worried.

In another second, something shorted out in his mind, a black, spreading sensation that lasted several seconds. With a sudden feeling of doom, he remembered that something devastating had happened here in this chair while he was working on this laptop. What was it?

His brain would not cooperate. His memory strained for an answer. Something had happened before the stroke. It had to do with money. And betrayal.

He could just barely recall being overcome by vengeful rage. And then sorrow. The emotions had been connected somehow.

No names came to mind. Except the president's. The neurologist would have applauded. He was frantic.

He paused, fingers above the keyboard, trying to remember passwords he'd never written down and never saved in the computer.

Again he drew a blank. His heart pounded. Mindful of his blood pressure and the likelihood of another stroke, he endeavored to calm himself by taking deep breaths. That left him light-headed.

What were his passwords?

He racked his brain, realizing with frightened certainty that parts of his memory were wiped as clean as the white-tiled walls of the hospital he'd just left. The stroke had been small, but he was more impaired than anyone seemed to think. Retrieving what he wanted without passwords would require help he couldn't summon in the middle of the night.

Montgomery sat and stared at the scattering of file icons displayed on the screen, opening each, finding nothing useful. But the last one was a video.

Distracted from his worries, he opened it, jolted by the familiarity of the background. A young woman walked through the old Montgomery mansion. He struggled to remember her name. He knew it. He had to know it. The sensation of pressure in his head eased and it came to him.

Erin Randall.

He slumped back with a sigh of relief. The artist from the historical society, of course. He'd commissioned her to portray his winning horse. That was why she looked as familiar as the hallway she walked through. But—damn it to hell. Some other memory connected to her nagged at him.

When had he last looked at this video? And why had she been recorded doing something that seemed perfectly innocent to him now? He clicked on various little icons, searching for information.

Last opened . . . he peered at the date in the list of information on the file. Aha. He'd looked at it on the day of his stroke. And he'd left it on his screen where he could easily open it again. So it must have been important.

Why?

Anger and frustration bubbled up in him. He paused the video and closed the file, then shut down the laptop, returning it to the hidden compartment with shaking hands, knowing that it held critical information he was in grave danger of losing.

Montgomery told himself not to fall into the holes in his head. Hardly a scientific description, but that was what it felt like to remember some things and not others.

His confusion exhausted him. He wanted to lie down and close his eyes and not think. Montgomery gripped the edge of the desk and got himself up, then walked stiffly out of the room. If he could make it to his bed, he might be able to sleep.

He felt somewhat stronger in the morning, but there still seemed to be odd gaps in his thoughts. Lying on his back and contemplating the ceiling soothed him a little. Montgomery roused himself with an effort and went into his bathroom, where he stared at his face in the mirror. He looked haggard and somehow lost. He rubbed the stubble on his jaw, not trusting himself with a razor just yet. But he was damned if he'd ask for help. Somehow he'd gotten into pajamas by himself last night. He didn't remember how.

Montgomery was glad the night nurse was gone. He usually sat alone at the breakfast table, so it didn't matter if he looked grizzled and old and sloppy.

He found a bathrobe and put it on, then headed for the stairs. Going down was a test of coordination and balance that made him tremble a little when he felt the parquet of the first floor under his bare feet. He had forgotten to put on slippers.

Like a beacon, the morning sun shone brightly out of the open doorway of the dining room where breakfast was always laid out for whoever wanted it. He went that way. A flash of fear hit him when he saw Vernette and Caroline sitting across from each other at the set table. His unsightly appearance was beside the point. He would have to make conversation. What if his mind went blank again? He would stick to short answers and not ask questions himself.

The nurses were paid to observe him—that was a routine part of their job. Caroline had her own reasons.

Look at her, he thought.

Caro had never come down to breakfast in all the years they'd lived together. Now she'd turned herself into a faux wife overnight. Full makeup. Hair blown smooth and tied back with a ribbon. Everything but the frilly apron.

She looked up when Monty came into the room, startled. Vernette rose immediately.

"Did you come downstairs on your own?" the nurse asked.

"Obviously." He took the chair she pulled out for him.

"You shouldn't have done that, honey," Caroline chided.

The nurse returned to her chair. "I apologize, Mr. Montgomery. It's my fault for not going up right away. The night nurse said you were sleeping."

"Yes, I was."

Caroline made a gracious gesture at a platter of scrambled eggs and bacon, and picked up a set of serving tongs, which she clacked at him.

"What would you like?" she chirped, as if nothing at all was amiss and today was just like every other ordinary day in his life.

"Coffee," he said. An insulated pitcher had been set on the table near Vernette. "With sugar."

"No problem." The nurse poured him a cup and sweetened it with a wink.

She didn't mean it to be flirtatious, just friendly. Vernette radiated kindness and practicality. Today she was wearing a different-colored scrub top, just as baggy as yesterday's, and the same thick-soled shoes. In a lot of ways she was the antidote to Caroline. He could use a friend in the house. "Thank you," he said.

Caroline clacked the tongs again, reminding him of her unwanted presence. "Mon-tee. Pay attention. Eggs? Bacon? What would you like?"

"Just eggs," he said. "No salt. And no bacon. Doctor's orders."

"You do have to get your blood pressure down." She served up his request and set the tongs on the side of the platter. "I hate to say I told you so."

"Then don't." Montgomery added a slice of dry toast to his plate and ate quickly.

Caroline and Vernette exchanged a look, which he ignored.

"Is there anything you'd like to do today?" the nurse asked him brightly. "I'm here to help."

Getting down the stairs had seemed like a major accomplishment. What was there for him to do while Caroline was awake and able to snoop?

"I-I'd like to visit the stables. By myself," he added with a glance at Caroline.

Caroline looked annoyed. "On your first day back? You should rest."

"I did. I won't stay in bed all day."

"If you go, you can't go alone."

He brushed a few crumbs from his mouth with a napkin and threw it down on the table. "Don't tell me where I can go and what I can do, Caro. Is that clear?" He rose unsteadily and Vernette was beside him instantly, offering unobtrusive assistance.

Caroline looked at him with open disgust. "You can't drive your-self, Monty."

She was right, but that sharp reminder of his frailty hurt. He stiff-ened his spine and tried to think of something to say.

"I can take you. Don't worry," the nurse told Caroline. "I'll stay with him every step of the way."

Caroline looked even more annoyed when Monty didn't argue with Vernette.

The task of dressing seemed almost too complicated to bear. But he managed most of it with Vernette's help. She held on to his shirt. Standing there, he wavered, then looked at her a little des-perately.

"Take a few minutes in the armchair," was all she said. "I'd like to get a baseline BP before we do anything else. Okay with you?"

He nodded and sat without objecting. Her matter-of-fact pres-ence was a comfort. Silently, Montgomery watched her unroll the equipment and get set to take his blood pressure.

A few steady squeezes inflated the cuff, and he matched his breathing to them. Nice and easy. Earpieces of the stethoscope in, she kept an eye on the gauge and a couple of fingers on the cool metal disk at his elbow.

She smiled down at him in a little while. "I like that number. You're good to go. But you have to let me help you. Skip the macho nonsense, okay?"

"All right," he muttered.

In another hour he was in the car, in the front seat to the right. Idly, he thought that he had never been a passenger in his own car. The sensation was a strange one.

Vernette checked the backseat, making sure she had what she needed as Montgomery stared through the windshield, ignoring Caroline, who'd come out to see them off and do some conspicu-ous fussing.

"Are you sure about this, Vernette?" she asked.

"He should be fine," the nurse replied. "Not like he's going rid-ing or anything. Just an easy walk through the stables and then we come back here, right, Mr. Montgomery?"

He gave a curt nod, throwing an angry look at Caroline. She backed away as Vernette slid behind the wheel and drove slowly forward on the circular drive.

She stopped and made a right turn onto the winding road that would take them out and away from the house. Montgomery leaned his head back and took in what he saw with a feeling of gratitude so strong it almost made him weep.

The dogwoods were in full bloom. Early flowers sprang at their roots. Green everywhere, unfurling on each twig of the taller trees and shooting up from the moist earth.

He was alive. He was going to make it.

"What a beautiful day," Vernette said. She seemed just as happy to be away from the house as he was.

"Yes, it is."

The warm atmosphere of the stables seemed to welcome him— Montgomery felt restored by the mingled smells of hay and horses and manure. One by one, the grooms and trainers stood when he walked by with Vernette, pausing in their routine to greet him the way they always did.

He stopped by the office of the stud operation, exchanging a few words with the two men and one woman there, people who'd been hired when the money was flowing like water. Not by him. Their names escaped him before he could introduce them to Vernette, but he didn't worry about it. His staff and stable employees were accustomed to lord-of-the-manor indifference from him. It would be a useful screen for his mental lapses. If he was too polite, he'd give himself away.

"Looks like you have work to do," he said pleasantly enough, waving to the three of them without going in and sitting down to chat.

"This is quite an operation," Vernette said. "I'm impressed." She was studying an enormous framed chart on the wall, faded but meticulously hand-lettered, that showed the bloodlines of the most famous Montgomery horses.

"All champions," he said. "Would you like to meet the latest in the line?"

"Sure."

He took the arm she offered and they walked slowly to where Take All was stabled. Vernette listened to him talk about the stallion's wins with interested patience.

Montgomery didn't have to brag when they reached the stall. The magnificent horse was being groomed by an older man who spoke to him softly, a hint of an Irish accent in the soothing words. Vernette stood and watched, fascinated.

"He gets the royal treatment," she said softly.

Montgomery nodded. "And he deserves it. He'll generate millions in stud fees when he retires from the track."

"Oh. That makes sense. Hey, next time he's entered in a race, let me know. I want to be in the grandstand cheering him on." She grinned at Montgomery. "I can't believe I got to see a famous horse this close."

"We can come again tomorrow." His stance wobbled a little and he reached for a thick beam to brace himself. Vernette offered her arm again and he took it, feeling an odd cloudiness begin to drift through his mind. The concerned glances that flew between the groom and trainer and the stablehands went over his head. But he had the last word. "Good work, Freddy," he said to the groom.

The man looked up, surprised. "Thank you, sir. Take's in fine fettle, as you can see."

Montgomery nodded and let Vernette lead him tactfully a little ways on.

"Do you want to sit down?" she asked.

"I think that would be a good idea."

She looked ahead to a wooden bench, but he shook his head. "Someplace a little less public."

Vernette understood about male pride. They went another thirty feet or so before she stretched up on tiptoe to look into an empty stall, one of several with no occupants. "How about a bale of hay? They're stacked two deep in here."

"Fine."

She glanced up and down the wide center aisle of the stables. No one was coming their way or even looking at them. Vernette unlatched the stable door and went in with him.

Leaning on her just a little more, Montgomery let her assist him and sat down heavily on the nearest bale.

He sighed with relief. "I really was tired. Thank you."

"You're welcome," she told him. "Do you want to go back? I can probably drive the car over to this wing of the stables."

"No. Not yet."

He breathed deeply and stayed where he was.

"Take it easy. Slow and steady. One day at a time."

"Now where did I hear that before?" he asked wryly, answering his own question before she could. "Oh, right. The neurologist. My memory is shot. Things that are supposed to connect just don't."

He stopped himself from saying more. His utter failure to re-member his passwords last night wasn't something he was going to share. Or that bits and pieces of strange dreams were getting in the way of rational thought. He was relying on a way of thinking he'd never trusted: intuition.

She smiled in a kind way that made him nervous. "It comes back. Don't try to think too much or do too much."

"Believe me, I can't."

"And try not to get angry with yourself."

He looked at her narrowly. "How did you know I was?"

"You want a straight answer?"

"I think I do."

Vernette folded her arms across her chest. "Brain events affect personality and perception. Moods can change like that." She re-leased one hand to snap her fingers. "Angry, happy, confused, sad—and they keep changing. Accepting help means admitting you need it. Men fight it."

Montgomery managed to laugh. "Is that bad?"

"Not necessarily."

Her brusque words made sense to him. "Okay. Thanks for the lecture. I needed that."

"Just so long as you remember it," she said dryly. "But this place does you good."

"Hmm." Getting away from Caroline had something to do with that.

Vernette looked all around her surroundings and up into the

rafters, then back at him. "I can see why. This is the first time I've been in an actual stable. Although I used to read a lot of horse books when I was a kid. That was as close as I got."

"I practically grew up in this one. My father taught me everything I know about horses."

"Lucky you."

He nodded, not wanting to go on and on like a foolish old man. But what he'd said was true. As a boy, he'd driven out in the morning from the family mansion with his father in the Packard. But not even that glorious car could compete with the horses they'd kept then.

Memories flooded his mind, made stronger by the setting. The way his father had lifted him up on a hay bale that scratched his bare calves between his short pants and his socks, making him wait so he could chat with everyone in the stable—or so it had seemed to him at the time. He'd been chucked under the chin and greeted by his nickname. Hughie. How he'd hated the sissy sound of it— and he'd hated getting his hair ruffled almost as much. Montgomery Senior never scolded him when he'd jumped down, eager to be off and hoping to talk a groom into saddling up one of the better-behaved ponies for him to ride.

And at the end of the day, sometimes even far into the night hours, his father would bring him along for one last walk around the barn, seeing that all was well and the horses settled. It was a ritual he'd almost forgotten about in the last years, though he had done the same thing on his own once his father had died.

Not that he'd ever brought his little daughter along. Ann was always in bed by seven. Occasionally she tagged after him during the day, hand in hand with her mother or her nanny. Keeping a respectful distance.

He'd always been too busy. And then, on that horrible night, she had been stolen from her bed. He hadn't been at home. His eyes filmed with tears that he forced back. He had never come to terms with her loss.

"Mr. Montgomery—"

"What?" His reverie came to an end. He looked at Vernette and heaved a sigh.

"Are you all right?"

He shook his head. "Maybe I should go home."

"Okay. If you're ready—" She broke off, startled by the appearance of the man who'd been grooming Take All. Freddy was looking over the stable door at them, his gnarled hands on the top, absently running over the bite marks of countless horses. "Hello. Where did you come from?" Vernette asked.

The groom jerked his head in the direction they'd come from. "From His Majesty's stall, of course. Sorry to startle you."

"It's all right. What is it, Freddy?" Montgomery asked.

"Ah—I just wanted to say, sir, that it's good to see you back."

"It's good to be back." But there was an underlying melancholy in his voice. The groom stayed where he was.

"Yes?" Montgomery asked.

"I was wondering, sir, about that Miss Randall."

"What about her?"

The groom looked from the nurse to his employer, seeming nervous. "She was here doing drawings of Take All—very good, they were. But when you took sick, Miss Loudon went on the warpath, so to speak, and had a few words with her."

Montgomery straightened and his eyes narrowed.

"Not very nice words, sir. Not nice at all," Freddy added. "I know you wanted Miss Randall to do a portrait of Take All, but Miss Loudon told her to go and not come back. She didn't think anyone heard, but I did."

"Thank you, Freddy," Montgomery said in a voice that held no trace of vagueness. "I'll look into that."

"I thought you would want to know." The groom tipped a cap he wasn't actually wearing at the older man and left them alone again.

Montgomery was silent for several moments, rubbing his forehead. When he looked at Vernette, his eyes were steely. "Did Caroline mention any of this to you?"

"No."

"What did she say?"

"Ah—mostly she talked about her concern for you. She wanted to know everything about your care." Vernette hesitated. "She did warn me that it would be tough to keep you quiet."

"Just so you know, she's not in charge, Vernette."

The nurse nodded.

"And neither is Dr. Xavier," he added. "I am fully capable of managing my life without those two. Although I like you."

Vernette gave him a wary look.

"Not in that way," he said bluntly. "But I think we understand each other. You seem very capable. Before we go, there is one thing I'd like you to do."

"Okay."

He smiled grimly. "Get me Erin Randall's phone number. I want to call her from here."

"But where—"

He forestalled her question with a raised hand. "Someone in the office will have it. They schedule her sessions. We don't let just anyone wander around, you know."

"If you say so." Vernette went to the stable door and looked down the aisle, then back at him. "Stay here," she said.

Montgomery braced himself on the tightly packed straw with an extended hand. He listened as she buttonholed a passing stablehand and told him to come back with Erin's number.

"Did you bring a cell phone?" the nurse asked when she came back in.

"No. Do you have one?"

She felt in her pockets and found hers. "Here it is. Just dial the numbers, then press the little green button that looks like a telephone receiver." She went to the door again and looked down the aisle. "This sure is a big place. I thought that was him coming back with the phone number—it isn't."

He wasn't listening to the second part of what she said. Her well-meaning instructions had angered him. "Believe it or not, I know how to use a cell phone," he said impatiently. "I'm not that old."

"I just wanted to be sure. . . . Mr. Montgomery, are you all right?"

Suddenly her voice faded, as if she were speaking from some distance away.

"I want to see . . ." He felt confused again, almost not hearing the end of his own sentence, though he had muttered a name.

"Come again? I didn't catch that."

He collected himself. "I want to see Erin Randall."

"Oh, okay. You said Ann."

"My mistake." He met Vernette's steady gaze. Did she know that sad story? Private-duty nurses got to watch a lot of TV. She didn't say anything else. He wasn't going to explain.

Last night had proved to him that his memory was not to be trusted. His hospital dreams of Ann and her mother might still haunt him now and then, but they were only dreams. Surely the way the lovely faces of all three had merged in his besieged mind was a side effect of blood on the brain.

He hoped the bleeding had stopped. Somehow he knew it hadn't. He noticed that the stablehand had returned. Summoning up all his strength, he took the slip of paper with Erin's number on it from the nurse. He waved her away, out into the stable's center aisle so he could make his call in something like privacy.

CHAPTER 17

Erin snapped her cell phone shut and put it on the coffee table. Excellent. Maybe the bad luck was ending.

She'd been hoping to get that call. Feeling better, she hugged herself. Charlie scrambled up from the floor, looking worried and coming over to her.

"It's okay, boy. I really did get the job." She sank her hands into his thick ruff and gave him a neck rub. The dog panted a little, enjoying the impromptu massage.

The cell phone vibrated on the coffee table before it rang again. She grabbed it and flipped it open without looking at the number on the little screen, assuming it was Bannon.

"Hey, guess what," she said softly. More than anything she wanted him to know she was okay. "The book cover is a go. The art director just called and—"

"Miss Randall?"

She started at the sound of the deep male voice. Not Bannon's. But familiar.

"Who is this?"

"Hugh Montgomery. On someone else's cell phone. I assume my number would have come up on yours."

"Yes, it would have—" Her eyes widened and she couldn't think of anything remotely intelligent to say for a few seconds. "Oh my gosh. How are you? I heard that—that you've been ill."

"I had a stroke," he said in a flat tone that didn't invite questions on the subject. "But I seem to be making a remarkable recovery."

"That's great," she said sincerely. "I'm really happy to hear it."

"Thank you." He paused as if he was collecting his thoughts.

Erin didn't jump in or talk for the sake of talking, but waited for him to speak. She was so surprised to hear from him that she couldn't have done anything else.

"I understand that Caroline Loudon chased you out of the stables."

"Ah—" She hesitated. "I wouldn't put it quite like that. But she did ask me to leave."

"She had no right to do that."

"Oh."

"I hope she didn't discourage you or scare you."

The truthful answer would be yes on both counts, but she replied as politely as she could. "Not really."

"Then you can proceed with the painting per the commission contract. I would like to view your preliminary sketches if you don't mind," he said, adding quickly, "Just for my own enjoyment, of course. You're the artist. I'm not looking for creative control."

Erin nodded. He was reaching out in a way she never would have expected.

"Sure," she said. "Uh, when? Are you home now or in the—" She had no idea if he was in the hospital or a rehab facility. He certainly sounded coherent. Almost commanding. She wasn't going to ask him for particulars. She didn't know much about strokes in general, and she knew absolutely nothing about the details of his.

"I'm at home—right now, I'm at the stables," he corrected himself. "Which is why I just heard about Caroline. I got the short version of your encounter."

"Let's leave it at that." Erin really didn't want to cross swords—or maybe it would be high heels—with Caroline again.

"I understand." There was a faint trace of amusement in his voice. "You won't have to deal with her in the future."

She didn't know what to say to that. Erin, thinking, reached out to stroke Charlie and look into his understanding eyes.

The man on the other end of the call gave a discreet low cough and Erin realized she hadn't responded to the last thing he'd said.

"Thank you, Mr. Montgomery." That covered all the bases.

"As far as meeting, you can pick the time. Since you're going to be at the stables again, that's probably easiest."

"Yes. How about, oh, two o'clock next Tuesday?" She picked the time and day because they rhymed, sort of. No other reason.

He seemed to be consulting a calendar. "That's fine," he said. "I'll see you then. Nice to talk to you, Erin."

"Yes—same here. Thank you so much, by the way. For every-thing."

She snapped the cell phone shut and put it in the center of the coffee table. If it rang again, she would let the call go to voicemail.

She pushed herself up and off the couch, going into the bed-room to look for her running shoes. Charlie could use the exercise and so could she. Erin needed to think, and she didn't do that too well cooped up inside four walls.

She put the shoes on and laced them tightly, then brushed her hair back into a ponytail. A sweatshirt got tied around her waist in case the weather changed.

Charlie responded to her whistle with alacrity. She didn't bother to clip on his leash, knowing that he would move by her side with military precision. Erin opened the condo door and they went out together. The dog did an about-face and sat when she paused to lock it.

She patted his head. "Good dog. Great move. I'd call that an about-snout, actually. Okay with you, Charlie?"

He wagged his tail and they began their run right there in the hall, dashing down it and outside.

She didn't see a short, stockily built man with a baseball cap pulled down over his eyes squatting between her rental car and Bannon's.

Jim Canver saw her, though. He stayed squatting even though it killed his aging knees, waiting until her bouncing ponytail was a block away before he completed the task of planting a GPS beacon in the wheel well of Bannon's car.

There was nothing to spying anymore, he thought, getting up with difficulty. These GPS babies were slap-and-stick easy. Of course, the thing might get scraped off on a rough road. But

Hoebel had told him to get a cheap one. The chief was feeling the economic pinch like everyone else in Wainsville. He'd complained about having to take some kind of a salary cut himself and forcing some of his non-uniformed staff to sign up for unpaid furloughs.

Tough luck for those guys. But more work for guys like him. Jim walked casually to his own car five spaces away and drove off.

Linc's house was near the Maryland border but he could see details of things hundreds of miles away. Bannon leaned over Linc's shoulder, looking at the inside of Erin's house on a really good high-resolution monitor. "I'm impressed."

The vidcam Bannon had planted on Erin's shelf was moving in place, following commands his brother entered into his computer, which were sent to hers and beamed out wirelessly from there to a tiny chip in the camera.

"It works great."

"Told you it wasn't junk," Link said.

"Sorry if I insulted you, bro. The thing looked pretty beat-up when I took it out of the box."

Link entered another command that made the vidcam swing from side to side. "So that's her place."

"Not at the moment. She's staying with me since the break-in. I boarded up the window."

Link shrugged one broad shoulder. "Maybe you should have left it the way it was. The creep could come back the same way."

"That's an idea. He could rip his guts out on the broken glass and hang there until we arrived."

"Nice way of putting it. And now she's with you? How's that working out?" He glanced up at his older brother. They resembled each other, though the scar that ran down Linc's cheek was one major difference. But the dark hair and strong build were a lot alike.

"Okay. I wish she wasn't so sexy. I keep trying not to notice."

"Succeeding?"

"Not often. Linc, it's not just that she's sexy. She's all-around amazing. A talented artist. Really interesting to talk to. Smart. Gentle. I could be in love."

"Requited or unrequited?"

Bannon thought. "She likes me. I think."

"A lot? A little?"

"Hey, the prowler scared her out of her wits. Right now, I'm playing it cool."

"You look like hell. Getting any sleep?"

"Not a whole hell of a lot, no. I'm bunking down on the sofa. She's got the bedroom."

Linc grinned. "What a hero. You get to toss and turn and fight with a cat who wants to sleep on your head while Erin gets to stretch out in a king-sized bed."

"She's worth it," Bannon said stubbornly.

"Huh. You're right. Could definitely be love." Linc rocked back in his chair. "She knows you're doing this, right? She approved the video feed in advance?"

"Yeah. Not in writing."

Linc rocked back up. "Don't you feel funny knowing her passwords?"

"She'd left everything on. I didn't need them."

"Even so."

Bannon found a chair and sat on it backward. "Basically she trusts me. That feels pretty good. All I'm looking at is the feed, and that's because she asked me to. Scout's honor."

"I'm holding you to that," Linc said. "A gentleman never looks into a lady's underwear drawer, reads her e-mails, or dates her friends. Unwritten law."

"Glad you remembered, considering I taught you all that when you were sixteen." Bannon returned his attention to the monitor.

"Ah, those were the days," Linc mused. "I didn't even have a cell phone. Or a computer."

"Who did?"

Linc got up and went over to the coffee machine. "I got the looks and I got the smarts. Just lucky, I guess."

"Yeah. I got the aggravation of having two younger brothers. How's Deke, by the way?"

"Fine, last I heard. He'll be in the DC area in another month, maybe two. We can go out together, just like the old days. The Bannon boys know how to raise hell." He lifted his cup of coffee in a toast to them all. "Citizens, lock up your daughters." Linc took a sip of coffee and added thoughtfully. "Of course, you and Erin could be a serious item by then. Sounds like it's the real deal."

"I want it to be. She's the girl of my dreams. Sounds corny, doesn't it?"

"Sounds like you."

Bannon didn't answer. He saw a shadow fall in the farthest corner of her living room. Then it vanished.

"Hey, I think I saw something. There." He pointed.

Both men were instantly alert. Linc took his seat and cut out that section of the feed with a keyboard command, enlarging it inside its own box. "Check this out. I coded that function myself."

Bannon looked intently at the enlargement. "Can you move left a little and do the same thing?"

"Sure."

There was the shadow again. Linc stared intently at the screen. "I see it."

He moved the box around, capturing different parts of the living room. The shadow proved elusive. Then, all of a sudden a contorted face filled the monitor, so close to the vidcam it blurred. The feed went black.

Linc shoved away from the computer and scrambled to his feet. "Let's go."

"In your car?"

"I picked you up in it. Coded government plates. We can go as fast as we want."

They scrambled for their jackets and grabbed a couple of guns in holsters almost as an afterthought.

The intruder was long gone by the time they arrived. He'd taken the trouble of picking the lock and had left the door open. They stood at the edge of the main room, examining the floor for prints, tracked mud, or other identifiers, seeing none.

"Doesn't look like he dropped anything."

Bannon snorted. "Too bad. Been known to happen. A driver's license would be nice."

"Then we wouldn't get to investigate."

"Linc, if I got a chance to use him for target practice, I would. He knows he was watched." He pointed his gun across the room before holstering it.

The vidcam was dangling from the shelf, its power cord yanked out.

"We can dust that for prints," Linc said.

Bannon nodded, going over to it without touching it. He'd put it on a high shelf. The man had been tall enough to reach it with ease.

"Where's the other one?"

Bannon looked around and spotted the second vidcam exactly where he'd left it. A quick look at the back of it showed that the light was out. For some reason it had malfunctioned.

He found a clean rag among Erin's painting supplies and used it to move the vidcam and lift the power cord.

"First rule of troubleshooting: check the freaking plug," his brother muttered.

"What I'm doing. Oh hell, will you look at that." The insulation on the wire had been nibbled. "Mice. Great."

Linc walked most of the way into the room.

"Hold on," Bannon said. He stopped his brother with an outstretched hand as he looked down. "Check out that piece of paper. Ten o'clock. Under the table."

Linc sighed. "Erin is an artist. Let me take a wild guess. She has paper. Lots of paper."

"Yeah, but that looks like a crumpled receipt."

"So?"

"Erin keeps things tidy. I don't remember it from the last time I was here."

"Pick it up carefully, dude."

Bannon used the same rag to retrieve the crumpled bit of paper, squatting and reaching under the table. He rose and opened it carefully.

Then he swore under his breath. "It's from a restaurant. And guess who signed it."

Linc lifted his chin inquiringly. Bannon smoothed out the receipt and showed it to his brother.

"Hoebel."

Linc came over to look at it. "Really? The chief?" He read the receipt aloud. "Pancakes. Two coffees. You think he's the guy?"

Bannon shook his head. "No. Our guy was tall. Hoebel isn't."

"And? Give me something to think about, bro."

"Erin said that the prowler looked in her window before Charlie went for him. I did a rough outside measurement on the height of said window and figured him for over six feet, more like six-five, most likely. He's got a helluva long stride and he's light on his feet, like a real runner. The footprints I found told me that. Two coffees means two guys, even with one entrée. So what I'm thinking is Hoebel plus one. And that one would be who's stalking Erin."

"On Hoebel's dime?"

"Yeah. My pal Doris told me Hoebel's a little too interested in the old case files on Ann Montgomery's kidnapping. She doesn't know why and I don't know why, but he is."

"So what do we do now?"

Bannon sighed. "Walk around the house. Observe. Did you bring a camera?"

His brother patted the gun in his holster. "I can take pictures with this."

Bannon looked at him with surprise.

"Lame joke. Sorry," Linc said. "Okay, lead the way. I never planned to live forever. In case the dude jumps out and kills me, I just want to say that it's been nice working with you and being your brother and all."

"Same here."

They did a standard recon around the perimeter of the house. Bannon noted the same distinctive footprints he'd seen the first time—long and dug in at the toe. The prowler had gone the same way toward the woods of the Blue Ridge.

"He could live up there somewhere," Bannon said to his brother, nodding toward the brooding mountains.

"No one lives up there. That's state park land, as far as I know. About a million acres. You can't see it all from here."

"He could be a squatter. Tent, shack, something like that—a roof over his head."

"Maybe. Who knows? Anyway, the two of us can't search an area that size on our own." Linc holstered his gun with a decisive shove under his arm.

Bannon followed his brother back inside the house. "I'm wondering if we should bring her computer and things back."

"I was just thinking that myself. Want to call her?"

"Not yet." The thought of how Erin would feel when she heard that the stalker had returned made him want to break the bad news nice and slow. "Let's just do it. Then I'll tell her."

"Okay," Linc said. "I can keep stuff in my garage until she needs it. You know the code if you want to pick it up. Don't forget to deactivate the alarm," he added. "The wah-wah-wah is seriously loud and the feds receive the silent one."

They disconnected everything that boasted a USB port, including the two vidcams, both of which got wrapped in yet another clean rag to preserve any prints, and carried it all out to the government car. Bannon went back in for a last look around. He went for the box of sentimental things first, the one with the scrapbook.

Linc was standing in the doorway. "Anything else?"

"You could grab those portfolios over there."

"What about her car?"

"Some other time."

In less than an hour, they had filled the car with everything they thought Erin might want, operating on an unspoken understanding that she was never, ever coming back.

Erin was in the shower when Bannon came in. Charlie rose to greet him and Bannon noticed that the cat had come out of hiding to perch on the upper part of the sofa.

"Hey, you two," he said. "Getting along better?"

Babaloo responded with a tongue-curling yawn.

"I see. Just bored. That works."

He slung his jacket over the chair and tried not to think about the creep who'd showed his ugly face.

There was a beautiful alternative to occupy his mind, and she was wet all over. He envied the lucky, lucky water that got to run over Erin's bare skin. The bar of soap—he was definitely jealous of the soap. He knew it made a generous lather that got everywhere on its own. A whiff of its spicy fragrance tickled his nose, carried there by floating steam.

Bannon tripped over the dog, who gave him a hurt look. "Sorry. Not your fault."

He went into the kitchen and looked into the fridge to see if he had anything that could be thrown together for dinner. Not really. Takeout, then.

The shower stopped. She must be drying off. Pat pat pat. Fluffy towels and a gorgeous naked woman he couldn't touch. Pat pat pat.

Shoot him now.

He distracted himself with a careful study of several different takeout menus. "Feel like eating Thai?" he called to her.

"You're home," Erin called back. "Sure, that's fine. I love anything noodly. With lemongrass and chicken."

"You got it."

Bannon was on the phone with a nice lady who didn't speak too much English as Erin came out of the bathroom, not looking at him. Her slender body was wrapped in one big towel, and her hair was wrapped in another twisted into a turban.

Was the towel-turban thing something women were born knowing how to do? He couldn't manage that to save his life. Face scrubbed absolutely clean, wet hair swept under the turban, Erin was even more beautiful. He stared when her back was to him, loving the way the big towel cuddled her rear. His old, roomy jeans were suddenly uncomfortable.

He figured out the order with the Thai lady and hung up. Bannon took a deep breath. "Dinner's on the way," he said to the steam in the air. Erin had made it to his bedroom—he heard the door close with a soft snick.

Bannon stuck a large glass under the fridge's ice cube dispenser, watched the ice rattle out, and moved the glass to the water side, filling it. He thought about pouring it over his head, but he drank it instead.

Refreshing and effective.

He made himself another glass.

The delivery arrived before she'd finished dressing. Not that she spent a lot of time fussing with her appearance. Maybe she was just lying down, Bannon thought, aching inside. He was glad he had something important to do, like paying the little guy holding up two plastic bags filled with Thai food. He shut the door and carried the order into the kitchen.

"Supper time," he called. He heard a faint okay.

Plates. Forks, spoons, knives. Napkins. A glass for her. He put the one he'd been drinking from by his plate. Being crazed with lust didn't mean he'd forgotten how to set a table. His mother would be proud.

"What would you like to drink?"

"Ginger ale," she replied. Her voice was louder. She must have opened the bedroom door. He wasn't going to look.

Bannon found a cold can and set it by her glass. Then he put the takeout containers in the middle of the table between the two plates.

"Ready when you—oh," he said. "There you are."

Erin was standing in the open archway of the kitchen, pulling down a light sweater over her hips. She'd combed her hair but it was still wet, dark chestnut strands clinging to her neck.

Bannon knew at that moment he was a goner. He would do anything for her. His heart was hers. A ring. A house. A puppy. Two kids. Whatever she wanted. Right now, he could start with killing the creep who'd tried twice to get to her. No problem.

He would do anything at all to keep her in his life, permanently. How to do it, what to say . . . He looked into the takeout bag.

"Want soy sauce?" he asked.

"No, thanks." She pulled out a chair and took a seat. They ate. She told him about her good news. He kept a lid on his.

Much later, after Erin had given him a lingering good-night kiss, he forced himself not to think about how good her body felt against his. He'd been the one to break off the kiss, not her, and she'd shot him a disappointed look over her shoulder when she'd gone into the bedroom. For now, that was how it had to be between them.

Protecting her was his first priority. He owed her that. It didn't matter if he felt guilty about playing detective when she hadn't asked him to, and worse, snooping in her stuff. Erin was in real danger and she had serious decisions to make.

What he and Linc had seen on the vidcam feed and found at her place told him the heat was on and rising. The new developments had an ugly side, and he knew they had to be connected to a lot of other things that were even uglier.

He wandered through the condo, feeling restless. This wasn't the safest place for her to be, not after today. She could hide somewhere else, under yet another name—he stopped that train of thought and sat down on the sofa.

No.

She'd said she wouldn't run. He'd been too slammed by all the crazy crap that had just gone down to think about what that meant.

For her sake and his own, he had to start figuring things out, including the right way to tell her exactly what he knew and what he didn't—and what he had guessed.

Bannon picked up a thin-tipped marker and propped a yellow legal pad on his knee, drawing a line down the middle of it to separate facts from conjecture. Then he started writing.

The man she thought of as her father undoubtedly wasn't. It was logical to conclude that Ernest Randall—inventor, tinkerer, oddball—had the skills to forge a document and a compelling motive to do so. Everything Bannon had learned about the man fit the bill. Her bogus birth certificate had been created with meticulous skill, right down to the official-looking seal. Getting the fake one filed in the hospital records department had to have been easy by comparison. He thought of the fifty he'd slid to the talkative clerk—worth it, for what he'd obtained.

Bannon frowned, tapping the yellow pad with the end of his pen. The final touch—the tantalizing words in Latin hidden in the state seal—was something that still baffled him. Why leave a clue at all? Guilt? Arrogance?

Her brother's birth certificate had obviously provided more than one template for Randall. Bannon jotted down a probable step-by-step. A die was made and engraved, then stamped onto a blank gold seal to falsify the first, crucial document of Erin's new life.

Truth is the daughter of time.

Had Ernest Randall left the motto for Erin to find someday? Or to taunt the Montgomerys? If she had been found and her abductors prosecuted for their crime, it would have been noticed during the forensic investigation. It occurred to Bannon that Randall would have felt a touch of pride to hear it read out in court. But he was dead and gone.

Both copies of the birth certificate in her scrapbook looked like they'd been there a while. Obviously, she'd never really looked at the official seal, but who did?

You, he answered his own question. But only because the identical sets of footprints on the two different certificates at the hospital had forced him to take a close look. He would have missed the changed motto otherwise.

The forger had been methodical to an extreme degree—and more than smart enough to plan an abduction that wouldn't leave a single clue. But there was little doubt in Bannon's mind that luck had somehow played a part. It always did. And from what he knew of such crimes, it was a safe bet that two people had taken Ann— and kept the secret between them all the way to their graves.

Ina Randall's role? All the little details, most likely. The freehand pen and ink on the certificate had probably been filled in by her. She was skilled at calligraphy and artistic. *Girl of gold.* Her phrase. *Ann's new mother.* Why announce it?

She must have been unhinged by the death of her little son. The passing years and the strain of hiding had only made it worse. Erin had made it clear that she wasn't very close to the woman she called mother.

He leaned back, thinking about her and the sentimental notecard, as well as the somewhat bizarre letter to the Montgomerys, apparently one of several. Well-established criminal profiles fit these two. Forced to hide from the world, they found peculiar ways to connect with it.

The only physical link he had between little Ann and grown-up Erin was the bear, if it was the same one. Hers was handmade.

When he got the visuals back from Doris, he was going to compare old Pinky to the bear in the photo, examining the stitching on both under the digital microscope. Old photos printed from high-quality studio negatives often provided more detail than pixels.

That could be interesting.

But the case couldn't be resolved once and for all without DNA testing. That would have to be up to her and—Hugh Montgomery. Bannon stopped writing and looked up at the painting of horses on the wall, letting his gaze move to the sketchbook she was currently filling up. Erin and Montgomery were getting to know each other, but that didn't mean Montgomery was going to hand over a sample of his oh-so-blue blood just to satisfy Bannon's curiosity.

He allowed himself a minute or so of idle speculation. Had Montgomery commissioned the portrait of his best stallion because he liked Erin's work, or because parental instinct was kicking in? Impossible to verify. He would do better to stick to the facts.

He wrote down the rest of the evidence, what there was of it, and pondered every item one by one, looking for connections, covering the paper with arrows pointing to this or that detail, circles around the important stuff, underlining and crossing out. What a mess. But then he'd never worked a case where the clues were nice and neat and everything seemed to make perfect sense. Life was sloppy. Evidence was worse. In a case this old, it was apt to be skimpy, contaminated, or simply nonexistent.

There was one very big question remaining, and he had no information whatsoever to help him answer it. The more he thought about it, the more curious he became. Where was Luanne Montgomery?

Doris hadn't said. Maybe she didn't know. But just about anyone could be found these days. Even when they didn't want to be.

He sat back, legal pad in his lap, thinking about the identity of the young woman now sleeping in his bed. What he knew and what he could prove were two different things, but they were drawing closer.

Bannon flipped the scribbled-up sheet over to the other side of the pad and jotted one more question on the fresh sheet of paper.

Is Erin Randall really Ann Montgomery?

The final proof would have to be ironclad. He couldn't jerk Erin around with a lot of theories and conjecture. What to say to her on the subject—he honestly didn't know.

In abduction cases, psychologists and social workers usually dealt with the families, taking over from the cops and detectives. The longer the separation of the victim and relatives, the longer the resolution took. Bannon knew that the reactions varied. Shock. Guilt. Anger. A flood tide of other emotions and a river of tears.

Some got through it and came out okay, when everything had been pieced together and the dust settled. People coped somehow, went on with their lives, got through the days.

What would happen to Erin when she found out where she really came from? He flipped back to the sheet of paper covered with complicated scribbles, reading it over. Lies inside of lies. Betrayals and selfishness. She had been an innocent child then and she still knew nothing of the deception that had changed her life forever.

Lucky you, he said to himself. *You get to tell her. You owe her that.*

The past couldn't be fixed, no matter what. The future was what counted. He wanted to share that with her. But this wasn't the right time to ask for a lot of things she wasn't going to be able to give.

He heard the bedroom doorknob turn very quietly and looked up to see her come into the room. Casually, he put the legal pad aside. No time to slide it under a cushion or crumple up the paper.

Bannon drank in the sight of her.

Sleepy. Hair messed up. Wearing an oversize T-shirt and leggings. A faint sheen of something that smelled great from where he was made her rosy skin gleam. His breath caught and his pulse quickened.

He couldn't bring himself to tell her what he had been working on, swearing mentally that he would do it in the morning.

"How come you're still awake?" she asked.

"I could ask you the same thing."

"The light under the door woke me up."

"Sorry about that."

She frowned at him and walked over to the sofa, sitting a cushion away from him. She leaned back and yawned, then rubbed her eyes.

"Anything on TV?"

Bannon reached for the remote and handed it to her. "No idea. Check the cable menu."

She leaned over to take it—and startled him with a bold reach over his thigh to get the legal pad. For more than one reason, Bannon tensed.

"Writing poetry?" she teased.

"Ah, no." He was doomed.

"What is all this? Mind if I look at it?"

"No. It's time you knew," he said resignedly.

"What?"

He got up and went into the kitchen. "Just go ahead and read. Then I'll explain. I should have told you everything as soon as I knew."

Bannon poured himself a shot and tossed it down. This wasn't going to be easy.

CHAPTER 18

Erin was too stunned to speak when he stopped his explanation halfway through. He began to apologize instead and realized she wasn't listening.

She stared straight ahead, her hands in her lap. She'd torn off the sheets of paper and held on to them. Now she let go. They drifted to the floor in front of her.

"Why didn't you tell me sooner?"

That simple question hit him like a steel dart, center circle. "I didn't know enough. Maybe I should have."

She didn't say anything more for a little while. "So. What now?"

"I'm not sure. Things are happening fast. You start turning over rocks and things crawl out." He gestured toward the boxes that Kelly had sent from the TV station. "Once the story hit the air—"

"That was your idea, right?" She pressed her lips together.

"Yeah."

Now he regretted it. He'd wanted to get the ball rolling, gain momentum before the chief could deep-six the Montgomery files and find a way to fire him at the same time. He'd had no idea that things would turn out the way they had.

"Have you looked at any of that stuff yet?" Erin asked shakily.

"No. It just came. I did review the e-mails Kelly forwarded at first. But the stuff in those boxes came in to the station later."

"Who else knows what you know?"

He hesitated for a few seconds. "Are you asking if anyone else thinks you're Ann?"

"Yes." Her reply sounded far away.

He wondered if she meant Hugh Montgomery. It was still hard for him to imagine that the two of them might be so closely related.

But Bannon hadn't been at the stable when she'd met him for the first time. If he ever got a chance to observe how the old man acted around Erin, another piece of the puzzle might fall solidly into place. What father wouldn't recognize his own child? An age-progression image created by a studio technician could be way off the mark, but not a parent's memory.

Which begged a lot of questions.

Uneasily, he reminded himself of the distinct possibility that there was evidence out there he didn't have, evidence that could prove beyond a shadow of a doubt that Erin was Ann, even without DNA testing. This case had it all. Family secrets. Money. People went to dangerous extremes to keep both.

"Well?"

The single word jolted him out of his thoughts. "It could be that someone else thinks that besides me. Exactly who—I can't say for sure."

"I could guess."

She didn't add anything to that blunt remark and he soldiered on. "The truth is going to come out." He hesitated. "Look, Erin, I didn't know what I was getting into. It's not like I was assigned to the case—I just got interested. And one thing led to another."

"Interested in what? Can you be more specific? This is my life we're talking about."

He picked up on the edge in her voice. *Tread carefully*, he told himself. He hadn't planned on telling her anything until he was absolutely sure. But when she'd come out of his bedroom and latched onto that legal pad, he hadn't had a choice. If she hadn't, would he have been able to look her in the eye and keep his suspicions to himself much longer? Not if her safety was at stake. He took a deep breath.

"Erin, when we were first getting to know each other, you told me some things about your family that seemed a little strange to me."

"Like what?"

"The brother who died before you. The baby pictures you didn't have. The way you grew up so isolated. Those things fit a pattern. We're trained to look for them."

"Right. You're a detective. Why do I want to forget that?"

"Sometimes I wish I could myself." His voice was level. "I don't want this to come between us."

"Too late now. Keep going."

"I minded my own business. More or less," he amended. "Then something cropped up that didn't fit a pattern at all—the notecard that said 'girl of gold.'"

"You mean the one in my scrapbook? What about it?"

He nodded. "I didn't think anything of it. Until Doris happened to see the same three words in a letter she found in the Montgomery files." He paused, gauging the effect of what he was about to say on Erin. "An anonymous letter. From a woman who called herself, quote unquote, Ann's new mother."

Erin's brow furrowed slightly. "'Girl of gold' is just a phrase. It must be from a poem or a song."

"I couldn't find it online anywhere. So I took the card—okay, sorry." He held up his hands in a placating gesture at her furious look. "You asked me to go over and walk the dog."

"I didn't ask you to snoop," she said heatedly.

"Well, after Doris told me about the letter—look, I knew it was wrong and I take full responsibility. I wanted to examine the card under a digital microscope. It was from a store, you're right about that. But the calligraphy inside was done by hand. I haven't had a chance to compare it to the writing on the letter."

He gave her a sideways look, about to confess all and dreading it. Erin was staring straight ahead, not at him.

"When I took the card, I photocopied your birth certificate to do a document check, compare dates, that kind of thing. Routine."

"Is it?" she snapped. "I don't remember you asking my permission. I don't even remember the certificate being in the scrapbook."

"It slipped out from behind the card. Took some doing to track down what I wanted to know. The hospital where you were born shut down years ago. So I went to the new one—"

"And flashed your shiny badge at some dumb clerk."

Good guess. It didn't seem like the right time to mention the fifty he'd flashed too. "Erin, I knew it was forged the second I saw your brother's birth certificate. And when I found a translation for the Latin words on the fake seal—"

"Truth is the daughter of time." She fell silent. "That rings true. My father liked puzzles. The harder the better."

"How well did he know Latin?"

She gave an infinitesimal shrug. "He could read it. He taught me a little."

"Were you familiar with that phrase?"

"No. I only learned a few words. Nothing like that." Her face was beginning to crumple with strain. "So what else did you find out?"

"Not much. I don't have a theory about how you were taken from your house and I couldn't truthfully say who did it. There wasn't a whole hell of a lot of evidence—practically none, if you want to know—and the reports in the files didn't speculate. "

"And you're sure I was taken. That I'm not Erin Randall."

It wasn't a question or a statement. More like an expression of profound pain. Her gaze moved involuntarily to the stacked boxes, as if the answer to all her questions was buried somewhere deep inside.

"Yes," he said quietly. "As sure as I can be without DNA evidence."

Erin turned to look at him. The piercing vulnerability in her blue eyes was almost too much for him to bear. "That's going to be tough. My parents—or the people I thought were my parents—died three years ago."

"I know that." He wasn't going to go into how DNA could still be obtained. Some other time. Let someone else tell her.

"But someone who knew them—knew me—might have seen the broadcast."

"That computer-generated image didn't look like you at all."

She shook her head. The movement made a couple of tears fall. Erin scrubbed them away viciously. "That doesn't matter. You said the case was all over the news back in the day. Somebody knew my parents from before—somebody might have figured out who I was. My mother had two sisters."

That fact distracted him for a moment. "Do you remember anything about them?"

"The aunties? Not their names. Just their old photographs. I was so young. I don't remember meeting them, if that's what you mean. I think one died and the other drifted away."

"Oh."

Erin's voice dropped to a bitter whisper. "But someone else might have noticed or guessed and didn't say anything."

"Like who?"

She shrugged, but the gesture was far from nonchalant. "My parents weren't always that isolated," she added. "So I'm thinking a distant neighbor or former friend. Someone who believed in minding their own business," she added acidly.

He reached out to reassure her with a touch, but she jumped up and walked away from him. She ran a finger along the packing tape on the top of one of the boxes, making a thin indentation in the plastic without slitting it.

Bannon wished he could make the damned boxes disappear. "Erin, most of those messages aren't going to pan out. People just want to be on TV or they're hoping to get paid for information or something. I'll consider myself lucky if I find one truthful reply in ten thousand—"

She whirled and pointed an accusing finger at him. "How would you know what's true and what's not? It's me they're talking about. My life. What's left of it."

"Don't talk like that."

Erin crossed her arms. He had the feeling she was fighting the urge to attack him physically. "Do you have any idea what it feels like to find out that everything about yourself is a lie?"

"No."

The silent standoff that ensued lasted for over an hour. She paced. He set his jaw against the pain of a world-class headache, found some paperwork to do, and let her walk it off. Even the dog kept his distance, settling his body against a wall and keeping his head up to watch both of them.

Bannon wished she would go into the kitchen and smash dishes. Or scream it out. She had incredible self-control. Or maybe she had just gone numb.

Finally she sat, glancing once more at the sealed boxes. "Did you tell that reporter about—"

"No," he interrupted curtly. "And I don't intend to. Ever. You're in charge from here on in when it comes to that. Kelly will probably contact me at some point, but I don't have to say anything."

"Good. Thanks."

Bannon looked up at her. He had detected the slightest possible softening in her tone. Not forgiveness. Call it a cessation of outright hostility.

"Right now, none of that is important. I don't have all of the answers, and I don't need them. We have other things to think about. I put you at risk. Now I have to keep you safe."

"We?" Erin looked down at her hands, which twisted nervously in her lap. "I know you were trying to protect me, Bannon."

He might have blown that. Big time. He had something to say and he had no idea how she would take it. "First things first. You can't go back to that house, Erin. Ever."

"I don't want to," she whispered. "But there's a lot of stuff still there that I need—did you think about that?"

"Of course we did. Linc and I disconnected the computer and peripherals and took it all with us. Plus a whole lot of other stuff. We stashed a bunch of boxes at his place. You could hide out there if you wanted—I don't think you're safe with me, to be honest."

She shook her head. "No. I said it once and I'll say it again, I'm not going to keep running."

Bannon could understand that. And she had a point. Wherever she went, she could be found.

The condo building was no fortress. There were no guards or doormen on the entrances or exits, and the doors were hollow-core junk. One kick and they'd splinter. There were decent locks on his, though, that he'd installed himself.

Charlie was serious protection, but he wasn't enough. Linc could set up new electronic security inside Bannon's place—oh, hell. He couldn't lock her up night and day.

He looked at her. She was silent.

Shut up and think, Bannon.

He reminded himself that he was up against the chief of police, who seemed to be hooked up with the psycho who'd appeared in Linc's monitor for less than a second before the vidcam had been torn out. Bannon was grateful Erin hadn't seen that face. She'd been terrorized enough for a lifetime.

At least they had that to go on. But Linc would have to pull off a miracle of pixel enhancement on an image from the vidcam feed or they would have no way of identifying him.

"You know what the worst part is?"

He snapped to attention. There was a world of hurt in her voice.

"Even if my parents—the Randalls—took me when I was too young to know better, that still doesn't make me a Montgomery."

"I thought about that too."

Erin reached down and picked up the folded yellow sheets of paper, crumpling them in her hands. "I feel like I don't exist." She threw them away from her and began to cry for real. He couldn't stand it. Bannon got next to her and held her tight.

She didn't use her fists on him this time. He kept on holding her. Charlie came over, keeping a respectful distance but clearly alarmed. Bannon had tears in his eyes too. A couple of the little bastards rolled down his face and into her hair.

Erin sobbed her heart out. He didn't know how many minutes went by before she cried herself out. For now, anyway.

The dog moved closer and put a paw on her thigh.

"I know that's not you, Bannon," she whispered into his soaked T-shirt.

He could almost feel her shaky smile through the wet fabric.

"No. It's not. Charlie, lie down." The dog obeyed, but he didn't move away, settling his big body protectively at their feet.

Erin lifted her head without looking at Bannon or the dog. She gave a raw sigh and buried her face in Bannon's neck. He couldn't adjust his position and his back was killing him, but he didn't care. He kept on holding her and stroking her hair. It seemed to help.

Linc's number flashed on the cell phone screen. Bannon flipped it open before it could ring.

"Hey. I called to see how you two are doing."

Bannon glanced toward the shut bedroom door. "She's not awake yet."

"Oh. Did you tell her about what happened?"

"Yeah."

"I guess she wasn't thrilled to hear that the creep came back."

"No, she wasn't." Bannon knew his brother was taking the situation seriously. Linc wasn't big on drama and emotions. He just got things done, like all of them. Their father had brought up his three boys that way.

He provided the barest outline of Erin's reaction. That was between her and him. His brother didn't need to know what they'd talked about. Or that she'd cried a river.

"You going to keep her there?" Linc asked.

"It's not a good idea. But she has no place else to go. You got the back story on her."

"Yeah, chapter and verse. What is it with you and stray cats?"

"Watch it, Linc."

"Sorry. You know I was about to say she can stay with me," his brother offered.

"I figured as much. In fact, I volunteered you. She's not interested in going someplace else."

Linc didn't seem surprised. "Not a problem. Here if you need me. Really. Look, maybe we can help her hide out of state somewhere or—at the cabin."

"It's too isolated, even if I went with her," Bannon said. "I thought of that too. Maybe I've got too many damn things to think about."

He could practically hear his brother analyzing pros and cons in his head. Linc had a knack for simplifying. Bannon could use some of that. His own head was spinning.

"All right," Linc began. "One. Erin is alive and safe. Two. All the rest can wait. The important thing is that we gotta get that guy."

"And when we do, the chief can hire some other thug. Speaking of that, did you get an image we can use from the vidcam?"

"Not yet. I did do a screen grab. But I have to amp up the pixels, smooth out the visual noise, and do some fairly sophisticated enhancement. Give me an hour."

"How about dusting for prints?"

His brother sighed. "I forgot I had all that stuff. Which box were the vidcams in?"

"One of them. It was brown cardboard."

"Thank you, Bannon. That's very helpful. We took out about twenty boxes matching that description."

Bannon cleared his throat. "Good thing you have that big garage."

"Yeah. Anyway, I get the picture. You want me to handle the forensics and come up with an ID. You defend the maiden and chop off dragon heads."

"What I want to do is confront Hoebel."

"With a receipt for his pancake breakfast? I don't think that's going to scare him, bro. His ugly mug didn't pop up on the vid."

"I'm following up on it today. You know, have a chat with the waitress, tip her a ten for a cup of bad coffee. She might remember a name, or at least what the guy who came in with Hoebel looked like."

"Better than nothing," Linc said.

"You can't find out everything on a computer," Bannon retorted.

Linc relented. "Don't I know it. Look, receipts are a gold mine of info. Time, date, items purchased, and bingo-bango, an authentic signature that can be tied to a credit or debit card. And speaking of not finding out everything, you'd better do a sweep of your car for bugs. Forgot to check that off. There's a gizmo for it in the box under your bed."

Bannon rubbed his aching head. "I believe you. Thanks for the reminder. And I'll do the dusting on the receipt. It's here, safe and sound. Somewhere."

"Don't lose it. Our guy's fingerprints might be on it. And why did he have it in the first place, hmm? Care to speculate?"

"Maybe he wanted to forge Hoebel's signature on something. Maybe it stuck to his shoe. Let's not get too logical. The guy is a psycho."

"Guess we're going to find out together." He heard Linc's swivel chair creak and knew his brother was leaning back. "Take care of yourself, Bann. And her too."

Hoebel pushed the budget projections away from him with one angry sweep. He preferred to have a clear desk—if any of the county or state brass showed up for a surprise visit, they'd get the impression that he was caught up. In charge.

Of course, most of this crap had come from them. Maybe they would want to see him nose-deep in their damned paperwork. They could have e-mailed him all of this and made it easier to ignore. He glanced at his monitor, which had gone dark, and poked a thick finger at a key.

The real-time data from the GPS beacon on Bannon's car appeared as a glowing line on a county map. The sonuvabitch was putting in some miles today. Fifty miles east, then a jog to the south. Then back to the west, not too far away. Keeping busy.

Too bad he couldn't just fire the guy. Keeping him broke was about the only weapon he had at his disposal. Bannon's continuance of claim forms were still waiting for Hoebel's signature. But he was a little surprised that Bannon hadn't found the thing yet. He'd pegged the detective as detail-oriented and dogged, a real never-say-die type. Intuitive too. And essentially fearless, which made him a serious threat to the chief's idea of law and order. He glanced at the icon for the GPS gizmo. It was moving along the county road that led out to Montgomery's stud farm. Was Bannon snooping around out there today?

At least Montgomery wouldn't be calling the office to give him hell. The old man's stroke had shut him up for the moment, although Hoebel understood that it hadn't been a biggie. Monty had been seen at his stables staggering around on the arm of some nurse, trying to show his underlings who was boss.

Pathetic.

One more reason for him to quit early, Hoebel thought. He

wanted to enjoy himself before old age whacked him in the back of the knees. Take the money and run. He made a note to call his favorite hacker tonight. Time to steal Montgomery's remaining loot.

As for Bannon—hell, he didn't have time to spy on the guy at the moment. Hoebel dragged the stapled reports and spreadsheets back in front of him.

The department was going to have to cut back. No overtime for the officers; involuntary furloughs for some of the non-uniformed staff. He could kiss the walnut paneling he wanted for his office good-bye—if he put in for a new pencil cup to go begging with, he'd be lucky to get it.

Like his jurisdiction didn't have enough problems. The beautiful rural country around Wainsville wasn't immune to crime, and the statistics confirmed it. The numbers for residential burglaries and related crimes were trending up—that made a lot of folks unhappy. Especially rich folks. They felt entitled to complain to high-level officials who could put him through the wringer because the corresponding numbers—for arrests—were down. The bad guys were getting smarter and they kept changing the rules of the game. Dealers in cheap black-tar heroin had abandoned the city street corners and come out here to sell to college kids and middle-class types who couldn't afford their painkillers—they were doing a booming business out of their cars, and they delivered. Tough to catch.

And don't even get him started on meth. The last lab his boys had busted had to have been bringing in a million a year. That kind of money was tempting, but he didn't want to work with tweakin' freaks. He glanced at the first page of that thick report and slammed a hand down on it.

Jolene chose that moment to come in with his coffee. He looked up, glaring at her, then saw that the unexpected noise had made her spill a little of it. She was brushing at the front of her dress.

Good. Once she'd put it on his desk, she would have to bend down and sop up the drops beading on the varnished floor with the paper napkin in her hand. He wouldn't mind watching her do that.

"Did I startle you?" he asked blandly. "Sorry. Put the cup right there." He moved a stack of reports aside.

Jolene set it down along with the napkin, then turned to walk out.

"You spilled some coffee," he said, stopping her in her tracks.

She cast a contemptuous look over her shoulder. "The cleaning service is here. I'll send someone in."

Hoebel grunted. How did she get to be so full of herself? But it wasn't like he could make her scrub floors. He returned to his perusal of the reports and budgets, in a worse mood than ever.

When he was done, he sipped the coffee. It was lukewarm by now. Asking Jolene to bring him another was asking for trouble. And he needed to stay focused. The chief took out a pad of paper and began making notes on who around here was going to stay and who he could do without. He chewed on the end of his pencil, thinking. His son-in-law he had to keep. But Doris could go on furlough. The archiving project wasn't that important. And he didn't like the way she spoke her mind sometimes. It occurred to him that she might be the one who'd been egging Jolene on. He thought it over and wrote down a few words. *Jolene—stay or go?*

He did like looking at her, even if she was a bitch sometimes. And she got along well with everyone else. He wrote the answer next to her name. *Stay.*

Hoebel leaned back, scratching his head. He couldn't make cuts in the ranks. And the officers were going to complain about the no-overtime thing, but that couldn't be helped. He knew most of them would keep on working hard anyway. The Wainsville PD attracted good men and women to serve on the force, some locals, some from away. The town itself was a pleasant place to live, affordable for civil servants and cops. But he wanted more than that—no, he deserved more than that.

For a second or two he felt almost ashamed of what he was doing on the side. Then he looked at the budget reports and thought that his pay might be the next thing on the cutting block. The chief blew out an irritated breath and the feeling of shame vanished.

All this paperwork was beneath him. But he had to respond to it. Hoebel turned to his monitor, which had gone dark again, and pulled the keyboard toward him. The GPS tracker map was still up but the icon that tracked the beacon's movements wasn't moving, just blinking. He grabbed the mouse and clicked on that part of the screen, enlarging it.

Blink blink. Jones Road at the intersection of Broad. What the hell—

Bannon wasn't out at the Montgomery stables. He was here.

Hoebel swiveled and looked at the door that Jolene had closed behind her.

"Go right in," he heard her say.

He stood.

"Hello, Bannon."

The young detective glowered at him.

"I haven't signed those papers." Why were Bannon's hands in his pockets? The chief was glad his gun was where he could reach it, in the top desk drawer. Locked and loaded.

"That's not why I'm here."

Hoebel stayed behind his desk. He wasn't going to sit down. Bannon was taller than he as it was.

"I'm not interested in a game of Twenty Questions. Don't waste my time," the chief snapped. "You can see I'm busy."

"Yeah. Seems like you get around."

Hoebel folded his arms over his chest. "What are you talking about?"

"I found a receipt with your name on it. From that café out on the county road."

"You going through garbage now?" He tsked. "Hard times. Things are tough all over."

Bannon gave him a fierce look and actually had the nerve to take a couple of steps closer. "You and somebody else went out for breakfast. Pancakes, two coffees. I talked to the waitress out there, confirmed that it was you. And a tall guy. She remembered that his hand was bleeding right through a dirty bandage."

"So?"

"I think he cut it on window glass."

Hoebel knew better than to take the bait and ask where. He said nothing.

"We got prints off the receipt and found a match on the national database."

"Who's we?"

"I'm talking, you're listening. Let's keep it that way."

Instant anger mottled the chief's face. "Don't talk to me like that." He dropped his arms and made a move toward the call button on his desk, but stopped when Bannon pulled out a small ziplock bag that held the receipt. He waved it at the chief.

It was like a red flag in front of a bull. Hoebel leaned over and made a grab for it, but Bannon stepped back. Hoebel used his meaty hands to brace himself on the desk and get his balance back. He wanted to wrap them around Bannon's neck.

Upright again, he stared at Bannon, breathing hard.

"Funny thing," Bannon began, "the day you had breakfast out there was also the day somebody—somebody tall—tried to break into a certain house. For the first time. The second time was when he dropped the receipt. We got him on vidcam for less than a second. Turned out that was all we needed. Want me to send you a printout of your friend's face? Suitable for framing."

"Up yours," Hoebel muttered.

"Same to you, Chief."

"You're fired."

"Not yet. And as far as the receipt, I'm assuming you didn't give it to him. The guy must have something on you, Hoebel."

The chief stared at him. "I don't know anything about this." Which was pretty much the truth. He didn't expect the detective to believe him. "But I have a proposition for you. You can be thrown out of here. Or thrown in jail. Take your pick."

Bannon stood his ground. "Don't screw around with me. Like I said, we got a positive ID on the guy. Not just fingerprints. A match on FaceBase."

"Good for you," Hoebel snarled.

"His name is Lee Cutt. You're hanging out with a parolee. An ex-cop with a hair-trigger temper who's done hard time. Bad to the bone."

"Do I know someone named Cutt?" The chief pretended to think.

"A ten-dollar cup of coffee says you do."

"Now that you mention it, he must be the guy who hit me up for a free breakfast."

"Yeah, right."

"That's my story." Hoebel barely controlled himself. "I don't have to explain or answer questions."

Bannon shrugged. "You will when the state commissioner starts asking them. Or a grand jury prosecutor."

The chief let out a vicious curse.

"Get one thing straight." Bannon pointed a jabbing finger at him. "Keep Cutt on a short leash. If I find him . . ."

Bannon didn't finish the sentence. He was too coolheaded to make a threat that would incriminate him. The detective turned and walked out, closing the door again. He came back in, holding up a small object.

"Almost forgot. Your GPS gizmo. I stomped it in the parking lot before I came in."

Bannon threw it at him, but the chief wasn't quick enough to catch it.

Out he went.

Hoebel heard Bannon say a friendly good-bye to Jolene before he dropped into his chair, cursing under his breath. What was going on and where was Cutt? A short leash wouldn't do it—hell, he was going to have to choke-chain the guy. The chief picked up the receiver of his desk phone, then replaced it slowly.

No. He'd call later, on a discount-store cell phone he could throw away. He didn't want Cutt's number traced here.

Calling the chief's bluff had felt damned good. Bannon was okay to leave it at that for now. He'd bought time. Erin would be safer. Not completely safe, not free to go back to the house. But safer.

Next step: Find Cutt.

Bannon wasn't going to do that alone. But he did want to go back to the house himself to try to find blood spots he'd missed. Fingerprints and DNA and the time-tagged vid image would be more than enough to put the crazy bastard behind bars for a long time. Judges didn't let parole violators slide too often. His gaze narrowed on the road ahead.

On the way home his cell phone rang and he checked the number. Could it be Linc, who'd called in sick to stay with Erin while Bannon paid his call on the chief? No, it was Doris. He couldn't tell her much, but he did want to talk to her. He flipped the phone open and put it to his ear.

"Hey," he said, "what's up?"

Doris answered right away. "Bannon, I wish I had good news. But it's bad."

He was instantly on his guard. "What's the matter? Are you okay?"

She seemed startled by the question. "Sort of. I mean, I didn't get hurt or anything. But I got furloughed, along with some other people."

Bannon blew out his breath. Not the end of the world, but even so.

"Budget cuts. We've been hearing rumors. So it wasn't that much of a surprise."

"That's not why, Doris."

She paused. "Want to explain that?"

"No. How'd you hear?"

"The chicken way. Not in person. Hoebel sent an e-mail to us lucky ones. Budget considerations, blah blah. Box your personal stuff and go."

"You did that?"

"Like I have a choice? Yes, I did. But it just so happened that Petey was grabbing lunch while I was clearing out my desk."

Bannon couldn't help smiling. He knew Doris. "Yeah? And?"

"So I let myself into the evidence locker and guess what I found."

"His dirty magazines?"

She sniffed. "No. The Montgomery photos. Do you remember all the ones you had to give back to me?"

"You talking about the originals with the little girl and Luanne Montgomery? Yeah, I remember them."

"I took those. And a bunch of other stuff I didn't have time to look through before I filled up the box and sealed it and put it in my car and drove away."

"You're amazing."

"Well, if I'm on furlough, I need something to do."

Her bad news was more than good. He had a feeling she knew it. "You home? Want me to get the box?" he asked.

"No, it stays here. Come on over later, Bannon. Pick a time."

He thought about that. "I'll have to call you back. But I want you to bring me up to speed on the case. Any new developments?"

"Several."

CHAPTER 19

Erin looked at herself in the bathroom mirror. Her morning routine was the same as always and she'd just finished it. Brush teeth, comb hair, deal with practically invisible flaws like every other woman did. And her face was the same.

But whose face was it? She didn't resemble Hugh Montgomery at all, if he was her father, and she had no idea what his wife looked like. She might never know. Now she understood why her parents—the Randalls, if that was their name—hadn't looked like her. When she was little, she'd thought that was because they were so much older.

Come to think of it, she couldn't remember ever hearing either of them say the usual things like, oh, that nose runs in the family, or you have your mother's beautiful eyes. Just . . . nothing.

Who were they? What Bannon had found out so far radically altered everything she thought she knew about the quiet couple who called themselves her mom and dad. Her brother, perhaps, was really their child. Erin was not.

There had been other cases like hers—the media usually had a field day with them. That she was somebody's long-lost daughter was a staggering thought. Not confirmed. But very likely so.

Montgomery's aristocratic manner didn't invite questions or confidences. Still, if it turned out that she did resemble his wife, then he probably had come to the same conclusion as Bannon. Or at least entertained it. She couldn't forget how unnerved she'd been by his scrutinizing gaze, or the odd sense of déjà vu she'd felt in his presence.

So the old Montgomery mansion might have been her first home. Her brief tour of the interior with Bannon had made her feel—was homesick the right word? And then there was the portrait of the little girl. Was it possible to look at your own face and not know it? It had been half in shadow. What had she said then? She couldn't quite remember. Or maybe she didn't want to.

It's like Ann is still here. Waiting.

Not anymore, apparently. Wait until everything hit the headlines. It occurred to her that she didn't want to be on the news. Let the inaccurate likeness be her public face. She'd survived. Let that be enough.

National news and tabloids blared stories for months of children taken, often hidden in plain sight not far from where they disappeared, raised by strangers who had to have them for one wrong reason or another. Some were found years later, often by chance. Sometimes because some dedicated cop or social worker took a second look in the right place and asked hard questions.

Some were never found at all, even when they lived. Worse things happened to abducted kids. The absolute worst had not happened to her. She'd been isolated. Lied to. That was all.

Erin felt numb. And hollow. Only Bannon could make both go away. All he had to do was hold her like he had last night. But right now he wasn't here, replaced by his brother. Linc's presence only emphasized the fact that the man in whose arms she wanted to be more than anything else in the world had left before she'd woken up.

Erin looked into the mirror again. She was tempted to pick up the bar of wet soap and rub it over the glass to erase her own reflection. She turned away and rested her head against the cool tiled wall.

No matter what, she couldn't fault Bannon. He had gone through her things without asking, true, but that wasn't the sticking point—she had showed him most of that stuff on her own. It was his nature to put two and two together when clues cropped up, and he had.

He had come when she needed him. Literally put his life on the line for her. The growing tenderness she'd been feeling for him was mixed with overwhelming gratitude. And fear.

Heaving a sigh, Erin bent over the sink and splashed cold water on her face, again and again, until it almost hurt.

She lingered in the bathroom for another few minutes, then went out and saw Linc sitting on the sofa, working on Bannon's laptop. The family resemblance between the brothers was unmistakable, but Linc had lighter brown hair, and his eyes were gray. Same cheekbones, though. Different chin. She wondered what the third and youngest brother looked like, and felt a flash of envy for their closeness. They didn't know how lucky they were to have each other.

He got up when she came into the room, looking a little awkward himself.

"Bann's on his way back," he said quickly.

"Okay." She gave him a tremulous smile. "I think I'll call him."

"Sure. Good idea."

She picked up her cell phone and headed into the bedroom, dialing his number on the way.

Bannon picked up in a hot second. "Erin? Hey. I'm almost home."

"Pull over."

"What's going on?"

"I don't want you to get stopped for distracted driving."

He snorted. "All right. If you say so."

The noise on his side of the call lessened. Maybe he'd done what she asked. "I don't know why you had to leave—"

"Erin," he said, "it had nothing to do with you."

"It's okay. I'm not that needy."

He was quiet for several seconds. "Both of us are lying."

"Forgiven. And forgive me. If you don't mind, I'm going to see Montgomery."

"That's up to you."

They left it at that.

Five minutes later, she came out of the entrance door of the condo building, noticing Bannon behind the windshield of his parked car. She waved, hoping he would stay there. Linc was still inside, for which she was grateful. Erin didn't want his brother to overhear. She used her hip to push against the door and hold it open as she went through, clutching the handle of the tackle box that held her art supplies and somehow holding the large sketchpad under one arm at the same time.

Bannon opened his door. "Hey, let me help you," he called to her as he got out.

"It's okay. I can manage," she said. She kept on walking to her rental car.

"You sure?" he asked. "What about when you get to the stables? Who's meeting you?"

"I'm going to Mr. Montgomery's house, not there. He isn't feeling strong enough."

"Oh."

"But he's okay mentally. He gave me directions that were right— Linc let me double-check them online. Montgomery made sure I knew the way."

Bannon wasn't so sure that was all they'd talked about. "Okay. But did you tell him—"

"Not about that. Not a word. He's recovering from a stroke, Bannon. Why would I?"

He drew in a breath, regretting his question. "Ah, I didn't mean to imply—"

Her troubled eyes met his concerned gaze. "He sounded so different. Kind of shaky. Bannon—"

"What?" He knew that she might experience another delayed reaction to what he'd told her at any time. Especially if she went to see Montgomery. He hadn't thought of that in time to say something when he'd pulled over.

"When I spoke to him, it hit me that now I know what he went through."

"Beg your pardon?"

"When he saw that broadcast—and you talking about his daughter—something must have snapped."

"What are you saying?"

The explanation came slowly. "For me and for him—what happened—that's our life. Not a news story. Not a case."

"I'm beginning to understand what you mean."

"I don't think you really can."

Bannon sighed inwardly. She was right. "Give me credit for trying, Erin."

"Fair enough." She bit her lip and didn't look at him. "The thing is, I have to stay with you. I mean, I appreciate what you're doing for me, but I don't want to talk about it anymore. Not with you, not with anyone."

"Got it." He reached out to take her by the shoulders, but she stepped back. His hands dropped to his sides.

"Not now. I have to get going."

"Right. What's the plan?"

Erin smiled ruefully. "Cucumber sandwiches and tea in the solarium, from what he said."

Bannon wasn't sure what a solarium was, but he was positive Montgomery's taste in refreshment ran more to bourbon and branch water. He caught himself. Not after a stroke.

"Is that okay with you?" Her tone was faintly needling and he realized he hadn't answered.

"C'mon, Erin. I said it's up to you. I just want to make sure you can deal with this."

"Don't look at me like that," she said bluntly. "Just tell me why I'm still standing here. No, don't." She seemed agitated, as if new feelings, not happy ones, were taking over. "I have to leave. It feels like my head's about to explode, what with—everything."

"I can understand that."

Erin opened the back door of her car and put what she was carrying on the backseat. She slammed the door shut and got into the driver's seat, starting the car and unrolling the window. Granted, the day was warm, but he had a feeling she was doing it not to lose connection with him.

He stepped back a few feet as she backed out of the parking space, not wanting to get his toes run over. "My brother didn't say anything obnoxious, I hope."

"No. He's a perfectly nice guy." Her eyes shimmered and she braked abruptly. "I just need time to think. And you have to give me that."

"Will do—you know that. But for your own safety, call me when you get to Montgomery's and call me when you leave. And come back here. Damn it, Erin, if you don't, I'm going out to that little house to get you. If I have to throw you over my shoulder, I will."

Erin continued to back out, looking over her right shoulder and not at him. She stopped one more time. "Oh yeah. That. I have to call Jenny."

"Who?"

"Jenny owns the house. I have to let her know I'm not going to be living there, right?"

With that, she made a sweeping reverse half-turn and zoomed out of the parking lot. Bannon looked after her as she drove off, rolling right through a stop sign.

Lost in thought, he jumped when an older lady spoke right beside him, looking up at him with brilliant blue eyes that contrasted with her white hair. "Lovers' quarrel?" she asked kindly.

There was no need to fill her in on the details. "Something like that," he replied. "Nothing serious."

"Oh good." She went on her way.

Bannon went back to his car and got in, draping both forearms over the steering wheel and resting his forehead on them. Had he done the right thing?

The answer was yes, but it was a tough, complicated yes.

There was no way he could've kept Erin in the dark for another day. And she might have accused him of playing hero if he'd told her about confronting Hoebel. He sure as hell didn't want to scare her any more than she was already scared.

He was doing what he had to do: let her go and hope to God she'd come back.

Bannon wanted to follow her, but it was a little too late for that. He turned the key in the ignition and headed for Doris's place.

* * *

Driving alone gave her a chance to think about him. She needed a distraction, badly. For the time it took her to get to Montgomery's house, she was going to focus on something positive.

They'd had something good going before all this happened.

The long curves of the well-maintained old road soothed her restlessness. Her mind was racing and she forced herself to drive slowly.

Bannon. He might be the man of her dreams, but he had opened up the door to a nightmare. She'd had no idea that the man she'd met purely by chance at the art fair was going to turn her life upside down. Neither had he.

Despite everything, she knew she still wanted him in her life, whatever it was going to be from here on in. It had to do with how she felt when he was around. Good. Happy. She'd been surprised to discover that the beginning of a romance could be that uncomplicated.

The physical attraction was strong from the start. Besides being great-looking, he was built. She relaxed fractionally, remembering what it had been like to draw him—he had the body of a male model without the professional detachment. His self-consciousness at being under her gaze for as long as she liked had amused her. Covertly, she'd studied every inch of him.

She'd known she wanted him, pretended to be diffident. He'd seemed to see through that.

From the start, his genuine interest in her art and what she'd accomplished so far got right through her usual reserve around men. It hadn't taken longer than a few hours in his company to figure out that she and Bannon had a few important things in common—the ability to observe the world around them in a unique way was one, their independence was another—but they were different enough to spark a fire that could burn bright.

Having him around her place those few times made the rented house feel like home for the first time. Seeing him come up the stairs with that long, easy swing to his stride, and a smile that said he could hardly wait to see her, was part of that feeling. Then, later, wallking over the fields in the golden late-afternoon sunlight like they'd been together forever—she could get used to that in a very good way. Just her and Bannon and a big dog, for starters. And that cat.

Nice dream. Wake up, she told herself.

The case was going to come between them. She had no way of stopping it. Erin's hands tightened on the wheel. She loathed the idea that a past of which she knew nothing could cause someone she liked so much to look at her differently.

She just didn't know. He didn't seem to pity her. But he was suddenly cautious around her, like she might break if he said or did the wrong thing. Funny how all she wanted to do was go into his arms and stay there. But instead she'd kept her distance, stunned by what he was saying.

Thank God he'd stopped explaining when he noticed her silence. One more minute of it and she would have started to scream. He had his theories, the boxes were probably full of a thousand more, and she didn't want to hear or read any of it.

Just hold me. She hadn't said it. Later, yes, he had let her cry it out in his big, strong arms. But something was different. He was doing the right thing, he was that kind of guy. That didn't mean it was what he wanted to do.

A sickening tension clutched at her heart. So much for distracting herself. Erin bit her lip and clutched the wheel, driving on without really looking at the road. The hell with it. She was almost there.

On her way up the semicircular stairs to the front door, Erin took a deep breath. She didn't know what she would do if Caroline opened it. Say that Mr. Montgomery was expecting her? Did the blonde even know she'd been invited?

She was relieved when a butler in a dark suit answered her knock. Erin bent down to pick up the sketchpad she'd leaned against her leg. The old tackle box clanked in her hand and only then did she realize how odd it must seem for a female guest to show up carrying that instead of a purse.

But the man smiled warmly at her. "I'll let Mr. Montgomery

know you're here, Miss Randall. He's been looking forward to your visit."

"Thank you." She entered and he shut the door with a quiet click, indicating by gesture that she was to follow him.

"Please come this way. And let me help you with your things."

"Ah—" She couldn't very well argue. Erin surrendered the tackle box. He took it carefully and carried it in the crook of his arm, as if she had entrusted him with a jeweled evening bag.

The house was impressive. She glanced up at a grand, curving staircase to the second floor. Evidently they weren't going that way. Erin noticed vases half her height on either side of the open doorway they were about to pass through. Branches on the verge of flowering had been artistically arranged in them—a mix of white-budded cherry and coral-colored quince. A few of the blossoms had already opened.

"Very pretty," she murmured to the butler.

He acknowledged her comment with a polite nod as they walked into the next room. On a mantel above a vast fireplace was a pair of smaller vases, holding long, slender stems covered with catkins. Erin stopped to touch one fuzzy bud with her finger. "Oh— pussywillows," she said softly.

A slight smile appeared on the man's otherwise impassive face when he stopped too and turned to her. She felt a bit embarrassed for sounding like a little girl. "Sorry. They're irresistible. And they always were my favorite."

"All our flowers are grown here," he said in a friendly voice. "Mr. Montgomery wanted to recreate the gardens of the old house where he grew up. I hear they were glorious."

Had she played under blooming shrubs there as a child? Her three-year-old self would have been nearly hidden. Maybe that was how she'd been abducted. A child's unheard cry, a swirl of falling petals—gone before anyone noticed.

No. Bannon had said she'd been taken at night.

"It's a beautiful place, but there are mostly lawns now. Not flowers. I've been there."

The butler nodded and began to walk on. "Mr. Montgomery

mentioned that you'd painted the mansion for the historical society. You'll be meeting him in the solarium. There are more plants
and whatnot in there. Some are quite rare."

Erin mumbled an appreciative reply and adjusted the position of
the sketchpad under her arm as she followed him. How big was this
house? Despite the spectacular floral arrangements, the décor wasn't
very welcoming. Whoever had been in charge of it was partial to
gold and silver brocade on the furniture and heavy window treat-
ments that blocked a lot of the light.

The butler turned and paused on the threshold of a hallway that
poured sunshine into the room they'd walked through. Her heart
lifted.

For some reason, with Mr. Montgomery recovering from a
stroke, she had imagined that he would be in a room with the
shades drawn and thick carpets that muffled sound. Soothing,
maybe, but also depressing. Erin just wanted to get through this
without having to think about last night's revelations or tears.

"The solarium is right this way," the butler said, gesturing for her
to follow him into the hallway.

A young woman in a loose cotton top over jeans waited for them
at a double door made of multi-paned glass. One side was open,
and through it Erin could see enormous plants and shrubs in pots
and part of a wicker settee. The woman came forward.

"Hello," she said to Erin, extending her hand. "I'm Vernette Adams,
Mr. Montgomery's nurse."

"Nice to meet you." They shook hands and for a moment all
three of them just stood there.

"Ah—let me go ask about the refreshments," the butler said.
"This belongs to Miss Randall." He handed the nurse the tackle
box.

Vernette's cheerful expression turned curious. "Are we going
fishing?"

"No." Erin laughed. "I keep my art things in it."

"Oh. That's great. I know Mr. Montgomery is eager to see the
sketches."

Erin patted the sketchpad under her arm. "Right here."

"I got a tour of the stables the other day," Vernette said, looking over her shoulder as Erin followed her into the solarium. "I don't think I ever saw so many horses all at once."

"It's really interesting, isn't it?" Erin said.

The nurse dropped her voice a little. "He loves it there, but he did get tired. That's why we're in here today."

"This is a wonderful space." Erin took in the view over rolling fields through the tall, floor-to-ceiling windows. The solarium seemed to run the length of the entire house. Though new, its design was reminiscent of a Victorian conservatory, and the butler had told the truth about all the plants. There had to be hundreds, arranged on open shelves of verdigris metal and sitting in handsome pots on the floor. The air had a fresh, loamy smell that revived her spirits.

Erin heard a deep but slightly shaky male voice call a hello from the far end of the room.

"Turn left at the tree fern," the nurse said, brushing aside delicate fronds that seemed to want to enfold her and holding them back for Erin.

She dodged through, noticing the large fiddleheads at the center of the giant fern, curving up to the sun that streamed through the high windows.

Bracing himself on one arm of a wrought-iron bench, Montgomery rose to meet her.

"Please don't get up," Erin said quickly.

"Too late." He was on his feet, holding out a hand to Erin.

She put down the sketchpad and took it, surprised by the strength and warmth of his grip. Then she realized that he was steadying himself by holding on to her hand. Vernette seemed to know it. She put the tackle box down on a table that matched the bench and took his arm.

"Feeling dizzy?" the nurse asked him.

"I'm fine. I can get up and down on my own." He gave her a mock glare and rested a hand on the back of a chair. "Please have a seat, Erin." He waited until she did to return to the bench and sit down himself, taking a deep breath as he settled in.

"Your good manners are going to kill you, Mr. Montgomery," Vernette teased him. "All right. I'll leave you two alone."

She went off in a different direction, bypassing the tree fern. Erin wondered where Caroline was. But she wasn't going to ask.

They made small talk until the butler appeared with a tray, which he set on the table, serving both of them bite-sized sandwiches and tea, then leaving them to it.

The thought of Montgomery being her father overshadowed her thoughts. She stole more than one sidelong look at him. That nose, that set to the jaw, the forehead—she didn't see herself. Erin told herself to concentrate on something neutral. The food, for starters.

There really were cucumber sandwiches. She'd never had one. Live and learn. Erin picked one up and nibbled at it, liking what the flavor of the delicate cress and mayonnaise did for the plain slices of cucumber.

"Is there any roast beef?" Montgomery asked. "Aha. Yes. Mrs. Horsham insists on serving vegetables, but I refuse to starve." He found what he wanted and devoured a small roast beef sandwich, then another.

Erin smiled politely. She was a stranger to all this and it all seemed unreal. Thinking while she ate another cucumber sandwich, she decided it was only different from the way she'd been brought up. Not necessarily better, just different. She selected a thin carrot stick from a celery-carrot mix in a cut-crystal container, and bit into it. The humble carrot tasted exactly the same.

"You and Take All share a fondness for those."

She smiled as she moved the tray of food and tea aside and picked up her sketchbook. "Yes, he did seem to get his share of treats from everyone. Your horses live well."

"Especially him. So—let's see what you have."

She picked up her sketchbook and opened it, turning the large pages slowly until she found the drawings she'd liked best. Then she positioned the pad so he could view it easily.

"Here he is. In bits and pieces."

Montgomery studied the unfinished sketches in silence, seeming very pleased. "These are wonderful, Erin. You have a great deal of talent."

"Thank you. I'm glad you like them."

"Very much."

She showed him other drawings, including some that really were bits and pieces. A hoof. Two oval ears turned in different directions. Flowing strokes that captured a tail flicking at a horsefly.

"He has so much personality. I can draw him without looking at him."

"Really?"

"Yes." To prove her point, she opened the tackle box and took out charcoal and a kneaded eraser to sketch the magnificent horse from memory—mostly his tricks, to amuse Montgomery.

Keep it light, she told herself. *No thinking allowed.*

No more than a minute went by and there was Take All on paper, balking on a lead rope with his hooves planted in the turf. Poking his head over his stable door, showing his teeth in an unrepentant grin at an exasperated groom waving a curry brush. She covered several pages as Montgomery watched with fascination. "You truly do know him, bad habits and all."

"Yes. And I keep a respectful distance." She laughed.

"When do you think you'll finish?"

"Oh—in a few months, if you're talking about the painting. It's great being able to study Take All close up. And I love the stables. There's so much going on. But there are quiet spots to draw."

He nodded. "A properly run stable is a fine place to be. So long as someone else mucks out the stalls," he added with a wink.

"I feel very much at home." How strange those words sounded in her mouth.

Montgomery smiled. "Did you have horses growing up, Erin?"

She swallowed hard and shook her head. "Not really. Unless you count our old plowhorse. He was too smart to work."

"Ah. I didn't know you grew up on a farm."

"It wasn't a working farm by the time we bought it."

"Tell me more. I really don't know much about you, Erin."

"There's not that much to tell," she admitted, especially since she wasn't sure anymore what the truth was. "My mother used to be a teacher, but I was homeschooled."

"You seem to have had a good education."

Did her voice sound as brittle as she felt? "Oh, I learned a little something about practically everything." She forced a smile. "My father let me hang around in his workshop. He was an inventor—we lived on the income from some of his patents."

"I see. Were you an only child?" The question rocked her. His vanished daughter had been his one and only. She hoped that he didn't see Ann when he looked at her, then chided herself for the thought.

"Yes, in a way. I did have a brother, but he died before I was born. He was only two, I think. Maybe three. My folks never talked about him."

Montgomery nodded. His next question was tentative and gently voiced. It was almost as if he'd guessed the answer before he asked. Stroke or no stroke, he was shrewd, she thought.

"Are they still alive?"

"No."

"I'm sorry," he said. "And I shouldn't pry."

"It was a while ago," she said.

"Yes." His tone grew curt. "But even so . . . some things don't get easier to bear. I—I suppose you know about my daughter."

A sudden, almost unbearable curiosity consumed her. She nearly asked why he didn't mention his wife. "Just what I saw on the news. I'm sorry—" She hesitated, not knowing quite how to express her concern. "I hope the case being opened again didn't shock you too much."

He didn't respond for a few moments, lost in thought. "Ann would have been about your age."

"I—I think I heard that." Erin's heart sank. Should she tell him? Ask questions? How much did he know?

Montgomery's eyes clouded over. "Gone. Not forgotten. Not ever." He paused to compose himself. "Well, let's talk of happier things. Mrs. Meriweather came by. She asked about you."

Erin didn't know whether to be grateful for the abrupt change of subject. She felt like crying. "I should call her. She's very nice."

"She happened to mention that you have a small house in the country—"

"It's not mine," Erin said quickly. "A girlfriend of mine owns it—she's living up in Vermont."

"I see. Mrs. Meriweather said she'd been driving through—" He stopped, looking confused. Erin supplied the name of the little town and he nodded. "That was the place."

"The house isn't in town, though," Erin said. "It's about five miles out. Maybe six."

"Oh. She said she stopped by and saw your car in front, but that you weren't there."

Remembered fear clenched at her insides. The thought of the sweet old lady out there alone after what had happened made her feel suddenly shaky. But she'd had no way of knowing that Mrs. Meriweather would pay a call. Thank God nothing had happened.

"If it was the afternoon," she said in a controlled voice, "I was out with Charlie."

Montgomery raised an inquiring eyebrow.

"He's my temporary dog—he belongs to a friend of mine."

"Oh."

She tensed, inwardly hanging on to her self-control and switching the subject herself. "I'm sorry I missed Mrs. Meriweather, though."

He didn't seem to want to ask any more questions, just let his gaze move over her face. Erin stopped talking, disconcerted.

"You remind me of someone," he said, catching himself. "That tilt of the head when you seem thoughtful, the way you did just then. Or is it—never mind. I might be imagining things. My memory has been playing tricks on me."

"Oh." She knew he meant his missing daughter. Her. But his quick dismissal of it as a trick of his memory told Erin the resemblance he spoke of wasn't to him. Her mirror had told her the same thing.

"The neurologist told me to expect memory lapses. He says it should improve in time. But he can't say when."

"That's too bad," she said sympathetically.

"Numbers escape me. And I can't quite connect faces with names."

"I understand," she assured him. "That happens to me sometimes. Although I don't have—any experience with what happened to you."

Montgomery's pensive expression grew sad. "And I hope you never will. My apologies. I didn't mean to bring that up."

Erin was glad that their conversation hadn't taken any wrong turns. She hadn't cracked or burst into tears. Even hinting at what she now knew could have derailed everything. She wanted to take her time. If she was his daughter, she wanted to hear him say it. That meant more to her than anything. The evidence didn't.

Vernette came back, her sensible shoes squeaking faintly on the tiled floor of the solarium. "Sorry to interrupt," she said quietly. "I just wanted to check on Mr. Montgomery."

"And for once I'm happy to see you," he said, teasing her before she could start in on him.

They seemed to have become fast friends. Erin was glad that he hadn't been left to Caroline's tender mercies.

Montgomery seemed tired, more tired than before, and there were gray circles under his eyes.

Erin gathered up her things and made her good-byes to both of them. He was nothing like he'd been at their first meeting. She was no longer intimidated, only sad for him. And for herself.

His mind might fade away before they could get to know each other as father and daughter. What if they ran out of time?

She followed the butler out the way she'd come in, not thinking too clearly herself.

CHAPTER 20

Erin maneuvered around the curves of the long driveway, back to the main road. But she didn't head in a direction that would take her to Wainsville. She drove out to the west instead, over roads she knew well, not paying much attention, lost in thought.

Spending time with Mr. Montgomery and seeing for herself the aftereffects of his stroke left her shaky. She hadn't been able to even hint at the things Bannon had gone over with her. If she had been abducted, if she were his long-lost daughter—she still couldn't get her mind around either one.

When she got back to Bannon's condo, she was going to open up those boxes from the TV station and try to take a long, hard look at everything now that she was calmer. Driving did help—once her hands were on the steering wheel, she could concentrate on the road and not her troubles. But the steady feeling might be something like the eye of a hurricane—a deceptive lull. What she didn't know and hadn't seen might knock her down.

Bannon wasn't going to stop investigating the Montgomery case, no matter the risk—and what had happened to her was next on his To Do list. Nice of him to care that much.

He did care.

Good going, she told herself ruefully. *You had to go and get mixed up with a detective*. He liked to live dangerously, she didn't. Finding out what people wanted to hide was a good way to get whacked.

She had been hidden for so long. That had taken thought and

planning and a measure of luck. Still, during all those years someone could have noticed that the little Randall girl seemed to have
appeared out of nowhere, even if no one ever went to the authori-
ties. There had to have been someone who'd glimpsed her once or
twice. She had a fierce need to believe that.

See me. Hear me. She had been too young to say those words
and no one had. She might as well have been invisible.

Their old farmhouse had been out in the middle of nowhere.
There was no return address on the letters her mother would write
from time to time. They sat in sealed envelopes for weeks, not
stamped, unsent. The post office was miles away and her father
never let her mother drive the banged-up car he kept in a garage
with locked doors.

Erin had had no idea at the time whom the letters were meant
for. She'd been old enough to read, but she didn't remember the
names or addresses on the front.

Those details were forever lost. The Randalls were dead, their
possessions destroyed.

Erin looked into the rearview mirror and saw that the road behind her was empty. She drove faster.

She had to see where she'd come from. Even though there was
nothing to see.

Twenty minutes later, she pulled over again. This time she was
well off the main road. The trees had grown back some since her
last visit here, but there was still an empty spot where the house
had stood.

The smell of ashes was long gone, but the black ruins of what
had been the Randall farmhouse were still there. She'd driven away
from the only home she'd ever known in a rattletrap car her father
had fixed up, on her way to college. Her parents were still living
here then, almost recluses, but they, too, were elsewhere on the
evening of the fire.

A conscientious deputy had called her, revealing a little too
much in his eagerness to be helpful. Her mom and dad had refused
to cooperate with the police investigation. The fire had been
chalked up to arson. Perpetrator unknown.

They had died within months of each other of natural causes

after their home had gone up in flames. Whatever clues to her real identity there might have been within its walls were ashes too.

Erin didn't stay long. The sight of the ruins affected her differently this time around. She literally couldn't stand to look at the scene now.

She still didn't head back to Wainsville. Erin just wanted to keep moving, and she did, for the better part of an hour. The roads changed but she stared straight ahead, thinking and thinking.

About Bannon, mostly.

She wanted him passionately. She had from the start. Why? Maybe it had something to do with the way he took care of her.

What lay ahead was anyone's guess. Erin sighed and turned off onto an intersection that looked familiar. Wainsville was about ten miles thataway. She'd been driving in an irregular circle many miles in diameter. It was time to go back.

Erin realized she hadn't called Bannon when she'd arrived at Montgomery's house. This long after her departure, it seemed beside the point, but she decided to text him. Easier than talking. He didn't have to know where she was right now, and if he asked, she could always say that the text had been delayed.

Got here @ 1 pm. Leaving in a while.

Not now. Not even soon. If he picked up on the fact that she needed more time and wasn't going to ask him for it, then good. The short message was meant to be vague.

Bannon's cell phone chimed in his shirt pocket.

"Excuse me," he said to Doris. "Incoming text."

She rolled her eyes. "Do me a favor," she replied. "If you and everyone else in your generation—"

"That's a lot of people," he said with a wink.

"Okay, then just you. If you would stop acting like you're guiding a jet with a blown engine down to an emergency landing on Runway Nine every time your cell phone makes noise, I would be very happy. Incoming, my bunny slippers. Want some coffee?"

"Sure." It was tactful of her to excuse herself, even if all he had to do was pick up the message, not listen or talk. He punched the button to read it, and frowned.

Got here @ 1 pm. Leaving in a while.

Not very informative. But it was better than nothing.

He turned back to the boxes Doris had brought from the police station. The two of them had been organizing all the evidence.

"Wait for me," she called. "I don't trust you to follow my system."

"Okay," he replied, lifting out more papers and photos anyway.

She came back in with two cups on a tray. "I knew you wouldn't listen."

Bannon looked at the cups. "They're empty."

"Yeah. On purpose. I'm not going to let you spill coffee on stolen evidence just because you get excited easily."

"You know I'm always careful," he said absently, holding up what he'd been looking for. "Yay. Here's the Ann Montgomery photos. I wanted to get a better look at those—do you know I have a digital microscope? And don't call me Sherlock," he added quickly.

"I won't. By the way, there are some new photos in there," she said, setting down the cups well away from the boxes. "Old but new to you, I mean."

"Got it."

Bannon looked through them all. The last one stopped him cold and his eyes widened. He double-checked the back of it for an evidence tag.

Yup, it was Luanne Montgomery. Young—too young, by his guess, to have had a baby. She was incredibly pretty. Slim. The bathing suit she was wearing clung to her skin. Her wet hair was pulled back, completely off her face, and she wasn't wearing any makeup.

He could have been looking at Erin, right out of the shower. The two women were nearly identical. Like mother and daughter.

Bannon had returned home by the time Erin walked through the door. He had brought back the boxes of evidence, placed them on top of the larger ones from the TV station.

"Hello," she said. From her closed expression, Bannon figured she wasn't inclined to talk. He wasn't going to press her. Seeing Montgomery must have been a strange experience, to say the least, considering that she knew he was almost certainly her father.

Her gaze moved over the room. Unfortunately, she seemed to notice the new boxes right away.

"What are those?" she asked without much interest.

"Doris found more boxes of evidence."

She nodded. "And she brought them home?" Her face turned to the new boxes, then back to him.

Bannon got up. "Yes. It's all from the Montgomery files. You can go through them if you like."

Erin's expression was noncommittal. "Okay. Maybe later."

He could take a hint. "I think I'll head out for a jog. I just walked Charlie, so he's good for a while." He moved toward the bedroom. "Gotta change, then I'm out of here."

She didn't look up when he came out in shorts and a T-shirt, and Bannon went straight to the door. "See you in about an hour. Maybe two hours if I have the energy to finish up with laps around the high school track."

"Okay." Erin leaned back as the lock clicked behind him. His casual attitude didn't fool her. There was something important in the new boxes that Doris had brought.

He wanted her to find it for herself.

One functioning strap was still attached to the crummy backpack slung over Paul's shoulder. He knocked and then fiddled with the other strap, which was torn, until Hoebel unlocked the door of the basement office for him.

"What's up?" he asked.

"You're late," Hoebel growled.

"So what?" Paul grabbed a metal folding chair and unzipped his backpack, taking out his laptop. The thing had acquired a few more skateboarding stickers on its aluminum case since the last time Hoebel had seen it.

"Can't you afford a better machine?"

Paul yawned and scratched himself under his sweatshirt. "No-body wants to steal an ugly one."

"You have a point, punk." Hoebel had to admit it. But some-times he had a tough time believing that he'd entrusted a kid like this with secrets that could put them both in a federal pen. "I was thinking of buying you a shiny new one. Part of your bonus when you hook the Montgomery money for me."

"Don't bother. I live in a dorm," Paul reminded him. "With nine million other punks."

"Did any of them ever hack you?"

"Lots of times. We do it back and forth to see if we can catch each other. Trojan horse attacks, mash-up malware, auto-porno in-stalls. It's fun."

Hoebel shot him a wary look. "Are you serious?"

The hacker rolled his eyes. "Dude, this particular laptop is pure."

"Really."

"Unhackable, if you want to know. I carry it with me everywhere. I sleep with it. So are you going out for pizza or what?"

Hoebel reached for his wallet and peered inside the leather flap. "Let me look—yep, two twenties. At least you're cheap to feed."

Paul nodded and opened his laptop, booting it up and picking a browser from five on the screen. "I pride myself on that. Pepperoni, extra cheese. Two cans of Coke. I need sugar and caffeine. This is going to take a while. And come back with a chunk of cash if you don't have any. You owe me."

Hoebel scowled and put his wallet back. "Maybe I should learn to do my own hacking."

The kid snorted with disgust. "You don't have what it takes."

"I could learn. You learned."

Paul shook his head as he pulled up a pirate music site. "Hey, I could teach." He made his voice sound like a late-night TV ad. "Are you under twenty-five, with a flexible sense of right and wrong? Study up on kick-ass code and break every law in the book for your degree in hackology."

"Ha ha."

"Don't laugh. I'm not going to teach you."

Hoebel opened the door and looked both ways down the hall. "Didn't think so. Get started. I'll be right back."

Paul's colorless eyes barely blinked as he heard the door slam shut behind Hoebel.

The chief unlocked the door while balancing a pizza box and a plastic bag of Cokes, paper plates, and napkins. He was thinking that it was nice of Bill, the security guard at the business upstairs, to loan them this room. Of course, Bill wanted to join the boys in blue and Hoebel would help him with that. Even if he didn't have a prayer of passing the exam or the background security check. Bill could man a desk and chow down on crullers with the best of them.

"Mmm. Smells like a heart attack," Paul said with satisfaction. He didn't turn around.

Hoebel kicked the door shut and slung the pizza box on a battered L-shaped desk that had been brought into the room and forgotten. "Let's eat."

"Throw a couple slices on a plate and bring 'em here," Paul said absentmindedly.

"You into Montgomery's account yet?" The chief pried open the lid and pulled at two greasy slices. Melted cheese on the hot dough stuck to his fingers and he blew on them.

"Not yet."

"Didn't I tell you to get started?"

"Food first. I'm looking up your creepy pal right now. Cutt."

Hoebel froze for a moment. Then he took a napkin and removed the slices, doubling the flimsy plates before he brought the pizza over.

"Did you think I was bluffing about him?" the chief asked.

Paul didn't look up when the pizza slices were shoved under his nose. "I like to check things," he said.

"Way to go."

"Yeah." The kid folded the plate into something like a half-funnel and held it over his face, lapping up a few drops of grease and then taking a bite from the part that slid down. He rested the mess in his lap and tapped a key to pull up a law-enforcement form that Hoebel recognized instantly. "Can I have a Coke?"

The chief brought one over and set it down, popping the tab. "Here you go. Sugar up."

Some soda foamed out but Paul just picked up the can and slurped off the excess.

"Thought I'd take a look at his rap sheet. You seen this, Chief? No misdemeanors. All felonies. Violent dude."

"I've seen it."

Paul took a break from his research to gobble the rest of the slices. "So where is he tonight?" he asked, wiping his hands on jeans that were already dirty.

"I don't know," Hoebel said curtly.

The hacker got up to get himself more pizza, then sat down after he ate it, tipping his head back to finish his can of soda. He crumpled the can and threw it in the direction of a wastebasket that never got emptied, and missed. "Oops. Oh, well. Not trying out for basketball," he said philosophically.

"C'mon, Paul." Exasperation laced the chief's gruff voice.

"Okay, okay. Back to work. You want Monty money. Here we go."

Hoebel watched the step-by-step hacking without much interest. He'd seen it fifty times by now. The thrill was gone.

Paul hummed. "Changes have been made. This looks different." "Like what?"

The kid clicked on the keys. "The two million is out of the reward trust." There was more clicking. "The forwarding code says— I don't recognize the number. Could be a bank he hasn't used before."

"I don't care. Grab it. Now."

Paul prowled through the connections he would need to make that happen, staying under software radar. But he stopped. "Ohhh, it went to that bank. No can do. Sorry, dude."

Hoebel straightened. "Why the hell not?"

"Look, technically, I can," the hacker said, with a note of smugness in his voice. "But I have a problem with where it is."

"Care to enlighten me?" The chief made the rubbing motion that indicated money, using his first two fingers and his thumb, putting his whole hand between Paul's face and the laptop screen so the kid couldn't ignore him. "Don't forget I have that cash you wanted. Right here, nice and warm, next to my gun. Do what I pay you to do."

Paul pushed away from the laptop. "Nope."

"Why?" The chief's face was starting to turn angry colors. He controlled his temper. Barely.

"Because the bank it got moved to didn't buy their security setup out of a box. It's custom."

"So?"

"The hacker who taught me went straight after his conviction. He ended up making more money on the good guy side, actually. Anyway, that's his. He wrote special code for this one bank. I know how he works and he knows how I work." He looked at an increasingly infuriated but silent chief. "Hackers are kinda like old-time jazz musicians. We recognize each other's riffs."

Hoebel grabbed the kid and lifted him out of his folding chair, then held him against the wall by his throat. "Don't give me that crap! Get the money out of there!"

Paul's breath hissed out, then in again. His glasses were askew on his nose and his pale eyes blinked furiously. His mouth tried to form words.

Hoebel dropped him. The kid coughed and choked, then vomited a sour torrent of coke and pizza all over the floor. The chief jumped back as Paul staggered to his chair and sat down, his head drooping. He rubbed his throat. Finally he managed to say something, a single word that hung in the nasty-smelling air.

"N-no."

Hoebel swore violently but hung back on his side of the disgusting mess on the floor.

"What's the matter?" Paul asked in a raw, low voice. "You afraid I'll spew some more? Don't want to get your shoes dirty?"

"Shut your mouth!"

Paul coughed and spat. "Sure. Pay me, and I'll keep it shut longer, if you know what I mean."

Slowly, with obvious reluctance, Hoebel moved to get out his wallet. He opened it and took several hundred-dollar bills, setting them on the table by Paul. The kid took the money and counted it. "Not enough. Go get more." He hit a key and turned the laptop to face Hoebel. "You're on webcam."

The chief's face turned livid as he stepped forward and whacked the laptop off the table. The kid grabbed it before it hit the floor, and scooped up his backpack, running right through the vomit to jerk open the door and get away.

Hoebel hesitated just long enough to let it happen. Then he stepped around the splashed pool of pizza and Coke and went out the door to the hallway. Empty. A blast of fresh air hit his face from an open, unseen exit to the outside at the top of the stairs to the basement.

He looked down at wet sneaker prints on the carpet. Hoebel glanced back into the empty room. He didn't have to explain anything to Bill. Let the guard deal with it.

Avoiding the prints, he edged along the wall and left. When he got outside, staying away from lights, he saw the bulky, unmarked SUV he drove. Someone was in it.

Hoebel was half tempted to collar the kid, bring him in on probable. The punk oughta spend a night in a holding cell with the fun people, he thought angrily.

Nah. He'd just rough him up.

He stuck to the dark side of the parking lot and reached the door, yanking it open. For a confused second, he thought the kid had gotten taller. Then he realized it was Cutt, slouched behind the wheel.

"Hi," the lanky man said in a cool voice. "You should lock your car. Someone might steal it."

"What the—what are you doing here?" The chief toned down the volume and the heat. After what Bannon had told him about Cutt, he had to be careful. Another problem he didn't need.

"I was driving by the lot and I saw your wheels. I parked around the corner." He lifted a bottle of cheap rye and waved it at Hoebel. "Did we have a meeting tonight? I forgot."

"No."

"Then how come I saw Paul run out? You two fight?"

"No again." An edge of exasperation crept into the chief's voice. "He had to leave."

"Don't you usually drive him back to campus?" Cutt said in a needling voice. He gave a belch that reeked of booze.

"Slide over," the chief replied. "Where do you want to go? You're drunk." He'd got lucky. Cutt wouldn't remember much of this.

The other man tipped the bottle over his mouth and finished up the dregs. He tossed it over the seat and it fell on the carpeted floor with a soft thunk. "Take me home. Down a country road. Um, wha' about my car?"

"I'll send a couple of guys out in a cruiser. They'll leave it at the lookout near your land." He added sarcastically, "Beautiful view from there. There's nothing finer than the Blue Ridge Mountains."

Cutt eased his lanky frame over to the passenger side. He bumped into the computer monitor fastened to the lower part of the dash and it came to life. Not focusing too well, he peered at the glowing screen and the map displayed on it. "Looky there," he said. "A GPS program. No icon. Did the suspect find it?"

"That case is closed."

The chief barely looked at Cutt as he slid behind the wheel. But he didn't like what he saw. The man's eyes were damn near going in circles. He wasn't just drunk. Cutt's mind was on the fritz and shorting out. Hoebel could almost hear the lethal buzz. It was time to end their association.

CHAPTER 21

Twelve hours later, Hoebel still had a headache. The struggle with Paul and the encounter with Cutt hadn't done his blood pressure any good. The chief waited at the front door of the Montgomery house, shifting from foot to foot. The ponderous brass knocker felt heavy in his hand, and the sound it made echoed as if the house was empty. Someone had to be here. The old man had servants, and a girlfriend in residence.

Not that he had ever met her.

Hoebel frowned and knocked again, wincing. His swollen, scraped knuckles hurt every time he bent his fingers. Things had gotten physical with Cutt last night when he'd fired the man. The crazy bastard was cruising for a bruising. The younger man had been drunk, which gave Hoebel a narrow advantage. The chief got him in a headlock and explained why he should stay away from Erin Randall—explained with his fists. Enough said.

An older woman in a housekeeper's uniform finally answered, opening the door only a crack to look at him suspiciously.

The chief raised a meaty hand and indicated his badge.

Cutt had swung a few wild blows, landing one below the chief's eye. His cheek hadn't shown a bruise when Hoebel shaved early this morning. Maybe blood had pooled under the skin. Or maybe the lady in the uniform wasn't impressed by a badge.

"Good morning, ma'am. Sorry to bother you—I'm Police Chief Hoebel. I don't think we've met. Is Mr. Montgomery in?"

Her eyes widened. "Has something happened?"

"Ah—I'd rather not say. Would it be possible to speak to him privately?" He anticipated her next question and answered it before her mouth opened to ask it. "No, he isn't expecting me."

He was a little annoyed not to be asked in right away, but the housekeeper finally did. "Please come in. He hasn't been well, but maybe he can see you."

"Thank you."

She indicated a chair in the foyer. "Would you like to sit down?"

"No. I can't stay long," he said. A not-so-subtle hint that might make her walk a little faster.

The housekeeper went to a grand staircase, going up and disappearing to somewhere on the second floor. A door opened on the floor he was on and he heard voices, both female, arguing heatedly.

"Vernette, you must get him to take his medication."

"If he won't, I can't force him to. This is his house, not a nursing home."

A ladylike but youthful voice responded with a couple of choice curses. The other woman didn't respond.

Who was Vernette? He'd already guessed that the ladylike one was Montgomery's girlfriend, Caroline. He'd written off a few DUIs for her daddy. Hamp Loudon regarded drinking and driving as his birthright, and he cursed a blue streak every time he got pulled over. Hoebel had read the police reports, thinking Hamp would be an easy shakedown, and he remembered them. He looked impatiently up the stairs to see if the housekeeper was returning.

"The night nurse said you spoke to her about it, Ms. Loudon. We're trying, that's all I can say. But I can't promise anything."

Hoebel mentally filled in the blanks. Vernette must be the private-duty nurse on the day shift. Was she in charge of the others? She sounded like it. So old Monty wouldn't take his pills. No surprise. But if he kicked the bucket, Hoebel was going to be good and screwed.

"Don't you walk away when I'm talking to you!"

More curses. Caroline Loudon was no lady. The housekeeper reappeared, frowning at the sound of the raised voices downstairs. She went very quickly down the stairs, only nodding to the chief as she went by him into a room he couldn't see and closing the door that had been opened. Hoebel couldn't really hear what she said in a very low voice, but the argument suddenly stopped.

She came back, her face expressionless. "Sorry to keep you waiting. Mr. Montgomery says he'll see you. His nurse should be with him, but—well, Mr. Montgomery prefers to speak to you alone. Please keep it to fifteen minutes if you can."

"Yes, ma'am. Thank you."

She didn't seem flattered by his politeness and he thought with a scowl that he shouldn't have bothered.

The housekeeper turned and led him up the stairs, to a room that seemed like a study. It held a big old desk with a computer on a stand next to it. A cabinet built into the wall was open, a key sticking out of a lock. The shelves behind the cabinet doors were in disarray, but Hoebel could see a wireless router inside, fully operational. Its little green lights were on, all in a row. Looked like it communicated with the laptop open on the sofa.

The man who was sitting by it was barely recognizable as the fierce old guy that Hoebel was used to dealing with.

Montgomery wore wrinkled striped pajamas and his hair was messy, as if he'd been running his hands through it. He made a move to get up but the housekeeper stopped him.

"Please don't, Mr. Montgomery. You need to rest. Chief Hoebel can only stay fifteen minutes." She straightened and gave Hoebel a gimlet look of warning.

"All right," Montgomery said in a dull voice. "Where's Vernette?"

"She's on her way upstairs."

The housekeeper began to walk out as Hoebel took the arm-chair opposite Montgomery.

So this was what the aftermath of a stroke looked like. Ugly. And pathetic. He'd heard that the old guy had been doing fairly well after his release from the hospital. Montgomery must be on the verge of a relapse. His skin seemed as gray as his hair. Hoebel felt an uneasy prickle and belatedly recognized it as conscience.

The hell with it. He had to get one last payoff from the old man, and it had to be big enough to go out with a bang. You couldn't blackmail a dead man, and the kid hacker might decide to turn him in any time.

"I know you're not here to ask about my health. If you are, I feel like I'm dying. So talk," Montgomery said in a monotone. He didn't seem to be joking.

Hoebel suppressed a smile. That sounded almost like the man he remembered.

"Yes, sir." Montgomery was easier to manage when you threw in a few sirs. "I'm sure you remember our arrangement. I'm here to collect what I'm owed."

"How much?"

Gee whiz. The old man was still sharp as a tack. Hoebel named his price, adding, "Final payment."

Montgomery thought for a while.

Hoebel stole a look at the laptop. A financial document of some kind was open on the screen—just by looking over Paul's shoulder, he'd learned to recognize most documents that Montgomery used. This was the trust.

He squinted hard at the line he was interested in. Ann Montgomery was still the beneficiary of the damn thing. A dead girl, on the mind of a dying man. *For cryin' out loud*, he thought with disgust. He looked up, startled when Montgomery cleared his throat and spoke.

"No. There's no more money. It's gone, Hoebel."

"But—"

"I said it's gone. All of it." Exhaustion overcame him and Montgomery leaned his head back and closed his eyes.

Hoebel fumed. He'd come a little too late for that final payoff and now he was screwed. It wasn't like he could rough up Montgomery. The housekeeper would hear, and whoever else was around to feed the old man strained bananas.

And even if he used force, he hadn't watched the hacker long enough to learn how to steal passcodes. If he knew how, he'd siphon the reward money in a heartbeat, the way he used to steal gas in high school. You had to suck it up just so. He'd have to try a different approach.

"Okay. Sorry to hear that. By the way, I have something to tell you," he said suddenly.

"What?" Montgomery's voice held no interest.

"We found some remains. Our top guy says child's bones. You know, small. Scattered. Looks like the animals got there first—well, never mind the details. The scatter area is close to your old house."

Not a bad lie considering he'd just made it up, Hoebel thought with twisted pride. It wasn't likely Montgomery would remember all of it—but it was only intended to scare him. Now that Cutt and Paul were out of the lineup, the only thing the chief could do to get his last payoff was play mind games with this pathetic old man. There was a fat wad of cash sitting in a new bank, and as far as Hoebel was concerned, he had grabbing rights, considering how the two others had betrayed him. Without the hacker to do an electronic transfer, the chief was on his own.

First step: Persuade the old man that the trust was pointless.

Hoebel knew like he knew his own name that the kid had to be dead. He'd read the book on appropriate responses from authority figures. Parents wanted—what was the word? Closure. Okay, poor old Montgomery was going to get closure. He'd probably break down and cry. Next move: Manly understanding. Quiet sympathy. Moving right along to mutual trust. The rules were the same as any other confidence game. The stakes were high enough to almost make it fun.

Montgomery sat up partway, breathing hard from the effort. "Is that true?"

"Yes, sir. The forensic team is out there now." He added a little more bogus information just in case Montgomery was thinking of taking a drive in his pajamas or having someone drive him. "They cordoned off the site."

The old man slumped and didn't talk for a moment. "I don't know why I keep hoping," he said in a faint voice. He picked up the laptop at an odd angle, and it almost slid off his lap. He held on to it and hit a few keys with a wavering finger.

"People do." Hoebel was angling for another look at the screen. His first move in the mind game was only meant to rattle the old man, in preparation for a careful shakedown when his servants and nurses and whatnot were busy elsewhere. Maybe not tonight, but he had to start somewhere.

Hoebel was startled to see a screen shot of Erin Randall at the original Montgomery mansion appear.

Montgomery gave him a crooked smile. "Not her bones you found. No. She isn't gone. The eyes. The eyes are the same," the old man said.

"Sir?" Hoebel wondered if Monty was about to blow another valve in his brain. He thought fast. A second stroke would really screw things up, if that was what was about to happen.

He looked closely at the old man. Hell, he was no doctor, but Montgomery looked pretty damn shaky. If he went back to the hospital, Hoebel would need to regroup, make a contact inside the new bank, give him or her a healthy cut so he could take the money and run—

At that moment, a woman in a scrub top and jeans walked in. "Time's up," she said briskly to Hoebel. "You must be the chief. I'm Vernette Adams."

Montgomery looked up at the sound of her voice and smiled tiredly. "There you are."

"How are you doing?" she asked him brightly.

"Still trying."

"Did you remember those passwords?" she asked him.

"Some. Not all."

"Well, that's a good sign. The rest will come back to you. You've got to take it easy, though."

"No. I'm running out of time. I can feel it."

"Are you up for another argument about your meds?" Her light tone made the old man smile again. But his answer made her frown.

"Vernette. No pills. I know Caro's been hounding you. I can hear her in my sleep."

The nurse cleared her throat and shot Hoebel a meaningful look over her patient's head. "I understand, Mr. Montgomery." She gestured toward the door for his visitor's benefit. "Chief Hoebel, nice to have met you," she said. "I'm sure you've got a million things to do. Thanks for stopping by."

There was nothing for it. The chief got up and expressed his obviously fake concern. Neither the nurse nor the old man seemed interested. He let himself out, not waiting for the housekeeper to do the honors.

Later that night, so much later that the rest of the household had to be asleep, Montgomery wandered back into his study. Vernette had won. He'd swallowed the first four or five in his prescribed regimen with a glass of water while she'd watched. He felt somewhat better. Not well. But more alert. He could remember things.

He found his laptop where he'd left it on the sofa, undisturbed but automatically shut down. In another minute he had the same image of Erin in front of him. He reached for the telephone on the side table and dialed a number he knew by heart. Not Erin's. Her mother's.

Several rooms away, Caroline picked up the receiver in her room and listened in. So quaint. No one else she knew had phones that were connected to actual wires in walls, let alone to other phones. The sound was excellent. Not a bit of static. There were a few advantages to living with a man who hadn't changed his ways since the year one. He'd kept the same damn number for the last thirty years.

Like his dead daughter was going to call him from the grave or something.

Whoever he was calling wasn't picking up. Tapping her foot impatiently, Caro listened to the rings.

His daughter. Hah. She'd had enough of that morbid charade. The past couple of months had been pure hell. That gung-ho detective had come out of nowhere and got his handsome face on TV to say he was reopening the case of darling little Ann, and Montgomery hadn't stopped obsessing for a second. So much for Caroline's marry-me campaign. Montgomery had made it all too clear before his stroke that he didn't want a replacement wife and baby. And now—well, she could just imagine the snickering if she cooed over his silver sideburns and talked about how sexy a mature man could be. She'd actually done that once upon a time. No more. His strength was gone and he couldn't even walk straight.

Let him lean on the nurse he liked so much. Caroline had a lot of things to do before she made her exit. Sneaking around with flash drives and whatnot had gotten her exactly nowhere. But she'd finally verified that the last substantial sum of money was tucked into that reward trust. Safer than a cookie jar. But not safe from Caroline.

A few days ago she'd done something so old-fashioned it was worthy of Monty: Hired a private investigator and paid him in cash. To do it, she'd had to return several designer dresses with no tags, demanding a full refund to her debit card and getting it after throwing a spectacular tantrum.

The PI knew his stuff and he specialized in financial chicanery, which was the reason why he'd demanded cash up front. He'd suggested she do some of her own digging to cut costs and had given her a few tips on how to do it. For his part, he'd unearthed a violent ex-con named Cutt, and quickly drawn a line from him to the police chief to Monty. And there were other lines. Montgomery Holdings was going belly-up. Not even Take All's potential stud fees were enough to make investors park their money in the Thoroughbred fund. And to think she'd helped him design the prospectus.

She had to protect herself. If she couldn't charm or bully Monty into giving her a reasonable settlement, there was always good old blackmail. His social standing and family name were precious to him. Hugh Montgomery would cling to both when all else was gone.

Damn it. The phone line clicked and the ringing stopped. Whoever it was didn't answer or hadn't wanted to talk to Monty. Caroline replaced the receiver quietly and went to the window, looking out at the dark trees against a night sky with no stars. Their high branches swayed in the wind. Bad weather was coming.

She picked up the receiver once more, just to check. Apparently he'd called again. Caroline was surprised to hear a woman's voice. Older. Low and sweet. She gritted her teeth, listening to the small talk between Monty and whomever he was talking to. Nothing of consequence.

Unthinkingly, she gave an angry sigh. Monty must have heard her.

"I'll have to call you later," he said to the woman.

Caroline hung up. He was nearly as sharp as ever. But why he'd used a house phone, knowing she might listen in—she didn't understand that. Unless the call was perfectly ordinary. Maybe the woman was a relative she didn't know about. No. The unfamiliar fondness in his tone didn't fit that theory.

She didn't know why he'd done it, but she was going to find out.

Bannon turned to greet Erin, who was coming in from the supermarket. Heavy bags were slung by their plastic handles over both her slender wrists. She lifted them so he could slide them off.

"Eggs and milk and OJ and bread," she said. "Everything we need for breakfast. Oh, and sausage." Charlie looked on approvingly as Bannon took the bags to the kitchen and set out the groceries on the counter. She watched him absently.

"I would've gone, you know," he said. Feeling thirsty, he didn't put the orange juice in the refrigerator, setting it aside and opening the tab top.

She gave him a slight smile. "I needed something to do."

He glanced outside the kitchen toward the boxes that Doris had brought. They were in exactly the same position atop the others. Bannon was sure Erin hadn't looked into them.

She hadn't touched any of the boxes last night either. He wasn't going to ask her why not; nor had he asked about her meeting with Montgomery. If and when she wanted to talk about that, it would happen. So far she'd said nothing.

"How was your run?" she asked him.

"Great," he said. "It's been a while since I had a chance to get out two days in a row. Feels good."

She nodded, turning her head to look at the rain suddenly spattering against the window.

"Here it comes," he said. "I saw the clouds piling up on the home stretch. Good thing neither of us got caught in it."

She came close enough for him to sense her warmth—damn. He was overheated as it was. "You looking for a hug?" he teased her. "I'd be happy to oblige but I'm all sweaty."

Erin touched her soft lips to his cheek. "Not there, you're not."

It didn't quite count as a kiss, but it was a start. "Hey," he said, startled. "I haven't shaved either."

"I don't care."

He wasn't going to argue. It was almost worth another night of frustration on the sofa to get a sweet surprise like that from her today. His brother had been right about his having to sleep with the cat, and good old Babaloo liked the arrangement just fine. But Bannon wasn't sure how long he could restrain himself.

He had to, though. The undercurrents of feeling between them— and the sensual attraction—weren't that important right now, not compared to what she had to be going through. And there was more to come. Who knew what revelations lay ahead? Bannon dismissed the idea of handing the photo to Erin without comment when the time seemed right. She had to decide what she wanted to do and when.

To see herself in Luanne Montgomery's young face was bound to be a shock. One thing at a time, he thought. One revelation too many might be more than Erin could handle.

She opened a cabinet door and reached up for a couple of juice glasses, a move that lifted her T-shirt just enough to show an inch of bare, velvety-looking skin above the top of her jeans.

Oh yeah.

He'd been about to ask if he could give her a real kiss in return, but when he saw her like that, the question was where. If the hem had gone a little higher, he could have started with her belly button.

He snapped out of it when Erin pulled her T-shirt back into place, not seeming to notice his interest. "Want me to make breakfast?"

"You shopped. I'll cook."

"Okay. That's fair." She poured herself some orange juice, then headed out to the sofa. Bannon really didn't want to stop looking at her just yet. He poked his head out of the kitchen in time to see her settle into the cushions, picking up on her sideways glance at the boxes as she drank.

So she was thinking about what was in them. Later for that, he suddenly hoped. He wasn't in the mood for life-changing conversations right now.

"Let's eat here." He indicated the table, then glanced at the stack of boxes. "You know, these are in the way."

Erin finished her juice, getting up to go into the kitchen when he came out. He heard her set the glass in the sink. "I agree," she called over her shoulder. "I was going to ask if they could go into a closet."

She was putting off the inevitable as long as possible. Bannon couldn't blame her. "No problem."

Erin came out of the kitchen. "If you want to know why, and I know you do, it's because I don't want to go through them, even though I have a feeling that was your intention."

"Sort of. I wasn't sure how you'd react to some of that stuff."

Erin leaned against the door frame, her arms folded over her chest. "It's all documents and old photographs, right?"

"Pretty much. There are police reports too."

There was a flicker of something in her eyes. Fear?

"What do they say?" she asked in a calm enough voice.

"Nothing much. There wasn't any evidence to speak of. From the night of the abduction, I mean," he amended. "And as far as what Kelly sent from the station, I haven't looked at any of it."

"Well, that makes two of us." She pressed her lips together for a second or two. "I'm just not ready."

"Then I'll put it all away for now." He made quick work of getting the boxes into the hall closet, taking his winter wear off hangers and bundling it onto the top shelf.

"Fine with me." She hesitated. "I assume you and Doris organized the material."

Was she asking if there was anything worth looking at? Hard to tell, especially when he was busy restacking the boxes and couldn't see her expression. "Uh, yeah. Everything's tagged and sorted out." He straightened, dusting off his hands and then closing the closet door. "Anyway, it can wait. I'm starving," he said cheerfully. "How about you?"

"More like moderately famished." She picked up the remote and cruised through the morning shows, keeping the sound way down low. He ripped open the sausage box and let the precooked links roll out into a frying pan, then got eggs started in another pan. Bread slotted into the toaster, pats of butter flipped on the plates. He opened the jam jar and stuck a spoon in it. A help-yourself breakfast was on the way.

"Do you think we could go out to my house?"

That stopped him cold. "What do you need?" His mind was still on the evidence. Maybe there was another scrapbook tucked away out there that held a definitive clue, one that really would wrap things up and make perfect sense. Just like TV, he thought, where it took thirty minutes to solve everything and get the girl.

"My easel," Erin said.

"That thing's huge. Linc and I didn't have room for it," he mumbled.

"I'm not blaming you, Bannon. Anyway, besides that, I need about a million other things. You wouldn't know what they are or where to find them."

Bannon turned the sausage with a spatula and flipped the eggs. "Hmm. You know, it might be a good idea if we—"

"What?"

Playing short-order cook wasn't going to get him out of answering. He really couldn't just tell her no. She had an assignment to complete, it would do her good to focus on that, and she needed her materials.

"Ah, I can't remember what I was going to say," he lied. "How do you like your eggs?"

Erin came into the kitchen. "Over easy. Those look fine." She gave him a curious look. "Let's go this afternoon."

"All right," he said. "Works for me." He turned off the browned sausages, slid her eggs onto a plate, and added the popped-up toast on the downbeat. "And thanks for not going alone."

"I wouldn't go without you, Bannon."

She took the full plate from his hand and set it on the counter. Bannon backed up, feeling as if the kitchen got a whole lot narrower as she came closer. He didn't bother to get a plate for himself. He couldn't. Her soft arms were around his neck and she was looking up at him.

"What are you doing?" he asked. "Not that I mind."

"Just thought I'd kiss the cook. For real. Thank you for letting me take my time, Bannon. And thanks for taking me in."

How about that. Every cop in the world knew the rescue-me fantasy was a potent one for a whole lot of women. But the good guys didn't take advantage of it.

Then her lips touched his. Once. Twice.

His hands slid down around her waist and somehow slipped underneath the warm, light material of her T-shirt, caressing the skin he'd glimpsed, but not going any farther than that.

Her mouth tasted of sweet juice and Bannon was damned if he was going to deny himself such an unexpected pleasure.

The embrace and the kiss itself were hungry and deeply satisfying at the same time, as if they'd waited a little too long for both. The tender pressure of her lips triggered a stronger, searching response from his. Her body moved against him, as if she craved being held and held hard.

It felt good. So good, he had to stop it. Bannon got her by the waist and moved her away from him with gentle force.

"Wow. Sorry. But you and I both know where this is going to end up."

"Tell me," she said, looking a little dazed.

"In bed. And you're not ready for that."

Erin stiffened and took a step back. Her blue eyes flashed with unexpected fire. "Are you going to protect me from everything?" she demanded. "Even what I want?"

He didn't dare reassure her with a caress. She looked like she was about to slap him. Instead, she stormed off into the bedroom and slammed the door. Bannon sighed. He wasn't going in there.

"Did you call your friend Jenny?"

They were still in the car but stopped, looking at the house from a rise at Bannon's request. It seemed the same.

They weren't. Not after that kiss. She'd come out of the bed-room eventually, acting as if it had never happened.

The afternoon light hit the windows in a way that let them look inside. The place seemed empty.

He was still going in first, and he'd brought his gun. He turned to glance at her, realizing that she hadn't answered. "You okay?"

There was a wistful look in her beautiful blue eyes. Home had to be a big deal to her. Now more than ever.

"Yes to both questions," she finally said. "And Jenny was great about it. She understood. All she wanted was for us to put timers on the lights. I told her we'd left my car here, and she said that was fine."

"Okay. Good. I can do that."

She collected herself. "Sorry. I should have told you before we got here. Just wasn't thinking, I guess."

"I understand."

They drove the last stretch of road in silence. He pulled up next to her parked car, not seeing one single thing different about it close up, except for the dust on the windshield. He'd take care of that and make sure the engine started. Then he'd move it to a dif-ferent position.

They still had not contacted the local police. Bannon had argued against it and she hadn't offered any resistance. Not having backup went against all his training. Coming out here with her was asking for trouble, even if it hadn't showed up. Hoebel knew that Bannon was on to him, and that went double for Cutt, who was violating his parole. Just because he'd tossed the GPS gizmo at Hoebel didn't mean they hadn't been followed. His instincts told him that. Mad-deningly, his other five senses weren't picking up a damn thing.

But here they were. If she needed stuff, she needed it.

"Ready?" he asked her with a sigh.

"Aren't you going to go in first?"

He grinned. "Yeah, I am. You really are getting to know me."

Erin settled into her jacket. "Go ahead. I don't mind. I like look-ing at the house from here."

He chucked her under the chin. "You're a sentimental one. It isn't even yours."

She waved him out, not replying.

Bannon did a fast perimeter check, seeing no new footprints. Today's rain and the intervening time had removed all traces of the old ones. He came around, raised a reassuring hand to her, and unlocked the front door. Without the boxes he and Linc had taken, and the stuff they'd grabbed, the inside of the house looked bare in spots. He hoped that wouldn't depress or scare her. He went from room to room, catching glimpses of her in his car through the windows when he could.

In another five seconds, he finished up and went back outside. "All clear," he called from the porch.

Erin got out and walked up the stairs to where he was standing. "Thanks for letting me take my time," she said.

"No problem."

She went right to her studio area and stood by the easel, running a hand over a side strut. "I love this thing," she said with a small smile. "I bought it with the money from the first painting I sold."

"Aha. It's not just a thing, then. It's a good memory."

Erin's eyes got shimmery. "You're right," she whispered. "I'm sentimental." He opened his arms and she went into them. Bannon just held her for a while, pressing his lips against the top of her silky head, murmuring words that he hoped would reassure her.

In her own time, she moved out of his arms, but the way her hands lingered just a little bit longer around his middle made him feel good.

"Guess I'd better think about what I want to take back," she said.

"You do that and I'll look around for some food."

She put a hand to her mouth. "Oops. The fridge must be a science project by now."

"It hasn't been that long. Providing it wasn't opened," he said.

Erin walked to the shelves. "I'm leaving it up to you."

"You shouldn't. I'm a man, and men will eat anything. You know that."

She laughed lightly as she found a bag and began putting small things and art tools in it. Bannon rummaged in the fridge and the pantry too, putting together cheese and crackers and some sliced apples. He ate and watched her collect things, offering a cracker now and then.

"Gotta keep your strength up."

"You're carrying the easel, Bannon."

He put up one arm at an angle and made a muscle. "Yeah. I know."

Erin seemed to relax as an hour passed, then a half hour. She even put on music to work by. The sun was setting when she finally announced, "I'm done."

He had taken the opportunity to figure out how to fold the easel, which wasn't as easy as it looked. The floor pieces were surprisingly heavy, which was why it was so stable, he guessed. But he had it flat and leaning by the front door before she was finished.

"Got everything?"

"I think so. I can always come back."

"No. We can always come back. As in you and me, or you and Linc, or you and me and Linc." He wasn't exactly pretending to be stern. "I don't want you here alone. Sorry to sound like a broken record, but I'm laying down the law."

"Understood," she said quietly.

They went out and she carried her bags to the car, then went back to lock the door while he carried the easel. Getting it into his vehicle was awkward, but it did fit with the backseat flipped down. She got into the passenger seat in front and dragged it forward by the top bar. "All right. It's in."

He went around to the driver's side, then realized that he'd forgotten to dust the windshield of Erin's parked car and start it up.

"Hang on," he said to her. "I want to move your car someplace else. Just so the place looks a little lived in."

"Oh. Okay. Good idea. Let me find the keys."

She looked in her purse and opened the door to toss them to him.

Bannon was glad to hear the engine start up right away. He used the wipers to dust the glass some, then gave it some squirts to get it cleaner still. He put the car in gear and rolled forward, turning the hatchback to point it in the opposite direction.

It was almost dark but he didn't bother with the lights, not wanting to blind Erin as she waited. He braked and put the car in park, hitting an unfamiliar button on the dash as he turned the key to off.

The hatchback flew open. He got out to close it, walking around to the back and slamming it down. Something hit him in the head at the exact same second, before he could think to reach for his gun. He went down.

He didn't hear Erin scream.

CHAPTER 22

The damp ground under his cheek felt like a cold compress. A vague memory of a high school game in which he'd been injured seemed to hover. Bannon reached out a hand and touched the muddy tire of a car. No. This wasn't football and he wasn't sixteen. He used the tire to pull himself up, seeing two huge, blinding lights rapidly retreating from where he was.

His gun was gone. Someone had her. In his car. He staggered to the front of hers and got in, fumbling for the key. The pain at the back of his head was unbelievably strong. He felt something crawling down his neck and slapped his hand over it. Blood. Not a bug. Soaking his collar now.

Couldn't be helped. He hoped like hell his skull wasn't fractured. But the blood wasn't running down his face. He could see.

Bannon started the engine and roared after the other car. It was darker now, but he kept the headlights off, hot on the trail of . . . he struggled to recollect the right name.

Cutt. Yeah. Tall and mean. The blow had come from above. Piece of wood. Pipe. He rubbed the back of his head where the blood was beginning to crust, feeling no splinters or jagged cuts. Okay, a pipe. Which meant Cutt hadn't hit him right, because Bannon wasn't dead and Cutt had to know it.

The guy was driving like the devil was after him.

Better believe it, Bannon thought fiercely. He wanted to step on the gas, but he kept to a following distance that reduced the likelihood of being seen.

A quarter mile ahead, the other car swerved suddenly. Was she struggling? Hitting out? Maybe she'd caught a glimpse of her car and him in it when he barreled over the last rise.

The dips and long curves in the country road were on his side so long as he drove without headlights. He struggled to get his cell out of a pocket and speed dialed Linc without looking at the phone.

Pick up. Pick up.

"Hey. What's up?" his brother said casually.

Bannon's reply was punctuated by swerves. "Trouble. Big trouble. We went back to the house. Cutt jumped me and took Erin."

Linc drew in a sharp breath. "Where are you?"

"Not sure. The road's going up. Okay, I see a marker." He gave the road number and direction to Linc, then looked at his odometer. "I'm about seven miles away from Erin's house. Ow. My ears are popping. Maybe because I got hit on the head."

"You hurt? How bad? What about her?"

"I'll live. I don't know about her. Right now Cutt is driving. I'm tailing him."

"Keep the phone with you. I'll get someone here to geo-locate from it. I'm on my way."

"By yourself?"

"Not if I can help it."

"Stealth mode. No lights, no sirens, or he'll see you miles away. Hostage situation protocols. Make it fast," Bannon said.

The road gained elevation and he lost Cutt around a couple of hairpin turns, big ones. Bannon put the phone down to navigate. When he picked it up, Linc was gone. He hung on. Turn after turn. Mile after mile.

Cresting another rise, he pulled over when he saw Cutt do the same far ahead of him. He could barely make out a cabin. Bannon had guessed at a shack or a tent. The roughly built structure was nearly hidden, perched on a jutting cliff over a jumble of massive stones that covered the slope beneath. There was only one way in to the cabin—the faint track to its rough-hewn door—and one way out.

It was all he could do not to race down to where they were. The headlights on the other car were still on when Bannon saw Erin try to escape. The tall man dragged her back in and switched them off.

Darkness swallowed everything. Silence was essential when you couldn't see the enemy.

Bannon put the car in neutral and coasted down, ending up in a narrow ditch lined with broken stones and gravel. He left the hatchback there and ran the rest of the way.

A light went on in the cabin. Propane—he could see the butt end of a large white tank, even in the dark. Bannon moved fast, getting close to the cabin but dodging into pine trees when he heard the door open. Their dripping needles were cold and prickly. Spring hadn't gotten far up this nameless mountain.

"Got your girl tied up already," Cutt said into the empty air. "Want to see?"

Bait. Don't take it, Bannon told himself. He hadn't heard a gunshot. She was still alive. Probably gagged.

Cutt took a cop stance and braced his gun, firing once into the pines. Bannon ducked before the bullet hit the tree next to him. He caught a whiff of scorched bark and pungent resin.

"Guess I missed. Or maybe you're dead." Cutt squeezed off a few more rounds, then reloaded fast.

Bannon stayed down. The other man turned and entered the cabin, closing the door. A thin, uneven rectangle of light around the frame shone into the darkness. Badly built.

Maybe he could ram himself through that door. Suddenly he heard more gunshots. No screams.

Bannon went for it, slamming his body through the door, breathing in ragged gasps. The pain in his head intensified when he saw Erin tied to a chair, her mouth gagged and taped shut. No blood. Her eyes showed her terror.

There were holes in the wall. Cutt cocked the gun right at him. "There you are. Been wanting to talk to you."

Play for time. "What about?" Bannon asked levelly.

"You and Hoebel had a fight and my name came up. The chief was mad. I got canned the other night." He smiled unpleasantly. "That's not fair. I need to get paid more than he does. I got some bad habits and I owe money. A lot of money."

"Maybe I can help. Let her go."

Cutt shot him a disgusted look. "You buying her from me?" He lowered the gun and traced Erin's cheekbone with the muzzle. "I don't think so."

Bannon tensed. "What do you want, Cutt?"

"Nothing from you. I don't trust you."

A brief silence fell, interrupted by the other man's laugh.

"I shoulda shot Hoebel while I had a chance. Guess I'll start with you." He pressed the gun to Erin's temple. She closed her eyes and he prodded her. "Uh-uh, blue eyes. Keep 'em open." Cutt waited until she obeyed, then turned to Bannon. "I'm gonna shoot you in front of her. Teach her a lesson."

"Shoot me if you want to. But leave Erin out of it."

Cutt made a low noise when he looked at her, like something ugly was squirming in his throat. "She's pretty. I was watching her off and on. Until you brought that big barkin' monster. That damn dog gave me away."

Bannon didn't answer. Erin's eyes beseeched him to . . . do what? He didn't know what else to do but listen to this psycho and try to gain the advantage.

Erin strained against the gag and cords that kept her bound and silent.

"Good thing the dog didn't come along with you today. I checked through a window. You didn't see or hear me. All that happy music playing and the two of you busy packing."

Cutt had to have driven around the back of the house—but it no longer mattered. He'd stalked them and found them.

"Now back out that door, Bannon. Nice and slow. I changed my mind."

"Why?"

Cutt stared intently at him and moved the gun like he was marking points in the air. Bannon realized what the other man was doing—per police training, eyeballing the kill spots on an imaginary target. The real targets were printed with a picture of a man. He was the man.

"I don't want splatter on my walls. Don't forget I used to be a cop. I know the drill. Someone might come around here when you and her disappear."

"Let her go," Bannon repeated desperately.

"Nah. Me and her are gonna have some fun, aren't we, sweetheart? And then I'm going to use her to get the dough I need out of Montgomery." He pointed the gun at her again, then at Bannon. "But I'm tired of looking at you. Rain is hell on evidence, so you get to die outside. Slowly."

Bannon had no choice but to obey. He might beat Cutt if they weren't in the cabin, even without a gun. In the dark, fights got crazy. He could seize the advantage. Get the bastard by the throat.

An uncertain moon was coming up through a parting in the clouds. White light silhouetted the mountain ridge. Less than a minute to make a move, by his guess. He had to lead Cutt away. Give Erin a chance to free herself, even if Bannon didn't make it.

He dodged into the woods and lay flat on the ground under wet, dripping bushes. Cutt fired his way and missed. On purpose? He could be making Bannon move where he wanted him to go.

He crept forward, feeling the cool grittiness of rock under his belly when his shirt was dragged out of his jeans. The dried leaves and needles and twigs were suddenly gone—he was crawling into a clearing. A bullet hit the rock near his head and ricocheted, deafeningly. Bannon lay low and listened for footsteps. He wasn't out of shooting range but he wasn't easy to see.

Another bullet struck. By his foot this time. Bannon crawled faster, snagging his shirt on a low branch and letting it rip off his back. Suddenly he tumbled right over the edge of the bald rock, landing several feet down with a thump, a bone-breaker of a fall. Knocked the breath out of him. The old bullet in his back made him want to scream with pain.

He rubbed the place and kept his mouth shut.

He heard soft footsteps. Cutt knew this terrain. Bannon didn't. He scrambled away from where he'd tumbled, pushing hard with his feet. His legs worked. He hadn't broken them or his spine.

He could hear Cutt breathing up above him.

"Bannon? Try again." The soft jeering was infuriating. "Climb up. There's a handhold to your left."

Cutt knew exactly where Bannon was hiding. He'd probably freeclimbed this boulder fall hundreds of time, knew every nook and cranny.

Knew there was only one way out.

Bannon heard a noise like a thunk. An inside noise. Only place it could've come from was the cabin.

Erin. Had she tipped over the chair? Or gotten free? Cutt let out a low curse and backed away. Bannon waited a few seconds, then used his hands and feet to lever himself out of the crevice he'd wedged himself into.

He flipped onto his feet, off balance but standing. The moonlight vanished, swallowed by clouds again, and raindrops pelted his bare skin. Their coldness gave him fresh strength. He reached up the side of the boulder he'd tumbled from and spread out his fingers to hoist his hurting body up and over.

Heavy boots stamped viciously hard on his hands.

With a silent curse, Bannon dropped back down into the rat trap Cutt had forced him into. He kept moving, guessing the other man couldn't see him well or at all, not if he'd just come out of the light.

Going on instinct and pure fury, he step-climbed smaller boulders and pressed himself into a space between two big ones. Cutt jumped down. He landed badly—Bannon heard him groan. Torn ligament? He hoped so. He listened.

Cutt turned in different directions, listening too. Bannon stopped breathing. He wriggled up between the concealing rock like a snake, using abs, butt, legs, and feet. His whole body worked but it was his hands that dragged him up to the top of the rock.

The other man still had a gun. Bannon lay flat, drawing in badly needed breaths as quietly as he could, not feeling his scraped skin begin to bleed.

Then he heard footsteps. Cutt hadn't torn anything. He cursed himself for a fool and jumped up. In two seconds they were circling each other.

Why didn't Cutt just shoot him?

He had to ask. The bullet went wide. Bannon dived down, grabbing Cutt by the knees and taking him with him.

They wrestled. The rain stopped but they were slick with it, writhing in moonlight that made red blood look black. Streaked skin got scraped to rawness on the rock beneath it.

He had to get the gun. Bannon gasped. Cutt seized his chance and jammed the barrel into his mouth.

Gagging, Bannon wrenched his head desperately to one side and chopped hard at Cutt's arm before he could pull the trigger.

Cutt dropped it. They both reached. The taller man had the advantage. The gun was in his hand again.

Bannon clutched his wrist in a death grip. He forced the other man's hand down, knowing full well the weapon could go off in a split second, pushing the muzzle of the gun into his attacker's lean cheek. He held it there.

"Gotcha." His voice was a raw whisper.

"No," Cutt said in a dull, distorted voice. The pressure of the gun got in the way of the single word. Bannon jammed his thumb into the nerves and sinews of the other man's wrist, hard, paralyzing Cutt's hand.

With agonizing slowness, Cutt let go of the gun.

Bannon had it and kept it where it was. He intended to use it.

Pinned, Cutt stared at Bannon with fiery, silent hatred. In another split second he arched his back and bucked—and Bannon fired straight into his chest.

The explosive force of the shot knocked him off the other man, but he scrambled up, cocking the gun and pointing it at Cutt.

Still holding it with both hands, he lowered it slowly. The other man was dead.

Bannon kneeled beside him to make sure of it, staying clear of the dark blood that trickled over the rock. Raindrops splashed in it. Cutt's glassy eyes stared upward. He put two fingers to his scrawny neck. No pulse.

He raced back to the cabin and burst through the door. Erin had rocked the chair to the table and was using its edge to scrape at her bonds. He found a knife and sawed through them, releasing her curled hands. One swift cut and the gag was off. She gasped for air, her mouth too dry to talk.

In another minute, Linc and a guy from his crew came through the door. Bannon didn't look up. He was easing Erin out of the chair.

"One shot?" Linc said. Bannon nodded. "Thought so. Good work. She all right?"

Erin croaked an almost inaudible answer and burrowed into Bannon's arms. He held her tight. "Yeah," he said in a husky voice.

"Okay," Linc said. "The locals can get Cutt bagged and tagged."

"You do the talking."

"No problem."

CHAPTER 23

Erin was still inside an ER examination room when a nurse came out. "You can go in now," she said to Bannon, who stood waiting, his bandaged hands clasped in front of him. "Nurse Hartley is helping her with the release paperwork."

Erin was sitting up in an adjustable bed with the sides raised to a diagonal and talking in a low voice to an older nurse with a clipboard. The cruel marks of Cutt's bonds were hidden by the gauze wrapped around her wrists, but the residue of the gag showed—there were red streaks on either side of her mouth. The forlorn expression on Erin's face just about broke his heart, but she brightened when she saw him, reaching out instantly. "Come here," she whispered.

He obeyed, maneuvering around the medical equipment and leaning into her awkward embrace. "Careful. Everything hurts. The adrenaline wore off."

"Same here. But you got the worst of it, Bannon."

The embrace somehow turned into something more, despite the nurse's presence. He pressed his lips into her hair, and murmured joyful, incoherent words. They had survived. They had each other.

"Break it up, you two." The nurse smiled and unclipped a piece of paper, which she folded and set on the bed.

Bannon straightened but it cost him. He groaned under his breath.

"Miss Randall, the doctor reviewed your wound care with you, and here it is in writing for your reference. It'll come in handy later. You're going to feel punchy for a few days. Maybe longer." She gave Bannon a swift, professional once-over. "I assume you got something similar, officer."

"It's in my pocket. How did you know I was a cop?" he asked.

"Erin told me. And because you're a cop, I assume you haven't read it."

He grinned ruefully. She was right.

"Please do. And take care of yourself. Now, at the bottom of the sheet," the nurse went on, talking to Erin again, "you'll see contact information for counseling and other free services for victims of violent crimes. There can be delayed reactions—emotional, physical—of various types. You don't have to tough it out and it's best not to go it alone."

"Thank you," Erin murmured. She hung on tightly to Bannon's hand.

The nurse prepared to go, turning with a few last words. "Your primary care physicians can take over from here. But call if you need to. The hospital number's on the sheet too." She left the room to drop off the clipboard in her hand.

Erin nodded. He winced when her arms went around him again. "Ouch."

"Sorry," she breathed.

"Do it again. It's worth the pain—worth everything. I love you, Erin." Saying it right out loud gave him an incredible rush. He didn't know if it was too soon or not advisable under the circumstances or whatever, and he didn't care. "I really do."

"Oh, Bannon," she murmured, not caring who was looking. "I love you. But what am I going to do now?"

"We'll figure it out soon enough." He pressed a tender kiss to her pale forehead and bent his head down to look at the raw marks on either side of her mouth. "They give you something for that?"

"Antibiotic salve. Same stuff for my wrists. Other than that— you're the one who nearly was killed."

He brushed off her concern. "Nothing wrong with me that won't heal fast." His eyes glimmered suspiciously. "I had some really good reasons to win the fight. You being the most important one."

"Let's go home," she whispered.

Bannon helped her out of the bed. Her movements were slow and gingerly, but she managed to land on her feet by herself. She took the bent arm he offered to spare his hand and interlaced her elbow with his.

Briskly efficient, the ER staff and nurses parted to let them pass, already concerned with other cases. Then a code on the PA system spurred them to a run as someone on an ambulance stretcher was brought in, yelling and pulling at the binding straps.

They walked down a corridor, away from the commotion. Near the sliding glass doors that led to the parking lot, Bannon halted.

"What's the matter?" Erin asked anxiously. "Do you want to sit down?"

He glanced into the room where visitors and family were supposed to wait. "Just seeing if—yeah, he's still here."

"Who?"

He gestured to the doorway of the waiting room so she could see for herself.

Erin's eyes opened wide when she saw the tall old man sitting in a wood-framed armchair, not facing them, leafing through a magazine without reading it. She pulled Bannon back so they were out of earshot.

"I had to call Montgomery." Bannon gave her an apologetic look.

She swallowed hard. "What's done is done. I'm not going to ask why you did. Not after what all of us have been through. But—how much does he understand?" she asked in an agitated whisper.

"A lot. He definitely knows who you are—to him, I mean."

"How?"

"I didn't tell him. He said you were his daughter the second I got done briefing him on what happened out at Cutt's. I don't know how he knows. But, Erin, he cares, believe me."

Reluctantly, she looked into the room again. After a moment, she spoke. But not to Bannon.

"Mr. Montgomery—hello."

The old man turned at the sound of her shaky voice and rose. The motion was swift but without sureness. "There you are. Thank God." He steadied himself with a hand on the chair's flat arm.

"Did you come alone?" Erin asked.

He shook his head. "No. Vernette just went for coffee." He paused, searching her face, a haggard look on his.

"I appreciate your coming," she said hesitantly. "How are you?"

The older man was momentarily at a loss for words. "That doesn't matter. Look at you. You're hurt." He swayed a little.

"Sir, I think you should sit down," Bannon said.

"Yes, yes." Montgomery found his balance and eased himself back down with an effort. "This was a shock, of course. Are you all right? Is there anything I can do? Money is no object—every penny of the bill for treatment will be covered. It's the least I can do—"

Erin shook her head. "That won't be necessary."

"My driver and car are waiting outside. Whatever both of you might need, all you have to do is ask."

"Thank you, but no." She seemed to understand that they couldn't possibly leave him alone and took a seat across from him. Bannon stayed standing.

"I told Bannon something very important," the old man blurted out. He stared at her.

"I know," she responded hesitantly. "And I know that you think I'm your—your daughter."

"Yes. I truly believe that you are. Dear God, what a place for a conversation like this."

The rows of somewhat beat-up chairs and tables scattered with out-of-date magazines lent a strange impersonality to the moment. But Bannon knew that ordinary waiting rooms had a way of framing the extraordinary events of people's lives. Birth, death, and everything in between—hospitals were where it all happened.

"Erin, when you came to see me in the solarium, I didn't remember who you were—until you had left. I wanted to call you but something stopped me. Then this happened. And here we are," Montgomery muttered. "We could go somewhere else."

Erin and Bannon exchanged a concerned look. Almost imperceptibly, she shook her head. The older man didn't see.

"No—no, I can't, not without Vernette," Montgomery said distractedly. "Where is she?"

His hand fluttered against the arm of his chair, an involuntary motion at first. He clenched his teeth and turned it into a nervous drumming.

"I'm sure she'll be back soon," Erin soothed. "Did she drive you here?"

"Yes. Not Caroline. She left yesterday. Bag and baggage. Good riddance."

Bannon raised an eyebrow for Erin's benefit.

"My house is yours if you want to stay with me while you recuperate, Erin."

She pressed her lips together, fighting back tears. "N-no. I don't think so. I'm going to Bannon's apartment. I've been there for a few days. There's so much—I mean, I have a lot to think about. Let's give it time. That's best."

Montgomery studied her face. "I'm sorry. You're right." He spoke again after a pause. "But there must be some way I can help you now—just tell me. Please."

Erin shook her head mutely.

"Forgive me," he said, contrite. "I'm upsetting you, and that is the last thing I want to do. Maybe I shouldn't have come. Don't blame him." Montgomery gestured to Bannon. "He conveyed information, and that was all. Not an invitation."

"I understand. It's all right, Mr. Montgomery."

He shifted in his chair, grasping the arms of it with gnarled hands. "How strange to be called that, now that we both know—but I suppose it has to be that way."

Her eyes filled with tears that she blinked back. "Not forever. Just not yet."

The old man's careworn face brightened. "I understand. If there is anything else I can do—anything you might need—let me be your father—again."

The last few words tripped him up. But the tone of his voice was so genuine and so heartfelt that something changed in Erin's expression. "I'll be all right. But thank you—for wanting to be my dad." Once the word was out, the awkwardness melted away between the two of them. "Oh my. You are my dad. It feels amazing to say it out loud."

"And to hear it," he said with feeling. "I remember you singing out to me when you were a tiny girl—Daddy, Daddy—you were so happy about the littlest things. I gave up believing I would hear your precious voice again. Or see you."

His gnarled hand reached out again and this time she caught it and pressed it to her cheek. "I'm here," she said quietly. "I'm really here."

The connection between them seemed to vibrate in the air of the plain room, not to be broken ever again. She let go of Montgomery's hand and Bannon put an arm around her shoulders as a huge sigh shuddered through her. Erin didn't speak for several more moments. Bannon had the feeling that she was summoning up her courage. Against what? Montgomery seemed like a broken man to him.

"Now I have a right and an obligation to give you whatever you might want or need," Montgomery said, not quite teasing. "Don't deny me."

"There is one thing. Just one." Erin shrugged off Bannon's arm and leaned forward, clasping her hands together so tightly the knuckles showed white.

Both men kept quiet, looking at her with surprise, staying where they were.

"I want to see my mother," she blurted out. "Your—your first wife."

"My only wife." Montgomery was overcome by emotion and said nothing more. Several long seconds passed by.

"Is she even alive?" Erin asked desperately.

CHAPTER 24

Montgomery seemed at a loss for words. "I had no idea that you didn't know—but then, how would you?"

He cast a look at Bannon, who gave only a slight shake of his head in response.

"Tell me," Erin whispered. "Just tell me the truth."

"My dear, your mother is alive, very much so. I—I called her a few nights ago and again today, as soon as I heard from Bannon. Luanne is waiting to talk to you."

"At your house?"

"No. She lives in South Carolina. She wasn't sure if you were—if she should—" He broke down, unable to continue, then composed himself.

"I know how much she wants to meet you. But you have to think of yourself first." He studied her, seeming to notice the red marks on her cheeks for the first time. Anger flashed in his eyes as he stretched out a shaky hand toward her face, dropping it when Erin flinched.

"A good thing that bastard died," Montgomery said fiercely, turning to the younger man, "I owe you an apology, Mr. Bannon. I owe you everything. I might have lost my daughter forever, if not for you."

His aristocratic features could have been carved from stone, except for the tears that rolled down them. He stood there like a statue, proud and alone, until Erin took his hand.

"Thank you. Both of you," he said quietly.

*   *   *

A few days later, Erin entered the study just ahead of Montgomery, who was walking with unobtrusive assistance from Vernette. The nurse helped him into his chair and gave a friendly nod to his daughter.

"Okay, the butler brought up your water carafe." She filled a glass for him and took an amber plastic vial out of her pocket, placing it within easy reach. "And here's your blasted pills." She winked at Erin. "That's what he calls them."

"Damn right," Montgomery growled. "But I'm taking them."

Vernette nodded with approval. "You're all set," she said to her patient. "I'll leave you two alone." She exited quietly.

Erin was looking around the luxuriously decorated room with interest. Her father folded his hands on the desk and drank in the sight of her. His intent gaze made itself felt—she turned to him.

"Well—here I am," she said, striving for a light tone. "What was it you wanted to show me?"

He managed to smile. "I had it all planned. I was going to start with your baby book."

Erin's eyes got misty. "Oh. I never had one—at least that's what I thought. The Randalls said . . . never mind." She fell silent.

Montgomery spoke quickly. "I'm sorry. I didn't mean to upset you. Besides, I realized last night that your mother has the baby book—she always cherished it. I suppose I could make do with family photo albums, but—"

"Let's just talk," she said softly.

Montgomery seemed taken aback. "If you wish." He reached for the glass and took a sip of water. "I don't know where to start. You must have so many questions. I hope I can answer them. My memory still fails me sometimes."

"It doesn't have to be perfect. You were there. You're my father."

Hearing her say the word seemed to please him very much. "Yes. Twice in a lifetime. I'm not sure I deserve that."

She took a deep breath. "Here goes. I'll start with the usual. What was I like when I was little?"

He leaned forward, intent on answering her. "You were a treasure. Shy and sweet. The three years Luanne and I had with you were the happiest of our lives. We never knew how much it meant until you were taken from us." A bitterness tightened his features. Montgomery clasped his hands together to keep them from shaking.

"How did it happen?"

"No one really knew. You and your mother were alone in your part of the house. I was away on business—something for which I have never forgiven myself."

"How could you know?" she asked softly.

He rubbed his forehead. "No one could, I suppose. But the if-onlys never leave you. The police and the people from the FBI did seem to think your kidnapping had been planned in advance. Someone watched and waited for an unguarded moment—the fire gave them that."

"What fire?" she asked curiously. "That's the first I've heard of it. In the house?"

He shook his head. "No, no. Far away. In the Blue Ridge. An afternoon thunderstorm had hit—hail, high winds, lightning, you name it. By evening the ridge was on fire. I was told when the sun went down you could see a scarlet ribbon of flame that stretched for miles. A bad omen, I suppose."

"I don't remember it at all. I don't remember anything before the Randalls."

Hearing that name forced him to stop and compose himself.

"Your mother never would have let you see something so frightening, even from a distance. She called me to ask if she should drive to a friend's house in the next town, but we decided it was best if you stayed with her in the house. Most of our men left to fight it. Later, another storm came through, a tremendous downpour. There were flash floods all over the mountains, but it put out the fire on the ridge."

"Oh." Erin tried to imagine it. Her face was pensive.

"You were never scared of storms—you slept more soundly, if anything. Like your mother. She was a country girl." A thin, sad smile lifted his mouth. "The damned rain washed away what traces there were of you and whoever took you—the bloodhounds and trackers lost the trail within yards of the house once they were outside. Apparently you were carried out through a side door that had been left unlocked. It wasn't far from your little room." He looked at her. "I know you've been inside the house."

"Yes, briefly. I felt so uneasy there." She paused, collecting her thoughts.

Montgomery settled wearily in his chair, grasping the arms with gnarled hands. "I can understand why."

Erin hesitated. "You look tired. Do you want to talk about this some other time?"

"My dear, I would be happy if I never talked about it again, especially now that you're back in my life. But you need to know."

She nodded in acquiescence.

"I was half-crazy when I heard that someone had taken you in the night while I was gone," he continued. "I felt entirely responsible, as I said. Your mother was beside herself. I was afraid for her— I pretended to be the strong one."

"Go on," Erin said quietly.

"No one had seen or heard a thing. There was just your empty little bed when she went into your room the next morning. No sign of a struggle. It was as if someone had lifted you in your sleep and simply walked out. God only knows where you woke up." His eyes flashed with anger.

"Tell me more. If you can."

"Your mother helped with the investigation—she remembered every little detail about you. I felt ashamed that I didn't, but that was how it was back then. She was the one who noticed that bear you loved so much was gone too."

"Pinky. I still have her." Her answer was almost inaudible. He didn't seem to catch it.

"And that little painting of you on the wall," he went on.

Erin's breath caught in her throat. "I saw that. It was half in shadow—but it's hard to believe I was looking at myself and didn't know it."

Montgomery smiled slightly. "It wasn't much of a likeness. That wasn't the artist's fault. You hated to be photographed, let alone being made to sit still and be painted. Quite a wriggler, you were. And you refused to smile for her."

"Why did you leave the portrait hanging on the wall?"

"I couldn't bear to look at it. But I couldn't bear to take it down."

His forehead furrowed with concern. "Did you ever look at the files that Bannon borrowed from the archives? He told me that he had. We've talked a couple of times since I met you in the hospital."

"No," she answered simply. "I didn't want to. And I didn't look at the responses to the broadcast either. All those boxes—I just couldn't."

Montgomery leaned back in his chair, rocking a little. "I can understand why. After a while, I couldn't either. I couldn't bring you back. We worked with the police, the FBI—nothing. I was so desperate that I paid for help outside the law, hoping to track you down by any means possible—your mother knew nothing of that," he muttered.

Erin only nodded.

"She and I stayed on in the old house, but we were like strangers to each other."

"And then?"

Montgomery's sigh seemed to come from the depths of his soul. "You were her heart of hearts. Her grief was too much for me to bear. My own—well, that was more like anger. Icy anger. At everyone but her. I think the distinction was lost on Luanne. I know my coldness frightened her."

"I see," Erin whispered.

"Months—years—went by. The police didn't have any new leads. We received crackpot letters now and then, but only a few. Nothing like the responses a TV website generates."

"Did you see that broadcast?"

He scowled. "I did. It infuriated me. The image they used was nothing like you—and the story was sensationalist. It occurred to me that the renewed attention might even endanger you somehow if you had miraculously survived. My lawyer called Bannon in for a talk—I must say, he struck me as intelligent even then. And foolhardy. He had no idea what he was getting into. But that isn't a criticism. He risked his life for you. I would have done the same, but I never had the chance."

"Yes, well—" Erin realized that her long-lost father could be a bit jealous of Bannon and incredibly grateful to him at the same time. "About my mother . . . you were saying?"

"We agreed to separate," he answered bluntly. "I took care of her financially—I want you to know that. Your mother never had to worry. She wanted to go far away from here. I helped her do that. The divorce went through. Afterward, we talked now and then. Not often." His gaze grew distant.

Erin swallowed hard. "What is she like?"

Montgomery looked at her again. "Like you."

"How so?" she whispered.

"Luanne is an artist."

"I didn't know that."

His chair creaked forward as he sat up. "Years after you were taken, she began to draw and paint, discovered a talent she hadn't known she possessed. She has a gallery now. Rather well-known. But not under her name."

"Does she go by Montgomery?" Erin asked tentatively.

"No. She uses her maiden name. I'm going to let her tell you her side of the story, though, when you're ready to meet her. You know, I thought I had lost my mind when I saw you for the first time. You look so much like the photographs of her when she was young. I do have those—and some old videos of all of us. Somewhere."

Erin shook her head. "Not yet. I want to see her—the real her. Not photos. Not videos. My mother."

"Hold off a little while, Kelly," Bannon said. "That's all I'm asking. Don't send reporters to follow me around. Please. I'm down on my knees here."

"Like hell you are." He held the phone away from his ear when she laughed at him. "That will be the day, Bannon."

"How did you find out, anyway?"

"On the grapevine," she replied airily. "One of our freelancers happened to see Montgomery being driven to the hospital and followed him. At a discreet distance. What's up with Monty, hmm? You can tell me."

"I'm not going to. And I'd bet anything the station paid your freelancer to park at the end of his driveway. Not exactly discreet."

He could practically see her fiddling with a pencil. "Why would we do that?"

"Because you somehow got wind of—" He stopped himself just in time.

"You were saying?"

Bannon let several seconds pass. "Sorry. I had gum on my shoe. I was just scraping it off. You still there?"

"Try ice for that," she said sweetly. "It freezes the gum and then it cracks. Bannon, I know Montgomery wasn't admitted. Our contact said so."

"You mean the freelancer? I don't happen to recall anyone who looked like a two-bit, scroungy, ambulance-chasing reporter hanging around the ER."

"You have such a colorful way of expressing yourself, Bannon," she cooed. "No. Not him. We have a contact in the hospital computer system. He alerts us to interesting little things now and then."

"For example?"

"Do you need one? Here goes. Someone named Cutt got shot up in the Blue Ridge and delivered, DOA, to the hospital morgue. The shooting got a line or two in the police announcements the next day. Who cared, right? Cutt was an ex-con and a loner. A nobody. No family, no nothing. But then another contact inside the PD told me Chief Hoebel and Cutt were working together. What's going on in Wainsville? Does Mr. Montgomery have anything to do with it?"

"Go up a few levels. County, state. Ask around at internal affairs. I assume you know someone there."

Kelly sighed. "Actually, I don't. That's where you come in."

"Count me out, Kell."

She laughed again. "I was only kidding. You would never tell me why a hero cop, meaning you, and a young lady were treated in the ER at the very same hospital where Cutt's body arrived, at the same time."

"That's a coincidence."

"No, it isn't."

He could hear her tapping on a keyboard and wondered if she was taking notes on this conversation. "Kelly, you can think what you want."

"So many connections to make. So little time. You could make this easy for me, Bannon," she said coaxingly. "Tell me what you know."

"No way. I can't and I won't. There's a lot at stake here, Kelly."

"Like what?"

He was getting seriously irritated. "Like my job and—"

"The girl? Her name is Erin Randall, right? I looked her up on-line. She paints horses. Any connection to Hugh Montgomery and his famous stables? Is she his missing daughter or something? Wouldn't that be wild?" Kelly didn't seem to believe what she'd just said, which was fine with Bannon. "Never mind. I was just thinking out loud. But what is she to you?"

He silently marveled at Kelly's ability to put two and two together. "A friend."

The woman at the other end of the line fell silent. Kelly was more dangerous when she wasn't talking, Bannon reflected.

"Let's make a deal," she said after a few charged seconds. "I smell a major story. But I can't connect all the dots on my own. Yet."

"What do you want from me?"

"When you're ready to talk, you talk to me exclusively. Deal?"

"I'll think about it."

"Bannon—"

He knew she was fuming. He said a quick good-bye and hung up, hoping he'd gained a little time for Erin. Kelly's instincts were excellent. The return of Ann Montgomery was a major story.

CHAPTER 25

After a night in a forgettable motel near the state border of South Carolina, they checked out before dawn, eating a fast breakfast and getting back on the highway just as the sun was rising. Bannon didn't mind doing the driving. One hand on the wheel, he kept the car at a steady speed, looking over now and then at Erin, her eyes closed, snuggled deeply into a pillow. Peaceful.

They'd left the firestorm of media attention far behind them. Hoebel was going to walk the plank, Bannon knew that much. The state investigators had found a bunch of stuff in Cutt's rat-trap cabin that linked the chief to a lot of dirty deals. Looked like he was a shadow partner in more than one racketeering scheme and the violence that went with it. He was going to have to turn state's evidence unless he wanted to spend most of the rest of his life in jail. A squeaky-clean new chief had been hired but not sworn in. In the meantime Doris was back in the office, taking a lot of ridiculously long lunches with Jolene.

He had nothing to worry about either. Internal affairs brass had asked him a whole lot of questions about what'd happened with Cutt and seemed satisfied with Bannon's answers. He'd been granted several more weeks of paid leave to recuperate.

As for Erin's case, the FBI had collected every single damn one of the boxes and a bunch of old files and whatnot from Montgomery and taken all of it to Quantico. For further study, they said. They had a theory that the Randalls had cased the Montgomery house, the old one, months before the kidnapping. Swift and silent as the deed was, it had to have been planned in advance.

Let them figure it out. The agent in charge couldn't discount the possibility that the Randalls were linked to other abduction cases. They'd practically sworn on their government-issued pocket protectors to return everything within a year. Bannon wanted to believe that, but he'd swiped the photos for Erin before the feds sealed the boxes up and took them away. Who knew if Montgomery had copies of everything? Bannon smiled to himself, changing lanes when a set of halogen high beams flared behind him.

Road's all yours, he said silently to the tailgating jerk. *But one honk and I'll bust you. That's my girl nestled on that pillow.*

More than his girl, but Erin didn't know that yet. He'd bought a diamond ring, a big sparkly one that had set him back a small fortune. Worth it, for her. He wanted to have it handy when the right moment happened. Might be sooner rather than later. Bannon touched his shirt pocket, making sure the button on it was fastened. He'd taken the ring out of the little domed box so the shape wouldn't give him away.

Erin hadn't noticed. She had other things on her mind. He could wait. For a lot of reasons, it was probably better if he did. But he liked to be prepared.

She slept for most of the way, waking up when they'd reached the Low Country. He'd exited the highway before that, taking an old road that would bring them to the coast and the bridge to the island where her mother lived.

He wanted her to rest. There was no way to predict how the reunion would affect her. She stirred in her sleep and he reached out a hand to stroke her hair. She woke up all the way and stretched as best she could buckled up in the front seat.

Bannon took his eyes off the road to take in that fine sight, then swung his gaze quickly back when an old pickup with wooden-slat sides tooted at him to stay on his side of the yellow line.

"Where are we?" she asked drowsily.

"Not far. Almost there."

"It's nice here. Not a house in sight."

Bannon smiled slightly. "Oh, they're there. Back under the trees and by the creeks."

"How do you know that?"

"My dad took us three boys on a fishing trip near here."

She yawned and ran a hand through her hair. "Catch anything?"

"Catfish. Crawdads. Poison ivy."

Erin chuckled and looked up through the dash window at the venerable live oaks, their branches draped in delicate moss, that lined the back road and kept the drive well-shaded and pleasant.

"Mind if I roll the windows down?" Bannon asked.

"No. Go ahead." Erin breathed deeply. "Smells like the sea a little. How far are we from it?"

"I don't know exactly. I think that's a salt marsh up ahead."

The trees dwindled in size and then disappeared from the flat landscape that stretched for miles in all directions. A playful breeze rippled through deep-rooted reeds of green and gold that concealed the mud they grew in.

"Look at that. It's beautiful," she said softly. "I wish we could get out and walk."

"Not unless you're a wading bird." He laughed.

"I know. Most of Chincoteague is the same way."

In another hour, they had come to the bridge, and Bannon pulled into the parking lot to let Erin get ready. He got out and stretched, walking around, enjoying the intense warmth of the Southern sunshine. In another couple of hours, it might be unbearable, but right now it was working magic on muscles stiffened by several hours of driving.

He glanced through the window and saw her take a brush out of her purse, running it through her sleep-mussed hair with long, deliberate strokes. She caught his eye and smiled.

Take your time, his wink told her.

She nodded and went on freshening up, then opened her door and got out. The breeze had softened to a barely perceptible movement of the air, but it did something very pretty for her hair.

"What time is it?" she asked.

Bannon consulted his watch. "About ten. I don't think Luanne—

I mean, your mother—is expecting us until eleven or so. Want to have coffee?" He nodded toward a couple of attached shacks that served the locals as a café and bait shop.

"No. But thanks."

He could hear the nervousness in her simple reply and let the subject drop. "I'm going to get some to go. Back in a sec."

She nodded and Bannon went up to the open-air counter to order a cup. He was greeted by a friendly lady in gingham who was setting out homemade doughnuts in rows on a tray, then covering them with plastic wrap.

"Just out of the fryer and still warm," she said encouragingly.

"Sold." The sweet fragrance of cinnamon and sugar that wafted up to his nose was too much temptation for a mortal man. He couldn't remember the last time he'd had a homemade doughnut.

"How many?"

"A dozen."

She grinned and snapped a paper sack open, filling it with his order and adding one more.

"And a cup of coffee, please. Black."

The woman in blue gingham nodded and filled a cup, settling a plastic lid on it and handing it to Bannon. "Anything for the young lady over there?" she asked politely.

"Oh—" He turned around to look at Erin, who was shielding her eyes from the sun with one hand and studying the island that lay across the water, a distance of less than a mile. "She's going to need a doughnut, so thanks for the extra. But she didn't want any coffee."

"I see. So you plan to eat the whole dozen, then."

"Not all at once." The woman laughed as he plunked down cash for the doughnuts and stuffed the tip jar with a couple of extra bills.

"You have a great day," she said in farewell. "Enjoy the island. It's small and it's outa the way, but folks around here think it's paradise."

Bannon picked up the sack with the hand that wasn't holding the coffee. "I can see why. Thanks again." He nodded a good-bye and headed back to Erin before the friendly woman could ask who they were visiting or anything like that.

Erin turned to him. "Is that breakfast?"

"Yes, it is. Homemade doughnuts, no less. Can I tempt you? One won't hurt."

She smiled wryly. "When in doubt, carb out. Sure."

They got back into the car and he drank his coffee, eating three doughnuts to her two. She didn't seem to want to talk. Bannon drained the last of the strong brew and stashed the cup behind his seat.

"Ready?" he asked.

Erin only nodded.

He didn't try to draw her out. He had a feeling that she was on the verge of tears. Her blue eyes were suspiciously bright and her lips were pressed together. Bannon got busy consulting the printed-out map he'd gotten off the Internet.

"There's only one road, and it winds. We might find ourselves going in circles, but we'll get there."

Erin cleared her throat and stared out the side window. He started the car and left the windows down. The smell of the sea was stronger now, but the tang was nice. Going over the bridge took all of five minutes and then they were on the island. It seemed to be completely flat. They were plunged once again into a world of green. Palmettos rose above tangles of smaller trees and brush, but there was still an occasional undisturbed giant of an oak near a house.

"Slow down," she said suddenly.

Bannon looked at her with surprise, then checked the speedometer. He was doing a blazing seven miles per hour. A turtle could have passed him. "No problem," he replied.

He concentrated on the narrow road, looking now and then at the houses. There weren't very many of them. Mostly one-story frame houses, but always with a plank porch and rocking chairs that held a lazy dog or cat luxuriating on a sun-warmed cushion. Children played in unfenced yards, casting curious glances at the unfamiliar car and the two strangers in it, returning to their games when Bannon and Erin drove on.

The map in his hand fluttered in his grip as he held the steering wheel at the same time. He blew out a breath, not sure which house it would be. None had actual numbers, or at least not any that he could see.

Then a double-story house came into view around the bend and he pulled over. It was clapboard, like the others, simply framed. There was nothing grand about the double-height porch, supported by sturdy painted beams, not columns. Even from where the car had stopped some distance off, they could see a riot of colors. Quilts hung from the upper and lower railings, and found-metal sculptures in bright enameled shapes whirred and clanked in the yard.

"That must be her gallery," Bannon said.

"Yes."

He switched off the ignition. "Want to walk from here?"

"Just give me a minute to think."

"You okay?"

"I'll be fine."

He leaned back and studied the quilts, squinting at the crazy, joyful patterns.

"Let's go," Erin said suddenly.

Bannon sat up and opened his door, getting out. When she didn't move, he went around to her side and leaned in, giving her a kiss on the cheek. "If you want to go alone, I understand." He looked at his watch for a fraction of a second. "We're about half an hour early."

"Oh. I don't want to sit here. Come with me." She looked up at him with a touch of panic.

He opened her door and she got out, not bothering with brushing her hair or straightening her top. Erin reached for his hand.

There was no one on the porch when they got to the house and she seemed to breathe a sigh of relief. Then they heard a crash from inside. A quilt on the lower railing billowed out and a huge black-and-white cat shot off the porch in pursuit of a small critter that vanished in less than a second.

"Max, you're nothing but a nuisance! That was my new vase!" a kind voice said with a trace of annoyance. The woman who'd spoken opened the screen door and stepped outside, looking down at the swinging cat flap at the bottom.

Bannon just stared. Luanne looked so much like Erin, it took his breath away. Older, yes, with a few pretty wrinkles that said she liked to smile, with shorter hair, and not as willowy as her daughter—but just as beautiful.

Erin gave a low gasp and Luanne turned. It was as if Bannon wasn't there. The woman's blue eyes widened. Her hello died away.

"I—I remember you," Erin said slowly. Tears welled and ran down her cheeks. "I thought I wouldn't. But I do."

She stood there, stunned. Bannon took her arm to steady her but Erin brushed his hand away and took a step forward.

"Oh my God. It's you," Luanne whispered. "I told myself I wouldn't believe it until I saw you. It's true. You're really here."

Erin rushed up the stairs into her mother's open arms. Bannon didn't know what to say or do. He wasn't going to cry. But he wanted to.

Damn. Not like him. He went around the porch to find Max and get his jeans carefully sniffed for evidence of a feline rival. He would soothe the cat with a chin scratch. Something to do. They could hang out together for a few minutes. Mother-and-daughter re-unions like this didn't happen every day.

In a little while, he heard Erin call his name. Luanne's lilting voice joined in. He strolled around back to them, followed by the cat.

"I see Max has made a friend," Luanne said. She was a little more composed, but only a little. "He has good taste. So you're the famous Bannon, huh?"

"Guess so. What has she been saying?" He gave Erin a wary look.

"Only good things. Champagne or lemonade? I have both in the fridge."

Bannon looked into Erin's wet eyes and took her hand, giving it a squeeze. "Lemonade for me. I think we should save the champagne for later."

"Tell you what," Luanne said brightly. "You two can take the bottle and have a picnic on the beach at sunset all by yourselves. This celebration is just beginning. You aren't going home until tomorrow, right?"

"That's right. And a picnic sounds good to me," he said to Erin. "What do you think?"

She laughed and went into his open arms, resting her hand over the buttoned pocket. Erin looked up at him, then to her mother, who was leading the way into the house. The screen door closed behind Luanne.

"Bannon, what is that?" Erin murmured. Her finger traced the circle in his pocket until he caught her hand by the wrist.

"Um, that's the little thing that keeps falling off the other thing on the dashboard thing. I put it in my pocket while you were sleeping."

Erin gave him a dubious look. "I have no idea what you're talking about."

"That's because it's the first time you've been in my car. And you were asleep practically the whole way."

"But—" she began. He touched his lips to hers. She tried again. "It feels like a—"

Bannon bent down and kissed her until she stopped asking questions. Then they went up the steps with their arms around each other's waists, a little flushed and a lot happy. Luanne let the door swing wide, not minding the frosty pitcher of lemonade that sloshed in her other hand.

"My goodness." She chuckled. "Maybe I shouldn't say this, but you two certainly look like a couple."

"We are," Bannon said.

Erin pinched him on the side. He didn't bat an eye.

"Really?" Luanne looked delighted. "I couldn't be happier. Come on in and tell me more."

They went inside, laughing.

If you liked this Janet Dailey book,
don't miss
TO SANTA WITH LOVE!
Coming this October!

SOMETIMES YOU DON'T KNOW WHAT YOU NEED

Summer's over and the leaves are falling . . . and free-spirited
Jacquie Grey plans to head west and start a whole new life. Her
solo road trip is going great—until she collides with rancher
Choya Barnett in Arizona. Good thing that no one's hurt. But she
can't afford to fix her car until he proposes hiring her to take care
of his little boy and his house. Too bad it's only temporary—the
tall, handsome Choya is a *serious* temptation. . . .

UNTIL YOU FIND IT . . .

Jacquie and Choya begin an unlikely friendship, fueled by a fierce,
unspoken attraction and a desire to find something real they
can each hold onto. Before they know it, Christmas and all its
joys are around the corner—along with the wonderful gift
of lasting love. . . .